MIKE EVANS

SEVEN DAYS

TimeWorthy
BOOKS

P.O. Box 30000, Phoenix, AZ 85046

Published by TimeWorthy Books
P. O. Box 30000
Phoenix, AZ 85046

Seven Days

Copyright 2012 by TimeWorthy Books
P. O. Box 30000
Phoenix, AZ 85046

Design: Lookout Design, Inc.

USA:	978-0-935199-53-6
Canada:	978-0-935199-55-0
Hardcover:	978-0-935199-54-3

This novel is a work of fiction. Names, characters, places, and incidents are either the product of the authors imagination or are used fictitiously. Any resemblance to actual events, locales, organizations, or persons living or dead is entirely coincidental and beyond the intent of either the author or the publisher.

This book is respectfully dedicated to my dear friend,
Lt. General Moshe Ya'alon,
one of the most brilliant leaders in Israel, and yet one of the most humble. His life defines a small plaque I saw on President Ronald Reagan's desk in the Oval Office: "A man can become too big in his own eyes to be used of God, but never too small."

In 1995 Ya'alon was named head of Military Intelligence, a position he held when Yasser Arafat launched the second Intifada in September 2000. He was appointed Chief of Staff of the Israeli Defense Forces (IDF) in July 2002, a position in which he served until June 2005. His task: to halt the Intifada.

Moshe, a long-time friend, became a member of the Washington Institute for Near East Policy and was named a Senior Fellow at the Adelson Institute for Strategic Studies at the Shalem Center Institute for International and Middle East Studies. In Jerusalem, he is chair of the Center for Jewish Identity and Culture at Abeit Morasha.

In 2008, Ya'alon entered the primaries to run in the 2009 elections. He exited the process in eighth place, and took a seat in the Knesset. When Prime Minister Benjamin Netanyahu formed a government, he appointed Moshe Ya'alon as Vice Prime Minister and Minister of Strategic Affairs.

MAJOR CHARACTERS

ANDREW STANTON: Former U.S. Senator from Illinois, now President of the United States.

GLADYS MOYNIHAN: President Stanton's secretary.

PETE MCWHINNEY: President Stanton's Chief of Staff.

ANN JOHNSON: White House Press secretary.

LEON BAIN: Chairman of Andrew Stanton's re-election campaign.

AUBREY PRESTON: White House advisor. Takes over re-election effort when Bain is moved out.

RALPH LIGON: Director of National Intelligence.

ADMIRAL BEAMON: Chairman of the Joint Chiefs of Staff.

KATHLEEN BAKER: Former US Senator from Vermont, now Secretary of State.

HAYDEN UPCHURCH: US Secretary of Defense.

DICK ELSER: US Secretary of the Navy.

JEAN BROWN: The President's National Security Advisor.

PAUL CATLETT: Director of the CIA.

FRANK ATTWOOD: Deputy Director of the CIA for Middle East intelligence.

JOHN SLADEN: CIA operative. Dies mysteriously on the streets of Istanbul.

ALEX RUTLEDGE: Two-term Michigan governor. Republican Party nominee for president.

JAMIE WRIGHT: Advisor to Alex Rutledge.

YOSEF WEISS: Wealthy fundraiser for the Democratic Party.

ELAZAR YEDAYA: Prime Minster of Israel.

GABI HALUTZ: Chief of the Israeli Defense Force.

EFRAIM HOFI: Director of Mossad, Israel's intelligence service.

THE
FIRST
SEVEN

CHAPTER 1
RABAT, MOROCCO

SWEAT TRICKLED DOWN Jabbar Hamadeh's forearm as he sat behind the steering wheel of the lime green Fiat. Even with the windows down, the car was like an oven. He glanced down at his fingers wrapped tightly around the wheel. His knuckles showed white beneath the skin of his hands. He took a deep breath and forced his body to relax.

At twenty-one, he had recently come to Morocco from France, where he'd been enrolled at the Paris Institute of Technology. With intelligence well above average, he had little trouble landing a place at his pick of the best schools. He chose the Institute for its Physics Department and planned one day to return home to Yemen as a teacher. After a stellar first year, he came under the influence of Abdullah al-Salam, a Sunni cleric working from the Grand Mosque. In his second year at the Institute, Jabbar continued to do well in class, but he spent more and more time at the mosque, attending classes in classic Shi'a Islam and participating in a rigorous regimen of prayer and worship. By the third year, he was enrolled at the Institute only to maintain his visa. Instead of attending class there, he spent his days as part of a select group of ten young men being schooled in the meaning and political implications of radical Nizari Shi'a documents, including the 1985 Hezbollah Manifesto and ancient scrolls of the Hashshashin recovered from the ruins of a castle near Alamut in northern Iran.

Seated next to Jabbar that day was Nashwan Girgrah, a sixteen-year-old from Temara, a coastal city on the southern edge of Rabat. Jabbar recruited him to help load the heavy canvas duffel bags into the trunk of the car and brought him along to assist with navigating the crowded streets.

A camera rested on Nashwan's lap. He fingered a knob on the side and glanced out the window. "Think we can get a good picture of him?"

The young boy's eager look sent waves of guilt over Jabbar. For a moment he considered telling Nashwan what they really carried in the trunk of the car, then he thought better of it. "I am sure we will see him clearly. Can you hold the camera steady? The car shakes a lot at slow speed."

"Yes," Nashwan grinned confidently. "You will see. I take great pictures."

Jabbar turned back to the window. The camera was almost new and he had wanted to leave it for his sister, but Nashwan asked too many questions about the contents of the duffel bags as they lugged them from the corner of the bedroom. He was worried Nashwan would become suspicious of what they really held and refuse to participate. He needed Nashwan to show him the route from the house to the liaison's office. In an attempt to divert Nashwan's curiosity about the bags, he suggested the boy accompany him with the camera to take pictures. "My editor might find a photograph helpful for the article I'm writing," Jabbar had added. Nashwan readily agreed.

Out the windshield, the hood of the Fiat shook from side to side, moving in time with the engine as it sputtered and knocked in a valiant effort to maintain an idle. A gear shifter in the console between the seats tapped out the same rhythm. Jabbar rested his hand on the shifter knob to silence it.

From the corner across the street, a concrete wall stood ten feet high. It ran the length of the block to the corner on the opposite end, broken only by a pair of iron gates that guarded the driveway to the Israeli Liaison's office. Behind the concrete wall, a blue and white Israeli flag flapped lazily in the afternoon breeze. Any minute now, if Jabbar's information was correct, the iron gates would swing open and a motorcade of black SUVs would appear. The third one in line would bear the Israeli foreign minister.

Nashwan's voice broke the silence of the moment. "What does that do?"

Jabbar glanced to the right to see Nashwan's hand stretched toward a small electrical switch that dangled from two black wires protruding from an air-conditioner vent at the center of the dash. "It's nothing."

"What does it do?" Nashwan wanted to know as he leaned forward and reached for the switch.

"No!" Jabbar snapped, and he grasped Nashwan's wrist tightly. "The car is old," he forced a smile. "Not all the switches work." He relaxed his grip on Nashwan's wrist. "We will find out what it does later."

"Okay," Nashwan shrugged, withdrawing his hand. "I was just curious."

"I understand. But you must—"

"Look," Nashwan interrupted, pointing out the windshield. "The gates are opening."

As the gates swung out, a single black SUV came from the compound and turned left. Jabbar waited, expecting two more vehicles to appear, but as the SUV moved away, the gates swung closed. Jabbar hesitated, then put the car in gear. "There must have been a change," he mumbled.

Black smoke billowed from beneath the Fiat as Jabbar pressed his foot against the gas pedal. The car struggled forward, then picked up speed. As the engine whined through first gear, the rough-running knock in the engine disappeared. Jabbar shifted to second gear and the car moved even faster, its engine running smoothly. Up ahead, the SUV still pulled away but not quite so rapidly.

Jabbar shifted the car into third gear and now they were racing down the street, gaining on the SUV. He shifted into fourth gear and they were only a few meters from the SUV's rear bumper.

Nashwan picked up the camera and propped his elbow on the open passenger's window. "I thought there were three of them."

"I did, too."

"The windows are too dark to get a picture of anyone inside."

"I know." Jabbar's voice was tense and terse.

"What will we do?"

"It won't matter."

Jabbar turned the steering wheel to the left. The Fiat darted from behind the SUV. As the nose of the car drew near the SUV's front wheels, he reached for the switch hanging from the black wires that snaked through the air-conditioner duct.

"I thought you said don't touch it." Nashwan had a hint of nervous apprehension in his voice, as if he understood what the switch would do even though his mind refused to form the conscious thought.

A wide grin turned up the corners of Jabbar's mouth. "Allah will be very proud of us," he said in a loud voice, making sure he was heard over the noise of the car's engine. "And he will tell us so himself." Then, with a flick of his finger, the electrical switch snapped forward.

For an instant nothing happened, and in that moment Jabbar saw a look of terror on Nashwan's face. He reached out his hand and felt his fingertips brush against the shoulder of Nashwan's shirt. Then a wave of searing heat swept forward from the trunk. It was followed by a deafening roar as the upholstery burst into flames. Jabbar felt his body strain against the seatbelt, saw the roof of the car rip free from the doorposts. Blue sky appeared above them, visible through the smoke and flames that peeled his flesh from his bones. An instant later, smoke poured from empty spaces in the SUV where the windows once had been. And then Jabbar's world went dark.

CHAPTER 2
WASHINGTON, D.C.

ISRAELI PRIME MINISTER ELAZAR YEDAYA came from the West Wing of the White House. With three quick strides, he reached a Cadillac limousine that was parked on the driveway. As Yedaya approached, a guard opened the rear door of the car. Yedaya ducked inside and took his place on the seat.

Moments later, the door on the opposite side opened and Alex Talbot appeared. A two-term governor from Michigan, Talbot was the Republican Party's nominee for president in an election that was only months away. Though he was still fifteen points behind in the latest polls, he was certain his campaign could close the gap. Being seen and photographed with the Israeli prime minister would only help his effort to court the Jewish vote in places like New York, New Jersey, and Maryland.

When Talbot was seated, the car started forward, third in line behind a police patrol car and a black SUV. Behind them, another SUV followed, trailed by yet one more police car. They came from the White House driveway and turned right as they began the thirty-minute drive to Andrews Air Force Base.

Talbot glanced across the seat at Yedaya. "Have a good meeting with the president?"

"Your president," Yedaya scoffed. "I don't know."

"He's not my president, Mr. Prime Minister. He's the Democrats' president and the country's president. I'm from the other party."

Yedaya shook his head in frustration. "I have dealt with many American presidents. Some have been eager to help us and some of them have not understood the dangers we face or how those dangers threaten the United States." He raised his finger for emphasis. "But until this visit, I had never dealt with an American president who understood those dangers, clearly and distinctly, and willfully chose to disregard them." He cut his eyes at Talbot. "And he has taken that position solely for the sake of getting himself reelected to an office the power of which he refuses to use for anything, well or ill."

Talbot looked amused. "Can I quote you on that?"

Yedaya threw his hands in the air. "We are surrounded by enemies on all sides. Syria, Hezbollah, the Palestinian Authority, all of them financed and equipped by Iran, a country that is working day and night to develop a nuclear bomb solely for the purpose of destroying Israel. Your president understands all of this and yet he insists on doing nothing to help us."

"If it helps," Talbot nodded, "he treats his own nation the very same way."

"It defies the imagination." Yedaya clenched his fist and bounced it impatiently against his leg. "If we go down, there is no one left who will stand and fight with America. England, France, all the NATO countries – they are spent. The war in Iraq and Afghanistan has drained their people dry. We are America's only ally in the region. Saudi Arabia masquerades as a friend simply because the royal family needs American help to remain in power." He looked Talbot in the eye. "We are America's one true friend in the region. Our countries have no one but each other."

"I think somewhere deep inside, President Stanton understands that. He just doesn't like the consequences."

"You mean, a disruption in oil prices?"

"That and the fact that he campaigned for election on an anti-war message. He knows that if he acts, he'll lose the economy and his electoral base, and I'll win the general election."

"Then we must push him all the more to act," Yedaya grinned.

Talbot ignored the comment. "How did your meetings go with Haden Upchurch?"

"He and I got along well," Yedaya shrugged. "He's a competent secretary of defense, but even he is not a friend to Israel. I know he wants us to feel like he's a friend, but he's not."

"You're certain about that?"

"Yes," Yedaya nodded. "I have known Haden Upchurch since I was a student at Dartmouth and I know with all my heart he would like nothing more than to carve up Israel into tiny little pieces and feed us to the Palestinians. He truly believes the lie that the Palestinians are an indigenous people and that we are the interlopers."

"He doesn't talk like it."

"No. He doesn't," Yedaya agreed. "That's what I mean. I warned you about him years ago. He talks well, but he cannot be trusted."

"And the secretary of state? How did your meeting go with her?"

"She understands what we face and the consequences for the United States if Iran develops a nuclear weapon, but she is constrained by the president. And he doesn't respect her opinion or seek her advice."

"She was put in that office to end her political career."

"Politics."

"I'm not sure she'll be around if he wins a second term."

"Perhaps not." Yedaya turned away and stared out the window. "You must win, Alex." He glanced over his shoulder. "The Middle East cannot endure four more years of listless American policy. He understands our situation and chooses not to act. That is the worst form of treachery."

CHAPTER 3
BOSTON

SEYYED KHANSARI MADE HIS WAY UP Salem Street, walking at a deliberate pace, hands in his pockets, doing his best not to call attention to himself. Outside the Old North Church, he came to a blue Honda Accord, approached the car with purpose, opened the passenger door, and slipped inside.

Born in Tehran, Seyyed came to the United States in the 1970s as a boy when his father, a mid-level bureaucrat in the Shah's government, was assigned to Iran's staff at the UN. When the Shah was deposed by the Islamic Revolution, Seyyed's parents applied for asylum in the United States. The family was resettled in the Roxbury neighborhood of Boston. New to the country and ill at ease with American culture, Seyyed sought friends among children in the neighborhood and soon found his way to a mosque off Washington Street. As a teenager, he was intrigued by the rising popularity of the Islamic Revolution sweeping through the Middle East. He thought of going there to join the fight, but an imam suggested he could do more by remaining in the U.S. Seyyed did well in school, attended Boston University, and graduated with a degree in Computer Programing. He took a job with the telephone company, married, and began a family. All the while, he remained a faithful adherent to Shi'a Islam. Then came the call. "Now is the time," the voice said. And with that, Seyyed joined the fight.

On the opposite side of the car that day, Gordon Williams was seated behind the steering wheel. As Seyyed closed the door, Williams put the car in gear and started forward. He glanced around nervously, checking in every direction. "You bring the money?"

"Yes," Seyyed answered calmly. He opened one button of his shirt, revealing a plain white envelope tucked inside near the waistband of his trousers. "You have the number?"

"Yeah." Williams pointed. "Lay the money on the console."

Seyyed did as he was told and set the envelope on the ledge beside the shifter. Williams glanced down at it. Through a gap in the flap a stack of twenty-dollar bills was visible.

"Okay," Williams nodded. "That looks good." As he spoke, he reached inside his jacket and took a folded slip of paper from a pocket. "That's the number." He held it between his fingers. "But you didn't get it from me. Okay? I mean, I've never done anything like this before. I just need the money."

"Right," Seyyed nodded.

"I'm a little behind," Williams continued. "That's all. Just a little behind. This is just to catch me up."

Seyyed took the paper from Williams and opened it. Written inside were the numbers 2-512-3-79. He counted to make sure it included the correct number of digits, then refolded the paper and stuffed it into his pants pocket. "Make a left," he pointed out the windshield.

Williams turned onto Charter Street. He continued to talk but Seyyed paid him no attention. All he could think of was getting out of the car before it was too late. At the next corner, he pointed to the right. "Drop me here."

Williams looked puzzled. "I thought I was supposed to take you to Roxbury."

"Change in plans," Seyyed directed. "Just drop me here. I have something else to do."

"Okay," Williams shrugged. "Whatever you say. I didn't really want to drive out there anyway." He slowed the car and brought it to a stop at the curb. Seyyed opened the door and stepped out to the sidewalk.

As the car sped away, Seyyed walked toward Jackson Street, doing his best to appear at ease. At the corner, he took a cell phone from his hip pocket and placed a call. Seconds later, he heard a thud, followed by the unmistakable sound of shattered glass. Then he heard the blare of a car horn. He looked up to see the Honda smashed against a telephone pole two blocks down the street. While Seyyed watched, flames shot from beneath the hood. Moments later, thick black smoke filled the air above the car as fire swept through the driver's compartment.

Seyyed switched off the cell phone and started up Jackson Street, walking at a casual pace. Near the center of the block he came to a trash can. He dropped the cell phone into it as he passed by.

CHAPTER 4
WASHINGTON, D.C.

ALEX TALBOT STEPPED FROM THE ELEVATOR into the corridor on the fifth floor of the Morrow Building, a steel and glass high-rise off DuPont Circle. Accompanying him were Don Winslow and Curt Menard, his staff assistants. Behind them came the security detail. Down the corridor to the right was a receptionist's desk that sat outside the entrance to Talbot's campaign headquarters. He smiled at the young blonde volunteer behind the desk as he moved past with his entourage in tow.

Beyond the office entrance, he came to a large open space known to his staff as the War Room. After the Clinton-Bush election of 1992, every campaign had a war room. Theirs was no different than most—desks spaced in rows across a spacious room unencumbered by partitions, a dry erase board on an easel in the corner, maps taped to the walls, handwritten notes stuck to anything that didn't move. The bright young faces that worked the room looked up as he arrived. It took a moment for reality to set in—that it was really him—then they all stood and clapped.

Talbot acknowledged them with a grin and a wave. "It's been a while since I was last here. In case you haven't seen me in a while, I'm the Republican candidate, Alexander Talbot, and I'm running for president of the United States." The room erupted in loud cheers and laughter. Talbot let them go for a moment, basking in their adoration, then waved them down. "Okay, okay," he grinned. "I appreciate the applause. Now, back to work. With your help, we might actually win this thing." Laughter teetered across the room as everyone returned to their seats and Talbot continued toward the opposite side of the room.

As he made his way in that direction, Leah Davis appeared in the doorway outside a conference room. "We're ready," she said, her serious demeanor in stark contrast to the enthusiasm of the moment.

At thirty-two, Leah was a veteran of three national campaigns, having worked her way up from state volunteer in Kentucky to become one of the most powerful Republican operatives in the country. She joined Talbot's campaign shortly after he announced and quickly assumed responsibility for executing the campaign's day-to-day strategy. With her help, Talbot had risen steadily in the polls. Much of that success came from Davis' shrewd ability to capitalize on Andrew Stanton's missteps. Now, with the election only months away, she was looking for an opportunity to repeat that tactic.

Talbot made his way toward her and stepped inside the conference room where he found his chief campaign advisors gathered around the table. He acknowledged them with a wave and a nod as he took his place at the head of the table. When everyone was ready, Davis closed the door.

"Okay," she began. "I heard the prime minister wasn't happy about his visit at the White House."

"He was livid," Talbot grinned.

"That's good," someone called from down the table.

"No," another added. "That's great. Gives us a shot at voters in New York."

"You mean Jewish voters."

"I mean we have to turn this to our advantage."

Jamie Wright spoke up. "There are more than just Jewish votes at stake on the issue. Evangelical Christians are huge supporters of Israel."

"Generally," someone corrected.

"Conservative evangelicals," another added.

"You know what I mean," Jamie nodded. "We have a chance to look presidential on the issue. And it will play well in the South."

"That's why we're here," Davis interrupted. "I think we have an opening here and we need to make the most of it."

"Can we quote him?"

"The prime minister?"

"Yes."

"No," Talbot answered, shaking his head. "We can do everything short of it, but we can't quote him."

Rick Allen spoke up. "We could denounce the bombing."

Talbot looked puzzled. "What bombing?"

"The car bomb in Rabat."

"Rabat? There was a car bombing in Rabat?"

"Just outside the Israeli Embassy," Davis stepped in to explain. "They didn't tell you?"

"Tell me what?"

"I assumed someone had briefed the prime minister about it while you were there."

"Briefed him? On what?" Talbot's voice had a hard edge. "No one briefed us on anything. We rode in the car together to Andrews. Talked on the way. He got out and I came back. What are you talking about?"

"A car bomb exploded outside the Israeli liaison's office in Rabat. Killed at least four people. All of them from the Israeli Foreign Office."

A frown wrinkled Talbot's forehead. "Anyone take responsibility for it?"

"Not yet."

"What did the president say?"

"He hasn't issued a statement yet."

Jamie spoke up. "I wonder if we should wait for him?"

Everyone else at the table replied in unison, "No."

"Might look like we're taking advantage of the situation."

"How?" Allen challenged. "How is it any different from the president issuing a statement?"

"The president is the head of state," Jamie argued. "He's supposed to issue a statement. We're the challenger, vying for office. I'm just wondering if we'll look like we're out to score some cheap points off four dead people."

"No," Davis disagreed. "This is what we've been looking for. A chance to point the finger at Stanton's weak foreign policy. If he'd been tougher, this wouldn't have happened."

"That's not true," Jamie replied.

"Who cares if it's true?" Davis threw her hands in the air in a gesture of frustration. Her voice was loud and caustic. "It's an accusation. It doesn't matter if it's true. No one expects it to be true. It's a political statement." Davis paused a moment and took a deep breath, then turned to Talbot. "You need to go live, right now, with a statement. Denounce this bombing and lay it at Stanton's feet. Now. Before he has a chance to speak."

Talbot pointed down the table. "I thought Jamie made an excellent point. We'll look like hacks. I'll look like a hack."

"Not if you do it now, before the president says anything."

"Okay." Talbot sighed. "Okay. Call a press conference."

Fifteen minutes later, Talbot appeared before a hastily gathered gaggle of reporters. Dressed in a dark suit with a white shirt and muted tie, he looked dignified, serious, and presidential.

"Just hours ago, a car bomb exploded outside the Israeli liaison's office in Rabat, Morocco. I have come to you today to extend my heartfelt sympathy to the families of those who were lost in the blast, and to say to the people of Israel that I stand with you in this dark hour. Initial reports indicate at least four people were killed in today's attack. While the investigation into this incident is ongoing, and there is still much that we do not know about it, one thing is clear. The failed policies of the current administration have created a climate around the world in which terrorists now think they can conduct themselves in a flagrant manner, without fear of meaningful reprisal. Today, more so than at any other time in history, we stand on the brink of serious global unrest. Much of that problem comes as the result of our current weak stance on terror. Unless we do something quickly, we will see even bolder action and not just from terrorists but from the nation we know directly facilitates their conduct—Iran. That's why I recently proposed that we double our naval presence in the Persian Gulf and why we must insist on establishing a permanent presence in the region. Come this November, when I am elected president, there won't be any doubt about where we stand. There won't be any question about what we will do not only in response to terrorist attacks but also to prevent them from occurring in the first place. When I am your president, we will find these people before they find us. We will change the global climate on what is acceptable conduct, and we will bring an end to the era of terror our current administration has allowed to flourish."

CHAPTER 5
ISTANBUL, TURKEY

JOHN SLADEN STARED OUT THE WINDOW at the crowded street below. Even from five floors above, the blare of car horns caught his ear and with it came the memory of a day, long ago, when he was a boy growing up in Haskell, Texas. They lived in a house on Third Street with a yard that seemed as big as a ranch. The day was hot and dry and he'd been lying on the porch enjoying the shade when the sound of a horn made him look up to see Buddy McGregor roar past the house in a new Chevrolet. They went for a ride in it later that day and during a stop at the Double A Drive In saw Laurie with Tom, and that was the end of that. Three days later he signed a scholarship commitment with Baylor to play baseball. He left town with every intention of playing in the Major League but while completing a degree in History he got interested in other things. Now, two master's degrees and a PhD later, he was halfway around the world from where he'd begun.

All of thirty-five years old, Sladen was an employee of ENX, an energy trading company and one of the many proprietary firms established by the CIA in response to the 9/11 terrorist attacks. Using bona fide financial advisors and brokers, the company traded energy futures and petroleum contracts on markets and exchanges around the globe. Profits from the business remained in bank accounts far from prying congressional eyes. With it, the CIA funded the other half of the company's operations—rendition, kidnapping, assassination, and activities far beyond the bounds of treaty, law, or moral decency. Sladen worked for the company as an analyst, reading reports, newspapers, books, and scouring the web for ideas, threats, and plausible plots that might be used to uncover previously unknown terror groups.

"Something interesting out there?" a voice called from behind. Sladen turned to see Steve Bachmann standing near the door. Bachmann, part of the analysis group, had been with ENX since the beginning. He came there straight from Harvard, where he'd been a mathematics professor. Sladen was never quite sure what he did, but he was always in the SCIF, the sensitive compartmented information facility, designed for handling the company and the nation's most important information. Sladen had been in there only once for a video-conference briefing on undisclosed operations in Iraq that continued after the official withdrawal. But Bachmann was in there almost every day.

"No." Sladen turned away from the window. "Just traffic."

"Always traffic this time of day."

"Yeah." Sladen glanced at his watch. "Oh. Didn't realize it was that late." He came from behind the desk and took his jacket from a coatrack in the corner.

"Don't rush off on my account."

"No," Sladen smiled. "Meeting a friend for a drink."

"Oh. Okay."

Sladen paused. "Sure you didn't need something?"

"No. I'm fine. Just saw you here and stopped for a minute."

"Okay." Sladen moved past him. "Got to go. See you in the morning."

Sladen made his way from the office down the hall to the corridor and stepped into the elevator. When the doors opened at the lobby downstairs, his cell phone dinged. He took it from his pocket and glanced at the screen to see an alert telling him that someone had logged on to his computer. "I thought so," he sighed.

From the lobby, Sladen made his way out to the street. Two blocks to the left, he came to Simdi Café. He took a table in back and waited. A few minutes later the door opened and Bryan Ferguson entered. A waiter brought him to the table.

A fifteen-year veteran of the foreign service, Ferguson had spent the last three years at the US Embassy in Baghdad. He called earlier in the morning to say he was passing through and asked if they could get together for a visit. A few minutes at the café was the best they could do.

"So," Sladen began after they'd greeted each other, "what brings you to town?"

"On my way to D.C."

"How long will you be gone?"

"I'm not sure." Ferguson glanced around, as if checking to see who was watching, then leaned closer and lowered his voice. "Listen, is something about to happen?"

"What do you mean?"

"You know. Military action. Are we about to go to war?"

"I don't think so. Why?"

"Two days ago they came into my office and told me I needed to clear out."

"Clear out? You mean they fired you?"

"No. They told me I was being relocated to Washington and would receive a new assignment when I got there."

"Seems a bit unusual for the State Department. They aren't known for acting quickly on anything. Did they give anyone else the same news?"

"I checked around. We had people on vacation who were told not to come back."

"They were reassigned?"

"Yeah. As far as I know, no one has been fired."

"I heard they were reducing the embassy staff in Iraq. Was this part of that?"

"I don't think so." Ferguson shook his head. "This is more like bugging out ahead of trouble."

"You think something's about to happen?"

"I don't know," Ferguson shrugged. "But it just doesn't add up. We were in the middle of some very big projects. Water treatment plants, electrical generation. Projects like that take a lot of planning and the bid process is complicated."

"And they told you to leave it and go."

"Yeah. We had contractors ready to go on two of the projects and I was told to leave it."

"To cancel the jobs?"

"No. To leave it on my desk and walk away."

"Interesting. These other people who were told not to return from vacation, were they high-level people? Low-level people?"

"High, low. Whatever. Everyone who was on leave was told not to return."

"And they had no advance notice this was coming?"

"No. None of us did. Last month they told us they were going to cancel some proposed projects. Not anything that was already in the pipeline, just projects we had wanted to do but hadn't already started. Said they had reviewed the situation and decided we'd been too optimistic in our projections of what could be accomplished. But they made it clear we weren't dropping stuff that was already in process."

"What do you think's going on?"

"I don't know but it just doesn't add up. I mean, I'm not talking about small projects here. I was in the middle of several big initiatives. Have I missed something?"

"I've been asking that same question myself." Sladen shifted his chair away from the table and crossed his legs. "Two months ago, I read an announcement that we were closing the embassy in Syria. I thought, 'That makes sense. Lot of unrest in Syria. No need to unnecessarily put people in danger.' Then last month I read that we were reducing our staff in Iraq. One of those announcements alone would have gotten past me without raising a question but the two of them together caught my attention. I began to look into it. The kind of staff changes you've described is happening all over the region."

"The region?"

"The Middle East."

"Nowhere else?"

"No. In most other places, embassy staff is expanding. In the Middle East, embassy staff is rapidly shrinking. Drastically shrinking, actually. More like 'get out now.' Jordan, Egypt, Saudi Arabia—all down to less than half their typical staff size."

Just then Ferguson pointed over Sladen's shoulder toward the door. "That the guy you were telling me about?"

"Yeah. Richard Cruse. FBI. But don't tell him what we were talking about."

Cruse came to the table. Sladen stood to greet him.

CHAPTER 6
TEHRAN, IRAN

JALIL AMINI STEPPED FROM THE CAR outside Sa'dabad Palace and walked quickly up the steps. A guard snapped to attention as he approached, then reached out to open the door. Amini rushed past him into the building. Inside, the click of Amini's heels on the marble floor echoed through the corridor. Originally constructed as a residence for Mohammad Reza, the last Shah of Iran, Sa'dabad Palace now served as both a museum and the official residence for the president.

At the center of the building, Amini came to a wide rotunda. There he turned right into a narrower hallway. At the end of the hall was a desk. A woman seated there looked up as he approached. "He's waiting for you." Amini moved past her without comment.

At sixty-one, Amini had enjoyed a long career in the Iranian military-intelligence service. He had begun as a junior officer in the Army shortly after the Islamic Revolution of the 1970s. In the first years of Ayatollah Khomeini's reign, Amini volunteered for a select death squad organized to root out officials and intellectuals who remained loyal to the Shah. His exemplary service caught the eye of several generals. When the squad was disbanded, Amini was sent to the Imam Hussein Military Academy where he obtained a graduate degree in the History of Warfare. By the time Rasoul Moussaoui was elected president, Amini was director of Army Intelligence. Shortly after the election, Moussaoui made him director of VEVAK, the Iranian Ministry of Intelligence and National Security.

Beyond the hallway, Amini came to a set of large double doors. An aide was seated to the right. He rose as Amini approached, rapped on the door, then pushed it open and stood aside. The doors swung back to reveal the president's office. Moussaoui sat behind a large, ornate oak desk that stood in the center of the room. He glanced up as Amini entered.

"You have news?"

"Yes."

A grin spread over Moussaoui's face as he looked past Amini and gestured to the aide. Moments later, the doors banged closed and the two men were alone.

"Our attempt in Rabat was a success," Amini beamed. "A complete success."

Moussaoui leaned back in his chair. "And you're sure they can't trace it back to us?"

"Israel will say it was us," Amini shrugged, "but that is what they always say. The trail ends with Hezbollah. No further."

Moussaoui ran his hand across his chin as if thinking. "And the Americans? What will they say?"

"The president will denounce the attack," Amini replied. "But sources tell us they will let Israel do most of the talking."

Moussaoui gestured to a chair in front of the desk. "What about Talbot?"

"He is a politician." Amini took a seat in the chair. "We know what to expect from him."

"You saw his statement?"

"Yes. Typical American political rhetoric. It means nothing to them."

"You are certain of this?"

"Yes," Amini nodded. "It means only that Talbot is an opportunist."

"Have the Americans shared their intelligence about the bombing with the Israelis?"

"Not yet."

"Interesting," Moussaoui muttered. "Is that an intentional decision?"

"Perhaps. Stanton is worried the Israelis will drag him into a war."

"He is afraid to fight," Moussaoui nodded.

"Not afraid to fight." Amini shook his head. "Just afraid of what it will do to his reelection prospects."

"I thought the Americans liked a fighter."

"They do. But they love cheap gasoline even more. Even the mention of conflict with us drives oil prices higher. That pushes up the cost of gasoline, which has a negative effect on the American economy."

"Which is yet one more reason why we must do everything to see that tensions remain high." Moussaoui leaned forward and propped his elbows on the desk. "Tell me, what happened to the action we planned in Thailand?"

Amini's eyes darted away. "The bomb failed."

"It failed?"

"Yes," Amini's eyes focused on Moussaoui. "There was a problem with the detonator. They did not wire it properly."

"Stupid operatives," Moussaoui scoffed. "I thought using our own people was supposed to prevent this. What about the one in Los Angeles?"

"Our operative got lost on the way to the synagogue."

Moussaoui leaned back quickly, a look of disgust on his face. "These are the best people you could find?"

Amini's shoulders sagged. "They were both recruited by Farjami."

Moussaoui ran his fingers through his hair. "They should have shot him long before they did."

"Perhaps so."

Moussaoui stood. "We should wait for the Americans to move before we try again."

"Yes," Amini rose from the chair. "I agree."

Moussaoui came from behind the desk. He draped an arm across Amini's shoulder as they walked toward the door. "You will see that their families are rewarded?"

"Already done."

"Good," Moussaoui smiled.

CHAPTER 7
HERZLIYA, ISRAEL

A SCREEN ON THE WALL of the Mossad operations center came alive. Daphna Abergil, an analyst seated at a desk across the room, spoke up. "Something's happened in Rabat." Everyone in the center turned to watch as images of two burning vehicles appeared on the screen. "This is a live feed from a camera outside the liaison's office. That's our SUV on the right. This is what happened." The screen split with one half showing real-time images, the other playing video images from five minutes earlier. As the video played, the gates of the compound opened and a black SUV appeared. The SUV turned on the street as the gates closed behind it. Moments later, a green Fiat appeared on the screen. It approached the SUV from behind. While those in the room watched, the car pulled alongside the SUV and exploded.

The room was quiet as Abergil continued. "All passengers in both vehicles are dead."

Someone spoke up. "Do we know who was in the SUV?"

"Four staff members from the foreign ministry and their driver."

"When did this happen?"

"Images on the right are live. It happened just a few minutes ago. As you can see, the fire is still burning."

Just then, the door to the room burst open and Efraim Hofi, the Mossad director, rushed in. He pointed toward the screen. "Is this the latest?"

"Yes, sir," Abergil replied. "You're looking at a live picture."

"Any other cameras in the area?"

"We're working on that now," Abergil added.

"What's the casualty count?"

"Four passengers and the driver in the SUV. Two passengers in the car beside it, as nearly as we can tell."

"As nearly as we can tell?"

"The car is still burning, sir."

On the screen a fire crew appeared alongside the SUV and began hosing down the flames. Hofi watched for a moment, then called over his shoulder, "Any satellite imagery?"

"Still searching."

"Where's the prime minister?"

"Still in flight. On his way back from America."

"Who do we have on the airplane?"

"Dover Yavin."

Hofi turned to face Abergil. "Write up a public version of what we know so far. Get it to him. Tell him to brief the prime minister. We'll follow up with details when he lands."

Hofi stepped closer to the screen. Abergil rose from her desk and came to his side. She glanced over her shoulder to an operator near the center of the room. "Tighten up on the left, please." The image moved in on the car.

A frown creased Hofi's forehead. "Is that a body lying in the street?"

"Yes, sir. Apparently it's the driver of the car. The door is missing. Agents on site have determined he is dead. He must have been blown from the car in the explosion."

Hofi pointed to the screen. "Tighten up on that body." The image of the man filled the screen to show his face was turned toward the camera. "Zoom in closer." The image appeared even larger. Hofi glanced at Abergil. "Have someone sharpen that image. See if our face-recognition software can find him in the database."

Abergil returned to her desk and loaded the image from the screen into the face-recognition program. Moments later, the monitor flashed a hit. "We have someone," she called.

"Already?"

An analyst announced from across the room. "The man lying in the street is Jabbar Hamadeh. A known Hezbollah operative."

CHAPTER 8
WASHINGTON, DC.

ON THE THIRD FLOOR OF THE PENTAGON, Dick Elser sat at his desk reading the final report on a naval exercise conducted three weeks earlier off the coast of Japan. As secretary of the Navy, he'd become accustomed to dry and unimaginative memos, but this one was particularly difficult to read. When he reached the end of the first page he tossed the report on the desktop, leaned back in his chair, and rubbed his eyes.

The office door swung open and an assistant appeared. "Check the news," she blurted.

"What happened?"

She crossed the room and picked up a remote from a table in the corner. "Car bomb in Morocco." She pointed the remote toward a television set.

"Any Americans involved?"

"No," she said tersely. "Israelis."

Seconds later a newscast appeared on the screen. Elser watched in amazement at images of a burning vehicle outside the Israeli liaison office. "This is just what we'd hoped would happen," he whispered. As the news continued to play, he turned to a credenza behind his desk and opened a drawer. He flipped through several files and took out a folder. Inside was a fleet status assessment for the Navy's presence in the Persian Gulf. It had arrived three days earlier. He leaned back in his chair and rocked gently as he scanned the report, then reviewed a cover memo. A satisfied smile appeared as he read again the memo's proposed recommendation to move additional ships to the Persian Gulf and Indian Ocean. The president had been reluctant to discuss the matter, and Elser had held off making a formal request. Now perhaps he should go forward with the issue.

When Elser finished reading the report, he scooted up to the desk and took a pen from the top drawer. With a flourish, he added the current date at the top of the memo and scribbled his initials to one side of the document. Then, folder in hand, he stepped from behind the desk and started toward the door.

From his office suite, Elser walked down the E Ring corridor. As he rounded the corner toward the next wing of the building, he saw Hayden Upchurch, the secretary of defense, emerge from the third-floor command center. Upchurch caught sight of Elser and paused to wait. Elser drew near and flashed a confident smile. "See the report from Rabat?"

"Yeah," Upchurch nodded. "We were just monitoring it."

Elser leaned close and lowered his voice. "This is exactly the kind of thing we were hoping for." He handed Upchurch the fleet report. "Our assessment of naval strength in the Gulf. The Navy's official position is this: If you're going to ask us to defend, you have to give us the power we need to do the job."

"Good," Upchurch nodded once more. "I have a meeting at the White House this afternoon. I'll go over it with them then." He turned toward the door to his office just across the hall. "Come in. I have something I want to show you."

Elser followed. When they were inside the office, Upchurch closed the door, then moved behind his desk. "This came in the other day." He opened a desk drawer and took out a document. "I'm not sure you've seen it yet." He handed a document to Elser.

Elser scanned it, then glanced up, his eyes wide. "Where'd this come from?"

"Someone at ENX created it."

Elser looked puzzled. "ENX?"

"CIA group in Turkey."

"I thought Attwood had them under control."

"Attwood thought he did, too," Upchurch chuckled.

Elser glanced back at the document. "John Sladen? Never heard of him."

"They say he's been around awhile. Have him doing this kind of research as a routine matter. Looking for plots, ideas, things no one else is thinking about."

"How long has this report been floating around?"

"About a week."

Elser looked at Upchurch. "How did you get hold of it?"

"I have more than one source at Langley."

"What can we do about it?"

"I already spoke to Attwood. He thinks it won't be a problem."

"I don't know." Elser shook his head. "Things aren't like they used to be. We spy on everyone now. We spy on others and on ourselves. And we even spy on ourselves spying on ourselves."

Upchurch rose from behind the desk. "I have another meeting on this Rabat thing."

Elser gestured with the report. "You need this?"

"Keep it. I can print another copy."

They walked together to the doorway. Elser paused at the hall and gestured with the report once more. "Is this going to be a problem?"

"I'll talk to the director. I think it'll be okay."

"Will the Rabat thing be enough to do what we want?"

Upchurch looked confident. "Between the bombing in Rabat and the Mossad agent we're about to give them, I think it will be more than Israel can resist. They'll have to act."

"You really think Iran will take the Mossad tip seriously?"

"They're as easy to maneuver as the Israelis. They're both so focused on each other, they'll trip over themselves trying to be the first to blow up something."

"Well, let's hope the Israelis move first. If Iran goes first, our plan falls apart and we're in the midst of a war."

"Dick," Upchurch grinned, "we're always in the midst of a war."

CHAPTER 9
HERZLIYA, ISRAEL

HOFI OPENED THE DOOR of the operations center and stepped inside. "Okay." He moved toward the center of the room. "Where are we on the car bombing?"

Daphna Abergil glanced up. "Still processing the debris." She came from her desk and moved across the room to stand beside Hofi. "We don't have a report yet. But an initial test of residue at the site indicates the explosive material was Semtex."

Hofi glanced in her direction. "Not acetone peroxide?"

"No, sir."

Hofi turned back to the screen, pointing with his right hand. "This was the work of the Iranians."

"I would agree," Abergil nodded. "Difficult to obtain plastic explosives without a government connection. Or at least a commercial license."

"Get someone on it," Hofi directed. "Find out who in Morocco had access to Semtex. If that's really what they used, they must have acquired it locally. I doubt they tried to bring it into the country."

"Records there are sketchy at best. It'll be a long shot."

"Yeah, I know. But we might find something, too." Hofi nodded toward the image on the screen. "They used Hezbollah to drive the car, but this was the work of the Iranians." He glanced in Daphna's direction. "And we might just be able to prove it." He turned to face the others in the room. "Listen up. We need to gather every shred of evidence that points to the identity of the people who did this. We have people on the ground processing the scene.

They'll send us what they find. In the meantime, we need to do our part. Let's start with the basics. Do we have any other video from the scene?"

Nissim Karpin, an analyst seated to the right, spoke up. "Just a single traffic camera on the corner. We're analyzing video from it now."

"Good," Hofi nodded. "Any other cameras in the area?"

"None that we have found so far," Karpin continued. "Not many traffic cameras in Rabat. We were lucky to get this one."

"What about satellite imagery?"

"Nothing yet," Arnon Podell answered. "Still trying to pry it loose from the Americans."

"Well, work faster. If we want to make the case that Iran did this, working through Hezbollah, we'll need everything we can find. Begin with the images. We have a name for one of the men. Run with it and see what you can find. We'll get you information on the car as they get it on the ground."

The door opened and Hofi's assistant, Mara Moss, entered the room. "Sir, they need you on a conference call from Rabat."

Hofi pointed toward a screen on the wall. "Put it on the screen. I'll talk from here."

"Sir, this involves the Americans." Mara gestured over her shoulder. "They need you in the SCIF."

"Very well." Hofi started across the room. "Maybe now we'll get those satellite images."

CHAPTER 10
WASHINGTON, D.C.

KATHLEEN BAKER STOOD in the State Department situation room and watched video from the camera outside the Israeli liaison's office in Rabat—the same video seen by Hofi and his team of analysts at the Mossad operations center. Relayed by satellite, Baker watched as workers on the street battled to extinguish the blaze. When the fire was out, technicians moved through the scene processing the debris.

"They're Israelis?"

"Yes," an aide replied. "The ones in blue are Israelis. Two men behind them in brown uniforms are Moroccan."

At fifty-nine, Baker was only the third woman to serve as secretary of state. She came to the office from the Senate where she represented the people of Vermont and chaired the Foreign Services Committee. A graduate of Harvard, she held a law degree from the University of Virginia and a master's degree in International Relations from Georgetown. She was tall, slender, attractive, and very much at home in a world dominated by strong, powerful men.

She pointed to the video screen. "Has anyone taken responsibility for this?"

Crawford Woodside, the undersecretary for Africa, stood nearby, arms folded across his chest, feet planted in a wide, defiant stance. "Not yet, Madam Secretary. But I'm sure a video will turn up before long."

"Al Qa'ida?"

"No, ma'am. Al Qa'ida hates us. Hezbollah hates the Israelis."

"That's a rather bright line, Ford."

"The gray areas are easier to see that way."

"You have gray areas?"

"A few."

Baker continued to talk as she watched the monitor. "You think the Muslims divide the world like that? One group assigned to us. The other assigned to Israel."

"Actually, I think Hezbollah would evolve into a political party if Iran would leave them alone."

"Really?"

"That's how they took over Lebanon and the Gaza Strip. Didn't do it with a gun. Did it by convincing the people to follow them."

"Or die."

"Maybe so."

"What about the Israelis?" Baker gestured toward the screen. "What are they saying about this?"

"Not a word yet. Either official or unofficial."

"Interesting."

"Yes." Woodside nodded. "I would have expected—"

The door opened, interrupting their conversation. Alicia Kirkland appeared. "Madam Secretary, there's a call for you in your office."

Baker had a stern expression. "Take a message. I'll call them back."

Alicia arched an eyebrow. "It's Nancy Shatwell."

"Okay." Baker sighed. She called over her shoulder as she turned toward the door, "I'll be back in a minute, Ford."

Across the hall in her office, Baker moved behind the desk and picked up the phone. Nancy's voice was a whisper. "Secretary Upchurch is on his way to the White House to meet with Jean Brown."

"Wasn't this already on the schedule?"

"Yes, but Mr. Upchurch has a report with him."

"What is it?"

"Something about a fleet status assessment."

"Did you see it?"

"No, ma'am. Mr. Elser gave it to him this morning. I didn't get a chance to read it but I saw the top sheet when they came from the office."

"Is that one of the topics on the agenda for their meeting?"

"No. That's why I called."

"Thanks." Baker hung up the phone and came from her office. Alicia's desk sat a few feet from the doorway. She paused there. "I need time with the president. Preferably this morning."

"Yes, Madam Secretary. I'll call over there now."

CHAPTER 11
WASHINGTON, D.C.

HADEN UPCHURCH WATCHED from the rear window of the limousine as the car made the turn onto the driveway and rolled quietly toward the West Wing of the White House. As the car came to a stop he took a leather pouch from the seat beside him and waited patiently while a guard stepped to the car. When the door opened finally, Upchurch climbed out and made his way toward the building.

From the reception lobby, Upchurch walked down a hall to the right and came to the office of Jean Brown, the president's national security advisor. She was seated at her desk when an assistant opened the door. The two shook hands. Brown gestured to a chair. "Have a seat." Upchurch dropped onto a chair. Brown returned to her seat behind the desk. "Anything we haven't heard about this situation in Rabat?"

"I don't think so. We get our information from the same place as you. How's it look?"

"Israelis are in control on the ground. Moroccans are letting them take the lead. I'm sure we'll get some solid information soon."

"Finally catching our breath from Yedaya's meeting and now this," Upchurch smiled. "How was the final session?"

Brown shook her head. "I thought they were going to fight."

The smile on Upchurch's face broadened into a grin. "That would be a sight worth seeing."

"I'm not kidding," Brown insisted. "A couple of times they got so hot I thought Yedaya might hit the president."

"So," Upchurch needled, "is it war when the leaders of two countries engage each other in a fistfight?"

"We were close to finding out."

They shared a laugh over the banter, then Upchurch turned the conversation to the topic at hand. "Well," he leaned forward. "At least we got through that. Now, about the car bombing."

"Yes."

"We need to develop a response."

"We have a meeting of the National Security Team set for tomorrow to review our options."

"Right," Upchurch noted. "But you and I ought to get on the same page before then."

"Okay." Jean leaned back in her chair. "What were you thinking of?"

"One possibility is to move additional ships to the Gulf."

Brown winced with a disapproving look. "We've about worked that response dry, Haden. We already have two carrier groups over there. The water's getting pretty full."

"This isn't just about the ships."

"Oh? Then what's it about?"

"It's about making a response."

"You mean any response is a good response?"

"Sort of. The ships there now were sent in response to Iran's threat to close the Strait of Hormuz. They threatened; we sent ships. This bombing in Morocco is their response to our response."

"I'm not so sure," Brown replied, shaking her head. "This car bombing has Hezbollah written all over it."

"Right, Hezbollah is doing Iran's heavy lifting."

"But it was a strike against an Israeli target," Brown countered. "The threat to close the strait was a threat aimed at us."

"Not exactly." Upchurch pointed with his index finger for emphasis. "Iran sees the two of us—the U.S. and Israel—as one and the same."

"Maybe," Brown said with a shrug. "So what do you propose?"

Upchurch reached inside the leather pouch he carried and took out a folder. He handed it across the desk to Brown. "This is a fleet assessment prepared by the Navy. They are ready to submit a request for the president to send three guided missile cruisers to the Gulf. Three destroyers to the Indian Ocean. And another submarine, preferably deployed to the Gulf but anywhere in the region will do."

"That's a lot of firepower."

Upchurch slid back in his chair. "If there's trouble, we'll need all the firepower we can get. Have you talked to the president about a response?"

"Yeah," Brown scowled. "We've talked. And talked."

"What's he thinking?"

"It's a military situation. He's dragging his feet, as usual. Won't decide anything."

"I don't have to tell you, twenty percent of the world's oil passes through the Strait of Hormuz. If Iran blocks it, oil prices will go through the roof. The economy will tank. And your reelection chances will evaporate."

"Yeah," Brown nodded. "Lately that's all I'm hearing. Lot of people around here don't see the difference between politics and policy."

"Best way to keep Iran from attempting a blockade is to make it obvious they can't win. To do that, we need an overwhelming force ready to act."

"We don't know Iran's next move, but—"

"No," Upchurch interrupted. "And we don't know Israel's next move, either. But we don't want to get caught flat-footed. If Iran attempts to close the strait, we'll have to respond quickly and decisively."

Brown glanced over the report. "If that happens, we'll need another carrier in the region."

"Maybe. What will it take to get the president to move on this?"

"We should make sure Pete's on our side," Brown suggested. "The president is much more likely to go along if we have his chief of staff behind it."

"Then you agree?"

"Yeah," Brown nodded. "I agree. If the Navy says they need the ships, they ought to get them."

"Good," Upchurch smiled. "Is Pete in the building?"

"Yeah."

"Think we can see him now?"

"I'm sure we can." Brown glanced at her watch as she rose from behind the desk. "The president is about to make a statement condemning the bombing in Rabat. He'll be in the Rose Garden in a few minutes. We can see Pete when they get through with that."

"I saw Talbot beat you guys to the punch on the statement. I guess politics trumps protocol."

Brown's face went cold. "The president was livid."

"So much for allowing the head of state to set foreign policy."

"Exactly."

CHAPTER 12
NEW YORK CITY

DAVID HOLSTEN STEPPED FROM THE TAXI and made his way inside the Harvard Club. From the lobby, he rode the elevator to the third floor and walked down the hall to a meeting room on the front side of the building, overlooking Forty-Fourth Street.

At forty-two, Holsten had already enjoyed a stellar and lucrative career as a political and business consultant. A lawyer by training, he first assisted on a campaign when a friend ran for the Massachusetts State Legislature. When the campaign proved successful, Holsten was hooked. Three more local races followed, then he moved up to his first statewide effort helping an unknown legislator from Illinois named Andrew Stanton in a bid to become a United States senator. When Stanton won, Holsten left the practice of law to lead a four-year effort to convince voters Stanton should be their next president.

When Stanton took office, he offered Holsten his pick of White House positions, but he declined, opting instead to continue working as a consultant. Using his Washington connections, he built an impressive array of clients, including some of the country's wealthiest businessmen and investors, which brought him to the meeting that day at the Harvard Club.

Gathered in the room were Curtis McCullough, Dan Luckett, and Sidney Adkins. For the modest sum of five million dollars each, they all had become principal owners of an investment vehicle known as the Shale Oil Real Estate Investment Trust, a daring attempt to cash in on potential profit from an as yet unpublicized discovery of shale oil reserves found beneath parts of western South Dakota.

Holsten made his way across the room to a wet bar. He poured himself a drink and found a seat with the others. A few minutes later, the door opened and Michael Geller entered.

At sixty-one, Geller had made a fortune as a hedge fund manager, where he showed an uncanny ability to purchase shares of stock in publicly traded corporations just prior to the announcement of market-changing news. When gold prices reached an all-time high he sold short, betting that a debt deal for faltering European countries would ease the price. Days later, when the deal was announced, gold plummeted, netting Geller's fund a handsome profit. While others dumped shares of automobile manufacturers in the 2008 recession, Geller invested heavily and saw their value triple after the federal government implemented a rescue package for the companies. When federal regulators became suspicious and began an investigation, Geller brought in Holsten to manage the fund's response. After the matter was resolved without any fines or penalties, Geller placed Holsten on a permanent retainer.

Curtis McCullough looked up as Geller entered. "Did we get the final option?"

"Yes, we signed the papers this morning."

"That gives us control of the whole tract?"

"Fifteen thousand acres," Geller nodded. "Wilson is finishing up the details now."

"And the tests confirmed this last section has oil shale deposits?"

"Yes. At least as good as the others. The geologists signed off on the report last night."

"Good."

Luckett took a seat beside McCullough. "Well, gentlemen, I believe we are now the largest independent players in South Dakota shale oil. When do we start drilling?"

"A few more car bombs," McCullough answered, "and we can sell without drilling a single well."

"Hey," Adkins protested, "nobody said anything about drilling."

"Relax," Geller soothed. "We aren't getting into production. We're just in it for the appreciation in value."

"Speaking of which," Luckett turned to Holsten. "Think this situation in Morocco will bring a response from the president?"

"The people I've talked to think he'll respond, eventually."

"Eventually?" Luckett scowled. "We don't need eventually. We need it now."

"Oil prices are up."

"Yes," McCullough nodded. "But if he responds, prices will stabilize here and create a pricing floor. The next event will push them higher."

"Why does he always equivocate on military action?"

"He's a Democrat," Geller chuckled.

"But seriously, any idea what that response will be?"

"The Navy is ready to ask for more ships," Holsten answered. "I suspect he'll give them what they want."

"Ships," McCullough scoffed. "They did that the last time. He needs to blow up something."

Adkins spoke up. "I heard the meeting with Yedaya didn't go well. Think Israel will act against Iran on its own?"

"Perhaps," Holsten nodded. "But Yedaya is operating—"

"Those Jews," McCullough chortled. "They won't take anything off anyone."

Holsten continued. "The two countries formulate policy by two different assumptions."

"Ahh." Adkins gestured with a dismissive wave of his hand. "That's a lot of Washington nonsense."

"No," Holsten said, shaking his head. "This is the crux of the matter. The U.S. sees oil supplies as the most crucial priority shaping policy for that region and so the president is more focused on threats to the Strait of Hormuz. Israel is looking only at Iran's nuclear program, which they see as a threat to their existence."

"Which it is," Adkins nodded.

"Right. But Israel sees that threat as the immediate concern. The president thinks Iran's program is a long way from being able to produce a weapon."

"We should let Israel blow them up and just get on with it."

"Well," Holsten demurred. "That's an aspect of the issue that complicates the matter. Iran may have reached the point at which its nuclear facilities are no longer vulnerable to attack by anyone."

"We don't want word of that to get out," McCullough cautioned. "If news like that gets to the market, the tension of a pending attack will evaporate. Oil prices will drop like a rock."

Adkins pressed the point. "You mean we can't hit them with our bombs?"

"We could hit them, but we might not be able to find all the sites," Holsten explained. "They have multiple centrifuge facilities and numerous ancillary installations. That gives them a redundancy that makes it almost impossible to disable their program with limited air strikes."

"So, that brings us back to the first question," McCullough continued. "Will Israel act on its own?"

Holsten shot Geller a knowing look. "We're working on that right now."

"If they did," McCullough grinned, "that would be great."

"Yeah," Adkins groused, "and then New York would become a target for every extremist in the world."

Luckett gave him a doleful look. "We're already a target for them."

"Good point."

"They might try to hit us," McCullough beamed, "but oil prices would go out of sight."

CHAPTER 13
TUBAS, ISRAEL

FAR OUT IN THE DESERT near the Jordanian border, Chaim Sharett sat at his workstation inside a computer center operated by the Israeli Defense Force. Feet propped on the desk, his eyes were glued to a paperback novel. As he paused to turn the page, he glanced at his watch. He'd been on duty for seven hours. Only one more hour and then he could return to the barracks.

Years earlier, in an effort to obtain a negotiated peace with the Palestinian National Authority, Israeli forces withdrew from defensive positions in southern Lebanon. Though the effort was an attempt to obtain long-term security, it left Israel vulnerable in the short term to surprise attack from its neighbors. In an effort to address that problem, the IDF established a series of listening posts along the country's northern, eastern, and southern borders.

Through that effort, code-named Operation Jericho, an extensive array of antennas began intercepting transmissions from every frequency on the radio spectrum. At the same time, trunk lines and cables entering the country were spliced and cell phone towers were tapped, rerouting both domestic and international calls through three large computer centers. One of those centers was located in Tubas, where Sharett worked.

At the center, computers developed especially for the project created digital copies of every call, text message, and email before sending the transmission to its destination. Because of the speed of the processors, the interruption was all but imperceptible even to the most astute users. Once safely added to the computer's database, the files were then analyzed using software programed to detect key phrases. No phone call, text message, or email sent from or received by a device within Israeli borders escaped review.

As Sharett continued to read, his eyes grew heavy and his head tilted forward, pressing his chin against his chest. Suddenly a buzzer sounded. He moved both feet to the floor and sat up straight in his chair. On the screen, a message indicated the system had flagged one of the intercepted transmissions. Sharett followed a link on the screen and opened a file. In it he found a copy of a text message that contained the numbers 2-512-3-79. He picked up the phone and called his supervisor. Moments later Ariel Olmert appeared at Sharett's cubicle.

"What do you have?"

"That," Sharett said, pointing to the screen. "But I have no idea what it is."

"The system flagged it?"

"Yes."

"Let me check the source." Olmert reached past Sharett.

With a few strokes of the keyboard, a dialog box appeared. Sharett frowned as he read the text. "What does that mean?"

"Mossad."

"Mossad? We intercepted a call to Mossad?"

"No. The system flagged a text message." Olmert entered a command and a second screen appeared. "This was a text message from a number registered in Spain."

"But you said it was Mossad."

"The program flagged the content of the message."

"I don't understand."

"You don't have to." Olmert captured the data flagged by the computer and pressed a key on the keyboard. "There, now you can return to reading your novel."

Sharett glanced at the monitor to see that the screen displayed its normal image. "What did you do?"

"I did what I'm supposed to do." He patted Sharett on the shoulder. "Good job."

*   *   *

In Herzliya, Efraim Hofi was sound asleep in an on-call room at the operations center when someone shook his leg. He opened his eyes to see Arnon Podell standing at the foot of his cot.

"The center at Tubas got a hit on one of our cell phone numbers."

Hofi squinted. "Whose number is it?"

"Revach."

Hofi sat up, wide awake and fully alert. "He is still in Qom?"

"Yes, the number was included in a text message."

"Who sent it?"

"Someone in Spain sent it to a cell phone in Qom."

"One of our cell phones?"

"No." Podell shook his head. "The phone is registered to an Iranian."

"Where did the caller from Spain get our agent's number?"

"We aren't certain yet. They're still working on it."

Hofi rolled off the cot and stood. "Any way to contact Revach?"

"Not without using the phone."

"What about other people in the area?"

"We're working to reach them, but it takes time."

Hofi started toward the door. "When is Revach supposed to report in?"

"Tomorrow." Podell glanced at his watch. "Actually today. It's early."

"And when he reports, they will see the call."

"Yes, sir."

"And they will use the transmission to locate him." Hofi opened the door and stepped out in the hall. "Someone gave him up. Mine the data behind those calls and find out who did this."

"Yes, sir."

CHAPTER 14
NEW YORK CITY

MICHAEL GELLER DROVE ALONE down Thirty-Fourth Street and through the Queens Midtown Tunnel beneath the East River. He emerged on the opposite side and followed the Long Island Expressway east across the island. An hour and a half later, he arrived at Hampton Bays. Just past the Methodist church, he turned right onto Springville Road and made his way to a narrow driveway that led down to Smith Creek.

At the end of the drive he came to a rambling one-story house with white clapboard siding. Geller parked on a gravel court, stepped from the car, and walked up the path to the back door of the house. As he started up the steps, the door opened and a housekeeper appeared. She gestured for him to enter, then led him down a broad central hallway.

On the opposite end of the house they came to a study. Paneling made of knotty pine covered the walls, the wood burnished by time and sunlight to a rich brown color with a hint of red and orange. Windows along the wall to the right afforded a view of the creek and the bay beyond. Bookcases lined the walls to the left and at the end of the room opposite the door. In between was a desk with two chairs in front.

On the wall to the left of the desk was a shadow box. In it was a Nazi shoulder band. The red swastika contrasted sharply with the gray band. To the right, in between the windows overlooking the water, were framed black-and-white photographs showing scenes from World War II. The first was of German officers in the field with Hitler. Another showed them reviewing a map that was spread across the hood of a car. Still another showed Hitler with his head down, arms behind his back, as if listening to the others. The one closest to the desk was a picture of Hitler and two men apparently locked in a serious and earnest discussion.

In one of the chairs near the desk sat Franz Baer. At eighty-nine, he looked his age but did not appear frail. He held a tumbler in his right hand and tipped it up for a sip as Geller entered the room. "Join me," he gestured with the glass. "Ava will get you a drink." The housekeeper disappeared while the two men talked. She returned a few minutes later with a drink and handed it to Geller. When she was gone, Baer gestured to the chair next to him. "Have a seat. We have a few things to discuss." He reached behind him and pushed the door closed.

Geller dropped onto the chair. "I assumed that was why you called."

"I am disturbed by what I hear, Michael."

"What is it that you hear?"

"I hear rumors that you are involved in some grand scheme. Out to complete the work of the Führer or some such nonsense."

Geller stared across the room, avoiding Baer's gaze as he replied, "It would take the effort of twenty men to complete even a tenth of what the Führer envisioned."

Baer patted him on the knee. "Your grandfather would be proud to hear you speak so well of such a great man."

"My grandfather gave his life for the glorious principles." Geller glanced in Baer's direction. "I should be glad to do the same."

Baer pointed to the photo of Hitler talking to two men. "We were both ready to give our lives, your grandfather and I." The old man's eyes grew misty. "Your grandfather was a remarkable man. Whatever Hitler suggested, he found a way to accomplish." Baer paused to take a sip from the glass in his hand. "Hitler wanted to bring back Germans from the Netherlands. Your grandfather was the one who devised the plan to make it happen. Eliminated the Jews from Poland, relocated the Poles to the East, put our countrymen in their place. And he did it all at once."

"Must have been a logistical nightmare."

"It was a remarkable feat," Baer said with pride. He turned from the picture to face Geller. "You are equally as remarkable as your grandfather, perhaps even more so. But you must be very careful. Those of us who remain faithful to the cause have been very careful to do our work in anonymity. No one must risk exposure." He touched Geller on the elbow and looked him in the eye. "No one will allow it. We all swore an oath many years ago."

"We aren't going to expose anyone," Geller interjected. "The Society of the Broken Cross shall remain in the shadows, where it has been since the war ended."

"And I hope it remains so. Success will bring you a thousand friends. But failure—even the threat of failure—will turn your dearest friends into mortal enemies. You understand what I am saying?"

"I understand."

"Be sure that you do." Baer took a sip from his drink. "My friends tell me Yosef Weiss has been using his access to the president to press for military assistance for the Jews."

"I don't doubt it."

"They tell me the prime minister requested refueling tankers, and the president turned him down. Weiss has been making overtures to the Republicans as a way of pressuring Stanton to act. Do you think he will give in to the temptation of the Jews?"

"I am meeting with him tomorrow. I'll know more then."

"You have a meeting with Weiss?"

"No," Geller said, shaking his head. "The president."

"Good," Baer nodded. "Is he as stupid as they say?"

"No. He's actually very smart. His problem is, he just doesn't care about governing as much as he does about holding the office."

They sat in silence a moment, each sipping their drink. Then Baer leaned away and his eyes grew dark. "I believe you have been using Holsten to help you with this … project."

"Yes."

"Do you think that is wise?"

"Holsten is in a unique position to be of assistance."

"Yes," Baer nodded. "But he brings with him the background of a traitor."

His voice took a hard edge. "Many of our people were imprisoned because of his uncle's lies. Good German officers whose only crime was executing the orders they were given."

"The others provide financing and the cover of apparent legitimacy," Geller explained. "Holsten actually makes things happen. And besides, he had nothing to do with his uncle's testimony. That was long before he was even born."

"Yes," Baer nodded thoughtfully. "It was a long time ago, but we have a very long memory."

Geller had a questioning look. "Do you know something I don't?"

"Only that in a work of this nature, there can be no loose ends. Addressing that concern, as it relates to him, may prove … problematic. People might notice."

"I am aware of that."

Baer arched an eyebrow. "Are you certain you do?"

"Yes," Geller nodded. "There can be no loose ends."

"You may have to clean up some of those loose ends yourself. Are you prepared to do that?"

"When the time comes," Geller said confidently, "I shall do as the situation requires." He gave Baer a tight-lipped smile. "On that you have my promise."

CHAPTER 15
QOM, IRAN

MEHRAN GOLZAR, A SENIOR IRANIAN intelligence officer, entered the security center at the Fordow enrichment facility. Constructed on the outskirts of town, the plant was capable of refining uranium to twenty percent purity, a crucial step in the process of making a bomb. Golzar crossed the room to a workstation near the wall opposite the door and leaned over the shoulder of an analyst working there. "I have a number I want you to track."

"A phone number?"

Golzar nodded. "A cell phone number."

"You have authorization for this?"

"I am the authorization." Golzar pointed to himself. "You're getting this straight from me. No written orders. No email messages. I am telling you directly."

"Very well." The analyst turned to the computer on his desk and opened a program that monitored cell phone traffic in the region. "What is the number?"

Golzar took his cell phone from his pocket and glanced at the screen as he read the number aloud. "2-512-3-79." He looked up with a quizzical expression. "That is a valid phone number?"

"Yes, that is a valid number."

A dialog box appeared on the computer screen, indicating the program accepted the number. When the analyst closed the box, a second page appeared with information for the number. Golzar pointed. "What's that?"

"This shows activity for the number. A call was made from that number three days ago."

Golzar had a troubled frown. "Where was the phone when the call was made?"

"Here," the analyst replied.

"Here?" Golzar's troubled look turned to surprise. "At the center?"

"No. I mean here." The analyst gestured toward the monitor on his desk. "In our system. In the region."

Golzar relaxed. "You can tell me where the phone is located?"

"Not now. The phone is not turned on. I can tell you the cell phone tower that transmitted the previous call, but to locate the phone it must be turned on."

"It is not turned on now?"

"No." The analyst shook her head. "If it was on, the number on the screen would blink."

"But you are certain the number is valid? It is assigned to an actual phone that is operational?"

"Yes. The number is a working number."

"Good," Golzar nodded. "Notify me the moment it is turned on."

"I will."

"You have my number?"

"Yes."

"Call me the moment that cell phone is turned on." Golzar turned to leave. "Call me regardless of the time."

CHAPTER 16
ISTANBUL, TURKEY

THE CONVERSATION WITH BRYAN FERGUSON over coffee the evening before had only served to heighten John Sladen's curiosity about reduction of embassy staff in strategic Middle Eastern countries. When he arrived at the office that next morning, he set to work looking again for an answer.

Sladen, a conspiracy buff since high school, found it easy to imagine a grand scheme in which appointed officials created a government within a government, operating on their own agenda. Finding a scenario wasn't his problem. The trouble was in the details, and one of the things that troubled him most about what he knew of the reductions in embassy staff was the lack of an official order from the State Department.

Under normal circumstances, changes in personnel were implemented by a memo authorizing the action and a written plan, many of them, in fact, covering every aspect of the action along with detailed analysis of what to expect at each stage. For a movement of the size he'd uncovered, there would have been volumes of supporting documentation and a procedure for follow-up review to ensure the transfers were carried out in an orderly manner. That none of that seemed to exist created a conflict in Sladen's mind. On the one hand, conspirators would want the paper trail to be as thin as possible. On the other hand, no one below the level of a political appointee could carry out such an ambitious plan without supporting documents.

In the quest to find an answer to his dilemma, Sladen turned to a detailed organizational chart of the State Department bureaucracy. There, he stumbled across an obscure section known as the Office of Management Policy, Rightsizing, and Innovation. Undersecretary Richard Ware ran the office. Ware, it seemed, had the authority to assign personnel as circumstances and embassy needs required, but the reshuffling Sladen uncovered went far beyond the filling of routine assignments and occasional downsizing. He looked again at the latest embassy staff figures. "In Qatar," he mumbled, "they're down to barely meeting basic consular services."

"Talking to yourself again?" a voice called from across the room. Sladen looked up to see Steve Bachmann standing in the doorway. Bachman pointed to the files and documents that covered Sladen's desk. "You're into a new project?"

"No." Sladen was trying his best to convey his displeasure at the interruption. "Same one as before."

"That thing about transferring embassy personnel?"

"Yeah. But it's more than mere transfers."

"Oh? You've found something new?"

Sladen looked up at him. "What were you doing on my computer yesterday?"

"Oh." Bachmann's eyes darted away. "I needed to check on something … and didn't want anyone to see."

"Liar," Sladen said flatly.

"No," Bachmann insisted. "It's true. I didn't want anyone to see what I was doing and I was already in here."

"So you used my name and password."

"Yes. I was on and off in just a few minutes."

"How did you get my password?"

"It's in that notebook you keep in the drawer."

"You've been in my drawer?"

"Relax. I didn't read any of your files."

"I know; I checked." Sladen turned back to focus on the notes on his desk. "Next time, ask me before you do it," he growled.

"Okay." Bachmann sauntered across the office and took a seat in a chair near the desk. "You know, I'm sure all this must be intriguing—staff mysteriously sent home and all that—but operations is looking for someone to support a couple of priority projects." He gestured toward the papers on the desk. "It's not going to look too good if they find out you were in here doing this while they have people in the field."

"You say that like I'm wasting my time."

"Aren't you?"

"Not really." Sladen pushed back from the desk, finally resolved to the fact that Bachmann wasn't going to leave anytime soon. Rather than fight about it, he decided to use the moment to his advantage. "Let me ask you: Could they do this solely at the undersecretary level?"

"Could they do what?" Bachmann made no effort to hide the sarcasm in his voice. "I have no idea what you mean."

"At the State Department," Sladen began. "Could an undersecretary in Washington close the Syrian Embassy, drastically reduce the staff in Baghdad, downsize every embassy in the region, and do it all without the explicit written authorization of the secretary of state?"

"He couldn't close the embassy," Bachman shook his head slowly. "To do that, the ambassador has to be told to leave, and an undersecretary couldn't do that."

"What about the rest of it?"

"An undersecretary in the right department could move personnel around, but if he did it on the scale you're talking about, and did it without explicit authority, he'd be fired."

Sladen took an organizational chart from a stack to his left and laid it atop the papers on his desk. "Look at this." He pointed to the chart. Bachmann leaned forward as Sladen continued. "This guy right here, the undersecretary for management, has the authority to do it. To shift personnel without anyone's prior authorization. He's three levels below the secretary."

"Yeah. But someone would find out about it."

"Suppose they didn't find out. Suppose there is an organization within the organization."

"At State?"

"Within the government in general."

"Is this another conspiracy theory?"

"Maybe. But suppose you had a group of people within the government who were bound, not by a nefarious plot, but by ideology. They all share a particular belief about how things ought to be. And one person in a position of influence takes it upon himself to identify people with those commonalities in strategic positions in government."

"And?"

"They could influence official policy."

"You mean draw down our embassy staff in the Middle East as a way of affecting Middle Eastern policy?"

"No. I mean draw down the staff because something is about to happen. Something they are manipulating."

"How would anyone pull that off? You're talking about something big. Something that reaches across departmental lines." Bachmann tapped the organizational chart with his index finger. "This guy right here—your undersecretary of management—he and the man two levels above him could pull off a plan to bill the State Department for nonexistent services. They could do that because the paper flows between them anyway. But to get beyond their agency, they would have to first identify someone in that other agency who agreed with them. That would be difficult to do. There's no place where they would meet to even get acquainted with each other."

"There is one place."

"Where's that?"

"A political party."

"Ahh," Bachmann said with a wave of his hand. "You're way off base."

Sladen returned to the chart. "Look, this guy I'm talking about—the undersecretary. Someone like him could reassign staff-level people. Right?"

"Yes. But not very many of them at one time, and not political appointees at all."

"But he could move around the ones who actually do the work."

"Maybe. But you still have a problem."

"What's that?"

"If you're thinking they're about to pull off some military operation, they can't send in the military without the president's order."

"Right. But when it all comes down to it, the president relies on only a handful of people to help him decide what to do."

"So?"

"It's not very difficult to influence who gets included in that group."

Bachmann stared at Sladen a moment. "This is a little weird, even for you. Maybe the State Department analyzed the political situation, looked at their staff numbers, and decided they were overexposed in the region. Simply as a routine review matter."

"Maybe. Or maybe a review was ordered by someone at the senior-executive level. Someone who wanted that assessment not for security purposes but for some other reason."

"Like?"

"Having fewer people in the region means fewer people to notice what's really happening. Use the security issue as a cover for making sure fewer people are there to watch."

"Have you talked to anyone else about this?"

"I sent a report to Attwood."

"Attwood?" Bachmann's forehead wrinkled in a frown. "At Langley?"

"Yeah. Why?"

"You just sent it straight to Attwood?"

"Yeah. Why? What's wrong with that?"

"He's not your primary contact."

"No. But he's the deputy director for Middle East intelligence."

"When did you send it?"

"Last week."

"Heard anything in response?"

"No." Sladen paused to take a deep breath. "Think it'll be a problem?"

"I don't know," Bachmann shrugged. "Careers end over things like this."

"I'm just doing what they asked me to do."

"Yeah. I know," Bachmann sighed. "That's what bothers me most."

"Why does that bother you?"

"Because that's what I'm doing, exactly what they asked me to do, and maybe that will end up getting me canned, too."

CHAPTER 17
TEL AVIV, ISRAEL

PRIME MINISTER YEDAYA CONVENED a meeting of cabinet officials to discuss the car bombing in Rabat and to brief members of the government on his trip to the White House. He outlined the nature of his discussions with US officials and the substance of his conversations with the president, then turned to the car bombing in Rabat. "I suppose we should consider whether to respond and how." He looked across the table at Efraim Hofi. "Do we know for certain who was behind the attack?"

"As best we can determine thus far, the driver of the car was a man named Jabbar Hamadeh."

"You know this because …"

"His body was lying on the pavement beside the car. We obtained an image of him from video and ran that through our face-recognition program. The database provided his identity and his ties to Hezbollah. We have since confirmed that information. He is a known operative. We do not yet have an identity for the passenger."

"You are certain the driver is from Hezbollah?"

"Yes, sir," Hofi nodded.

Eli Barak, the minister of Internal Affairs, glanced around the table. "Is there really any question about whether to respond? We can't let this go unanswered. Certainly not if the evidence points to Hezbollah."

"But how?" Orit Erdan, the education minister, shrugged his shoulders. "Against whom do you suggest we respond?"

"I can answer that," Moshe Noked, the defense minister, spoke up. "If this was the work of Hezbollah, then the Iranians cannot be far away."

Erdan was taken aback. "You are suggesting a military strike against Iran as a response to a car bombing?"

"Yes," Noked nodded slowly. "We should have hit them long ago."

Barak looked over at Hofi. "The bombing in Rabat took planning and considerable effort to arrange. Surely there is evidence of others who were involved."

Yedaya glanced at Hofi and pressed the point. "Is there any evidence indicating who else might have been involved?"

"It's very early in our investigation, Mr. Prime Minister. We're hoping for satellite imagery from the Americans. If we get that, perhaps we can find out more."

Yedaya's eyes narrowed. His forehead wrinkled in an angry scowl. "They still have not provided satellite images?"

"No, sir."

"The more I know about the Americans, the less I like." Yedaya leaned back from the table. "Stanton is one of the weakest presidents we've ever confronted, and the people he has appointed to office are just like him. He's more interested in retaining his office than in using its power. Afraid he'll offend the Arabs and, in the effort, offend his friends."

Barak looked down the table. "Does he really believe Iran is not planning to weaponize their stockpiles of uranium?"

"I think he has convinced himself of that position. Believing it allows him to justify delaying any serious action until after the election."

"I would think a strong military response would improve his chances with voters."

"Yes," Yedaya nodded, "except for the economic consequences. The American election has become a referendum on the way Stanton has handled the economy."

"The US economy is improving."

"But if there is an attack on Iran now, it will drive oil prices higher."

"Double them."

"Right," Yedaya agreed. "And that would seriously impede economic progress in the United States. The price of gasoline directly affects almost every American household. Higher prices would be bad for Stanton's reelection campaign."

"The Americans have the luxury of making assessments that bear little relationship to reality. They are not the target of Iran's nuclear program."

"Well put," Yedaya noted. "Now, I think ..." He paused to glance around the table before continuing. "I think the time has come for us to make our own decisions about what is in Israel's best interest and move forward. Perhaps the Americans will join us as the wisdom of our position becomes evident." Yedaya arched an eyebrow. "But we can no longer attempt to coordinate our plans with their interests. That simply is not going to work now."

"What does that mean? For us? For now?"

"To begin with, it means no more sharing of information with your American counterparts. If the United States won't give us the satellite images we requested, then we are under no obligation to tell them what we know or give them advance warning of what we plan to do."

"In the past," Erdan argued, "they convinced us to forgo development of our own satellite program under the promise they would provide the data we need. They agreed to share their intelligence and we agreed to coordinate our actions with theirs. Are we now revoking that agreement?"

"There is no need to take a public position on the matter." Yedaya sounded irritated. "Simply instruct your people to stop the routine sharing of information. Look, we face a grave situation. New facilities in Iran rapidly reduce the amount of time it takes them to purify their uranium. We need to keep all of our options open, without having to defend against U.S. interference."

Barak spoke up once more. "Will the Americans respond to this incident, beyond the president's statement?"

"Who knows?" Yedaya sighed. "I'm telling you, the president is almost totally focused on winning reelection. That is the lens through which they view everything now, even more so than before."

"What about the others, the officers of government? Will they see the bombing as an incident related to Iran, requiring a significant military response?"

"No one has told us anything officially, one way or the other," Hofi offered. "Our contacts at the Pentagon say the choice right now is to send more ships to the Persian Gulf."

"More ships," Noked scoffed. "Is that all they can do?"

"What kind of ships?" Barak asked.

"Three cruisers. For public announcement."

"And what are they asking for in private?"

"Those three plus three destroyers and another submarine."

"Why the cruisers?"

"Antisubmarine warfare. They're focused on the strait. They think that if Iran follows through on its threat, the Iranian Navy will use submarines to patrol the region."

Noked arched an eyebrow. "Not a bad analysis of the situation, as far as it goes."

"We have a much larger problem than merely keeping the strait open to tanker ships." "We should look at this car bombing in terms of the bigger picture, rather than merely responding to that single incident. We must focus on the state of Iran's nuclear program." Barak turned to Hofi. "Where do things stand now?"

Hofi looked across the table. Yedaya gestured for him to answer. "The new facility in Qom more than doubles their capacity to refine uranium," Hofi explained. "Worse for us, it also shrinks the time necessary for achieving weapons-grade material."

"How long do we have?"

"At this point, that remains uncertain," Hofi equivocated. "We're working on an estimate."

The discussion continued before culminating in a decision to move forward with the development of specific options. When the meeting concluded, Hofi lingered as the others filed out. Once they were gone, Yedaya turned to him. "You have something you wish to discuss in private?"

"The facility in Tubas flagged a text message sent to a cell phone in Iran.

The message contained the cell phone number for one of our agents working at the facility in Qom."

"They know he's there?"

Hofi nodded. "Apparently they do."

"How did they find out?"

"Someone gave him up."

"Who knew he was there?"

"We're tracking down that information now. In the meantime, the only way we can warn him is to contact him by cell phone. But if he turns on his phone, he'll expose himself."

"When is he scheduled to report?"

"Today."

"So when he checks in, they will find him, and then he will die a slow and painful death."

"Yes," Hofi sighed. "Most likely."

"We have to find him."

"Yes, sir. We have people looking for him, but it takes time to exchange messages in a way that doesn't endanger our other assets. I just wanted you to know. If they capture him, they may go public."

"Right," Yedaya nodded. "Keep me informed."

CHAPTER 18
QOM, IRAN

OHAD REVACH PULLED THE PROTECTIVE jumpsuit over his street clothes. Made of rubberized cloth, it was heavy, hot, and two sizes too large. Already as he zipped the front closed, his skin was damp with sweat. An attendant helped close the openings at his wrists and ankles, then slipped a pair of thin latex gloves over his hands and rubber shoes over his feet. Finally, suited and ready, the attendant opened a door that led to an air-lock chamber. When Revach moved inside, the door closed behind him. Then, as that door sealed shut, a door on the opposite side opened. Revach stepped through the open doorway and into the main room of Building A.

The building, one of ten at the site, housed rows and rows of gas centrifuges. Contained in tall, cylindrical tubes, they rose eight feet above the base to which they were mounted on the floor. Inside each tube, high-speed motors spun uranium hexafluoride, a radioactive gas, using centripetal force to separate uranium-235 isotopes from heavier elements in the material. Once extracted, the lighter, purer uranium particles produced in Building A were sent to Building B, where the process was repeated with the resulting product moving on to yet another building. When working properly, the site generated a steady stream of material finally resulting in a finished product of twenty percent pure uranium-235.

Ensuring that the process operated without interruption required constant attention. Revach was one of the technicians charged with that responsibility. Working in five-hour shifts, he and five other men kept the motors running, adjusted, and properly aligned to make certain everything functioned at optimum efficiency.

As Revach walked along the narrow rows between the centrifuge tubes, he slid his hand inside the pocket of his work suit. An opening at the bottom of the pocket allowed him to push his hand through the suit and reach into the pocket of the pants he wore underneath. With practiced effort, he curled his fingers around a razor-thin cell phone and drew it from his pants into the pocket of the work suit.

The phone, manufactured by Apple especially for Mossad, had a camera lens with accompanying software that allowed it to take sharp, clear pictures from variable distances without the need to adjust the focus. An additional application in the phone's software package automatically compensated for motion, light, and shadow. From the edge of his pocket, doing nothing more than pressing a button on the edge of the phone case, Revach could produce pictures sharp enough to read the license plate of an automobile from any distance up to seventy-five meters away, in almost any lighting condition.

Revach slowly worked his hand partway from his pocket and cocked his arm to one side, resting the weight of his arm on his fingers, pressing them against the outer edge of the pocket in a pose that suggested his arm was in a relaxed position. All the while, the camera was tucked safely out of sight between his palm and the fabric of the work suit. As he walked along, he aimed the lens between his index and middle finger, then used his thumb to press a button on the phone. Quietly, the phone snapped picture after picture as he made the rounds through the building.

Five hours later, a buzzer sounded. Revach glanced up to see yellow lights blinking overhead, a sign that his shift had come to an end. He made his way to a green door on the opposite end of the room and waited. When the buzzer stopped, the door opened revealing yet another air-lock chamber. Revach stepped into the chamber and spread his arms wide apart. The door behind him closed and latched tightly. He heard the seal seat against the steel frame, then a pump motor hummed and a fine mist filled the air in a procedure designed to wash away any particles that might have adhered to the suit. When he was sufficiently decontaminated, a green light on the wall began to blink. Revach stripped off the suit, opened a door to the right, and stepped into the change room.

An attendant met him as he entered and checked the radiation tag on the lapel of his shirt. The exposure registered on the tag was noted in the building log before Revach was allowed to leave. Outside, he walked along an unpaved drive that ran between the buildings toward a barracks that stood on a hill near the northern edge of the compound. Officially known as the Fordow facility, it was referred to by most people simply as Qom, the city that stood just a few miles to the west. As Revach strolled along, he took the cell phone from his pocket and scrolled down a thumbnail list of pictures, three hundred in all. *Uploading all of those will take a while,* he thought to himself. Still, he was scheduled to report and there was nothing to do but send the pictures. He selected them for attachment, then sent a text message to the command center in Herzliya. When he was certain the call was in progress, he returned the phone to his pocket and continued toward the barracks.

*   *   *

On the opposite side of the compound, Arash Modiri sat at a workstation in the Fordow security center and watched a monitor as it displayed the real-time results from a software program that tracked communications into and out of the facility. Whether by cell phone, landline, satellite, or cable, the center's system trapped all of it and monitored it for content, much like the system Israel used at the facility in Tubas. When Revach's cell phone came on, the number appeared on the list. As it began to upload the content of the message, the phone number flashed red and an alarm sounded.

Arash moved the cursor over the phone number and clicked on it. A fresh page opened with a map of the area. A dot with the number beside it appeared on the map. Arash picked up the phone and placed a call to his supervisor.

"We have a phone flagged for special attention operating near Building E."

"What is the number?"

"2-512-3-79."

"Call Mehran Golzar."

"Golzar? You want me to call him?"

"Call him immediately," the supervisor insisted. "He placed the alert on the number. We have no way of knowing why, so we can't do anything until we talk to him. Call him."

Arash placed the call. Minutes later, Golzar entered the center. "Where is he? Show me." Arash pointed to the screen. Golzar checked the position. "Okay. He is moving toward the barracks?"

"Yes," Arash assured. "He's almost to the barracks now."

"Where?"

Arash pointed out the barracks on the map. Golzar nodded. "Call security. Tell them to meet me at that location. I'm on my way there now."

"Who is this?"

"He's an Israeli agent."

Arash's eyes were wide. "Mossad?"

"Yes."

"A Jew observing our operations?"

"Yes." Golzar pointed to the screen. "And from the size of that message file he's sending, I'd say he's been taking pictures of it." He turned away and charged toward the door. "Call security!" he shouted. "Tell them to meet me there immediately."

CHAPTER 19

HERZLIYA, ISRAEL

AT THE MOSSAD OPERATIONS CENTER, analysts continued to work on the Rabat car bombing, reviewing details from video images and information retrieved by investigators who sifted through debris at the scene. Hofi, however, was preoccupied with Revach. He glanced at his watch to check the time, then turned to an operator seated near the center of the room.

"Have we heard from Revach yet?"

"No, sir." She shook her head.

"Is he late?"

She retrieved a file that logged his calls. "I don't think so," she said as she scrolled down the list. "He doesn't have a regular time."

Hofi turned toward the others in the room. "Who's working on the cell phone call from Spain?"

"I am," Nathan Goldstein spoke up.

Hofi crossed the room to his desk. "Show me what you have."

Goldstein turned to the laptop on his desk. "The message began here." He pointed to a line at the bottom of the screen. "That's a number assigned to a cell phone. The phone was activated in Mexico, but someone used it to send a text message from Boston."

"That's the message we're trying to trace?"

"Yes, sir," Goldstein nodded. "The message originated from that cell phone, transmitting it from Boston to a cell phone that was in Aruba." He moved up the screen. "The phone in Aruba forwarded the call to a phone in Dubai. From there it went to a phone in Germany, then to France, then to the phone in Spain. Someone using that phone then forwarded it to a phone registered in Iran."

"Do we have names for any of the people who owned those phones?"

"No, sir. I've been trying to get that information but it's a slow process."

"Is that information available?"

"The original phone, issued in Mexico, was a throwaway. I found records that show when and where it was activated but there's no name associated with it. The others are even more obscure. We'd have to ask each individual phone carrier."

"The only reason someone in Iran would want that cell phone number would be to use it as a way of locating Revach."

"Or to call him."

"Not much chance of that." Hofi pointed to the screen. "They wouldn't have sent the text message around the world unless they were trying to hide the real recipient."

"Then someone in Boston gave him up?"

"Yes. But that person probably went to great lengths to hide his identity, too."

"You want me to work on the Boston end?"

"As you can," Hofi nodded. "But this is going to be over before the day ends. When Revach turns on that cell phone, they'll know he's there."

"And when he sends a transmission, they'll know exactly where he's calling from."

"How exactly?"

"They'll identify the tower that's relaying the call immediately. That will locate him inside a particular geographic area. Then, depending on how their software is set up, it could take a minute or two for them to analyze the signal strength from the phone to the tower. That will narrow his location to a box about fifty meters square."

"You can see the same information?"

"Yes, sir." Goldstein opened a tab for the page behind the one they were reviewing. "When he turns on the phone, I'll see his location right here."

"Tell me as soon as that happens." Hofi stepped away from Goldstein's desk and walked back toward the middle of the room. "Anything from the Americans on the situation in Rabat?"

"No, sir," Daphna Abergil answered.

"What about the satellite images? They told me they were sending them."

"We haven't received anything from them."

"And they wonder why we are developing our own capabilities. What does our satellite show? Anything helpful?"

"It shows images of the area an hour before the blast."

"Have we checked them for the Fiat?"

"Yes."

"Anything useful?"

"Nothing definite."

"What about the British? Don't they have satellites that cover that region?"

Abergil came to his side. "You want us to ask the British for assistance?"

"We need images from somewhere."

"They'll consult with the Americans first, then deny us access."

"Well," Hofi sighed, "I suppose we could try the French."

"They're worse than the British."

"But they won't run to the Americans first." Hofi paused for a moment. "Ask them, ask them all. The French, the Russians. Ask anyone you can think of. We need to know who—"

Goldstein shouted from across the room, interrupting their conversation. "We have pictures from Revach in Qom."

Hofi rushed toward Goldstein's desk. "His phone is still on?"

"Yes, sir. Still downloading pictures."

Hofi watched a moment as thumbnails of each photo appeared on the screen. "How many has he sent so far?"

"About a hundred."

"You're certain his phone is on?"

"Yes, sir." Goldstein pointed to the screen.

"Send him a message. What's the distress word?"

"If we send him a message, they'll know it came from us."

"If they're tracking him, they already know he called us. What's the distress word?"

"Masada," Goldstein answered grimly.

"Send it." Hofi patted him on the shoulder. "And then data-mine the text message for every possible bit of information you can find."

"Already on it."

Hofi called over his shoulder as he stepped away, "And make sure those photographs get downstairs for review. That man is about to give his life to get them to us. We don't want to waste it."

*   *   *

At the Fordow facility, the sound of a truck caught Revach's attention. He glanced over his shoulder to see it coming toward him. Three men stood in back, armed with automatic rifles. Revach stepped to the left, behind a building, and quickened his pace. He was almost to the opposite end when the truck turned the corner. One of the men standing in the truck shouted at him, "Halt! Halt or we will shoot!"

Revach darted around the end of the building and took the cell phone from his pocket to check the screen. A note indicated his message had been sent. He shoved the phone into his pocket and ran to the far corner of the building, then turned right and ran. From the opposite side of the building, he heard the crunch of gravel as the truck turned the corner. Moments later the engine roared as the truck made the second turn and started toward him. Then bullets struck the ground around him. Shots ricocheted off the wall to his right.

Twenty meters ahead, a motorcycle leaned against the building. By the time Revach reached it, the truck was closing fast. He grabbed the handlebars and threw his leg over the seat, then reached below the fuel tank for the ignition switch. He felt only the bare metal of the frame. He leaned to the right to see and found the switch had been removed. Wires dangled from the place where it had been. He twisted them together and put his heel against the starter lever. "I hope this works," he growled, and shoved down with his foot. Instantly the engine came to life.

Dust filled the air as the truck slid to a halt beside him. Men jumped from the back, their arms outstretched to grab him. Just as they were about to seize him, Revach pressed the toe of his right foot against the gear shifter, released the clutch, and twisted the throttle. The motorcycle shot forward, leaving the men grasping at nothing but air.

At the end of the building, Revach leaned to the left, worked the clutch with his left hand, and shifted to the next gear. He guided the motorcycle around a trash barrel, darted past a car, and headed toward the gate. When he was just thirty meters away, a truck shot from behind a building and slid to a stop, blocking his path. Revach threw his weight to the left in an attempt to avoid a collision. As he did, the motorcycle leaned beyond the center of gravity and the wheels lost traction. The motorcycle slid sideways toward the truck. Revach struck the truck with his shoulder and fell to the ground. The motorcycle continued on beneath the truck, emerged on the opposite side, and slammed into the fence near the gate. Before he could move, men from the truck surrounded him, rifles at the ready, pointed at him.

Mehran Golzar pushed past them and leaned over. "I must say, you gave it quite an effort." He glanced at the men standing nearby. "Give Mr. Revach a hand up from the ground."

The men grabbed Revach and bound his hands behind his back with a zip tie. One of them looked over at Golzar. "He is a Jew."

"I think we shall find Ohad Revach is many things." Golzar bent over and picked up a cell phone from the ground. He held it up for Revach to see. "I assume this is yours?" When Revach did not reply, Golzar switched off the phone and gestured to the men with a nod of his head. "Put him in the truck. I will show you where to take him."

The men lifted Revach from the ground and dropped him into the bed of the truck. Then they climbed in back with him.

*   *   *

At the Mossad operations center in Herzliya, all eyes were focused on the wall screen as they watched a green dot on the map follow Revach's movements. When it disappeared from view, Hofi turned to Goldstien. "What happened?"

"The cell phone has been turned off."

"Show me where he was the entire time the phone was on. Can you put that up on the screen?"

A series of dots appeared on the screen forming a trail. Goldstein highlighted one of them in red. "This is where he turned on the phone and began transmitting the pictures. The remaining dots track his movement while the phone was on."

"He moved in a circle, then in a straight line?"

"Yes."

"What was he doing?"

The screen changed to a satellite photograph of the area. Hofi squinted at the screen. "Tighten up on that," he said, pointing. The picture zoomed in closer. Hofi once again turned in Goldstein's direction. "He was running."

"Yes, sir. That's what it looks like." Goldstein walked from his desk. "That long building is one of the centrifuge arrays. He walked past the end of it, turned right, went all the way to the opposite end, then came back down the other side. He went around the end, back where he began, turned right, and went straight for the gate." Goldstein turned away and hurried to his desk. Moments later, the image was cluttered with numbers beside each of the green dots.

Hofi frowned at him. "What's all that?"

"These are the times for each location." Goldstein once again came from his desk and stood near the screen.

"So," Hofi asked, "what does it mean?"

"A much longer time passed between the dots as he circled the building."

Hofi's eyes lit up. "He was walking."

"Yes, sir. But when he got to here," Goldstein said, pointing to a spot on the screen, "he began to move in a straight line, and the interval between the dots becomes much shorter."

"He was running?"

"No, sir. More like riding."

"In a car?"

"Hard to say. Car, truck, motorcycle. But he was definitely moving faster than he could run."

"Did he try to contact us, other than sending the pictures?"

"No, sir. We picked him up when he sent the photos. The system had his identity from that call and continued to track his position, but the phone was simply on."

Hofi stared up at the screen. "They were chasing him," he offered quietly.

"Perhaps."

"No perhaps," Hofi said with assurance. "I know it."

"How?"

"I've been in that situation before." Hofi turned to the operator. "Do we have other assets in the area?"

"Yes, sir."

"Have they been contacted?"

"No, sir."

"Contact them," he barked. "Find out what they know and do it now. Revach's in trouble."

Abergil came to Hofi's side and spoke in an even, quiet tone. "Is it really worth the risk?"

Hofi looked puzzled. "What do you mean?"

"Revach is most certainly in their hands. He may already be dead. Do we really want to risk the others to find him?"

Hofi thought for a moment, then shook his head. "I'm not leaving him." He glanced back at the operator. "Contact the others. Find out what happened to Revach."

CHAPTER 20
WASHINGTON, D.C.

KATHLEEN BAKER GLANCED AROUND the cabinet room as members of the president's national security team gathered. Paul Catlett, director of the CIA, stood near the door talking quietly with Ralph Ligon, the director of National Intelligence. Jean Brown, the national security advisor, was seated at the table to the right of Upchurch. On his left was Admiral Beamon, chairman of the Joint Chiefs of Staff.

In a few minutes, Pete McWhinney, the president's chief of staff, entered the room. Behind him was President Andrew Stanton. Everyone stood as Stanton worked his way toward the table. "If you'll take your seats," he said in an authoritative tone, "we'll get started."

When they were all in place, Stanton glanced over at Baker. "Kathleen, give us the latest on the situation in Rabat."

"The Israelis have taken charge of the investigation. Moroccan authorities are providing assistance but they have agreed to let an investigation team from the Israeli Foreign Service take the lead."

"Does that mean Mossad is calling the shots?"

"Yes. But no one is saying that publicly."

"Do they know who was behind it?"

"The Israelis have confirmed that the driver was Jabbar Hamadeh. He has known ties to Hezbollah."

"So the Israelis think Iran was behind the attack?"

"Yes, sir."

"Any indication how the Israelis will react?"

"No, sir. They seem to be focused on the investigation right now."

Upchurch spoke up. "Mr. President, there can be little doubt that Iran was behind this. And I don't think anyone in this room doubts that Israel will respond with force."

"We don't know that for certain," Baker responded. "There's been no indication that Israel is either contemplating or preparing for a military response."

Stanton looked across the table at Upchurch. "Does defense intelligence have any hard evidence, other than the Hezbollah connection of the driver, that links this to Iran?"

"No, sir. But everyone in the intelligence business knows who was behind it." Upchurch propped his elbows on the table and leaned forward. "It's very simple, Mr. President. Last month Iran threatened to close the Strait of Hormuz. We responded by sending a second carrier into the region. And now they're responding to our move, only this time they gave us that response in Rabat."

"They responded to us by making a hit against Israelis?"

"Yes," Upchurch nodded. "For them, our policy in the Middle East is all about Israel."

"Theirs is, too."

"That may be so, but I am certain this bombing was about our response to their threat to close the strait."

Baker shook her head. "This is—"

"If I may," Paul Catlett interrupted. "I think Haden is correct, but I don't think that's the extent of their response. I think the bombing in Rabat was a distraction to keep us from seeing something else." He reached into a briefcase that sat beside his chair and retrieved a manila envelope. "Our satellites found this." He took three photographs from the envelope and laid them on the table. "These are photographs of movements within Iran." He pointed to the first picture. "This is a photograph of an area inland from the strait. It was taken three days ago." He used a pen as a pointer. "That one shows nothing unusual." Catlett slid the photo aside and pointed to a second picture. "This one shows the same region two days ago. And that right there," he said, pointing, "is a mobile missile battery." He laid the third photograph on top. "And this is a picture of the same location three hours ago." Everyone leaned forward. "As you can see, a dozen mobile launchers are now at that site."

"Couldn't that be a staging area?"

"Yes. I'm sure it is. But the point is, those missile launchers have been relocated within striking distance of the strait."

Baker cleared her throat. "Weren't they already within striking range?"

"Not these. Iran has larger missiles that could reach the strait from anywhere in the country. But they carry a much larger warhead and are of a more strategic nature. These mobile units use smaller, tactical missiles."

"So," Stanton summed out, "you're saying the larger missiles could reach the strait but using them would be more complicated than these smaller ones."

"Yes, Mr. President. It would be like using an ICBM to take out a tank. You could do it but why would you want to waste the larger missile when a smaller, less-expensive one would do at least as well, if not better?"

"Okay," Stanton continued. "What do you suggest?"

"I think we have to make a response."

"I issued a statement denouncing their latest threat. We sent the second carrier. And I issued a statement denouncing the car bombing. Are you suggesting a military response?"

"Yes, sir."

"We need a tangible military response," Upchurch added.

"With all due respect," Baker argued, "a military response will only add to the tension in the region."

"Not exactly," Jean Brown spoke up. "This is a game of tit for tat."

Stanton gave her a puzzled look. "What do you mean?"

"Game theory," Brown explained. "When the first player moves, the second player must match that move in order to maintain equilibrium. If not, the first player perceives the second player's lack of response as a sign of weakness and the first player becomes more aggressive."

"But if we match their move," Baker countered, "aren't we both becoming more aggressive?"

"Yes, to an extent. But if we maintain the equilibrium of our relative positions, hopefully we will raise the stakes so high both sides will see the absurdity of the situation, neither will be willing to follow through with their threats, and both players will begin searching for a way to back down."

"This is crazy!" Baker sounded exasperated. "This is the kind of argument that got us into Iraq and every other mistake we've made."

Upchurch bristled at the comment. "You think going to Iraq was a mistake?"

"Yes, I do."

"So you'd rather see Saddam Hussein in Baghdad than what we have now?"

"No, but that doesn't answer the question."

Stanton waved them off and looked in Upchurch's direction. "So, what do you suggest we do?"

"They have the missile batteries on shore, which our two carriers can more than cover. Their other prime weapons for closing the strait are three Kilo Class Russian submarines. They were specifically designed for this kind of action."

"Have they deployed those submarines?"

"We don't know for certain where they are. They are not in port."

"Any indication of where they might be?"

"Nothing definite. One put to sea three months ago and hasn't been seen since. Two others put to sea last month. One of those docked in Indonesia, the other in China, but they have both put to sea again."

"So we don't know where any of these subs are located."

"No, sir."

"Which brings us back to my question. What do you want me to do?"

"Deploy three guided missile cruisers to the Persian Gulf."

"Don't we have cruisers and destroyers escorting the carriers?"

"Yes, sir. But their primary mission is just that—protecting the carriers. Additional ships in the area give us the ability to search the region for the submarines."

"Are these Iranian subs nuclear submarines?"

"No, sir."

"Kilo Class submarines are diesel electric."

Admiral Beamon spoke up. "Mr. President, their primary power comes from a diesel engine, but they operate on batteries while submerged. They have a range of about 400 miles traveling under water. Then they have to surface and recharge their batteries."

"How many days do they have?"

"Running solely on diesel, they have to refuel every forty-five days."

"All right." Stanton turned back to Upchurch. "When do we need to deploy?"

"Now would be best. Sooner rather than later."

"Mr. President," Baker interjected. "This is the wrong move, at the wrong time, in the wrong place. If we add those ships it will only provoke the Iranians to do more in response."

"What do you suggest?"

"Negotiate."

"Never!" Catlett erupted. "We are not negotiating with terrorists."

Baker ignored his outburst. "Mr. President, Iran is a member of the United Nations. They're a recognized sovereign government. You wouldn't be negotiating with terrorists. You would be negotiating with the authorized leader of a recognized country."

"This is an election year," Jean Brown added. "No one's going to be caught saying anything to Muslim extremists except how much we want to blow them up."

"Okay," Stanton said, holding up his hand for quiet. "I think I've heard enough." He slid back from the table and stood. "Thank you all for coming. I'll give you my answer this afternoon."

Everyone stood and waited while Stanton left the room. When he was gone, Upchurch pulled McWhinney aside. "He has to do this. You have to talk him into it. He doesn't have an option."

"You mean *you* don't have an option."

"Time is running out."

"You'll know when I know."

Upchurch made his way to the lobby on the west side of the building and walked out to the driveway, where he found Catlett waiting for his car. "I hear we have a problem with one of your people."

Catlett gave him a knowing look. "You saw the report?"

"Yes. I saw it."

"Apparently this John Sladen guy was sharper than Attwood anticipated."

"I'm taking care of it."

"Make sure you do. This thing is about to come to a head. We don't need any distractions now."

A limousine came to a stop a few feet away. Catlett crawled into the backseat. "Need a ride?"

"No, I'm fine."

As the car moved away, Catlett took a Blackberry from his pocket and sent a text message to Jean Brown. "He's still wavering."

Almost instantly she replied, "I'll contact Weiss."

CHAPTER 21
NEW YORK CITY

ALEX TALBOT STOOD BACKSTAGE and waited while the moderator introduced him. Through a gap in the curtain he saw the crowd seated in the auditorium. Known as the American Israel Public Affairs Committee, the group assembled that morning represented many of the nation's most important Jewish leaders. Most of them were politically active, donating thousands of hours and millions of dollars to political campaigns for candidates of both parties. To have a shot at winning the presidency, Talbot needed to capture as much of that support as possible.

As the moderator concluded his remarks, Talbot straightened his suit coat and squared his shoulders. Then, to polite applause from the audience, he strode across the stage, shook the moderator's hand, and turned to the podium.

"Thank you," he smiled at the audience. "Thank you very much." The crowd applauded a moment longer, then the room grew quiet. "Let me say as I begin, as I also said yesterday, I am appalled at the attack in Rabat and I extend my deepest sympathy to the family, friends, and fellow countrymen of those who lost their lives yesterday in the cause of Zion and in the protection and well-being of the people of Israel. No one can doubt that terrorists around the world have been working diligently to destroy the nation of Israel and to eliminate the Jewish race. I want those terrorists and all the world to know that I am committed to doing everything in my power to see that that never happens!"

Talbot's remarks were greeted with enthusiastic applause as he pressed on. "If I am elected president, I will marshal every available asset to see that those who perpetrate such acts are brought to justice and the countries that harbor them are forced to cease providing sanctuary to them. And if I am not elected president in November, I shall do everything in my power as a private citizen to see that end accomplished.

"Just as no one can doubt that terrorists have as their primary goal the elimination of Israel and Israelis, so also no one can doubt that these latest attacks are the work of terrorist elements emboldened by the weak and aimless policy put forth by the current administration. Chief among those so emboldened is the nation of Iran."

A roar of approval went up from the audience as applause once more interrupted the speech.

"Iran," Talbot continued, "has ignored international efforts to inspect their nuclear program—a program no reasonable person could conclude is aimed at anything other than the creation of nuclear weapons. They have refused international demands for inspection and this administration has done nothing in response. All he has given them is words, words, and more words. And if we continue to insist on accountability for Iran's program, Rasoul Moussaoui says he will close the Strait of Hormuz to all shipping traffic. He says this while funneling millions of dollars from the Iranian oil trade directly into accounts controlled by Hezbollah, an organization that uses its money to fire rockets into Israeli settlements, indiscriminately killing men, women, and children. Can there be any doubt what they would do should they succeed in achieving their goal of obtaining strategic nuclear weapons? We must never let that happen!"

The audience leapt to its feet, applauding and shouting wildly. Talbot stepped back, basking in the moment and doing nothing to dampen their emotion.

*   *   *

At the White House, Pete McWhinney came down the hall and made his way into the office of Gladys Moynihan, the president's secretary. There he found Stanton standing with the staff, staring up at a television that was mounted to the wall above the door. Stanton glanced at him, then gestured toward the television. "You see this?"

"I caught part of it in my office."

"Talbot just makes this stuff up as he goes."

"Yes, sir, he does a pretty good job of selling it, too."

Stanton shot a glare in his direction as he turned away and started toward the Oval Office. McWhinney followed after him and closed the door behind them. Stanton continued to the chair behind the desk. "You think I ought to go after him?"

"I think we should talk about those ships we discussed earlier."

"I know," Stanton growled.

"The Navy is asking for them."

"I know." Stanton's voice was growing tense.

"So, we have to send them."

"You think?" Stanton snapped sarcastically.

"It's our only option."

"Why?" Stanton shouted. "Why is that our only option? Because it's an election year? Because Talbot is finding an audience for bashing me?"

"Because it's the Navy," McWhinney said calmly. "And it's the right thing to do."

"No, it's not the Navy," Stanton countered, wagging his finger for emphasis.

McWhinney's forehead wrinkled in a frown. "It's not the Navy?"

"No. It's Upchurch and Dick Elser. They're the ones who came up with that plan."

"Sir, if we refuse their request, we'll be in an untenable position. Talbot is attacking us as weak. Yedaya thinks we've lost our collective mind. The voters don't recognize you anymore."

Stanton cut his eyes in McWhinney's direction. "I told you never to talk politics in this office."

"I'm not talking politics. I'm telling you the truth. Talbot is calling us out as weak—calling you out as weak—and it's getting traction with voters because it's the truth."

"And you think I should send the US Navy in to protect your job."

"I'm saying maybe Talbot is getting traction because we are weak."

"Does the view look black and white from over there, Pete?" Stanton came from behind the desk. The two men stood face-to-face. "If the voters want Talbot in this office, they know how to make it happen. And if you don't like the way I govern, you know what you can do about it, too."

"Mr. President—"

"It's my name on the order that sends soldiers and sailors off to die for your latte. If you want things done differently around here, run for office yourself."

"Mr. President, I'm only saying—"

"I'll make my decision by this afternoon." Stanton turned away to face the window.

McWhinney backed away from the desk, then turned and opened the door. As he moved down the hall, he took an iPhone from his pocket and typed a text message to Jean Brown. "Nothing is definite."

CHAPTER 22
WASHINGTON, D.C.

A LITTLE BEFORE NOON, Yosef Weiss arrived at the White House. Not quite six feet tall, he wore a dark gray handmade suit with a shirt made especially for him by a tailor in London. His tie came from Italy, as did his shoes. His salt-and-pepper hair was trimmed neatly above his ears and when he smiled he looked as if he'd stepped from the pages of a fashion magazine. Even at seventy-five, he found women younger than his grandchildren attracted to him.

Weiss, the sole heir to a family fortune made in the textile business, lived the life of a well-connected fundraiser for the Democratic Party. He came to town that morning directly from the American Israel Public Affairs Committee meeting in New York. A limousine brought him to the White House gate, where he passed unhindered through building security and arrived at Gladys Moynihan's desk looking as sharp and handsome as ever. "I was wondering if the president had a few minutes to see me." The tone of his voice made it clear he wasn't asking.

"I don't think so." Moynihan avoided eye contact. "He's really busy, Mr. Weiss."

"Mrs. Moynihan," Weiss said imperiously, "the president is always busy." He gestured with his right hand. "Would you check with him? Perhaps he has a minute for an old friend."

Gladys rose from her desk and disappeared inside the Oval Office. A few minutes later, Stanton emerged, followed by Pete McWhinney. Stanton greeted Weiss with a smile. "Hey, Yosef. We're on our way over to a meeting at the Capitol Hilton. I'm giving a speech at noon." He gave Weiss a friendly pat on the shoulder. "Ride with me."

As they came from the office, the phone on Moynihan's desk rang. Weiss heard her calling after them. "Mr. President. It's the secretary of state."

"Not now," Stanton answered over his shoulder.

"She called yesterday too, sir."

"I know. Tell her I'll see her this afternoon. When I get back. I'm late."

Weiss walked with Stanton down the hall, through the reception lobby, and out to a car waiting on the driveway. Once they were seated inside, Stanton glanced in Weiss's direction. "How much did we raise at the event last week?"

"That's not why I'm here."

"I know why you're here," Stanton scowled, his face suddenly red with anger. "Look, Yosef, they aren't going to close the Strait of Hormuz. It's just a bluff."

"They already know that."

"Then tell them to back off," Stanton insisted. "What's the problem?"

"We think this is a distraction from their real plan."

"Which is?"

"To attack Israel," Weiss said flatly.

"Ahhh … that's ridiculous," Stanton scoffed. "They might talk about it, just like they talk about shutting down the strait, but they would never do it."

"People in Jerusalem and Tel Aviv are taking the situation seriously. I am sure you heard this from Prime Minister Yedaya."

"That's all I heard from Yedaya, and he wasn't taking it seriously, either. He just wants to manipulate me into giving him the refueling tankers."

"Refueling tankers are essential to our defense, but he was not trying to manipulate you. He was telling you the truth about the situation we face."

"If I give him the refueling tankers," Stanton explained, "Israeli planes can reach targets in Iran. Everyone knows that. It would be viewed by the world as notice that we're giving Israel free rein to attack Iran."

"Israel already has the capacity to attack Iran," Weiss answered. "The refueling tankers Yedaya requested simply make it easier for the pilots to return safely to their families." He turned to look Stanton in the eye. "Rather than bailing out over Syria where the pilots and their planes would fall into the hands of all our enemies."

Stanton's eyes opened wide. "You guys have to get this under control. Iran is crazy, but they aren't crazy enough to launch an unprovoked attack on Israel. They know what will happen."

"If by that you mean an all-out retaliation by the United States, many in Israel are no longer certain America has the will for such a response. Many Americans are no longer certain of it, either."

"You have polling data to back that up?"

"I have Alex Talbot and the reaction he is generating."

"Traction," Stanton scoffed, shaking his head. "That's all I hear anymore. Alex Talbot has traction."

"Do you support Israel, Mr. President?"

"How can you ask me that?" Stanton's voice was loud and sharp. "Are you suggesting AIPAC might actually put its support behind Talbot?"

"AIPAC will support those who support Israel," Weiss nodded. "Do you support Israel?"

"Yes," Stanton replied in an exasperated tone. "Yes. I support Israel. But I don't have my head in the sand."

"Israelis look at your response thus far and see only two ships."

"Two carriers," Stanton argued. "Carrier groups, I might add. We have enough firepower in the Persian Gulf right now to end World War II."

"But we are not fighting World War II," Weiss countered. "Israel is fighting for its life."

The car turned onto the drive at the hotel, where a crowd had gathered. "And if I don't get elected, you think Talbot can give Israel more than I do?"

"We raised over two million dollars for you last week, Mr. President."

By then Stanton's eyes were focused out the window on the supporters waving campaign signs near the hotel entrance. "Two million?" His voice sounded distracted.

"We would have raised more if you had been there."

"I had a thing in Florida." Stanton stared out the window. "Couldn't be avoided."

"Next time, see that you avoid it. Our people in New York need to see you."

Stanton jerked his head around. "You keep the money coming, Yosef. That's what I need from you. Not campaign advice. Not foreign policy advice. Just keep the money flowing." Then the car came to a stop and the rear door opened. Stanton slid from the seat and made his way to the rope line, where he greeted the crowd.

*   *   *

Late that afternoon, Stanton ordered three US Navy cruisers to the Persian Gulf. His press secretary issued a public statement announcing the move. Without public announcement, he also ordered four destroyers to the Indian Ocean and detailed two additional submarines to the region.

A little before five, after the news outlets had their stories and the ships' crews had been informed, Kathleen Baker appeared at the Oval Office. Stanton looked up from his desk as Mrs. Moynihan led her into the office.

"Thanks for coming by," he said, still seated in his chair.

Baker waited until Moynihan was gone, then turned to Stanton. "I see you made your decision," she began. "I wanted to talk to you before you did that."

"Sorry, there just wasn't time."

"You realize what's happening, don't you?"

Stanton leaned away from the desk. "I'm the commander in chief, commanding his army."

"In an election year," Baker said, her mouth turned up on one side in a look of contempt.

"Are you suggesting campaign considerations are affecting my decisions?"

"I'm suggesting Upchurch and Elser are using it against you and I don't think you realize it."

"Madam Secretary," he snapped. "I am a graduate of the University of

Chicago and Harvard Law School. Do you think I can't read two men like Upchurch and Elser?"

"I would hope you could, sir," Baker responded.

"I would, too." Stanton rose from his chair and came from behind the desk. "But thank you for your concern." And with that, he walked out the door to the promenade and disappeared.

CHAPTER 23
NEW YORK CITY

THAT EVENING, ALEX TALBOT appeared on *Political Perspective*, a cable news talk show aired weeknights on CNN. Mattie Lewis, the moderator, got right to the point. "Governor, this morning you delivered a scathing attack on President Stanton's Middle East policy in your speech to AIPAC. Is it your—"

"Excuse me, Mattie, but I didn't attack the president's Middle East policy. That would presuppose that he actually *had* a Middle East policy. I don't think he does. What I attacked was the anemic response he's made to rising Iranian militancy and its quest for nuclear arms."

"And what was the point of your position?"

"We can't just send in ships to deter a rogue nation from acquiring weapons of mass destruction. The Navy alone can't solve this situation."

"You're aware the president ordered three more ships to the region?"

"Yes. I saw the report."

"We already have two carrier strike groups in the Persian Gulf." Lewis glanced at his notes. "I'd just like to bring our viewers up to speed on what that means. Each of these carrier strike groups consists of an aircraft carrier, two guided missile cruisers, two antiaircraft warships, and two destroyers equipped for antisubmarine duty, as well as a ballistic missile submarine. Eight ships in all and we have two of these groups operating in the Gulf for a total of sixteen ships from these two units alone. That's a lot of firepower in the area already and now the president is adding still more. Yet you still call this a weak response. Why is that?"

"Because it's all smoke and mirrors. To solve the situation militarily we have to put boots on the ground."

Lewis looked startled. "Governor, are you calling for an invasion of Iran?"

"No. I'm saying the president has to actually *do* something about the situation. All he's doing is inching us toward war. If he keeps adding ships to the region, without some coherent policy to actually change the situation, then one day someone is going to feel compelled to actually use all that military power placed in that location."

"What would you do?"

"First, I would put together an international coalition to seize Iranian bank accounts and the accounts of every entity tied to Hezbollah. Not just in the United States but in every nation. I would make it impossible for Hezbollah to receive funds through the international banking system. Then I would assist Israel in blockading Gaza and destroying the tunnels used to smuggle weapons from Egypt in the south and Lebanon in the north. And that would be a good start."

"Blockading Gaza has already been tried and Israel could destroy those tunnels anytime they want. I fail to see how that would change Iran's strategic position."

"I said it was a start," Talbot repeated. "It would limit Iran's ability to project regional influence through its ties to Hezbollah and it would be a significant step toward ensuring the continued safety of Israel. Once we accomplished those two goals, I would engage our partners in the area in an effort to assist us in finding a solution. A few leaders in the Palestinian Authority actually want a functioning government that is not an arm of Hezbollah. I would find those people and put them to work. Then I would work out a plan to ease border restrictions to allow Palestinians to travel freely to and from the territories controlled by the Authority."

"I still don't see how that would help the situation with Iran."

"Those changes would allow Palestinians to work and for their businesses to trade with Israel as well as the outside world. As they did years ago. These measures would incrementally make Iran irrelevant and, in conjunction with current sanctions, would work to isolate Iran from those forces in the region that enable its expansionist approach. We'd use these measures to put an end to Iranian hegemony."

"You would force Israel to cooperate?"

"No. Israel is a sovereign nation. I would never force them to do anything. These measures are consistent with their own policies and with the goals of the Yedaya administration. I would simply use the power of the United States to assist them in making it happen."

CHAPTER 24
CHICAGO, ILLINOIS

LEON BAIN STEPPED FROM THE SUV to the curb and made his way inside the Edgewater Beach Hotel. Until two years ago he'd enjoyed a productive career with Larchmont & Castille, Chicago's premier advertising agency. Then, with Andrew Stanton facing reelection and David Holsten no longer available, Bain had been hired to develop marketing strategy for the campaign. From there he had risen quickly to become the president's chief political advisor. When Stanton formally announced his bid for a second term, Bain was put in charge of day-to-day operations.

As Bain crossed the hotel lobby, a reporter stepped out to greet him. Microphone in hand, he stepped ahead to block Bain's path. Klieg lights came on and a cameraman appeared.

"Mr. Bain, were you aware the president ordered three more ships into the Persian Gulf this evening?"

"The president has every intention of protecting our national interests in the region and that includes ensuring strategic stability for Iran's neighbors."

"Did he consult with you before issuing that order?"

"I'm not commenting on the nature of my conversations with the president."

"Were you in the loop?"

"I operate the campaign." Bain reached the elevator and pressed the call button. "I don't dictate foreign policy."

"We've heard rumors that the president ordered more than the three ships he publicly disclosed. Are you aware of additional ships that were secretly ordered to the region?"

The elevator doors opened and Bain stepped inside. "You'll have to contact the White House press secretary for comments on that." He pressed a button for the eleventh floor. When the doors closed, he took his cell phone from his pocket and called Aubrey Preston, the president's deputy chief of staff, at the White House.

"Are we sending more ships than we publicly disclosed?"

"What are you talking about?"

"The White House announced we were sending three ships to the Persian Gulf. Reporters are asking me about rumors we secretly sent more than that. Is it true?"

"I can't talk about that, one way or the other."

Bain shouted at the phone, "Why wasn't I informed?!" He jammed his thumb against the "end call" button, then placed a call to the Chicago campaign office. "Get me on a plane to D.C., now!"

*   *   *

Not long after the White House announced its response to Iran's latest threats, Michael Geller boarded a private jet at LaGuardia Airport. An hour later, he arrived at Reagan National Airport. A car met him there and took him to the White House, where he was ushered to the residence on the second floor. After drinks and a brief discussion about sports, Geller turned to the topic that was most on his mind. "I understand Weiss came to see you today."

"Yes," Stanton nodded. "Disrupted my day, but what can I say? He does a lot for the Party."

"Throwing his weight around again?"

"Trying to."

"You must remember," Geller said, gesturing with his finger for emphasis, "Weiss can give you New York, but we gave you the country."

"I haven't forgotten. It's just that—"

The president's private cell phone rang, interrupting their conversation. He stepped away to take the call but returned a moment later. "That was Leon

Bain. He's on his way up." Stanton cut his eyes in Geller's direction. "It would be better if he doesn't see you here."

Geller set aside the glass he'd been holding. "Is there time for me to leave?"

"No." Stanton shook his head. "He's downstairs in the lobby now. Just go to the other room while he's here." Geller stood and started across the room. A few paces from the chair, Stanton stopped him. "Here," he said, handing Geller the glass. "You better take this with you."

A moment later, there was a knock at the door. Stanton opened it to find Bain standing in the hall. "Leon, come in," Stanton said, his voice more tense than ususal. "Didn't know we had a meeting tonight. I thought you were preparing for a push next week in California."

"Well, something came up. I thought we should talk."

"Sure," Stanton agreed. "Have a seat."

Bain settled onto the chair where Geller had been sitting and began at once. "What are you planning to do in the Middle East?"

"That's defense policy, Leon. Not politics."

"It all converges in an election year."

"It's just a couple of ships."

"I got a question this afternoon from a reporter who wanted to know if there were more ships."

"More ships?"

"He said he'd heard a rumor that you secretly sent additional ships to the region. Did you?"

"Come on, Leon. We said we weren't going to ask each other direct questions like that."

"Mr. President, they're pushing you toward military intervention. I bet Weiss came to see you today, didn't he?"

"You know," Stanton shrugged. "He comes to see me often."

"He runs a pro-Israel lobbying group. Of course he comes to see you. He talks about politics but what he wants is for the U.S. to intervene, or to at least tacitly approve their own military plans."

Stanton looked away. "Yosef Weiss raises a lot of money for us—money that pays your salary, by the way—and he's the key to winning New York, which is essential to our reelection plan, in case you don't remember."

"They want you to order an attack on Iran's nuclear sites."

"Upchurch thinks it's a good idea."

"Upchurch is the secretary of defense," Bain argued. "He thinks any war is a good war."

"You're right about that."

"Mr. President, we have to stay out of the Middle East. You have to stay out of the Middle East. At least until after the election. If you don't, and trouble starts, oil prices will go through the roof. The economy will tank. Your approval ratings will plummet. And all of us will be looking for new jobs after January."

"That's what everyone keeps reminding me."

"You've seen the reaction Talbot is getting?"

"Enough about Talbot," Stanton snapped. "That's all I've heard."

"What he's saying sounds good, but it's a trap. Americans are tired of war, especially war in the Middle East. They want our troops home and if they can't come home they at least want them out of harm's way. You start sending soldiers over there, for another war with no end in sight, and Alex Talbot will be downstairs in the office that should be yours."

For the next thirty minutes they argued about Iran, Israel, and a campaign message that talked tough without making any further military commitments. When Bain was gone, Geller stepped from an adjoining room. "Intense young man."

"We used to be that intense." Stanton refilled Geller's glass. "Back when we were young."

Geller took a seat. "I think he thinks he's actually advising you on the campaign."

"He's good with details," Stanton smiled.

"Just make certain you remember who pays for all this."

Stanton's lips curled ever so slightly at the corners. "You and your investors will get plenty of return on your dollar." He looked away as he continued. "How's that oil shale deal going, by the way?"

"The less you know about that, the better."

"Probably so."

"This thing is building in the Middle East."

"I know."

"Have you thought about an end game?"

"I haven't thought about a beginning game," Stanton answered sarcastically.

"Bain is right about one thing...."

"What's that?"

"You should think about where you want to go. Otherwise, you'll just get sucked into something you don't want."

"Any suggestions?"

Geller leaned forward, his elbows propped on his knees. "Think about this as an opportunity to solve the real Middle Eastern conflict."

"And what's that?"

"The Jewish-Palestinian conflict."

"Now, that's the real third rail of American politics," Stanton replied dismissively.

"Think about it," Geller continued. "The Jews have been at the center of problems in that region since the time of Abraham."

"They weren't around until Abraham."

"That's what I mean. They've been a problem since the beginning."

Stanton had a questioning look. "You really think this could give us a chance to solve that issue?"

"I think all the players are aligning themselves in perfect position. If Israel makes a preemptive strike against Iran, the world will view Israel as the aggressor, bringing us to the brink of disaster. We can step in to resolve that problem and, at the same time, force Israel to make strategic concessions that are necessary to once and for all resolve the Palestinian question."

"And if they don't attack Iran?"

A smile turned up the corners of Geller's mouth. "Do you really think they won't do it?"

"I really don't care. But I wonder what the president of Iran thinks."

Geller's eyes were wide with surprise. "Oh?"

"If we're trying to play him, chances are pretty good that he's trying to play us."

"Leave that part to me," Geller said with confidence.

"To you?"

"Foreign policy is susceptible to the same solution as any other issue."

"Which is?"

"The proper application of capital resources." Geller set aside his glass and stood. "That, I can manage very well."

CHAPTER 25
WASHINGTON, D.C.

BAIN WALKED OUT OF THE WHITE HOUSE and across the lawn to the northeast. From there he made his way to the corner at Fifteenth Street. After a short wait, he hailed a taxi and rode to Wisconsin Avenue in Georgetown, then walked two blocks north to a townhouse rented by Aubrey Preston. He arrived a little after midnight and rang the doorbell, then banged on the door with his fist. A few minutes later, the door opened and Preston appeared.

"It's late," he growled. "Couldn't this wait until tomorrow?"

"No. It can't wait." Bain pushed his way inside. "I need to know exactly what happened."

"What happened when?"

"Don't get cute with me," Bain replied in a curt tone. "You were supposed to make sure everyone at the White House stayed on message. And if not, you were supposed to at least give me a heads-up before anything happened."

Preston leaned against one end of the sofa. "You are out of your mind."

"No," Bain wagged his finger. "You dropped the ball."

"I'm a White House staffer. Not a campaign employee."

"Were you not in the loop on the decision about sending more ships to the Gulf?"

"Yeah," Preston admitted. "I was in the room."

"Then why didn't you call me?"

"You're with the campaign. I'm White House political liaison."

"Yeah. That's why I left you there. So you could keep things under control."

"Leon, this is policy and governing. Not reelection."

"It's about surviving."

"Look, I said I would do my best to coordinate policy with the campaign message, but I never said I would ride herd on what the president says and does. I can't do that. Pete McWhinney can't even do that and he's chief of staff."

"I'm gone for a week and the whole thing goes down the toilet. And all I see is Alex Talbot on television going on and on about some nonsense he thinks will solve all the problems in the Middle East. If we don't get past this, we're not going to get reelected."

"Get past what?"

"This obsession with Iran and the Middle East."

"And that is precisely why the campaign can't be run from the White House."

"Don't be naïve," Bain smiled sarcastically. "Every campaign of every incumbent president has been run from the White House."

"I'm not being naïve. I'm being realistic. We can't shape policy to suit your campaign needs."

"Listen to me." Bain leaned closer. "If you don't keep this under control, there won't be a campaign. There won't be anything to campaign for."

Preston folded his arms across his chest. "Why are you so upset? Because we didn't give you a heads-up before the announcement?"

Bain moved away. "That would have been nice, but that isn't the problem."

"Then what is?"

"Israel and Iran."

"Yeah. Well, great minds have tried to solve that problem for three thousand years." Preston started toward the door. "You're with the campaign. So, you deal with the reelection. We'll handle the rest of the world."

"This is a powder keg." Bain pointed with his finger. "If you guys keep on, it's going to blow up. You have to keep Weiss away from the president."

"And what do I do with him?"

"Send him to me."

"The president won't like it."

"Yeah, well, I'm with the campaign and this is a campaign issue, so I'll deal with that."

CHAPTER 26
QOM, IRAN

OHAD REVACH SAT ON A WOODEN CHAIR, his arms held fast to the armrests by plastic zip ties, his legs tied tightly by ropes to the frame. He squinted through the narrow slits of his swollen eyes to see Mehran Golzar standing in front of him. He knew Golzar from working at Fordow, where they had been friends. Now Revach's blood dripped from Golzar's knuckles as he leaned closer. "I want to know who else is here with you."

Revach stared at him a moment, letting his eyes focus on Golzar's. He had no hope of convincing Golzar to stop, only to delay the inevitable a little longer. Finally, when he was certain Golzar would wait no longer, he forced open his mouth to speak. "I am an Iranian citizen." Revach forced the words past his parched lips. "I am a technician at Fordow nuclear facility."

WHAP!

Golzar struck him with the back of his hand. "I want answers!" he shouted. "Real answers. We know you are Mossad. We have your phone. We saw the pictures you took and the number you sent them to." He leaned over Revach once more, his hot breath even fouler than the stench of feces in the air. "You will tell me, or you will do more than wet your pants."

"I am an Iranian citizen," Golzar repeated much too quickly. "I demand my rights."

"Rights?" Golzar roared. "Jews have no rights! Only the right to die a painful death." A toolbox sat on the floor to the left. He reached inside it and took out a pair of pliers. "This is your last chance. And I give you this chance only because we once were friends."

"I am an Iranian citizen."

Golzar held the pliers near Revach's left hand. "Who was working with you?"

"I am an Iranian citizen. I am a technician at the Fordow nuclear facility."

Golzar grasped Revach's index finger by the nail with the pliers and pulled. Pain shot up Revach's arm and he screamed. Golzar held up the pliers with the bloody nail firmly gripped between the pincers. "You have nine more fingers before we get to your toes. I suggest you start talking. We know you had accomplices helping you."

Two hours later, Revach sat slumped to one side in the chair. The zip ties dug into his arms as his weight pressed his flesh against them. His left eye was swollen shut. Through the hazy image of his right eye he saw blood dripping from his nail-less fingers. On the floor he felt something sticky beneath the soles of his bare feet.

Golzar, his shirt splotched with blood and wet with sweat, lugged a twelve-volt car battery into the room and set it beside the chair. A moment later he returned with electrical cables. He fastened one end of each cable to the battery, then attached the other end to a capacitor. When the device was wired and ready, he turned to Revach. "We are nearing the end. You really should consider talking now."

With great effort, Revach smiled up at him. "I am an Iranian citizen. I work at the Fordow nuclear facility."

Golzar dropped the electrical leads, reached over and ripped open Revach's trousers, exposing naked flesh. "You will tell me the names of those who helped you," he yelled. "Or you will die." Revach squirmed as Golzar attached the wires to the most vulnerable region of his body.

CHAPTER 27
HERZLIYA, ISRAEL

EARLY THE FOLLOWING MORNING, Mara Moss knocked on the door to Hofi's office, then pushed it open and leaned inside. "Eyal Portman is here to see you."

"Good," Hofi nodded. "Show him in."

Mara backed away and Portman appeared. "I came as quickly as I could." He stepped inside the office carrying a large brown envelope. Hofi pointed to it. "Are those the photographs?"

"Yes, some of them. We're still working on most of them but you said you wanted to know what we found as soon as we found it."

"So," Hofi said insistently, "let's have it."

Portman laid the envelope on the desk and took out the first photograph. "This one shows a surface-to-air missile battery." He laid it on the envelope and pointed to it while he spoke. "From the date stamp on the image, it was taken about six days ago. It's located inside the Fordow facility."

"You mean, inside the perimeter fence?"

"Yes, sir." Portman moved his finger to a spot near the center of the picture. "These are the missile tubes on the launcher." He traced with his finger. "Those black lines are lead lines coming from a panel on the side. As best we can determine, the tubes are empty."

"Why would they be empty?"

"The unit is not operational. It could function—they could load it with missiles and operate it—but," he paused again to point, "these lead lines should be attached to an integration unit that connects the launch system with a satellite dish."

"And the lines are not connected."

"No, sir." Portman shook his head. "They are not."

"Do they have the dish?"

Portman took a second photograph from the envelope and laid it on the desk. "This is the dish." He turned the photo on the desk for Hofi to see.

"It looks complete," Hofi scanned the picture.

"Yes. It looks complete, but it's not." Portman pointed. "You see this piece right there on the ground?"

"Yes."

"That is conduit that comes up from the ground. The narrow black lines protruding from it are cables with the ends wrapped to protect them."

"They aren't connected."

"No, sir, they are not connected."

"How long would it take to assemble this system?"

"It could be connected in a matter of an hour or two. But I do not think that is the problem."

Hofi leaned back from the desk. "Then what is the problem?"

"We think these pieces of equipment were parked there to give the impression that the defense system is functional. That's all. Just to give the appearance. They could have finished assembling the parts into a cohesive unit with no special equipment or expertise, but they did not." Portman paused a moment for effect. "I think," he continued, "it's because they do not have a satellite to which they can connect the system. This was a system designed solely for use with an integrated battle system and I think that system is not available."

A smile crept over Hofi's face. He leaned to one side and rested against the arm of the chair. "This isn't a system based on radar."

"No, it is not." Eyal laid three more photographs on the desk. "These are radar-based mobile units. They use a radar signal to locate and track targets. From the terrain in the background, these appear to be located beyond the Fordow perimeter, about two kilometers north of the site. These units are operational and fully functional, but they're based on targeting information generated by a radar unit."

"When they turn those units on, our planes would know it."

"Yes," Portman nodded. "Active or passive, they will light up like a neon sign."

"Does Iran have any functioning satellites in orbit?"

"So far they have placed two small satellites in space."

"But do they function?"

"Yes. One produces usable images of the earth and has been helpful in predicting the weather. The other—the earlier one—doesn't do much of anything. But they are not capable of tracking incoming targets, providing real-time battlefield data, or anything like that. In the world of satellites, the ones they have up there now are only slightly more sophisticated than an orbiting battery-powered camera."

"Do they have anything in the pipeline?"

"There are rumors that the Iranian Space Agency is preparing another Safir-1B rocket for launch later this month. We are attempting to determine precisely the payload for that mission but so far we have been unable to obtain any information about it." Portman took one last picture from the envelope. "This is a photograph of the launch site near Semnan, east of Tehran. As you can see," he said, pointing to the photo, "these two vehicles are trucks carrying stages of a Safir-1B rocket. The photographs were taken last week as the trucks arrived at the site."

"How long before that missile is ready to launch?"

"Three weeks. Maybe four. Could be a little longer, depending on how quickly they wanted to get it up."

"And after they launch, how long before their satellite would be available?"

"Assuming they have a satellite, and assuming that the lack of one really is the reason why they have not made the missile batteries at Fordow fully functional, it would take about two days after launch to get the payload properly positioned. And then probably a week to get most of the bugs out of the system."

"So they would be functional two weeks after launch?"

"Yes," Portman nodded. "If that is what they are actually doing, and barring a catastrophic failure, they would be operational within two weeks of launch." He stepped back from the desk. "If we were deploying a system we would take longer, but as a matter of determining the shortest possible time in which the system could work, two weeks is as quick as they can do it."

"And they don't have any other satellite capabilities?"

"They are able to monitor NASA satellites that provide information generally to the scientific community."

"What do those satellites provide?"

"Data regarding climate conditions, some mapping images, basic navigational aids, land-use information, thermal images for crop studies. Transmissions from deep-space probes are usually available after the initial mission is completed and they have access to images from the Hubble Space Telescope. That sort of thing."

"Nothing strategic?"

"Nothing that we know of as strategic."

Hofi looked puzzled. "What does that mean?"

"Sanctions have forced Iran to become unusually resourceful. For example, they needed sun sensors and several other sophisticated devices to complete their most recent satellite. International sanctions prevented them from obtaining those parts on the open market. So they produced the items themselves."

"So, bottom line, if they wanted to get this satellite system functional, and assuming they don't have a satellite that could do it right now, how long from now before they are able to use this surface-to-air system?"

"I'd say we're looking at a maximum of two months, on the long end. On the short side, four weeks, maybe six."

They talked a few minutes more, then Portman left the office. When he was gone, Hofi picked up the phone and called his assistant. "Mara," he said tersely, "I need to see the prime minister."

CHAPTER 28

ISTANBUL, TURKEY

WITH A RARE DAY OFF, JOHN SLADEN came from his apartment and walked up the street. He had errands to run and planned to spend the afternoon watching tourists while they shopped at the grand bazar. Observing people was one of his favorite pastimes.

At the coffee shop on the corner, he stopped in for a cup to sip while he walked. As he came from the store, he turned left and continued toward a bakery in the middle of the block. *A pastry might be nice, too,* he thought. As he came to the shop, he paused to let a woman pass by on the sidewalk. While he waited, someone bumped into him from behind. He thought nothing of it—a pedestrian caught unawares as he came up short. Then he felt a stinging sensation against his neck and reached up to rub a spot just beneath his ear. He glanced behind him in time to see a man dressed in a black collarless shirt with a brown jacket.

Sladen opened his mouth to speak but before he could form the words, a wave of nausea swept over him. He doubled over in pain and struggled to control his stomach muscles but found it impossible. With a spontaneous, gut-wrenching spasm, the contents of his stomach erupted from his mouth and splattered onto the concrete sidewalk. Droplets of brown liquid spattered over the tips of his shoes and sprinkled the legs of his trousers. Before he could collect himself, bone-jarring pain shot up his left arm. His chest tightened and he gasped for breath. Then he felt his knees buckle. The weight of his torso pushed him to the pavement as his body collapsed. His right elbow landed hard against the sidewalk, striking just a few inches from the curb. Before he was prone, his weight shifted and he tumbled into the street.

Someone screamed. Someone else was talking—a voice he was certain he'd heard before. Then all around him faded from sight.

*   *   *

Thirty minutes later, a phone rang at the FBI desk of the US Consulate in Istanbul. Richard Cruse, a special agent assigned to the office from New York, answered the call.

A veteran of twenty years with the FBI, Cruse had entered the bureau after graduating from George Washington University's law school. Following special training at Quantico, Virginia, he was detailed to the Washington, D.C., office. While there he obtained a master's degree in Terrorism Law from Georgetown. The following year he was sent overseas, where he worked first in Dubai, then Qatar, and Kabul. He became fluent in both Arabic and Farsi and quickly became one of the FBI's most experienced international investigators. Dedicated and conscientious, he was twice offered command of the FBI's Counterterrorism unit in New York but turned it down to stay in the field.

The caller on the phone that day was Taner Umar, a detective with the Istanbul police department. Cruse knew him from previous cases. "Mr. Cruse," Umar began, "we need to talk. In fact, you need to come see me as quickly as possible."

"What's up?"

"We have a dead body in the street."

"An American?"

"I think so. He has a US passport in his pocket. But that's not what makes him interesting."

"What does?"

"He has your business card in his wallet."

"Who is it?"

"As best we can determine, his name is John Sladen. Do you know him?"

The words struck Cruse hard. He and Sladen had known each other since graduate school and had maintained their friendship in spite of assignments that took them to opposite sides of the world. Now that they were posted to the same city, they were enjoying time together exploring the city and surrounding region. The thought that Sladen was dead left Cruse feeling sad and empty. "Where are you?" he stammered, then fumbled for a pen as Umar gave the address. "I'll be right there," he said finally, then hung up the phone.

Seated across the room was Sandra Lyman. Ten years Cruse's junior, she was an intelligent, capable agent. Unlike Cruse, who was a special agent from the New York office, Lyman worked from the FBI field office housed on the embassy campus in Ankara. She was in Istanbul on special assignment investigating a case that began in the Ankara district. Still, Cruse felt uncomfortable going to a crime scene alone, especially one that involved the death of a friend.

"Lyman," he said in a gruff voice. "Get your gear. You're with me."

"Excuse me?" She looked at him quizzically.

"If you want to sit in my office, you can help out, too." Cruse stood and slipped on his jacket. "Get your stuff and come with me."

Lyman grabbed her pistol from the drawer, shoved it into the holster on her hip, and took her jacket from a coatrack in the corner. She slipped it on as she hurried toward the door. Cruse was in the hall by the time she caught up with him. "What's this about?"

"I'll tell you when we're outside."

"No." She grabbed him by the sleeve. "Tell me now. I'm not supposed to be working with you like this. They told me not to get involved."

"Well, I'm telling you differently." Cruse pulled his arm free. "We'll talk about it in the car."

With Lyman in tow, Cruse made his way downstairs to the motor pool. A blue Chevrolet Impala was parked a few spaces from the door. Cruse got in behind the steering wheel and started the engine. Lyman took the passenger seat.

"Okay," she insisted as the door slammed shut. "Tell me what's going on."

"John Sladen is dead."

"Sladen?" She frowned. "Your friend at ENX?"

"Yes."

"Why? What happened to him?"

"I don't know." Cruse steered the car from the garage to the street and turned left. "Taner says he collapsed on the sidewalk."

"Who's Taner?"

"Taner Umar. An Istanbul detective."

"Was Sladen ill?"

"I don't think so." Cruse kept his eyes focused out the windshield as he drove through heavy traffic. "I just saw him last night. We met for a drink."

"Anything unusual happen?"

"We had a few drinks. That's about it."

"Run into anyone?"

"There was another guy there. I didn't know him. Didn't know he was going to be there. I thought it was going to be just me and John. But he was all right. Works for the State Department."

"What was his name?"

"I can't remember."

"Do you really think someone killed your friend?"

"I don't know." Cruse threw his hands in the air in a gesture of frustration. "I don't know any more than I've already told you."

"ENX is an energy company," Lyman continued. "Sladen was a trader."

"And your point is?"

"He's not a government employee. He's a US citizen who works in a foreign country. Isn't this something for the local authorities to handle?"

Cruse jerked the wheel to the right and steered the car to a stop at the curb. He turned to face her. "Look, ENX doesn't just trade energy."

She had a puzzled look. "Then what do they do?"

"It's a proprietary organization."

"Proprietary." The frown on Lyman's forehead deepened. "You mean, as in the CIA?"

"They're analysts, among other things."

"What other things?"

"You have to ask?"

"Why would the CIA create a front for a group of analysts?"

"Plausible deniability, insulate the official organization from whatever the front company does. Plenty of money to be made in the energy business."

"So the CIA funds itself now?"

"Not exactly."

"But why—"

"Stop!" He cut her off. "Do I have to explain everything to you? The CIA set up ENX as a self-sustaining, independent company. They trade energy futures and make a fortune. That's one side of the company."

"And the other side is covert operations."

"Yeah, one that operates completely off the books. Total deniability. No one on Capitol Hill knows about it. Hardly anyone at Langley has a clue what they're actually doing over here."

"Do you have a clue?"

Cruse put the car in gear. "I know enough to be worried." He checked the mirror for a break in traffic, then steered the car away from the curb.

CHAPTER 29
TEL AVIV, ISRAEL

AN HOUR LATER, EFRAIM HOFI ARRIVED at Yedaya's office carrying the large brown envelope he had received earlier. Yedaya was seated at his desk when Hofi arrived. "It sounded urgent when you called." He pointed to a chair. "Have a seat."

Hofi ignored the chair near the desk and stood while he talked. "We have a preliminary report on the photographs we received from Qom."

"What's the latest on the agent?" Yedaya seemed genuinely concerned. "Have we heard from him since he sent the pictures?"

"We've been unable to contact him."

"Do you have other people in the area? Someone who might be able to locate him?"

"Yes, they've all been alerted. Took a little while to get them up, but they're searching for him. Discreetly, but searching nonetheless."

Yedaya laced his fingers together in a thoughtful pose. "But you don't think they'll find him."

"Not alive." Hofi shook his head sadly. "If the Iranians have him, they'll torture him and then they'll kill him. They aren't going to let him live."

"Then we should honor him," Yedaya said with a tight-lipped smile, "by making good use of what he sent us."

"My sentiments exactly." Hofi took several photographs from the envelope and spread them across Yedaya's desk. "These first two photos show parts of a surface-to-air missile system. The equipment is in place but it is not yet operational."

"What's lacking?"

Hofi pointed to the cables and the satellite dish. "This is a system designed to obtain its targeting and guidance information from a satellite. These cables should connect the launcher to the dish, but they have not been connected to anything. Our analysts think it's because Iran does not yet have the satellite capability to support this system."

"Yet they have the system."

"Apparently they ran into some unforeseen delays and simply parked this equipment in place to give the appearance it was operational. We suspect the problem is with the satellite technology. Sanctions have limited their ability to purchase components on the international market. They've been forced to develop much of the technology from scratch."

Yedaya tapped the picture with his finger. "What's in the launch tubes?"

"Nothing; they are empty."

"This is one of their standard launchers?"

"Yes. A Russian launcher using their own missiles."

"Can't they operate it with a radar system?"

"Yes," Hofi nodded. "They could." He took another photograph from the envelope. "And they have those units positioned farther out, beyond the site." He pointed to the picture. "This one is about two kilometers north of the Fordow facility. Same launcher loaded with missiles, ready to go, only the targeting information for it is acquired from a radar system."

"But our drones could jam this radar-guided system."

"Yes, sir. Our drones could render their radar ineffective. But if they gain the ability to program their defenses from a satellite, we might not be able to disrupt that so easily."

Yedaya frowned. "We can't intercept their signals?"

"Intercepting is only half the problem. We could intercept the transmissions, but using them and making sense of them would depend on how well they encoded the information. We can receive signals from US satellites, but we have no ability to decode the signal."

"What about the guidance system onboard their missiles?"

"For missiles that use radar to guide them to the target, we could render them incapable of receiving that information. But our technology for doing that is not one hundred percent efficient. For a system that takes its coordinates from a GPS grid, we would have much less success."

Yedaya pointed to the pictures on his desk. "When did you receive these photographs?"

"Yesterday."

"Our agent did a good job," Yedaya said thoughtfully.

"Yes, sir." Hofi nodded. "He did an excellent job."

Yedaya picked up one of the photographs and studied it a little longer. Then he laid it back on the desk and looked over at Hofi. "So, what are you telling me?"

"Based on our current information, if Iran launched a satellite today capable of supporting the system in these photographs, these surface-to-air batteries could be fully functional within a month."

"Can they do that? Do they have such a satellite?"

"That is the key question." Hofi took one last photo from the envelope. "This is a picture from their launch site near Semnan."

Yedaya leaned forward for a closer look. "Those are stages of a rocket."

"A Safir-1B. The kind they used to put their most recent satellite into orbit."

"But that satellite can't support this system."

"No. It does very little, actually. But from the information in this picture, we feel they are preparing to launch something into space. If it is a military satellite, and it works properly, this missile defense system would be operational within four weeks."

"Anything to suggest they have such a satellite?"

"Nothing definite."

Yedaya sensed the hesitancy in Hofi's voice. "But what?"

"There is a facility near Shiraz in southern Iran. We have tried repeatedly to infiltrate the staff, but have been unable to do so. The Iranians are particularly careful about it."

"You are certain this site is related to their space program?"

"Yes. We have confirmed that. But we have not been able to get a look inside."

"What about the nuclear facilities? Can we penetrate them?"

"Without question, for most locations. A few are now buried underground but most of those are in cut-and-cover facilities. They dug out a hole, constructed the building below grade, and covered it with several feet of earth."

"As opposed to building it inside a mountain."

"Correct. But the nuclear development sites are only part of the equation. And perhaps the lesser part."

Yedaya looked puzzled. "The lesser part?"

"If we hit them hard at those sites, we can slow down their nuclear development program. Perhaps put off the attainment of nuclear weapons by a year or more. Maybe as long as two years. But if we do not hit their space facilities, they could develop military satellite capabilities and then we would lose the ability to strike any of their targets."

"We know where these space program facilities are located?"

"Yes. And if we should strike at Iran, I would put those sites at the top of the list. A satellite in geosynchronous orbit over Iran would give them the ability to see over the horizon in every direction. No one would be able to sneak up on them."

"That would change things," Yedaya nodded in agreement.

"Even now, if we attacked today, there would be no guarantee the Russians or the Chinese wouldn't tell them we were coming. But once they get their own satellite system operational—even with a single satellite—they'll be able to see our every move well in advance and their nuclear program will be as secure as it can possibly be."

"So instead of targeting just their nuclear sites, you're suggesting we need to hit their space program equally as hard?"

"Yes, sir," Hofi nodded. "If we don't hit their space program now, we may never get another chance at this."

CHAPTER 30
ISTANBUL, TURKEY

CRUSE AND LYMAN ARRIVED to find Sladen's body covered with a white cloth but still lying at the edge of the street. Uniformed policemen directed traffic around the scene, and yellow tape across the sidewalk forced pedestrians to gawk from a distance. Cruse pushed his way through the bystanders and ducked under the tape. Lyman followed.

Taner Umar saw them and moved in their direction. "Thanks for coming." He guided them toward the body, then stooped over and gently raised the sheet. "Do you know this man?"

"Yes." Cruse winced at the sight. "I knew him."

Umar covered the body. "What can you tell me about him?"

"Not much. Met him once or twice. You know," Cruse shrugged. "He was an American. I'm an American. We mostly talked about things from home."

"His documents show an address on the other side of town."

"Yeah," Cruse nodded. "I suppose they do."

"Any idea what he was doing all the way over here?"

"Can't really say." Cruse knelt beside the body and raised the sheet once more. "Any indication of trauma?"

"None." Umar leaned over. "Looks like a heart attack. No blood. Not even the slightest sign of a wound."

"Right." Cruse lowered the sheet back over the body and stood. "I assume you'll do an autopsy."

Umar's eyes darted away. "We'll send you a report."

As they talked, an ambulance arrived and came to a stop just a few feet away. Paramedics stepped out and began unloading equipment to retrieve the body. Cruse stepped back and watched a moment, then caught Umar's eye. "I'll be waiting for your report."

"Right," Umar nodded.

Cruse turned away and walked slowly toward the corner. Lyman walked at his side. When they were far enough away to avoid being overheard, she glanced up at him. "You lied to him."

"Yeah."

"Why did you do that?"

"He lied to me."

"About what?"

"He knows Sladen didn't die from a heart attack."

"Well, if we're going to investigate this case, we should have one of our people at the autopsy."

"There won't be an autopsy."

"Why not? I thought he was sending you a report."

"We're in Istanbul," Cruse explained. They reached the corner and turned right, then continued down the cross street. Lyman moved to the left to avoid a man sweeping the sidewalk. "Sladen is a US citizen. In spite of what you read in the papers and online, the Turks aren't really that interested in us."

"How deep will they have to dig before they find out who he really works for?"

"I suspect Umar already knows."

"I thought the point of the company was to shield the organization."

"Did you see anyone there from the CIA?"

"No. At least, no one officially."

"Right." Cruse paused to look up at the building to his right, then continued walking. "No one official. Maybe we should leave it that way for now."

"I still think it would be better to have one of our people do the autopsy."

"You're probably right, but we don't need an autopsy to know what killed him."

"We don't?"

"Looked like a professional job to me."

"How can you tell?"

"Just a hunch."

"A hunch."

"Yeah."

"So what do we do now?"

"Go to Sladen's apartment."

"But the car is back that way." Lyman gestured over her shoulder.

"I know," Cruse replied as he pointed in a different direction. "But the apartment is down here."

"Here?" Lyman looked startled. "I thought that guy said it was on the other side of town?"

"It used to be. Sladen moved a couple of weeks ago."

"Where to?"

Cruse came to an abrupt halt. "Here." He turned to face a building to the right. "On the third floor."

They made their way inside and walked upstairs to the third floor. Lyman watched while Cruse took a lock pick from his pocket and worked it into the keyhole. She glanced around nervously. "Is that legal?"

"We're in Istanbul."

"The law doesn't apply here?"

"Not really."

"Well, shouldn't we leave this for the local police to do?" Lyman glanced around once more. "I mean, if they're taking the lead."

"Sladen didn't just die on the street." Cruse worked the tumblers in the lock. "And anyway, we are the police."

"How can you be sure no one's inside?"

"Shouldn't be." Cruse twisted the doorknob. "Sladen wasn't married." He pushed open the door and gestured for her to enter.

Lyman stepped inside the apartment and glanced around. "Is this how you got assigned to an office on your own?"

Cruse pushed the door closed and followed her. "I learned from the best."

"Who was that?"

"Foster Goodall."

A hallway led from the door, past the kitchen, to a living room on the opposite side of the apartment. On the far side of the living room, a second hallway led to a bathroom and bedroom. Cruse stepped toward the living room. Lyman turned aside into the kitchen. "Where's Foster now?"

"He's in charge of the New York office."

"He's your boss."

"Something like that."

"What are we looking for?"

"Anything interesting."

Cruse moved on through the living room and into the bedroom. A few minutes later, Lyman called out, "Found something." He returned to the living room to find her standing at a desk near a window along the back wall. A drawer was open and Lyman pointed. "Looks like a laptop."

"Take it out." Cruse started toward her. "Let's see what's on it."

"You don't think the police would want to see it first?"

Cruse reached around her, lifted the laptop from the drawer, and set it on the desk. "Open the lid and see what you can find."

While software on the laptop booted up, Cruse looked around the living room once more. A minute or two later, Lyman called him over, "You should take a look at this."

Cruse came behind her and glanced down at the screen. "What did you find?"

"Your friend Sladen was into a lot of things."

"Like what?"

"Energy. Iranian scientists." She scrolled down the file directory. "Spent a lot of time working on something to do with embassies."

"Whose?"

"Ours." She pointed to a file on the list, then clicked on it and scanned down the page. "Here's a report about the closing of our embassy in Syria. Reduction of staff in Iraq. Analysis of embassy personnel changes in Jordan, Qatar, and Saudi Arabia."

"Interesting, but it doesn't seem like anything that would get someone killed."

"Which reminds me," Lyman noted, "if ENX is a CIA front, why isn't someone here right now wiping down this apartment?"

"I don't know, but if we—"

A sound from outside interrupted him. Cruse glanced out the window at the alley, then hurried to the bedroom. From the window on the front side of the apartment, he looked down at the street below. A car was parked to the right. Two men dressed in jeans and T-shirts came from it and walked toward the building entrance. Cruse rushed back to the living room. "They're here now."

"Who?"

"CIA. Bring the laptop and come on. We'll get someone to analyze it at the office."

"We're taking evidence?"

"Just get the laptop. Come on."

Lyman grabbed the laptop from the desk and followed Cruse to the front door. They paused there, listening. After a moment, Cruse eased open the door, turned to the right, and walked toward the back of the building. At the end of the hall they came to a stairway. He led the way down to the ground floor and outside to the alley. When they reached the corner, they turned right and walked quickly away from the building.

"What about the car?" Lyman asked.

"We'll get it later."

"Won't they find it?"

"Probably, but it's better they find the car than find us. Come on. We'll take the bus."

* * *

Harmon Hodges sat in a car parked across the street from the alley behind Sladen's apartment building. A camera lay on the seat beside him. As Cruse and Lyman emerged from the building, Hodges picked up the camera and snapped a photograph. He continued to take pictures as they reached the corner and started away from the alley.

When they were out of sight, Hodges took a cord from his pocket and plugged one end into a port on the side of the camera. He connected the other end to a Blackberry, then used the keypad on the phone to create a text message. With the message prepared, he attached photos from the camera and sent them on their way.

CHAPTER 31
TEL AVIV, ISRAEL

LATER THAT DAY, YEDAYA MET WITH Gabi Halutz, chief of the Israeli Defense Force general staff. Together they reviewed the pictures received from Hofi and discussed the intelligence assessment they both had received.

"I understand the argument Hofi is making," Halutz replied. "He and I went over it several times, both of us yelling and shouting at each other. But you must understand, Mr. Prime Minister, sites regarding Iran's space program are not currently on our targeting list."

Yedaya leaned back in his chair. "Which means what, exactly?"

"Which means," Halutz explained, "we would have to reprogram some of our missiles to account for those locations."

"Or hit them with planes," Yedaya suggested.

Halutz's brow narrowed and his voice lowered to a rumble. "We were trying to keep the planes to a minimum."

"I tried to get the refueling tankers from them." Yedaya put up his hands in a defensive posture. "I gave it my best. So much so that the president and I nearly came to blows." Halutz glanced up at him with a skeptical look. "I'm not kidding," Yedaya insisted. "We were on the verge of a fight when Jean Brown stepped between us."

"Someone should knock some sense into his inexperienced head."

"Believe me, I was ready to do it."

"We need those refueling tankers in order to launch a strike that brings the greatest possibility of hitting all their sites, and brings our planes back safely. We will only get one opportunity to do this."

"I tried to convince them," Yedaya repeated. "But Stanton wouldn't budge."

"Stupid Americans," Halutz sighed. "I have heard the same thing from them." He shifted positions in the chair. "Have you considered an alternative?"

"We discussed this earlier, before my trip."

"But what about the French?"

"The French?"

"Airbus is pushing their version of a refueling tanker. It's already flying and much better than Boeing. The French use it and they fly NATO planes."

"Where would we get the parts to fit it for our jets?"

"That's what I'm saying. We are using the same version of airplanes as the French. They are NATO planes. I think the French can supply us with their fittings. I'll check on that, but would you be willing to purchase from Airbus if we can make the modifications with parts from France?"

"Yes." Yedaya's eyes were bright with enthusiasm. "But there isn't time for that now. Can we use our own 707s?"

"The 707s will work, but they are much more vulnerable than the ones we requested. There is no certainty they can return."

"If they're lost, then so be it. We have little time to wait."

"Yes. I agree."

Yedaya changed the subject. "What kind of time frame are we looking at to be ready for an attack?"

Halutz's face was serious once again. "If we attacked Iran with the sites already loaded in our system, we could fly in two days."

"And if we hit their space program?"

"To account for sites regarding their space program, we'd need an additional week. Plus, to hit them all, we would have to add additional aircraft, most of which we would lose to the lack of fuel."

"So we could move in two weeks' time."

"Easily. And we could still add some of the additional targets even with that short window. But beyond that, we would also be saying that the planes and pilots for that mission are expendable."

"I understand."

"We must know precisely which targets to hit by tomorrow evening—noon the following day at the latest." Halutz leaned forward. "And Mr. Prime Minister, I know this is a tough decision, but I think we must attack immediately. Even if it means losing men and equipment. The planes and pilots are no good to us if Iran develops a nuclear bomb."

"I agree," Yedaya nodded. "But not everyone is onboard yet and if we attack now, we will do so without American help."

"If we don't respond to this latest bombing of our embassy staff, all our enemies will see us as weak. Hezbollah will become more aggressive from Lebanon, Iran will be less inclined to reign in its nuclear ambitions, and those in Egypt who hate us will gain the upper hand."

Yedaya seemed to agree. "Can we destroy the facility at Qom?"

"Assuming the defenses are as Hofi has suggested, we should have no problem leveling all of the buildings at that location."

"It's at the top of the list?"

"Yes. But what about the space program sites?"

"Can you prepare for them without delaying preparations for an immediate attack?"

"Yes, if you let me select the targets. And understand, we will not hit every site related to that program."

"Then let's do that." Yedaya stood. "I agree with Hofi's assessment. If Iran obtains military satellite capabilities, we may be prevented from striking them again. But if they obtain a nuclear weapon, nothing else will matter."

"Well put, Mr. Prime Minister." Halutz rose from his chair. "We shall proceed with preparations and hope our friends see the wisdom of our decision."

CHAPTER 32

TEHRAN, IRAN

ON THE WEST SIDE OF THE CITY, Jalil Amini watched from the backseat of the car as Azadi Stadium came into view. Guards waved the car across the parking lot and into a private space near the stadium entrance. When the car came to a stop, an attendant opened the rear door and Amini stepped out.

Briefcase in hand, he walked quickly to the elevator and rode up to the mezzanine level. There he made his way to the president's private suite. Security agents stepped aside as he approached. Someone opened the door for him.

Inside, he found Rasoul Moussaoui alone and seated near a large window that looked out over the field below. Dirty dishes and cups littered the room, but all the guests had been cleared out. A soccer game was in progress and the stadium was filled to capacity. Noise from the crowd reverberated through the walls, creating the perfect cover for what they were about to discuss.

"I am sorry to interrupt, Mr. President, but we have a matter to discuss that can't wait."

"Certainly," Moussaoui nodded. "What is it?"

"Yesterday one of our security officers, acting on a tip from credible sources, captured a man believed to be a Mossad agent who was working at the Fordow facility."

"What?" Moussaoui blurted as he jerked his head around, his eyes wide with surprise. "A Mossad agent? At Fordow?"

"Not so loud, Mr. President. Others might hear you."

"They don't even know we're alive." Moussaoui pointed over his shoulder to the crowd. He was on his feet now and moving toward Amini. "Tell me you knew he was there already. Tell me those Jews didn't just walk into the building and make themselves at home." He took a deep breath and shouted, "Tell me he didn't walk right past our security measures!"

"We were tracking him," Amini said sheepishly. He inched backward as he spoke. "Our sources had tipped us."

"I doubt that," Moussaoui snapped. "More like a lucky guess. Where in the facility did he work?"

"Building A."

Moussaoui's face was red with anger. "He was in one of the centrifuge units?"

"Yes," Amini nodded.

"How did this happen?"

"We are not sure, but we have ordered a review of all security procedures at every location."

"As well you should." Moussaoui paused to collect himself before continuing. "What has happened to this Mossad agent?"

"We are holding him at a secure location."

"And he is actually from Mossad?"

"Yes. We have confirmed he is Ohad Revach. Born in Haifa. Educated in the United States."

"Where did you get this information?"

"We have a contact with access to the FBI database."

"Really." Moussaoui's shoulders relaxed and a grin spread over his face. "The FBI? In America?"

"Yes."

Moussaoui shook his head in disbelief. "What was this Mossad agent doing there, in our facility?"

Amini lowered his gaze. "He was taking pictures."

"Pictures!" Moussaoui struck the table with his fist, then held his breath in an effort to control himself. "What did he do with them?"

"He transmitted them right before we captured him. But we have his phone."

"How could this happen?" Moussaoui shouted. "How? How? How?"

"He was using a cell phone. He had a security clearance that gave him access. Someone on the inside must have helped him."

Moussaoui placed his hands on his hips. "Someone on the inside. Just as we have someone on the inside there."

"When he made the call," Amini explained, "his number appeared in our system. One of the operators caught it and notified our agents, who were able to locate him on the grounds."

Moussaoui turned away, arms folded across his chest. When he spoke, his voice was firm and even. "What has happened to this agent since he was captured?"

"We have been questioning him."

"What has he told us?"

"Nothing, except to insist he is an Iranian citizen."

Moussaoui looked over his shoulder in Amini's direction. "Is he?"

"He has papers, but no one seems to know for certain yet whether they are authentic."

"But you are sure he was born an Israeli?"

"Yes."

"Does he know anything helpful?"

"Perhaps," Amini shrugged. "But if he was going to tell us, he would have talked by now."

"Is he alive?"

"In a manner of speaking."

Moussaoui folded his hands behind his back and gazed down at the game on the field. "You must get rid of him."

"Yes, Mr. President."

"If the world press finds out about this, we will look like idiots. A Jew right here under our noses, and no one noticed until now."

"Yes, sir. We will put him—"

"No," Moussaoui interrupted. "Not in the usual manner. Send him home to Israel."

Amini looked perplexed. "Send him home?"

"Yes." Moussaoui looked Amini in the eye. "Send him home in a way the Israelis will understand."

CHAPTER 33
WASHINGTON, D.C.

BEFORE THE PRESIDENT'S DAY BEGAN, Miles Parker, an officer from the CIA and Ralph Ligon, the director of National Intelligence, appeared in the Oval Office for the morning intelligence briefing. After a review of regional issues in Asia and South America, Ligon turned to the Middle East.

"Mr. President," Ligon began, "we have been informed that a Mossad agent working in Iran is now missing and believed to be captured by Iranian intelligence operatives."

"This is the first I've heard of this." Stanton's brow was heavy with a look of concern. "Where was he working? Do we know? It's a man, right?"

"He was at the Fordow facility just outside the city of Qom."

Stanton sat up straight in his chair. "You guys didn't tell me Mossad had an agent inside their nuclear program."

"Actually, we did," Parker replied with a grin. "We just didn't tell you about it."

"You told me, but you didn't tell me?"

"We gave you the digested version," Ligon added.

Stanton gestured with his hands. "So when you said 'sources,' this is what you were talking about?"

"Generally."

"Has Iran acknowledged they have him?"

"No," Parker answered.

"Will they?"

"That's not likely. Mossad has agents and operatives working in all phases of Iran's … essential programs. That's how they know so much about it. If they—"

"Essential programs. I like that. Has a nice ring to it. Better than 'thermonuclear bombs' or 'weapons of mass destruction.'" Stanton rested his elbows on the desktop. "So all that stuff Yedaya was telling me was actually true?"

"Most of it," Parker answered.

"Except the parts we deliberately fed them," Ligon added, "to slow them down."

Stanton frowned. "We do that?"

"Not officially."

Stanton picked up a pen from the desk and twirled it through his fingers. "Do they really need those refueling tankers?"

"As we mentioned in the briefing before Yedaya's visit," Parker explained, "if they wanted to strike inside Iran with airplanes, and get the planes and pilots safely back to the bases in Israel, they would need to refuel at least twice. Once on the trip over, to enable them to get in, loiter near the targets while engaging, and then get out with a margin for error. And then they would need to refuel at least once on the flight back home."

"Tell me about this Mossad agent." Stanton returned to the subject at hand. "You're pretty confident he's in Iranian custody?"

Ligon nodded. "Which means he is being tortured and will likely be killed."

Stanton raised an eyebrow. "But he won't talk."

"No, sir," Parker answered. "I don't think so."

"Mr. President," Ligon interjected. "In addition to the Mossad agent, yesterday an employee of ENX died on the street in Istanbul."

Stanton looked perplexed. "ENX?"

"An energy-trading firm," Parker added hastily.

Ligon gave him a disapproving look, then turned to Stanton. "It's a CIA proprietary company, Mr. President."

"What happened to him? I mean, how did he die? Did he just drop dead?"

"Apparently," Parker concurred. "But they're still investigating exactly what happened."

"Okay."

"And," Ligon continued, "we're still monitoring the car bombing in Rabat."

"Are the Moroccan authorities being helpful?"

"Yes, sir. As we mentioned yesterday, they are allowing the Israelis to take the lead role."

"And by Israelis you mean Mossad?"

"Yes, sir."

"How long before Israel retaliates?"

Parker hesitated. Ligon jumped in. "That's a little troublesome, Mr. President."

"Troublesome because we don't know?"

"No, sir. Troublesome because they haven't indicated any response at all, which means they could be planning something big."

Stanton leaned away from the desk. "They would tell us first, right?"

"That isn't certain."

"Then what is certain?"

Parker and Ligon exchanged looks. Stanton tipped back his head and rested it against the back of the chair.

"We can tell you what has happened, Mr. President," Ligon explained. "We can't predict the future. Normally when the Israelis are planning something, they give telltale signs of what they're up to."

Stanton closed his eyes. "Troops on alert, that sort of thing?"

"Yes, but we usually see things even before that. Essential personnel confined to base. Additional deliveries of fuel and food. And other things, but you get the idea. We've seen none of that. Everyone is still coming to work on regular hours, going home on regular hours. No entertainment canceled. Nothing that would indicate something is in the works."

"Are any of these incidents related?"

Ligon looked unsure. "Which incidents, Mr. President?"

"The Mossad agent, the CIA employee, and the car bombing."

Parker spoke up. "We don't think the Rabat incident is related to the ENX employee. We're not sure about the missing Mossad agent. He appears to have been a target of opportunity, but we won't know until we get a little farther into the investigation."

"How did they find him?"

"That's the mystery."

Stanton opened his eyes. "This other guy, the employee, with ENX—he was a CIA agent?"

"Not really an agent, sir," Parker explained. "ENX is a separate corporation."

"But owned by the CIA."

"Technically, yes."

Stanton looked perturbed. "Am I going to hear about this from Alex Talbot at one of his rallies or the next time he appears on one of those cable news shows?"

"We don't think they're related," Parker assured.

"You didn't answer my question."

"Everything was compartmentalized," Ligon responded. "We're taking steps to keep it that way."

Stanton leaned back in the chair and closed his eyes once more. "Talbot has friends, you know."

"That won't be a problem."

"I wish there was a way to shut that guy up. He just talks about whatever pops into his head. Half of it is so far off base it's nearly impossible to refute."

Ligon was taken aback by the comment. "Mr. President, we should be careful about how we talk about shutting people up. He *is* the Republican Party's nominee and this is the White House."

"Relax, Ralph." Stanton opened his eyes and straightened his posture. "I'm just saying, Talbot is so good at being their nominee, I hope the voters choose to keep him right there and make him their former nominee on Election Day." He rose from his chair. "Anything, just as long as they don't elect him president."

CHAPTER 34
NEW YORK CITY

DAVID HOLSTEN WAS IN THE LOCKER ROOM at the New York Athletic Club when his cell phone rang. He checked the number and saw the call was from Michael Geller.

"We need to talk."

"Meet me for lunch," Holsten replied. Geller ended the call without saying more.

From the club, Holsten walked four blocks south to Carnegie Deli on Seventh Avenue. The place was crowded but Geller was alone at a table in back.

"You look worried," Holsten said as he took a seat opposite him.

"We have a problem." Geller reached in his pocket for his cell phone. He paused while a waiter set two glasses of water on the table.

"What now?" Holsten asked when they were alone again.

"Someone has been in the apartment." Geller checked the phone, then passed it across the table. Holsten took it and scrolled through a series of pictures showing a man and woman walking down a street. He recognized the location from the buildings in the background. Geller pointed. "Do you know them?"

"No."

"How do you know they were inside?"

"The person who took those pictures saw them. Can you find out who they are?"

"I have a friend who might be able to help." Holsten forwarded the pictures to his own phone, then handed Geller's back to him. "I'll check with him and see what he thinks."

"Do that." A waiter appeared to take their order. When he was gone, Geller continued. "You should have had them wipe the apartment clean."

"They did. Our people arrived within minutes."

"Then how did these two," Geller said, gesturing with the phone, "beat your team to the scene?"

"I don't know." Holsten took a drink from the water glass. He stared at Geller while he swallowed, then set the glass gently on the table. "You spying on me now, Michael?"

"What?"

"The photographs," Holsten explained. "Did you have someone following me?"

"I didn't." Geller arched an eyebrow as he spoke. "But I'm not the only one interested in how things turn out."

"Baer." Holsten had a knowing look.

"They are concerned," Geller nodded. "As well they should be."

"I should have known they would be watching." Holsten retrieved his phone from his pocket and checked to make certain he had received the pictures. Then he scrolled down his contacts list to a number for Duncan Robinson and forwarded the pictures to him. "I'll find out who they are."

Geller looked across the table at him. "We need to know what's going on."

"Relax," Holsten assured him. "My guy has access to this kind of thing. If he can help, he will."

"Another one of your illustrious contacts?"

"Yeah," Holsten nodded. "Something like that."

"You were supposed to take care of this before it happened. That is what we are paying you for … among other things."

"It's under control."

"These people are serious about maintaining their anonymity."

"Tell Baer his secrets are safe with me."

After lunch, Holsten walked up the street to his apartment on

Sixty-Fourth Street. On the way, he sent Robinson a text message. "I need names to go with the faces." Moments later, Robinson sent a message in reply. "I'll let you know what I find out."

A few hours later, Holsten received a second text from Robinson that said simply, "Meet me."

From his apartment building, Holsten took a taxi down to Battery Park at the lower end of Manhattan. Robinson was seated on a bench near the Castle Clinton monument. Holsten took a seat beside him. Robinson didn't wait for a greeting.

"The man in the photograph is Richard Cruse. Woman's name is Sandra Lyman. They're FBI agents stationed in Turkey. Why are you interested in them?"

"Business."

"Well, that's all I can help you with on this one. Whatever else you need you'll have to get from somewhere else."

"You sound shaken."

"Not shaken," Robinson answered. "Just not interested in giving up information about federal agents."

"Protecting your own?"

"Protecting myself." Robinson turned in Holsten's direction. "Cruse has been with the bureau for twenty years. Guys like that have plenty of friends with long memories. I don't want them knowing my name."

"No one's going to know you helped."

"I've been with the Marshals Service long enough to know better than that." Robinson rose from the bench. "Someone always knows," he said, and then walked away.

Holsten sat on the bench, watching a flock of pigeons peck at a potato chip bag that lay on a patch of grass a few feet away. As the birds fought for scraps from the bag, he stole a look, first to the left, then to the right, and scanned the park to make certain no one was watching. What he'd learned from lunch with Geller left him feeling paranoid. Baer could be ruthless, but he was nothing compared to his friends. If they were interested enough to obtain photos, they were much too interested for comfort.

After a while, Holsten tired of watching the birds and he'd seen no one watching him in the park. Finally he rose from the bench and walked back toward State Street. He paused at the curb to check for traffic before crossing to the opposite side. While he waited, a black Lincoln came to a stop in front of him. The rear window lowered and he could see Geller sitting in the backseat. Holsten opened the door and climbed inside. "You following me now, too?"

"I always monitor my investments. What did you find out?"

"They're FBI agents."

"Then why did they leave the apartment in such a hurry?"

"Good question."

Geller took out his cell phone and retrieved one of the pictures. He enlarged it on the screen and pointed to an object in Cruse's hand. "Recognize that?"

"From the emblem on it I'd say it's an Apple laptop."

"I think we have a problem." Geller closed the phone and returned it to his pocket. "Otherwise, the FBI agents would have stayed and your team would have been sent away. Or arrested."

"It's not a problem."

"They suspect something."

"Probably just curious."

"Or they were already on to Sladen."

"I don't think so." Holsten shook his head. "Attwood assured me no one else received the report. Without it, no one outside ENX could know what he was doing."

"If those two agents have Sladen's laptop, they have his report now," Geller argued. "And most of his research that went with it."

"It'll be okay," Holsten assured him.

"Why do you keep telling me that?" Geller frowned. "It's not okay. This is a mess. One that could have terrible consequences."

"Look, this will be over long before the FBI figures out what's happening. Once it starts in motion, events will roll over everyone. Anything those two agents know will be buried in the clutter."

Geller folded his arms across his chest. "For your sake, I hope you're right."

*   *   *

That evening, Geller drove from his midtown apartment on Lexington Avenue across the Williamsburg Bridge into Brooklyn. Beyond the bridge, he turned onto Grand Street and brought the car to a stop outside a brownstone near the corner at Graham Avenue. In a few minutes, a man appeared beside the passenger door. Geller pressed a button for the lock and the door opened. Ahamad Sair slid into the front seat. He closed the door and gave Geller a sullen look. "Three ships. It would have been nice to know about that beforehand."

"Too risky."

"Even for a friend?"

"Three ships is only part of it. They're also moving four destroyers into the Indian Ocean and sending two more submarines into the region on patrol."

"That is good information."

"I thought you would want to know."

"What is their primary concern?"

"Your submarines."

"Good," Sair nodded. "That is why the imam insisted we purchase them."

"Your people are moving forward?"

"Yes. You can keep the president on board?"

"He is moving up each time your forces move."

"Good. And the Israelis? What about them? Will they be as unpredictably predictable as usual?"

"We have no direct control over them, but I cannot imagine them failing to move on the information their agent supplied from Qom. Especially after that car bombing."

"That was a stroke of genius from our people. And a blessing from Allah. Finally we are working together. You, the direct descendent of Hitler's closest confidant. And me, the direct descendant of Haj Amin el-Husseini, the Grand Mufti of Jerusalem."

"As the Führer envisioned all along. Perhaps now you will get what he promised to your forebears—a homeland of your own, free of the Jews—and you as the Grand Mufti of Jerusalem."

"We shall see."

Geller glanced across the front seat at Sair. "There is one risk for which you have not accounted," he noted in a serious tone.

Sair looked concerned. "What is that?"

"Iran must first survive an Israeli attack."

"Oh." Sair looked relieved. "We will survive," he laughed nervously.

"With enough remaining to launch a counterattack?"

"We will have more than enough," Sair boasted. "You are certain your president will strike a deal?"

"I am positive," Geller nodded. "Israel will attack, the U.S. will support, the stakes will go up, and our president will ask your president what it will take to end the conflict. It's the American way. Can you get your president in the room when the time comes?"

"We will have him there," Sair assured. "And you?"

"Consider it done."

CHAPTER 35
WASHINGTON, D.C.

LEON BAIN CAME FROM HIS LAST MEETING of the evening and walked out to the street. Suitcase in hand, he waited at the curb for the car that would take him to Reagan National Airport. He checked his watch. If he hurried, he might get home to Chicago in time to catch the last edition of the news.

As the car approached, Bain's cell phone rang. He took it from his pocket and was surprised to see the call was from Kathleen Baker, the secretary of state. "Have you left town yet?" she asked.

"About to take the car to airport now, ma'am."

"Don't go yet."

"Why not?"

"We need to talk." Her voice sounded serious.

"Now?"

"Yes," she insisted. "Now would be great. Come to my office."

When the car came to a stop at the curb, Bain tossed his suitcase on the backseat and climbed in after it. "Change of plans," he told the driver.

"Where to now?"

"Foggy Bottom."

"Yes, sir." The driver put the car in gear and steered it into the evening traffic. Twenty minutes later, they came to a stop at an underground entrance beneath the State Department building, a few blocks west of the White House. Bain climbed from the car, took his suitcase, and trudged across the walkway. As he approached the entrance, a guard opened the door and helped him inside. Bain was cleared through the building security checkpoint and took the elevator to the fifth floor. Baker was waiting for him when he arrived.

"I took the liberty of ordering dinner." She guided him toward a dining table that stood to one side of the room. Bain deposited his bag to one side and took a seat at the table. Stewards appeared and began to serve the meal. While they were in the room, Baker and Bain talked about the events of the day but with little more detail than was available in the news. When the stewards were gone, Baker got to the point of her earlier phone call.

"We have a problem," she began. "And if we can't fix it, I think the president's chances for winning reelection may be lost."

"Let me guess. This has something to do with Yedaya's visit."

"Yes," Baker nodded. "Sort of. Upchurch, Dick Elser at Navy, Jean Brown, Paul Catlett at CIA, and several more are all pushing hard for a military response against Iran."

"I knew about Upchurch and I suppose I could have guessed about Elser."

"And Yosef Weiss," Baker added. "That man spends more time at the White House than the president."

"I told them to put a stop to that."

"Well, they've totally frozen me out of the process," she lamented. "I learned about the president's decision to send additional ships to the Gulf when I heard it on CNN."

"Pete needs to get a handle on this. He's manipulating the schedule and making sure that those who favor diplomacy get as little time as possible with the president. That lets him shape the president's thoughts. I don't like it."

"What do you think we should do?"

"We have to diffuse the nuclear issue," Baker insisted. "Take the air out of the issue. To do that, the president has to sit down with Rasoul Moussaoui. Face-to-face. At a neutral site. And talk. Just like we did with the Russians."

"Not sure I would agree with that. At least, not before the election."

"With Upchurch and the others shutting everyone else out, there isn't much chance of it anyway."

"You want me to do something about it?"

"I want you to get McWhinney off his game. Andrew Stanton and I have been friends for years. When I talk to him, he listens and he uses his brain. He has to think his way through this. He can't just reach for a ship or bombs or troops. He has to think. But when Upchurch comes in with his military lingo and the whole shock-and-awe routine, the president's eyes glaze over and he just goes along with whatever they say."

"You really think meeting with Moussaoui is a good idea?"

"It is the only thing that will work. This thing is already spiraling down toward the military option. We have to find a way out that doesn't involve blowing up something." She put down her fork and looked Bain in the eye. "Get McWhinney to back off and give me some time with the president. I think we can rescue the situation. Otherwise, you and I are going to be out of a job at the end of this term."

CHAPTER 36
ISTANBUL, TURKEY

WITH CRUSE WATCHING FROM across the room, Lyman reviewed the contents of the laptop they took from Sladen's apartment. A quick scan of the directory led to the files most recently viewed. Lyman scrolled through them, opening each one as she went. "Most of the ones he was working with over the past month or two contain information about embassy staff in the Middle East." She continued talking as she read. "Here's one about the State Department closure of the embassy in Syria. Another about changes in Iraq." She looked over at Cruse. "They are seriously reducing staff in Iraq, you know."

"I heard," Cruse acknowledged.

"They'll be down to less than half their previous strength by next month."

"What else is on there?" Cruse sounded irritated by the discussion.

"Staff lists from embassies and consulates in Saudi Arabia, Qatar, Jordan, Egypt, and Israel." She squinted at the screen. "This was from last year." She moved on to the next file. "This one is from the year before that." She opened yet one more new folder. "Here we go. A comparison of the last five years. Wow. He was right."

"About what?"

"All of those locations are way down on personnel and most of it happened within the last six months."

Cruse set aside the work on his desk. "Did he do anything with that information? Is there anything on there that looks like a report?"

"I can't tell." Lyman scrolled farther down the screen. "Here's a note that indicates he filed a report. Sent it to Langley about two months ago, asking for a check of other agencies to see if military action in the region was pending or if a major policy shift was planned. He didn't receive a response and there isn't a copy of the report on here."

"So maybe that's not what got him killed. I mean, if he filed the report two months ago and someone just now killed him, that wouldn't seem like the two were connected." Cruse leaned back in his chair. "Maybe he wasn't killed. Maybe he just died of natural causes."

"Except for this." Lyman pointed to the screen. "Take a look."

Cruse rose from his chair and came to her desk. "What did you find?"

"This," she gestured.

On the screen was a memo to the file written by Sladen. Cruse read it quickly. "Didn't get a response. Began his own check. Polling major agencies that operate in the region … That's a little obsessive, don't you think?"

"Sounds like he was definitely into it." Lyman moved the cursor down the page and picked up from there. "Found no other agency or entity had changed personnel strength in the region except for the addition of Navy personnel aboard several ships that have been moved to the region."

Cruse took a step back from the desk. "Anyone working with him on this?"

"Not sure anyone actually helped him. But there's an access log over here." Lyman opened another file. A list of dates, files names, and numbers appeared. She ran her finger down the left side as she scanned across the screen. "Looks like someone else accessed some of these files." She moved her finger along a line of information to the right side of the screen. "Someone named Steve Bachmann."

Cruse leaned closer once more. "You sure about that?"

"Yeah, there's the name and date right there. Accessed some of them as recently as yesterday."

"Who is he?"

"Apparently he's an employee at ENX."

"Think we ought to talk to him about this?"

"I don't know," Lyman shrugged. "Not really any indication of a crime."

"Just a young, healthy CIA analyst who collapsed on the street in Istanbul."

"Okay." Lyman pushed back from the desk and stood. "Let's go talk to this guy."

"I thought you weren't supposed to be working on our cases," Cruse grinned.

"I'm curious now. I don't know if a crime was committed, but I'd like to meet Steve Bachmann and hear what he has to say."

From the consulate, Cruse and Lyman drove across town to the ENX office. A receptionist escorted them to a room in back. Bachmann was standing at the window, gazing out over the city, when they arrived. He turned to greet them as they entered.

"Mr. Cruse." He reached out to shake hands. "I've heard a lot about you. John used to talk about you all the time."

Cruse introduced Lyman and then got right to the point. "We wanted to talk to you about John and the projects he was working on."

Bachmann looked concerned. "You think something happened to him?"

"We're not sure," Cruse answered. "Just following up on some loose ends."

"Yeah, I'll do what I can. It seems such a waste, him dying on the street like that." A frown creased his forehead. "Do you really suspect foul play?"

"Like I said, we're not sure what to suspect right now, but given the nature of his work, we thought we'd take a look."

"Well," Bachmann began. "I worked with John on several projects." He turned back to the window and gazed off into the distance. "He … uh … he liked to keep most of it to himself."

"We noticed he had conducted quite a bit of research into embassy staffing levels. Did he talk to you about that?"

"John had an idea that—" Without warning, Bachmann wheeled around to face them. He moved to the corner of the desk. "You know, maybe we should do this in the conference room." He gestured toward the door. "We can walk down there and have plenty of room to spread out." As they moved in that direction, he glanced over his shoulder toward the window. When he realized they noticed, he turned back quickly to open the door. "I'm sure you have things we need to discuss."

Cruse and Lyman followed Bachmann out the door and down the hall to a windowless conference room. A table ran down the center of the room with a dozen leather chairs arranged around it. Cruse and Lyman took a seat near one end. Bachmann closed the door and joined them at the head of the table.

"Sorry for the interruption. You just never know who might be listening." He adjusted his position in the chair and turned to Cruse. "Now, you were saying …"

"What can you tell us about the projects John was working on?"

"To tell you the truth, I'm not really sure exactly what he did. John was pretty much a loner, which fit in well here. Nobody really tells you what to do. You just find something that interests you and dig in."

"We've been through his laptop. We know the most recent files he used were related to embassy closings, reductions in staff. What was that about?"

"Hard to say." Bachmann rested his hands on the table. "Most of us here spend our day reading and interpreting articles and reports about other governments, but John started doing the same thing to our own government. Read everything he could find from our own agencies. Came up with all sorts of theories about what we were really doing over here."

"Any idea what caused that shift in his focus?"

"Not really," Bachmann shrugged. "I don't think it was sinister. I remember one day he saw an article about embassy staff reductions in Iraq. We talked about it and how maybe the State Department people were finally coming to their senses. Then a few weeks later he saw an article about closing the embassy in Syria. I told him it had to do with the uprising and the Syrian government's crackdown and safety for our personnel, but that wasn't enough for him. He started digging into information about other embassies in the region to see what they were doing. That's when it got interesting. It looked like they were all shrinking their staffs."

"Right."

"And in an unusual way."

"How so?"

"Normally when the State Department wants to reduce an embassy's staff, they do it like any other big company. Send out notices. Give you a chance to apply for other positions. Take their time. Then coordinate the moves. Not this time." Bachmann shook his head. "This time they just dropped the hammer. Had people on vacation who were told not to return to their duty station. Things like that."

"They were fired?"

"No. They were reassigned. From what I hear, the State Department never fires anyone. They just move them around. But the abruptness of it was odd. I heard they wouldn't even let them come back for their belongings."

"You mean, they had to leave stuff behind?"

"They hired someone to pack it up and move it out."

"So one day you're at Grandma's and get a call. Don't return to … Saudi."

"Right," Bachmann nodded. "Stay there. We'll send your belongings later."

"That's very disruptive for a family."

"And we found a number who were quite distraught."

"We?"

"He," Bachmann corrected himself. "I'm sorry. John. This was John's project."

"User logs on the laptop indicate you accessed some of the files. Were you at John's apartment?"

"No," Bachman shook his head. "If I accessed any of his files, I got to them from the computer in my office. We have remote access."

"Why would you need access to his files if you weren't working on the project with him?"

"We try to check up on each other." Bachmann's eyes darted away. "We all have pretty much free rein to do what we want and sometimes it's easy to get lost in your own world. We keep tabs on each other to make sure no one goes off the deep end on anything."

"So you were just being a friend?"

"A thoughtful coworker. John and I weren't exactly pals, but we got along."

"I saw mention of a report John prepared, but we didn't find it on his laptop."

"He did the report here, at the office," Bachmann explained. "He didn't want it on his laptop."

"Why not?"

"John was a conspiracy buff," Bachmann grinned. "He was always coming up with these wild ideas about who was pulling the strings behind the scenes. When he first started working on this embassy idea, it seemed like just another one of his conspiracies. Then we found some hard data. And then he got a little paranoid."

"He had a theory about what was going on here?"

"Yeah," Bachmann nodded. "He wondered if there was an organization within the federal government, orchestrating events in the Middle East, working to overthrow Iran."

Cruse arched an eyebrow. "We need to see that report."

"I'm not sure I can do that."

"We need to know what he was working on."

"Right." Bachmann stood. "Let me check on that."

"Did he file that report?"

"Yeah." Bachmann moved toward the door. "Sent it to his contact at Langley."

"Who was that?"

"Frank Attwood."

"Did he respond?"

"No. As far as I know, no one did." Bachmann opened the door. "Let me see about that report."

When he was gone, Cruse looked over at Lyman. "Was it just me or was that a little strange?"

"It was more than a little strange."

"Didn't do much to convince me to drop it."

"Me, either."

CHAPTER 37
TEHRAN, IRAN

RASOUL MOUSSAOUI SAT ON THE SOFA in his residence at the presidential palace. Seated before him that day were the heads of the major branches of the Iranian military—Jalil Amini, the director of Intelligence and National Security, Air Force General Akbar Imjanian, Army General Parsa Karimi, and Navy Admiral Iraj Shirdel.

"Our Supreme Leader, Ali Tafresh, suggested that I should meet with you, apart from the Supreme National Security Council, to discuss our views on the current state of affairs with Israel, the United States, and our regional position."

"This is irregular, meeting like this," Admiral Shirdel noted. "With all due respect, Mr. President."

"Highly irregular," General Imjanian added. "But these are irregular times."

"You understand," Moussaoui continued, "no one is suggesting that we decide anything definite." He said that for their benefit, but everyone in the room knew their discussion that day would be treated as acquiescence to anything Moussaoui might decide. "However, if a response is necessary to the current situation, it will require the action of those of us gathered here today. We are the ones who must execute that response and we have already been engaged in this matter for some time. Our Supreme Leader thought we should continue that process without being constrained by the Council's participation in matters arising from these latest circumstances." He'd rambled on too long, but he was certain they understood his meaning.

Amini spoke up. "Mr. President, what is it you wish to discuss?"

"I am concerned about all I'm hearing from Israel and about what I am not hearing. They should have responded to the car bombing by now."

General Karimi spoke up. "I think the new American ships being sent to the Gulf was their response."

"What does that mean?" Shirdel frowned.

Imjanian shook his head. "You think the Americans are going to respond, and not Israel?"

"America and Israel are like two sides of the same coin," Karimi explained. "They are one and the same. Almost no difference at all. One controls the other. American ships. Israeli bombs. They are all the same."

"I do not think this is the full picture." Shirdel tried to move the conversation forward. "We must assume Israel is planning to attack."

"And if they attack," Imjanian added, "they will hit our nuclear sites. The Americans will send their ships and loiter off our coast for years, but not the Israelis. If they attack, they will strike at the things that matter most to them."

"As they did in the past," Shirdel nodded.

"Are our defenses fully operational?"

"Not yet," Imjanian replied. "As you know, we ran into some delays with the satellite system."

"What was it this time?" Karimi wondered. "Were the Russians slow in supplying necessary equipment?"

"You know what happened," Imjanian retorted.

"Stupid Russians," Shirdel interjected. "They are worse than the Americans and only slightly better than the Jews."

"Perhaps they are all working together," Karimi said, needling them yet again. "Another of your conspiracies, perhaps? All of them trying to delay us as long as possible."

"But we have alternative systems." Moussaoui showed a hint of irritation at the way things were going.

"Yes," Imjanian answered. "We have deployed surface-to-air missile batteries at all the major installations. However, in the event of an attack, those missile batteries would be highly vulnerable."

"As soon as we turn them on," Karimi said seriously, "their position will become obvious to anyone who can read a radar screen."

Moussaoui nodded thoughtfully. "Where are we in terms of the ability to launch a counterstrike?"

Imjanian was still defensive. "We have already moved our aircraft out of sight."

"Perhaps we should fly them to remote locations," Shirdel suggested.

"If we do that," Imjanian explained, "the Americans will see us and tell the Jews where we have put them. Better to secure them at the bases where they are already deployed."

"Why are we talking this way?" Karimi blurted out. "Why are we talking about Israel's attack, our counterattack, the American position on the subject? Why are we talking about those things? We have missiles. We have airplanes. Why not launch a first strike and get on with it, like the Americans did in Iraq and Afghanistan? Israel is a threat to our existence. They are meddling in our affairs. We have a right to defend our interests, the same as any other nation."

"That sounds good," Moussaoui nodded. "And I like the spirit of your suggestion. But if we strike first, the Americans will unleash all their power against us. Many of their leaders are simply waiting for such an excuse to attack us. And if they do, we will be crushed. Many millions will die. Many more millions will be injured. Our country will be destroyed." A sly smiled spread across his face. "But if we wait and let Israel strike us first, they will not be able to destroy everything and we will be able to respond with a counterstrike. And with our agents working inside America, we will bring that response to the doorstep of every American family."

"We will be justified in our response," Amini added confidently.

"Yes," Moussaoui continued. "We will be justified in our response and the world will not condemn us. Instead, Israel will be blamed. Then, after we launch our attacks in New York, Chicago, Los Angeles, and a hundred other places in their country, the Americans will give us Israel on a platter to convince us to stop." Moussaoui smiled and let his gaze move around the room, looking each of them in the eye before focusing on Amini. "Is that not right?"

"In Iraq," Amini nodded, picking up the train of thought, "they gave us what we wanted in order to stop the insurgent attacks, so they could leave the country. In Afghanistan, they gave us what we wanted so they could go home. And now they will give us what we want to stop their people from crying in agony."

"But we have worked hard to develop our programs," Imjanian argued. "Complex facilities like the centrifuges, the rocket programs, our satellite technology. If Israel attacks, they will hit those sites. All of that will be lost."

"Not all of it," Amini interrupted. "They cannot penetrate our hardened locations, and most of the sites are at places they don't even know about."

Moussaoui kept his eyes on Amini and changed the subject. "Are our agents in Mexico ready?"

"Some have already begun to move into position near the border."

"Very well. Have them prepare, but take no action until my order. We have worked many years getting them into place. We don't want to reveal them too soon." Moussaoui let his eyes wander to the others. "But if the Americans should be so brave as to move against us first, or assist the Israelis, we will strike them in the heart."

"Are you certain this will work?" Imjanian seemed skeptical. "This seems like a great risk for an operation of dubious potential."

"Dubious potential?" Karimi railed. "Osama Bin Laden was a dog, but he proved one thing—the Americans are more vulnerable than they think. One more airplane and they would have been dealt a lethal blow."

Imjanian rolled his eyes at the suggestion, but before he could respond, Shirdel stepped in. "Mr. President, I do not think Israel will attack without further provocation."

Moussaoui glanced in Amini's direction. They both knew that what they had already done, capturing the Mossad agent and returning him to Israel as a message, would be more than enough to provoke an incident with Israel, but neither of them wanted to speak of it, especially not to the men gathered around the sofa that day. Instead, Moussaoui smiled at Imjanian. "As you know, there is risk in every plan. We, however, have no choice but to refrain from taking the offensive. Allowing an attack, if it comes at all, to be generated first by Israel is our only hope of success."

They talked awhile longer. Then, as the meeting ended, Moussaoui gestured for Amini to remain behind. When the others were gone, Moussaoui drew him near. "I want you to meet with Admiral Shirdel and have him relocate our submarines to the Mediterranean."

Amini looked surprised. "We do not need them in the strait?"

"Forget the strait," Moussaoui barked with a dismissive tone. "We were never going to attack there. But if Israel attacks us, we must be in position to counter their moves with a surprise."

"The submarines cannot remain there long. They have forty-five days at most. Then they have to recharge and resupply."

"We will address that after they have been moved."

"Yes, Mr. President," Amini turned to leave.

Moussaoui pulled him back. "And keep an eye on Imjanian. I am not convinced he is with us on this."

CHAPTER 38
ISTANBUL, TURKEY

IN SPITE OF HIS INITIAL RELUCTANCE, Bachmann provided Cruse and Lyman with a copy of Sladen's report. When they returned to the office, Lyman went to work reviewing it. What she found left her with more questions than when she began. "This report was sent to Frank Attwood at Langley," she said finally. "I can't believe no one responded."

"Anything sensitive in it?"

"Not really. And it doesn't lay out the full theory of a conspiracy, like Bachmann suggested. It's more like a report, telling them what he found, giving dates and figures to back it up, and just asking if anyone else has seen similar information." She looked over at Cruse. "They get these reports all the time. Someone usually responds one way or the other."

"Any way to find out what Attwood did with it?"

"I don't think so." Lyman shook her head. "CIA has never been interested in sharing anything like this. Think we should ask anyway?"

"Not yet," Cruse cautioned. "Let's go deep on Attwood first, find out who he really is. Then we'll think about asking them what happened to the report."

"Attwood is deputy director for Intelligence," Lyman countered. "Do you really think we can get away with digging into his past like that? You're talking about investigating the deputy director of the CIA, on our own."

"Look, I know it's a little out of our league—"

"You think?"

"Listen," Cruse insisted. "The trail led us to Attwood. If this was any

161

other case, we'd dig into him and see where it leads. So," he shrugged, "let's go deep on Attwood and see what we find."

Just then the door opened and Taner Umar, the Istanbul police detective, entered the room. He started talking as he came through the doorway. "We ran a check on that dead American. John Sladen." He looked up, his eyes narrow and focused straight toward Cruse. "Found out he recently moved."

"People do that sometimes," Cruse countered, now certain that Umar knew all about his friendship with Sladen.

"We searched his apartment," Umar continued.

"Find anything?"

"Looked like someone got there ahead of us. Sladen's laptop was missing."

"How do you know he had one?"

"Found the power supply on the floor. Found this, too." Umar reached into his pocket, took out a photograph, and handed it to Cruse. The picture was of Cruse standing next to Sladen at a bar. "I'm assuming you have the laptop," Umar added.

"I may know where it is," Cruse answered.

"When you get through with it, we'd like to take a look."

"I'm not sure that's going to be possible."

"Why not?"

"Some of the files on there are quite sensitive."

"This is a murder investigation," Umar argued. "And I think we both know what's going on here."

"What about the autopsy?"

"Oh," Umar said with mock amusement. "You want me to give you information, but you don't want to share yours?"

"It's a little sensitive," Cruse answered, trying to explain.

"Right," Umar nodded. "It always is." He turned and started toward the door. "But our judges take a dim view of Americans plundering items from a crime scene. You should call your attorneys and put them on notice."

Cruse waited until Umar reached the door, then called out, "Okay." Umar turned to face him. "Sladen was working on a project for the government."

"What kind of project?"

"It was research."

"The judge will want to know more than that." Umar reached for the door.

"Our embassies," Cruse corrected. Umar paused once again and turned to face him. "He was conducting research on our embassies."

"Sladen was researching your embassies?"

"Yes. He came across information that indicated our embassies in the region were reducing their staff. He wondered why. Started asking questions."

"What kind of person spends their time researching things like—" Umar caught himself in midsentence. "Oh. I see." He had a knowing look. "Why didn't you tell me you knew him earlier?"

"I didn't know what was going on then."

"And now?"

"I still don't know, but I need the results from your autopsy."

"Then this is your lucky day," Umar smiled. "The preliminary report shows there were traces of prussic acid in Sladen's blood."

"Prussic acid?" Lyman spoke up. "What are you talking about?"

Umar glanced in her direction. She'd been sitting quietly until then and the sound of her voice seemed to catch him off guard. "Residue from cyanic poisoning."

"Like that guy in Belgium," Lyman replied. "Last year."

"Right," Umar nodded.

"So," Cruse said, "this wasn't a heart attack or death from natural causes."

"Doesn't look like it. They tell me prussic acid dissipates rapidly, but our technicians are certain this is how he died." Umar turned to the door one last time. "I'll let you know what the final report says. Get me some details about who might have wanted him killed." He opened the door. "And I still want to see that laptop." Then he stepped into the hallway and disappeared.

When he was gone, Lyman looked over at Cruse. "We can't give him what he wants."

"I know," Cruse sighed. "But we need his help."

Lyman spent the remainder of the day searching for information about Attwood. Using the FBI's database and authorization under the Patriot Act, she obtained access to his financial records along with copies of disclosure forms he was required to file with the federal Office of Government Ethics. That information was helpful but most of it was of a routine nature and led nowhere. When that proved fruitless, she turned to Attwood's family.

Using readily accessible public records, she learned that Attwood was married to Nancy Geller. With just a few simple searches on the Internet, she learned that Nancy and her brothers were beneficiaries of the Geller Family Trust. That interest had not been disclosed on Attwood's federal forms and there was no public information about it. Stymied with that attempt, Lyman turned to the Geller family lineage. Not far into that effort she ran into a wall with Nancy's parents. "This is frustrating," she complained.

Cruse looked up from the work on his desk. "Problems?"

"I keep hitting a dead end. There's plenty in the FBI database about Attwood—school, career, family, but nothing else. He's clean. At least on paper. So I took a look at his wife, Nancy. There isn't much there, either, so I tried to branch out into the family. And now I've hit a wall with her parents."

"There's nothing about them in Attwood's file?"

"No."

"And nothing in our database?"

"No."

"Curious."

"It's like they didn't exist."

"What are their names?"

"Max and Katherine Geller."

"German? French?"

"I don't know," she answered. "It's like they don't exist."

"Name change," Cruse suggested. "I'll look into it. You keep going on the family."

By the afternoon, Lyman had learned of Nancy's brother, Michael Geller, and his successful career as a hedge fund manager. She also uncovered his ownership interest in something called the Shale Oil Real Estate Investment Trust.

"We should get someone in New York to check this out." Lyman stared at the monitor on her desk.

Cruse came to her desk and looked over her shoulder. "What have you found?"

"Attwood's brother-in-law, Michael Geller."

"Just request the records on him."

"I already have records."

"What do they show?"

"This trust," she said, pointing to the screen. "Shale Oil Real Estate Investment Trust. It owns only one asset. An option to purchase ten thousand acres in South Dakota."

"What is it? A real estate development trust?"

"Better," she indicated. "The land they have an option on holds a large reserve of shale oil."

"Interesting."

"I've checked probate records—deeds, leases, agreements. I've looked at all the documents. Everyone seems convinced the oil is there."

"And they own the option?"

"Yeah."

"Who set it up?"

"A lawyer in Pierre did the paperwork. I'm sure Geller put it together."

"Attwood is a government official and he has an investment like that?"

"It's not his. This belongs to the brother-in-law."

"I don't know," Cruse mused. "Michael Geller and his brother-in-law Attwood at the CIA. And no disclosure."

"I haven't found any paper trail that connects them."

"They wouldn't leave a paper trail. Attwood didn't get where he is doing something that reckless. How did you find him?"

"You said go deep on Attwood. That led me to Attwood's wife, and then to her siblings, which took me to Michael and the trust."

"That's a lot of land."

"And a lot of value. Shale oil is more expensive to recover than most deposits, but it's oil just the same."

"If Sladen is right—that something is about to happen in the Middle East—the value of that shale oil would skyrocket."

"Think Attwood's using his position to help Geller?"

"Seems a little thin, but we should get someone from the New York office to look into it. See if they can get hold of the manager's records."

"If we're doing this, we should go have a look for ourselves."

Lyman frowned. "You don't think New York can do it?"

"I think maybe you should go to New York and see ... what's the manager's name?"

"Henry Wilson."

"You should see Wilson and I should go to Langley and talk to Attwood."

"You want to tip him off that we're looking at him?"

"I think as soon as you talk to Henry Wilson, he's going to call Attwood and then the cat's out of the bag anyway. If I'm there, I can at least get to him before he has time to figure out a response."

"I don't think we'll get very far without a warrant."

"We can get what we want under the Patriot Act without a warrant."

"We'd have to involve the New York office to do that. I thought you were trying to avoid them."

"Yeah, maybe not a good idea. But I can get a search warrant without them."

"That might get a little ... problematic. Don't you think?"

"What?"

"A search warrant for the offices of a financial representative who manages this kind of investment pool." She had a skeptical look. "These guys are well-connected."

"We can work around it," Cruse shrugged.

"Work around it?"

"Yeah. Look, I think we have to go and see what happens. At the least, we'll find out for certain who the players are."

"The players? You've already decided a crime has been committed?"

"I've decided something is up, and we won't get to the bottom of it by staying over here wondering. If this doesn't work out, we'll try something else."

"Yeah. Like a new job."

"It won't be that bad. At least not for you. You're with me." Cruse turned toward his desk. "I'll clear it with your office in Ankara."

CHAPTER 39
TEL AVIV, ISRAEL

ONCE AGAIN, YEDAYA CONVENED a meeting of Israeli cabinet officials to discuss the situation with Iran.

"I wanted to bring you up to date on the latest information," he began. "And I have asked Efraim Hofi to brief us on some new developments."

For the next ten minutes, Hofi outlined what they knew about the car bombing in Rabat, details about the driver, and the names of others who were his most likely accomplices. Then he turned to the matter of Revach, the pictures from the Fordow centrifuge facility in Qom, and attempts by Iran to build its own satellite network.

When he was finished, Eli Barak, the minister of Internal Affairs, glanced around the table. "I ask again, as I did at our last meeting, is there really any question about whether we must act, and act now?"

"I still have reservations," Orit Erdan, the education minister, responded. A collective sigh went up from those in the room. Erdan tried to explain. "We can't possibly remove every site they've developed."

"But we can destroy enough to stop them," Barak argued. "At least enough to push them back a few years."

"So our children can live now with what the Iranians will do in response?" Erdan looked angry. "Have you thought about that? They will respond."

"I am certain they will respond," Barak conceded. "But it is better to deal with their response than to live with a nuclear sword always over our heads."

Moshe Noked, the defense minister, cleared his throat. "There might be reprisals," he began quietly. "I would expect them. But Eli is right. We can't let them continue to develop their nuclear and satellite systems. Even if we are unable to destroy every single facility, we can hit the ones that matter most. And if our children must take up the fight, then let them. And their children. And the ones who come after them."

Erdan shook his head. "I made the point before, but I say it again, we are suggesting a military strike against Iran as a response to a car bombing."

"No," Barak corrected, "not because of a car bombing. But because they are on the verge of obtaining the military capability to carry through on their threats against us."

Yedaya moved to cut them off. "After our meeting two days ago, I discussed our situation with Hofi and with Gabi." Gabi Halutz, chief of the Israeli Defense Force general staff, was seated at the far end of the table. Yedaya glanced in his direction. "Tell them where we are in developing plans for action."

Halutz stood. "As you are all aware, we have preplanned target packages that account for Iran's critical sites—the known centrifuges and reactors, plus their producing mines. If we use only those packages, we can launch an attack in two days. That action would remove eighty percent of their critical facilities."

"Eighty percent of what?" someone asked. "Eighty percent of twenty percent of their total capacity?"

"Something like that," Halutz agreed. "Perhaps."

"So they would have ninety percent of their military capacity still intact?"

"The attacks we're discussing don't include conventional military targets. These are only targets related to their nuclear program." Halutz glanced over at Hofi. "And if we have a list by the end of the day, we can add the most critical elements of their space program."

"So they would be fully capable of launching a counterattack."

"They would have the military hardware for it. Our current plan of attack would disable their communications systems and electrical grid. It would take some time for them to recover."

"Time?" Erdan was growing more uncomfortable. "Are we talking days, weeks, months? What are we looking at?"

"Days."

"Not weeks?"

"No."

Barak leaned forward. "And we would use only missiles?"

"We would have to use airplanes in conjunction with the missiles in order to inflict enough damage to push back their program."

"Can the planes complete the mission and return safely?"

"It will be marginal. As you are aware, the U.S. refused to give us the refueling tankers we wanted. Our 707s will work, but they are quite vulnerable and much less effective."

"I regret the loss of any life," Barak lamented, "but that is the price we must pay to ensure our people are safe. They are not safe right now."

Someone down the table spoke up. "We have been discussing this at length and we have yet to mention our most important partner."

"Which is?"

"The United States."

"And there is a good reason we have ignored them in this discussion." Barak's eyes blazed. "They have chosen to ignore this threat."

"If we are to attack, we must inform them."

"No!" Barak snapped. "We must not. If we tell them, they will only pressure us to delay. And if we refuse to heed them and continue with our plans, they will tell the Iranians what is about to happen."

Erdan could hardly contain himself. "You act as if the decision to attack has already been made." He was all but shouting. "If we attack now, we will be viewed as the aggressor. All the nations of the world will line up against us."

"And if we do not attack," Noked countered, "our enemies will see us as weak. And they will pursue their own nuclear ambitions."

"The time has come." Yedaya leaned back from the table. "If we are to do this now, we need to determine the final target package today. We must decide." He paused a moment, as if to let the gravity of their decision sink in, then he stood. "All in favor of moving forward with a comprehensive strike against Iran's nuclear program, signify your approval by standing."

All at the table stood, except for Orit Erdan, who remained seated. "I do not agree," he said softly. He sat with his eyes fixed on the tabletop as he spoke. "You have the votes. We are about to launch an attack. But I fear it is the worst mistake we've ever made. And one that will have a most tragic consequence for our nation and our children." While the others remained standing and silent, he pushed back his chair, stood, and walked out of the room.

*　　*　　*

Late that afternoon, Mara Moss returned to her desk outside the door to Hofi's office. On the floor near her chair she found a cardboard box sealed with packing tape. It bore no name or address and had no postal markings. At first she paid it no attention, but on a second look she noticed a dark stain on one side and the cardboard was dirty. Grimy fingerprints showed on one side. "Telltale signs of a bomb," she whispered to herself.

With practiced calm, she rose from behind her desk and walked quickly down the hall to the nearest office. There she placed a call to the building security office. Minutes later, two guards appeared and walked with her back to the office. "It was there when I came in just now." She pointed to the box on the floor.

"Did you move it?"

"No, I didn't do anything with it."

"You don't remember it from earlier in the day?"

"No, I'm sure it wasn't there."

With no choice but to treat the box as a threat, security agents began evacuating the building. In a matter of minutes, the complex was emptied of employees. While they all stood outside watching, a team of bomb technicians arrived.

Using a motorized robot, members of the team retrieved the box from the office and brought it outside. A steel blast-resistant container sat on a flatbed trailer in the parking lot. Technicians maneuvered the robot up a ramp and onto the trailer, then dropped the box inside the container. By then Hofi had arrived. He stood near one of the technicians as the lid on the steel container slammed shut. "What now?" he asked.

"We'll take it to the field and detonate it," the technician replied.

"What's inside it?"

"We don't know."

"Let's have a look," Hofi suggested.

"Too dangerous."

Hofi looked perplexed. "You can't x-ray the box to see what's inside?"

"That would be risky," the technician said, dismissing the notion with a scowl. "There's no way of knowing what it contains."

"I know," Hofi responded, making little attempt to hide his growing frustration. "And the only way to find out is to have a look. So have someone x-ray the box."

"I can't," the technician said flatly.

"I wasn't asking you," Hofi retorted. "I'm the director of this agency." His voice grew louder with each word. "I'm ordering you to x-ray that box."

"We can't do that," the technician insisted. "We'd have to take it to the warehouse and that means transporting it down the street. We'd endanger every person we passed."

"With that thing?" Hofi pointed to the container on the truck. "You could detonate a five-thousand-pound bomb in that container and no one would ever know it."

"Okay." The technician's shoulders sagged. "But this is your call."

"I'll take responsibility for it, if that's what's bothering you."

"All right, guys," the technician sighed as he turned to the others on the team. "You heard the man. Pack it up and let's go see what's inside the box."

Reluctantly, the bomb squad prepared to do as Hofi requested. While they packed their gear, the trailer truck inched from the parking lot and began the slow journey from the operations center. Before it was out of sight, the bomb technicians left, too. Hofi climbed in an SUV and followed after them.

Twenty minutes later, they arrived at a warehouse about a mile from the operations center where the box had been found. When the truck was parked inside the building, three of the bomb technicians donned their safety gear. Three more set up a folding table at the far side of the room near the doorway where they brought the truck inside. They put a laptop on the table and brought out the motorized robot. Using a joystick to control the machine, they watched on the screen of the laptop as they guided the device up the ramp and onto the trailer. When it was in place, they pressed a button to open the lid of the container and used an arm on the robot to retrieve the box. Then, with the box firmly in the robot's grasp, they backed it down the ramp and set the box on the warehouse floor a few feet from the truck. Technicians positioned the panels of a scanner on three sides of the box and moved quickly away. Everyone else gathered around the table to see images from the scanner on the laptop.

Technicians stared at the screen, carefully studying views from all four sides of the box. "I don't see anything inside that appears to be explosive," one of them ventured finally.

Hofi glanced at the image. "What do you think it is?"

"This looks like bone," the technician said, pointing to a thin line that appeared inside the box. "But I have no idea why it would be in there or what the substance is that surrounds it."

Hofi felt sick to his stomach. "No wires?"

"No sir," the technician answered. "No wires or detonators. Nothing metal of any kind."

Hofi stepped back. "Open it," he ordered.

The technician looked startled. "You mean the box?"

"Yes. Open it," Hofi repeated.

"You can't be serious."

"I am serious," Hofi insisted. "Open the box."

"I can't risk it." The technician shook his head from side to side. "I can't ask my men to take any more risk with this. We've done far more than we should have anyway."

"Then clear your men out of the way," Hofi declared. "I'll open it myself."

As the technicians stared in disbelief, Hofi strode confidently across the room toward the box. When he reached it, he took a knife from the pocket of his pants and sliced the packing tape with the blade. Using the end of the knife, he lifted back one flap for a better view.

Inside the box he found a plastic bag filled with what appeared to be rotten flesh. A foul stench filled the air. He gagged and turned away, trying not to vomit. "Send it to the lab," he choked.

"The lab?" someone asked in dismay. By then all their faces were twisted in a bitter scowl as the smell wafted across the room.

"I want to know precisely what that substance is," Hofi charged. But inside he already knew the answer.

CHAPTER 40
WASHINGTON, D.C.

LEON BAIN ARRIVED at the White House without an appointment. He entered through the West Wing lobby and walked briskly down the hall to the office of Pete McWhinney, the president's chief of staff. McWhinney was startled to see him. "Thought you left last night for Chicago."

"We need to talk."

"I'm rather busy."

"I don't care if you're busy," Bain replied with an edge. "We have to talk."

"Okay, if you feel that way, have a seat."

Bain pushed the office door closed and took a seat near McWhinney's desk. "We have to get a couple of things straight about how we're handling things for the next few months."

"You're really going to do this?"

"Do what?"

"Inject domestic politics into White House policy."

"The White House has always mixed the two," Bain smirked. "It's a myth that the two could ever be kept separate."

"Maybe so, but we can keep campaign strategists and consultants from meddling in what we do here in the White House."

"Look," Bain countered. "We can argue about this all day, but here's what we're doing." He slid forward on the seat and leaned closer, an earnest look in his eye. "We're running a campaign based on our record of an improving economy."

"The president's record," McWhinney corrected.

"Whatever." Bain tried not to get lost in the details. "An improving economy. That's it. End of story. The country was in a recession when we came to office. We fixed it. Every analysis of every Republican proposal shows their plan would have a negative impact on the economy. That's our message from now to Election Day. We fixed it, they want to ruin it just to give a break to their rich friends. Your job is to find a place for that message in everything the president does and says."

McWhinney took a condescending tone. "You want to do my job, too?"

"Listen to me," Bain insisted. "There are a lot of people running around this town and this building talking about war in the Middle East. Talking about using a military option against Iran. Yedaya was just here. I'm sure he told you all about how it could work." Bain paused to take a breath. "War is not part of our campaign strategy. War is not part of the country's agenda right now. They're tired of it. War will kill us in November."

"What if it's part of the strategy to defend the nation?"

"We can't afford a war with Iran. Not now." Bain leaned back in his chair. "After November, you, Brown, Upchurch, all the others, can do whatever you want. Until then, I'm calling the shots. And I'm saying we can't have a war before Election Day."

"You're president now, too?" McWhinney's eyes bore in on Bain. "Is that what this is about? You're just taking over now? In addition to doing my job, you're doing the president's job, as well?" McWhinney slid forward in his chair. "Get out of my office."

"Listen to me," Bain snapped, raising his voice once again. "The president likes you. He chose you. He wants you as his chief of staff. But he wants to be reelected to a second term and if that means getting rid of you to do it, he won't raise a single word of protest to defend you. You can either get on board with this reelection or you can find another job."

"We're through here." McWhinney pushed back his chair and stood. "If you don't leave, I'll have the guard escort you from the building."

"You don't want to go toe-to-toe with me on this, Pete. An attack on Iran wouldn't be like a brief incursion into Panama, or a three-day operation on Grenada. This is the Middle East and it's Iran—nuclear arms and oil. If we hit Iran, if Israel attacks Iran, oil prices will instantly double, even triple. That will spark fear in the American consumer, and the economy will drop like a rock with no end in sight. We can't risk the election on that. No war. And from now until November, no more open access for Weiss."

McWhinney came from behind the desk. "And what do I tell Weiss? He happens to be a friend of the president's and one of our party's best fund-raisers. He's in here two or three times a week."

"Send him to Aubrey Preston."

McWhinney paused, a curious look in his eye. "Aubrey?"

"He'll know what to do."

McWhinney opened the office door. "Next time you come to my office, call for an appointment."

*   *   *

Aubrey Preston was seated in his office, reviewing a draft of the president's remarks for an upcoming Party leadership conference. As he waded through the text, Pete McWhinney appeared in the office doorway.

"I just had a visit from Leon Bain."

"Leon? Shouldn't he be on the road somewhere, setting up a rally or making phone calls or whatever it is he does?"

McWhinney moved farther inside the room. "Someone has tipped him off."

"About what?"

"About Iran."

Preston laid aside the paper he was reading. "That shouldn't be too hard to figure out."

"I have a pretty good idea who it was." McWhinney took a seat in a chair near the desk. "He thinks you are on his side."

"Why do you say that?"

"He told me that if Weiss calls or comes by, I should send him to you. That you'd know what to do with him."

"Yeah," Preston nodded. "Leon came to see me about that two nights ago. He told me it was my job to keep everyone on the same message as the campaign and to make sure Weiss didn't see the president anymore until after the election."

"Well," McWhinney chuckled, "now he's telling me that's my job."

"I would have told you about what he said but I just assumed it was Leon talking. Not really something to worry about. And anyway, if Weiss showed up in my office I was taking him to the Oval."

"We have to take care of this."

"Right," Preston agreed.

"You know what to do?"

"Yes."

When McWhinney was gone, Preston walked down the hallway to Jean Brown's office. He found her office empty but as he turned to leave she appeared from around the corner. "Looking for me?"

"Yes."

"Talk to me while we walk. I have a meeting in the Roosevelt Room."

"Leon Bain came to see Pete."

"When?"

"Just now."

"I thought he was back in Chicago."

"So did everyone else."

"What did Mr. Bain want?"

"He wants us to stop talking about a military response to Iran."

"Oh?" Brown arched an eyebrow. "That's a little beyond his job description, isn't it?"

"He threatened to fire Pete if the chatter about it didn't stop."

"What does he want us to do, ignore an international nuclear threat?"

"Pete sent me to see you."

"I'll take care of it."

*   *   *

Paul Catlett stepped from the SUV onto the tarmac outside a hangar at the airport in Miami, Florida. A Gulfstream Jet was parked a few yards away, awaiting his arrival. As he made his way toward the plane, his cell phone rang. The call was from Jean Brown.

"We have a situation."

Catlett stopped in his tracks. "Another car bomb?"

"No, sir. Leon Bain."

"That's a domestic matter. You shouldn't even mention his name to me."

"He came to see McWhinney."

"When?"

"Just now. He told McWhinney to back off until after the fall."

"These people think they can mix politics and policy."

"I think we do that all the time. The real question is whether politics trumps national security."

"Exactly."

"You'll take care of it?"

"I'll take care of it," he sighed. Catlett ended the call and then continued toward the plane. When he reached the steps he turned to an aide. "Find Michael Geller for me."

CHAPTER 41

NEW YORK CITY

DAVID HOLSTEN ARRIVED at the Harvard Club and took the elevator up to a room on the third floor. He was there for yet one more meeting of the Shale Oil Trust investors. By the time he entered the room, Henry Wilson, Curtis McCullough, Dan Luckett, and Sidney Adkins were already gathered in the corner around the wet bar. Luckett acted as bartender. He caught Holsten's eye. "Any new information?"

"Our contact in Tehran says the package will be delivered tomorrow," Holsten answered.

"And they're sure that will be enough to get the ball rolling? Force Israel to act?"

"That's what they say."

"Well," Luckett snarled, "maybe those idiot Jews will take the bait and we can get on with it."

"Yes, but I've been thinking," Adkins spoke up. He was on his third drink and it was beginning to show. "What if Iran really has a nuclear weapon and they use it?"

"All the better," Luckett growled. "Blow the kikes into the Mediterranean where they belong."

"But," Adkins continued, "what if they use it against us?"

"The Iranians are crazy," McCullough said with disdain, "but they aren't stupid. They would never try such a thing." Geller entered the room while they were talking. McCullough caught his eye. "Isn't that right, Mike?"

"Whatever you say, Curt."

Adkins kept going. "What if they're playing us as much as we're playing them?"

"Oh, I think we're all getting played," Geller chuckled. "One way or the other."

"So, the box arrives tomorrow?" Wilson steered the conversation to the point of their meeting. "How long after that before events take their course?"

"Three or four days, I suspect," Geller guessed.

Wilson turned to Holsten. "Anyone hearing anything from Israel that might confirm this? Any signs of planning or preparation?"

"Nothing," Holsten replied. "Not even a hint."

"No one ordered to their base? No hold on leaves?" Wilson had a quizzical look. "Isn't that the kind of thing you look for?"

"I'm not hearing anything from any of the usual sources."

Adkins picked up his earlier question. "What happens if Israel attacks, Iran counters, and the U.S. responds with an all-out attack on Iran?"

"This president would never do that," Geller answered.

"Why not?"

"Because he's not George Bush," Luckett laughed.

"His immediate reaction will be to ramp up our involvement," Holsten explained, "but once Iran responds and he sees the stakes are getting way too high, he'll back off. That's why Tehran's response is important."

McCullough looked over at Geller with concern. "Do you think they understand that?"

"Yes," Geller nodded. "I'm quite sure they do."

"You explained it to Sair?"

"Ahamad Sair and I have discussed it on several occasions. He assured me just last night that everyone was clear on how this would proceed."

"Isn't it a little late to be discussing this now?" Luckett needled. "We've been over all of this a thousand times. It either happens or it doesn't, but we've done what we had to do."

Holsten and Geller exchanged looks. They both knew that no one in the room but the two of them had lifted a finger to orchestrate the events they were all now so eager to discuss.

"I know," McCullough replied, "but I want to make sure we're set. While there's still time to stop."

"We're way past the time to stop," Holsten responded. "This thing is in motion."

"Think of it this way," Geller added. "Israel moves. We support. Iran pushes back. All hell breaks loose. We cave. Business as usual."

"And in the meantime," Luckett smirked, "we make billions on our oil investments."

"Absolutely," Geller grinned.

"It seems illegal," Adkins chuckled. "Which makes it fun."

"I assure you," Geller added with confidence. "There's nothing illegal about taking financial advantage of a situation. It's the American way."

"Relax," McCullough patted Adkins on the back. "We'll make more money at this than we've ever made before, and we won't even drill a single well."

*   *   *

When the meeting ended and the others started toward the hallway, Geller lingered behind and took Holsten aside. "We have a problem with Leon Bain."

"What's he doing now?"

"Do you know him?"

"Yeah. I know him. I don't like him, but I know him. He worked for us on the campaign four years ago."

"He's pushing McWhinney to put the brakes on things in the Middle East. Making a real mess. Threatened to have McWhinney fired. Wants to limit Weiss's access to the president, tone down the rhetoric until after the election."

"He can try all that, I suppose," Holsten grinned. "But this thing won't wait that long. Israel is ready to move. Yedaya is convinced the president won't act no matter how strong the evidence or how severe the threat from Iran. They're moving forward with an attack on their own. I don't think we could stop them now, even if we wanted to."

"Yeah, well, this whole thing is like a Chinese puzzle box. Get one thing in place and another falls out. And all this hand-holding and coddling." Geller nodded toward the door as the last of the group stepped outside. "They act like they're doing so much but all they've done is write a check. And Bain. I don't understand him." Geller paused and took a sip from his glass. "If we let one piece slip out of place, this whole thing will collapse. And if that happens, it'll fall on our heads." He gestured with the hand that held the glass. "Yours and mine."

"Look," Holsten soothed, "everything is set for now and we're in a delicate spot, I understand that, but most of this is out of our hands now."

"Not quite," Geller cautioned. "Not quite."

"What do you need?"

"Can you take care of Bain?"

"Yeah," Holsten nodded. His eyes darkened. "I can take care of him."

"Good." Geller set aside the glass he'd been holding. "Get on it right away." He gave Holsten a pat on the shoulder as he started for the door.

From the Harvard Club in Manhattan, Holsten drove an hour north of the city to the Monticello Raceway, a horse track located in the foothills of the Catskill Mountains. He parked the car in the lot, entered through a turnstile like any other patron, and made his way down to the track. At the end of the front stretch he found a spot along the outside rail near the first turn and focused on the horses just coming from the paddock.

In a little while, Rick Dwyer appeared beside him. "They said you wanted to see me." Tall and lean, Dwyer had a rawboned, rugged appearance. He had a square jaw and eyes that seemed always to notice every detail. Of all the fixers Holsten knew, Dwyer was his favorite.

Holsten took an iPhone from his pocket, scrolled through the icons on the screen, and opened a photograph of Leon Bain. He handed the phone to Dwyer. "You know who that is?"

"Yeah."

"You're sure?"

"David, I know who Leon is. I've been doing this a while."

"We need something on him."

"Something big? Just enough to cause a problem? What did you have in mind?"

"Something big enough to get him out."

"Can I manufacture it?"

"No. I want you to find something. Something that will hold up. People are going to check it out, ask questions, and plumb it all the way to the bottom. It has to hit hard and it has to hold up."

"Okay," Dwyer nodded. "No problem."

Holsten finally looked him in the eye. "This has to stick."

"If I bring it to you, it'll stick."

"We can't mess up."

"I understand."

Holsten took an envelope from his pocket and handed it to Dwyer. "That ought to be enough to get you started."

Dwyer turned back the flap and looked inside. "Yeah, that'll get me started. But this one has some risk. If I find something, I'll have to step out for a while. It's gonna cost you more."

"You find what we need, and we'll make it right," Holsten guaranteed. "Get busy."

CHAPTER 42
HERZLIYA, ISRAEL

HOFI STOOD IN THE OPERATIONS CENTER, his eyes darting back and forth between the screens at the far end of the room. Since the cardboard box had arrived at the center, he had resigned himself to what he was certain would be obvious when the lab ran tests on the contents—Ohad Revach was gone. While he waited for final results from the analysis, he threw himself and his staff into the hunt for those responsible for the bombing in Rabat.

"Okay," he said, to no one in particular. "We have video of the car." He pointed to the screen. "This was taken two blocks away, ten minutes before the bomb exploded."

"Are we certain that is the same car?"

"Yes," someone answered. "We were able to read the license plate off an image from that video. It matches the partial number we got from the car that exploded."

"And we have the driver's name. Jabbar Hamadeh. Anything new on that?" When no one answered, Hofi looked around with a perturbed expression on his face. "Am I the only one interested in this? Do we have anything new on Jabbar Hamadeh?"

Daphna Abergil spoke up. "We have a report from one of the teams in Rabat. Witnesses identified him from a photograph. They claim to have seen him in a car matching the description of the one that exploded. They saw him as recently as two days ago on a street off Avenue Moulay Rachid, in Temara."

"Where is that?"

"It's a community south of the city."

"Do we have someone checking that area?"

"Yes."

"Do we have anything else from that area? Security-camera footage. Optical scans from police cars. Anything?"

"This is Rabat, sir," Abergil replied. "They don't have all that. I'm surprised they have even this much."

"Hey!" an analyst called from across the room. "We have satellite images from the U.S."

Hofi hurried across the room. "The sanitized version or the actual feed?"

"Looks like the real thing."

"Are they working on this downstairs?"

"I'll send it to them now," the analyst answered. "It just came in."

"Great." Hofi leaned over her shoulder to watch. "That's the car, follow it." Images on the screen jumped from one frame to the next, and the angle of the view changed with each one, but the analysts and Hofi were able to track the car backward through the streets of Rabat. "How many of these images do we have?"

"I think we have what they have. They get about two pictures per second during a twenty-minute window."

"Incredible."

"Yes it is."

"But these aren't going to give us what we need."

"What do you mean?"

The analyst pointed to the screen. "You can tell by the angle of the first image, these pictures caught the car as the satellite was moving away. So we're on the far side of the time window, not the near."

"Which means?"

"Which means the satellite was ahead of the car. It's as if the camera was looking back as it dropped over the curvature of the orbit."

"How far back can you take us?"

The analyst closed in on a photo sequence and pointed at a spot. "I can get you right there. That's at the corner of Rachid and Avenue Tarik Ibn Ziad.

"That's good," Abergil said. "That's in the same neighborhood where witnesses say they spotted that car."

"We need to concentrate on that area." Hofi was excited about the possibility of a new lead. "Talk to people on the street. Show them a picture of Hamadeh. See if anyone else recognizes him."

Moshe Perez, one of the young analysts, was skeptical. "You think the people in that car were living in that area?"

"If a witness saw them there two weeks ago, I'd say there's a good chance of it."

"But will they talk to us?"

"Will who talk to us?"

"The people on the street. Moroccans. The ones who live in the neighborhood. When they see the people we send are Jewish, will they talk to us?"

"Don't send our people," Hofi countered. "Ask the Rabat police to question people in the neighborhood."

"We'll be telling the police what we know and they'll realize we had help with it. Can we trust them?"

"Look, Moshe," Hofi snapped. "I appreciate your thoroughness, but we have no choice. This is the best lead we've found so far." He turned to walk away. "Stop talking and make it happen."

CHAPTER 43
NEW YORK CITY

WITH A FEW PHONE CALLS, Cruse found a seat for Sandra Lyman on a State Department jet bound for New York. After an overnight flight, she landed at La Guardia Airport early in the morning.

Outside the airport terminal, she walked to the taxi stand and waited for a car. Half an hour later, she arrived outside an office building on Lexington Avenue. She entered through the main lobby and rode up to the ninth floor. A brass plaque on the wall opposite the elevator indicated Henry Wilson's office was down the hall to the left. Lyman made her way in that direction.

When she pushed open the office door she found a receptionist seated behind an antique desk on the far side of the door. Rugs covered a hardwood floor. Original artwork hung from the walls. The receptionist, an attractive redhead, kept her eyes focused on a computer screen that sat atop her desk and when she spoke she sounded at once both sullen and aloof. "Was there something you needed?"

"I'd like to see Henry Wilson." Lyman flashed her credentials to the receptionist.

"Oh," the receptionist replied, her eyes suddenly alert. "I'll get someone right away." She rose from her desk and disappeared down a hallway to the right.

Moments later an office assistant ushered Lyman to a conference room. She took a seat at the conference table and waited. Wilson appeared shortly. He entered looking distracted and aggravated as he took a seat across from her. "They said you needed to see me?"

"Our office is investigating an entity known as the Shale Oil Real Estate Investment Trust. I understand you manage that property."

"Uhh, yes." Wilson's demeanor suddenly changed from harried to focused and concerned. "What's this about? I had no idea anyone even knew that trust existed."

"What can you tell me about the trust?"

"I'm afraid not very much."

"And why is that?"

"Any information I have about that entity would be confidential. I can't give you client information without a court order."

"Mr. Wilson, under the Patriot Act, I can get what I want with or without a warrant."

"Under the Patriot Act you'd have to be investigating an act of terrorism. Shale Oil is an American investment trust. It does nothing except hold an option on raw land in South Dakota. It couldn't possibly be involved in an act of terrorism."

Lyman leaned forward and tapped the tabletop with her index finger as she spoke. "Here's what you need to know. Without a warrant, you get to stay open while I have a look around. If I have to get a warrant, I'm coming back with a crew and we'll haul off all your records and you'll be out of business."

Wilson leaned back in his chair. "You can't do that."

"Watch me."

"Well … I …" Wilson struggled to find the words. "You'll have to let me make a phone call," he said finally.

Lyman let her eyes bore in on him. "You'll have to give me those records now."

"No," he said, shaking his head vigorously. "No. You can't do that."

"I can and I will."

"Not with my participation. And certainly not without making a phone call to my lawyer."

"Then I'll be back." Lyman rose from her chair. "And it won't be pretty." She made her way out to the hall and down to the elevator. While she waited, she used her cell phone to place a call to Cruse. When he didn't answer, she left a voice mail message and sent him a text. "Need a warrant." Then she rode the elevator to the lobby and walked outside. A coffee shop was located at the corner on the opposite side of the street. She started in that direction.

*   *   *

Meanwhile, the FBI Gulfstream carrying Cruse landed at Dulles and rolled to a stop outside a private hangar near the end of the runway. A car was waiting in the parking lot behind the hangar. Cruse got in and drove toward the airport exit.

Forty-five minutes later, he came to a stop outside Attwood's house in Bethesda, Maryland. He switched off the engine, climbed from behind the steering wheel. He took a leather satchel from the backseat and walked to the front door. To his surprise, Attwood answered the doorbell.

"Good morning, Mr. Attwood." Cruse flashed his badge. "We need to talk."

"Why is the FBI interested in me?"

"John Sladen is dead."

Attwood looked puzzled. "Who?"

"John Sladen. One of your analysts at ENX. In Istanbul."

"Oh. Right," Attwood nodded. "I heard about that. Friend of yours?"

Attwood backed away from the door and led Cruse to the living room. He dropped onto the sofa. Cruse took a seat on a chair near the end. "Before he died, Sladen sent you a report."

"I'm afraid I don't remember Mr. Sladen or his report," Attwood replied. "We're a rather large agency, you know."

Cruse reached inside his leather satchel and took out a copy of the report. He handed it to Attwood.

"Where'd you get this?" Attwood scowled as he glanced over the report.

"You remember it?"

"Yes. Vaguely. Some question about embassy staff in the Middle East."

"What did you do with it?"

"Read it, about as thoroughly as I have just now."

"And then?"

"And then nothing."

"Did you respond to him?"

"No. I mean, it's an interesting observation but a little outside the realm of possibility to suggest that somehow there's a government within the government and it's about to engage in military activity."

"Did you look into it?"

"Why would I?"

"One of your analysts—whose job is to speculate about potential threats—raises the possibility there is an organization within the federal government. A nefarious organization. Working to overthrow the Iranian government. Maneuvering the U.S. into striking at targets inside Iran. And the CIA doesn't want to investigate whether that might be true?"

Attwood's eyes darted away. "I'm afraid I can't answer that."

"Can't, or won't?"

Attwood looked smug. "I take it you're hoping for a nice long career with the FBI."

"Are you threatening me?"

"No, I'm not threatening you. I'm suggesting you've been around long enough to know that if I did respond I couldn't tell you about it, and even if I could I wouldn't."

"Then tell me about your wife's trust. That's not a CIA secret, is it?"

"How do you know about that?"

"Not difficult to find," Cruse answered. "Does she own an interest in her brother's shale oil business?"

"You'd have to ask him."

"Did Sladen know about that? Is that what got him killed? He found out you were using your office to benefit investments made by your brother-in-law?"

"They told me he died of a heart attack. No one said anything about killing him."

Cruse looked skeptical. "You don't really expect me to believe that, do you?"

"Now, listen here." Attwood leaned forward. "If you want to know about my brother-in-law's business you can ask him. And as for my wife, she manages her own affairs. I've given my life to government service without spot or blemish on my record and I don't appreciate your accusations."

"Yet even after he was killed you did nothing to find out why."

Attwood stood. "Unless you have some evidence to support these wild speculations, I have nothing more to say."

"Sladen got curious about shifts in State Department personnel and then he was murdered. You don't —"

"I told you," Attwood insisted, "they said he died of a heart attack. That's all I know about it."

Cruse stood. "Whoever killed Sladen wanted it to look like a heart attack. He was poisoned with cyanide."

"Oh," Attwood moaned. "I didn't know they found that."

"So, was he murdered because of what he found out about the embassies, or because there really is a plot like the one he suggested? Or was it to cover up your use of your office for personal benefit?"

"You'd have to ask State about their embassies. CIA doesn't have any control over what they do with their employees. And I told you, I know nothing of my brother-in-law's business dealings." Attwood's face was red with anger. "Now get out of my house!"

"Are you trying to overthrow the government of Iran, or are you trying to force Israel to cut a deal for peace?"

"You're crazy." Attwood pointed toward the door. "I said for you to leave."

"You're not answering my questions."

"Do your superiors know you're here?"

"Either plan would work," Cruse continued. "Eliminate Iran and you take away the support for Hezbollah. That puts an end to unrest in Lebanon and Syria. Makes the Palestinian Authority much weaker and easier to deal with. Trouble over there makes all that South Dakota oil your brother-in-law

MIKE EVANS

controls worth a lot more. I'm curious to know how much you stand to make off that deal."

Attwood leaned close, his face just inches away from Cruse. "I know what you're trying to do. You think you can get me mad enough that I'll say something incriminating. And if that doesn't work you're hoping I plant my fist on your jaw so then you can arrest me for assault. Well, it won't work." He stepped back and opened the door. "Now you've said what you came to say. It's time for you to leave."

*   *   *

Cruse walked from Attwood's house and made his way to the car. He tossed the leather satchel on the seat and got in behind the wheel. As he steered the car from the curb, he placed a call to Lyman.

"How did it go with Wilson?"

"He threw me out. Told me he wouldn't give me the files without a warrant. How about you? Did you see Attwood?"

"I saw him, but he didn't want to talk."

"Imagine that."

"Yeah. Well, now we'll see who the real players are."

"You think?"

"I'm thinking Attwood is on the phone right now to someone. And pretty soon someone will be on the phone to us."

"Yeah. To tell us we're fired."

"So, you need a warrant."

"If you're serious about going through with it. I mean, this is a major undertaking. Most of the files will be electronic and we'll have to find a way to copy them."

"Okay. You go to a store and find the biggest external hard drive you can. Buy two of them. No," he caught himself. "Get three. And a couple of USB cables. I'll take care of the warrant."

"You're really going through with this?"

"Yeah. Why?"

"Doesn't seem quite up to the FBI's standards. We're usually a little more sophisticated than this."

"And we miss a lot by doing it that way, too."

Cruse ended the call with Lyman, then telephoned Charlotte Stillwell, a friend from law school who worked in the Manhattan office of the U.S. Attorney.

"Charlotte," he spoke when she was on the line. "I need a favor."

"Goodall's looking for you."

"Already?"

"Yeah."

"I need a search warrant."

"Where do you want to search?"

"The office of Henry Wilson."

"What? Are you out of your mind?"

"I need it, Charlotte."

"Wilson is one of the top financial managers in the city. Maybe in the country. He has lots of friends, you know. Who authorized this?"

"I did."

"Another one of your maverick ideas?"

"This is really big."

"No. This is the kind of thing that ruins promising careers."

"I need it."

"Okay," she sighed. "Send me what you've got and I'll take a look at it. But I'm not promising anything. And if anyone asks about it, I'm not lying."

"Thanks. Check your email."

CHAPTER 44
WASHINGTON, D.C.

AT THE WHITE HOUSE, Pete McWhinney's assistant appeared at his doorway. "There's a call for you."

"Who is it?"

"Yosef Weiss."

"Okay." McWhinney reached for the phone.

The assistant came closer and lowered her voice. "Didn't Leon Bain say we should send him to Aubrey Preston?"

McWhinney gave her a cold stare. "You were listening to our conversation?"

"No," she shook her head. "He talked to me. Told me that if you weren't around I should know that all of Mr. Weiss's phone calls should go to Aubrey. And then he said something about Mr. Weiss having too much access to the president."

McWhinney's face turned red. "You work for me," he hissed. "Not Leon Bain. You do what I say. And if he ever tells you something like that again, tell me about it immediately."

"Yes, sir."

McWhinney snatched up the phone. "Yosef," he said with a pleasant tone. "How are you today?"

"I am not good."

"What's the matter?"

"I just got off the phone with Henry Wilson. He says an FBI agent was at his office this morning. Wanting to see his records."

"What for?"

"Something about an investigation."

"Into Henry?"

"Into one of his investment vehicles."

"You sure it wasn't the SEC?"

"No. It was the FBI. You know anything about that?"

"No. I don't. I'll make some calls, see what I can find out, but you know they're very sensitive about this sort of thing. We can't tell them who or what to investigate."

"I understand that. But Henry's never broken a law in his life. And now they're threatening him with a subpoena if he doesn't open his files."

"Who came to see him?"

"A woman. I have it right here." There was the sound of shuffling paper. "Her last name was ... Lyman. Sandra Lyman."

"I'll find out."

No sooner had McWhinney hung up the phone than it rang again. This time the call was from Frank Attwood.

"An FBI agent just left my house," Attwood sounded serious but not excited. "He was asking all kinds of questions."

"Who was it?"

"Said his name was Richard Cruse. From the office in Istanbul. He's supposedly investigating the death of an ENX employee."

"What is ENX?"

"One of the proprietary companies."

"Oh."

"I made a few calls after he left," Attwood continued. "I understand his partner has been asking questions in New York."

McWhinney glanced down at his notes from the conversation with Weiss. "A female agent named Sandra Lyman?"

"You know about this already."

"Yosef Weiss called a few minutes ago."

"I assume you can look into it."

"I'll make some calls," McWhinney offered.

When he finished talking with Attwood, he reached for the phone to call the FBI. Then he paused. If he called the director, he would generate an inquiry that would run the full extent of the bureau. *That's too much attention,* he thought. And it would take too long to produce a response. But if he contacted someone in New York, he would be going past the director and meddling in Bureau affairs. That's the kind of thing that gets leaked to the press. Still, the matter had to be dealt with, and soon. "I'll deal with the fallout," he grumbled. He contacted the White House switchboard, got an outside line, and telephoned the FBI's New York office. His call was routed to Foster Goodall, the special agent in charge.

*   *   *

McWhinney was brief and to the point. Agents from overseas FBI offices were threatening a New York funds manager and an official with the CIA. No one was trying to interfere with an investigation, but the White House was in the process of evaluating several policy issues, and McWhinney wanted to be briefed on the nature of the investigation.

When the conversation ended, Goodall called Mark White into his office.

"Close the door."

White pushed the door closed and turned to face Goodall. "Something wrong?"

"Richard Cruse is in town."

"Oh? Is he looking to get reassigned back here? I thought he liked it overseas."

"It's not that." Goodall looked concerned. "Apparently he has an agent from the Ankara office with him. Sandra Lyman."

White raised an eyebrow. "What are they doing?"

"I'm not sure. He called me yesterday to arrange a flight. I tried to find out what he was up to but he put me off. Said he didn't want to talk about it yet." Goodall gestured toward the phone. "I just got a call from the White House. Whatever Cruse is up to, he's getting noticed."

White's eyes were wide. "The president called you?"

"No. His chief of staff. Pete McWhinney."

"You want me to find Richard and bring him in?"

"Find him," Goodall nodded. "Take Billy Dobbs with you. See what Cruse and Lyman are up to. But don't try to stop them. Cruse is a good agent. If he's on to something, there's probably a good reason."

"Right."

CHAPTER 45
HERZLIYA, ISRAEL

ONCE AGAIN, HOFI STOOD in the operations center and stared at the screens on the wall. This time the images he saw were from an IDF special missions unit in Rabat. Cameras mounted on unit members' helmets and on their weapons provided live video and audio. Images appeared on three separate screens as the two SUVs in which the unit was riding turned down a dusty street.

"We're sure this is the address?" a voice asked from inside the first SUV.

"Yes," someone replied. "We checked it twice."

"Pull up over there," another ordered. "That's our spot."

The first SUV lurched to a stop. One of the cameras caught a glimpse through a side window of the second SUV as it moved past.

Images on the three screens jumped up and down and shook from side to side as the soldiers stepped from the SUVs. Then the first two cameras showed only the ground and the tops of boots. A third focused on a house a hundred meters away.

A voice spoke in a hoarse whisper. "Everyone ready?" Someone inquired but the words were inaudible. Seconds later, the first voice spoke again. "Get your teams in position and wait for my order."

The first camera showed a team of three men as they moved down the left side of the house. A second team was visible to the right.

A few minutes later someone said quietly, "Alpha Team in position."

"Bravo Team," another whispered. "We have the back."

"Okay. Let's go."

At once, teams approached the house from the front and back. They hit the doors at the same time, kicking them in to the sound of splintering wood and breaking glass. In only seconds, soldiers poured through the open doorways, filling the central hallway from the front and then the kitchen from the rear. A quick search revealed the house was empty.

"We missed them," Hofi sighed.

A frown wrinkled Daphna Abergil's forehead. "This was too easy."

"No," Hofi argued. "Just bad intelligence."

Abergil came from her desk. "I don't think so. More like a—"

"Hey," a voice called from inside the house. "We found something."

Hofi stared intently at the screen as the camera moved down the hallway and into a room to the right.

"A note," someone said. And the camera focused on a wooden table. In the center of the tabletop was a plain white sheet of paper.

"Give me a shot of that note," Hofi called. The image tightened on the paper and the words, written in Hebrew, came into focus. תומל םיכירצ םידוהיה לכ

Abergil's eyes squinted as she stared up at the screen and slowly read the words aloud. "'All Jews must die.'"

Hofi repeated the phrase. "All Jews must die," he said softly. "All Jews must die." Then his eyes opened wide. "Get out! Get out! Get out!" he shouted. "It's a trap!"

Images on the screens jumped violently as the soldiers scrambled to get out of the house. There was a thumping and scraping sound of footsteps banging against the floor. Someone shouted. Then another. The front door appeared. Getting closer and closer. And then a roaring sound. The doorframe seemed all at once to zoom closer. Smoke and ash swirled around the hall. Then the screen went blank.

Hofi looked around, his eyes alert. "What happened?"

"I think there was an explosion," Abergil guessed.

"Anyone got another view? We had half a dozen cameras on the scene," Hofi shouted. "Can't one of them work?"

"Three, sir," someone corrected.

"What?"

"There were three helmet cameras. One with each team."

"I don't care how many there were. Can we get something from just one of them?"

"We're looking."

Moments later an image appeared on one of the screens. There was the muffled sound of someone panting. Then a voice. "I can't believe it." The camera swung around to show the house engulfed in flames. "It went up in an instant."

"They knew we were coming," someone said.

"All those leads were nothing but lies."

"Should have never put it out on the street like that."

"All right," a voice commanded sternly. "Knock it off. Give me a count. Anyone hurt?"

"Three wounded, sir. And there's Olmert."

"Olmert? What about him?"

"He was hit pretty bad."

The camera swung around to show a soldier lying on the ground, his face bloody, his chest torn open. A soldier beside him looked up. "I think he's dead."

CHAPTER 46
WASHINGTON, D.C.

PETE MCWHINNEY LOOKED UP from his desk to see the president, Andrew Stanton, standing in the doorway. "I have stumbled across a moment," Stanton smiled, "that has become all too rare to me in the past several years."

"What's that?"

"A moment when I have nothing to do." Stanton entered the room and dropped onto a chair across from McWhinney. "No meetings. No telephone calls. Nothing at all."

"That won't last long."

McWhinney's assistant entered the room. "You should see the news."

"I'm in the middle of a conversation," McWhinney complained.

She ignored him, picked up a remote control from the desktop, and switched on a television set on a shelf to the right. Images of a house in flames appeared. A voiceover said in a solemn tone, "No word yet on the number of casualties. All we know is that witnesses say a team of soldiers approached the house, went inside, and then it exploded. First reports indicate the soldiers were from the Israeli IDF, but we have yet to confirm that."

Stanton's eyes were wide. "Where is this?"

Just then Aubrey Preston burst through the open doorway. "Rabat, Mr. President. They're in Rabat."

"The IDF had troops in Morocco?"

"Yes, Mr. President. They were following up on a lead from Mossad. Someone tipped them that the house was the location where the car bombers had lived. The unit raided it, but when they were all inside, the house exploded."

Stanton looked over at McWhinney. "Pete, this can't possibly turn out well."

McWhinney pushed back from the desk and stood. "We should get downstairs to the situation room."

Suddenly the image on the television switched to a town square. Tall oak trees shaded a lush green lawn. A caption at the bottom of the screen identified the location as Courthouse Square, Newnan, Georgia. The camera showed a picture of the courthouse entrance with a brick front, white columns, and marble steps. Then the tall oaken doors opened and a tall man in a dark gray suit appeared.

"That's Alex Talbot." Stanton pointed to the television. "What's he doing?"

While they watched, Talbot walked purposefully down the steps to a bank of microphones. With shoulders squared and his jaw set, he began.

"I'm sure you've all heard by now that there has been a second bombing in Rabat. This one involved an Israeli special missions unit. Operating in conjunction with Rabat police, they have been investigating the recent bombing at the Israeli Consulate office. The unit and Rabat police followed up on several leads and received a tip that a house south of the city was the site where the bombers lived before the attack and the location where they created the bomb and planned their cowardly assault. When the special missions unit entered the house, they found it was empty except for a note on the table. Written in Hebrew it read simply, 'All Jews must die.' A few seconds later, the house exploded."

A reporter spoke up. "Were there any casualties?"

"I've been advised," Talbot announced, "that we should let Israeli and Moroccan authorities answer those questions. I'm sure from the video we've all seen that there were injuries, but I don't have specific information about that and I'm sure the proper authorities would rather handle the details with you themselves."

A second reporter raised a hand. "You seem to be better informed than the White House on this. How is it that you know more than they?"

"Who was that?" Stanton fumed. "That was a softball question. This whole thing is a setup. Who was that reporter?"

"Wait," McWhinney said. "Let's hear this."

"The White House," Talbot responded, "has been out of touch with conditions in the Middle East ever since President Stanton's inauguration. That's part of the reason we face incidents like this. Not all the reason, but certainly the president's reluctance to confront the root causes of unrest in the region has led to a situation in which terrorists feel emboldened to act as they please."

The same reporter followed up. "Are you suggesting President Stanton is to blame for this and the earlier bombing in Rabat?"

"Look," Talbot explained, "all I'm saying is, when you live in a hostile world with your head in the sand, it produces consequences. Bombings, like those we've seen the last few days, are just one of those consequences."

"He doesn't mean sand," Stanton shouted angrily. "He doesn't mean I've had my head in the sand. He means I've had my head up my—"

"I know what he means, Mr. President." McWhinney picked up the remote control from the desktop and switched off the television. "Let's get downstairs." He came from the desk and took Stanton by the arm.

"Yedaya gave him that information," Stanton argued as they started toward the door.

"I'm sure he did."

"I know he did," Stanton retorted. "Yedaya thinks I'm weak and indecisive. He told me as much right before Jean Brown jumped between us."

McWhinney ushered him into the hall. "Let's get downstairs to the situation room."

CHAPTER 47
NEW YORK CITY

THAT AFTERNOON, HOLSTEN WALKED down to Foley's Restaurant on Thirty-Third Street. He made his way past the bar and took a seat at his regular table in back. Ten minutes later, Rick Dwyer arrived. A waiter brought him over. When the waiter was gone, Holsten turned to Dwyer.

"You have something for me?"

Dwyer took an envelope from the pocket of his jacket and laid it on the table. "I think that's what you're looking for," he said. There was no emotion in his voice and his face seemed unexpressive.

Holsten took the envelope from the table, reached inside with his fingers, and pulled out three photographs. The first was taken through a doorway opened just wide enough to snap the picture. It showed Leon Bain with a female who appeared to be no older than a teenager. The girl wore blue jeans and a shirt that buttoned up the front. The buttons were undone and the shirt gapped open. The second photograph apparently was taken just moments later as they fell backward on the bed. Both were wearing even less clothing. The final picture was even more revealing.

"You're sure she isn't his wife?"

"That girl is so young she could be Bain's granddaughter," Dwyer scoffed.

"And you're certain she's not his wife," Holsten repeated.

"Positive."

"Who is she?"

"Megan Lewis. She's a campaign intern."

"You know that for a fact?"

Dwyer took a second envelope from his pocket. "Took these because I thought you'd ask."

Holsten opened the envelope and found pictures of Lewis working in one of the Stanton campaign offices. "Where were these taken?"

"New Hampshire."

"You did that in less than a day."

"Got lucky, they weren't far away."

Holsten flipped through the first set of photographs once more, then looked over at Dwyer. "Good job."

He stuffed the photographs inside one of the envelopes and put it in the inside pocket of his jacket. Then he reached in his outside pocket and took out another envelope. He laid it on the table and slid it across to Dwyer. "That should cover it."

Dwyer opened the enveloped, glanced inside, and smiled. "Pleasure doing business with you. Call me anytime."

Holsten remained at the table after Dwyer left and ordered a drink. When he finished it, there was still time for one more. He sipped on it and watched while the afternoon crowd slowly drifted through the door. By the time he was ready to leave, most of them still hadn't gotten any farther than the bar. They were gathered there in a cluster drinking and talking with the sound of their laughter slowly growing louder and louder.

Holsten waved the waiter over to his table and asked for the check, but the waiter just smiled. "The manager said for you to have a good day."

"You tell him I'm grateful." He handed the waiter a twenty and started toward the door.

A car was waiting at the curb when Holsten stepped outside. He crawled onto the backseat and relaxed as they drove across the river to Teterboro Airport in New Jersey. A Learjet was parked on the tarmac outside a hangar on the far side of the runway. The door of the fuselage was open and the steps were down. An attendant waited at the top.

The car came to stop near the wing of the plane and Holsten climbed out. He hurried up the steps and disappeared inside the fuselage. As the attendant closed the door behind him, the plane's engines began to whine. Minutes later it rolled toward the runway and was gone.

CHAPTER 48
NEW YORK CITY

CRUSE BOARDED A SHUTTLE FLIGHT in Washington, D.C., and arrived at La Guardia an hour later. He rented a car and drove to the coffee shop in Manhattan where Lyman was waiting. He brought the car to a stop at the curb out front and waved to her through the window. She came from the shop carrying two plastic bags.

"What's that?" he asked, gesturing toward the bags.

"I got four," she replied.

He had a blank look. "Four?"

"External hard drives."

"Oh. Yeah." Lyman tossed the bags in back, and Cruse put the car in gear. "Think we'll need that much space?"

"Who knows?" she shrugged. "But with the program on this," she held up a flash drive, "we can tell his computer to download the files and then all we have to do is change out the hard drives as they fill up. Maybe we won't look too much like amateurs."

Cruse had a sheepish grin. "This is going to get unmanageable, isn't it?"

"Rather quickly, I believe."

"Maybe Wilson has some paper files, too."

"Not many." Lyman gestured out the window. "Where are we going?"

"To get the warrant."

They drove across town to Broadway, then turned south. At Wall Street, Cruse steered the car into an alley and brought it to a stop in the delivery zone beside Trinity Church. "Stay here." He opened the door. "I'll be right back."

Cruse climbed from the car and entered the church through the front doors. He found Charlotte Stillwell seated on a pew a few rows up. "Interesting choice of meeting places." He slid onto the bench beside her.

"Here." She handed him the warrant. "You can email me the return when you're finished."

"You'll actually file a return?"

"Not unless you go forward with a case." She glanced over at him. "Goodall is looking for you."

"You talked to him?"

"No. But I hear he has his agents scouring the city for you. If they ask me, I'm saying I thought it was legit and didn't have a clue there was a problem until after the fact."

"Do whatever you have to." Cruse turned to leave but Charlotte grasped his forearm. "We're even now."

"Yeah," he nodded. "We're even."

From the church, Cruse and Lyman drove back to Lexington Avenue and arrived at Wilson's office a little before four that afternoon. As they approached the receptionist, Cruse held the warrant for her to see. "I'm Richard Cruse with the FBI. I have a search warrant. I'm here to see your files on the Shale Oil Real Estate Investment Trust." He tucked the warrant into his pocket. "You can have someone show the files to me, or I can seize the office and lock you all out. Which would you prefer?"

"Just a minute, I'll get someone." The receptionist rose from her chair and scurried down the hall.

Lyman had a disapproving look. "Do you always do it with such care and concern?"

"Gets results every time."

Moments later Henry Wilson appeared looking angry and upset. "What is the meaning of this?" he demanded. "I told you people to—"

Cruse held up his badge and the warrant. "I have a search warrant. I want to see your files on the Shale Oil Real Estate Investment Trust."

Wilson pointed toward Lyman. "I told your assistant—"

"She's not my assistant," Cruse said sharply. "She's an FBI agent."

"I don't care what she is. I've made some calls about you. And I don't have to—"

"Mr. Wilson," Cruse interrupted, "we can do this the easy way or the hard way. Easy way, you show me the files I'm asking about. Hard way, I seize the office and lock you and your staff out until I find what I'm looking for. Which is it going to be?"

"Why, I never …" Wilson stammered. "I've done nothing wrong."

"No one has accused you of doing anything wrong, Mr. Wilson. Not yet. But if you don't show me your files, I'll arrest you for obstructing a federal investigation. Now, what's it going to be?"

Just then a woman appeared in the hallway. Dressed in a business suit and heels, she looked like a person in charge. "Henry, what is this about?"

"The FBI," he growled.

She stepped closer. "I'm Peggy Newman. The office manager." She looked past Cruse to Lyman. "You're the one who was asking about the Shale Oil Trust?"

"Yes."

Newman called over her shoulder, "Mary, get me those files on Shale Oil."

Wilson cut his eyes at her. "I've already called," he seethed. "Just wait. We don't have to do this."

"I'm not going to jail over it, either." Newman looked back at Cruse and Lyman. "Right this way." She gestured for them to follow. "We maintain a database on all our clients. I believe you can get what you need from our client file package."

Cruse took the lead as they followed her down the hallway and around the corner to a cubicle. A young woman was seated there. The manager glanced at her. "Mary, you have the file?"

"Yes, ma'am." Mary pointed to the monitor on her desk. "This is the account file. The profile is on the next tab." Cruse leaned over her shoulder to see. Mary stood and gestured toward the chair. "You can sit here."

Cruse took a seat and scrolled down the screen. Then he clicked on the second tab and scanned the customer profile. "This is all you have?"

"There's a trading file, too. We have one for every client that shows their trading history." Mary leaned over his shoulder to the keyboard and opened a third screen. The file appeared but showed no activity. "It's empty because this account doesn't trade. It holds a single asset." She flipped back to the client profile and scrolled to the bottom of the screen. A dozen items appeared in a list. "Actually," Mary explained, "it shows them as multiple tracts but that's all the trust owns. Real estate. It doesn't trade securities."

Cruse gestured toward the screen. "Can I get a copy of this?"

Mary shot a quick glance in Newman's direction. Newman nodded her approval. Mary opened a desk drawer and took out a flash drive. She slipped it into a USB port on the server beneath the desk and entered a command on the screen. Moments later, she took out the flash drive and handed it to him. "There you go," she smiled.

Cruse put the flash drive in his pocket. "Do you have any hard files?"

Mary glanced up at Newman once more. Newman checked her watch, then nodded to Mary.

Mary turned to a cabinet behind them and opened a drawer. "These are the permanent files."

"This single drawer?"

"Actually, there are two drawers," Mary explained. "This one and the one below it."

"I need them both."

"We can make copies for you," Newman offered.

"No," Cruse said, shaking his head. "I need the files."

Newman appeared upset. "You're going to take them?"

"Yes."

"O-okay," she stammered. "I'm not sure what to say."

Cruse lifted a file from the drawer. "I need a couple of boxes."

Mary left the cubicle and disappeared down the hall. She returned a few minutes later with cardboard boxes. By the time Cruse finished unloading the drawers, he'd filled four. Lyman looked over at him. "How are we getting these downstairs?"

"I'll take two. You get one." Cruse glanced at Mary. "You get the other one."

"I don't think I'm allowed—"

"I'm conscripting your help," Cruse ordered. "Get the box and let's go."

Boxes in hand, they trouped back through the office. Newman was waiting for them at the receptionist's desk. "We need a receipt for those files."

Cruse set the boxes on the floor and grabbed a notepad from the desk. He scribbled a general description of the files, dated it, and signed his name. Newman glanced at the sheet of paper. "I think we should list each file individually."

"I'm not—" Cruse stopped in midsentence with a knowing smile. "It won't work." Then he picked up the boxes and started toward the door.

"I need a list of those files," Newman demanded.

"You're just trying to delay us. But it won't work."

As the elevator doors opened, Wilson appeared in the hallway behind them. "Wait!" he shouted. "Your office is on the phone."

"Tell them I'll talk to them later," Cruse replied as they stepped into the elevator.

"But they said you should wait," Wilson continued.

By then the doors were closed. Lyman looked over at Cruse. "What was that about?"

"Nothing."

"It didn't sound like nothing."

"I'll tell you later."

In a few minutes, the elevator reached the lobby. The doors opened and Cruse stepped out. He glanced around warily, then started toward the street. "Come on, we might just make it."

When they reached the car, he opened the back door and set the boxes inside. Lyman got in the front. Cruse moved to the driver's door and glanced over the top of the car to Mary. "Thanks for your help." Then he got in behind the wheel and started the engine.

"Where are you staying?"

"Sheraton on Fifty-Third Street," Lyman answered. "But what was all that with Newman about trying to delay us?"

"They called while we were in there. Goodall is on his way."

*　　*　　*

Cruse and Lyman reached the hotel room without incident. They set the boxes on the bed and Cruse began working his way through the documents. Lyman placed the flash drive in the port on her laptop and started through the electronic files.

"Okay," she said moments later. "We have a list of investors. Michael Geller, Henry Wilson, Curtis McCullough, Dan Luckett, and Sidney Adkins. Any of those names mean anything to you?"

"Maybe. Geller is a hedge fund manager. We should run down information on all of them before we go back. Be easier to do it here than in Turkey."

"But we need a better place to work," Lyman suggested. "This hotel room is going to get expensive. And you can't stay in here with me."

"Yeah, probably not a good idea." Cruse picked up a menu from the hotel restaurant. "And room service is expensive, too."

"I thought we were working on these files."

"We are, but I'm hungry," Cruse replied. "You want something to eat?"

"Yes, now that you mention it."

"I'll go get something for us. You keep working."

Cruse came from the room and rode the elevator to the lobby. As he started toward the front entrance he glanced outside to see a black SUV come to a stop near the hotel entrance. Then the passenger door opened and Foster Goodall stepped out. Cruse turned around quickly and ran back to the elevator. Minutes later, he burst into the room.

"They're here. Pack up everything."

Lyman looked confused. "Who's here?"

"Foster Goodall and a couple of agents."

"I thought you said he was your friend."

"He is but if he finds us, he'll take all these files and we'll never hear about this case again." Cruse began stuffing files back in the boxes.

"We aren't even sure there is a case," Lyman argued.

"Sladen is dead. It wasn't an accident." Cruse was adamant. "The answer is somewhere in these files or with the people, or something."

"You don't know that." Lyman closed the laptop and returned it to its case.

"Why else would the FBI know we're here?"

"They are some wealthy, well-connected people." Lyman turned to the bed and placed a lid on one of the boxes. "You said so yourself."

"Look, Goodall is my boss. But he isn't going to ruin his career for this and I'm not going to ask him to, either. So get moving."

"Goodall is your boss? You work out of Istanbul. We're accountable to the agent in Ankara."

"You're accountable to Ankara. I'm in counterintelligence. I work out of the office in Istanbul. I cooperate with the office in Ankara, but my supervisor is the head of the New York office. And that person is Foster Goodall. And Foster Goodall is headed to this room."

"That's who Newman called."

"I'm just surprised it took them this long to locate us."

Cruse retrieved a luggage cart from the linen room down the hall and brought it back to the room. He stacked the boxes on it, then he and Lyman hurried from the room to a service elevator on the opposite end of the hall. They rode down to the first floor and stepped out to a storage area behind the kitchen. The space around the elevator was crowded with delivery carts and extra chairs. Cruse maneuvered the luggage cart past all that to a loading dock in back, then went for the car. Ten minutes later, they were once again driving through Manhattan with the boxes on the backseat.

Lyman let the seat back and closed her eyes. "So, what do we do now?"

"I have a friend."

"You have lots of friends."

"That's how I get things done."

CHAPTER 49
DETROIT, MICHIGAN

HOLSTEN EXITED THE LEARJET and made his way down the steps to the tarmac. A black SUV was parked just beyond the plane's wingtip. He opened the passenger door and climbed inside to the second row.

The driver caught Holsten's eye through the rearview mirror. "They're at the Cadillac Hotel."

"Okay," Holsten nodded. "Let's go."

From the airport, they drove downtown and turned onto Washington Boulevard. As the hotel came into view, Holsten placed a call to Bain. "We need to talk."

"I'd love to, David, but I won't be in New York anytime soon."

"I'm here," Holsten replied tersely. "At the hotel. Come downstairs. Black SUV. Parked out front." He ended the call without waiting for a response.

A few minutes later, the SUV came to a stop at the hotel entrance. Bain appeared in the doorway. A bellman opened the car door and Bain got in beside Holsten. When the door was closed, the SUV started forward.

"What's this all about?" Bain seemed aggravated. "We're right in the middle of a big push. I was headed to a staff meeting."

"I know about your staff meetings," Holsten scoffed. He took the envelope from his pocket and handed it to Bain. "Take a look at these."

Bain sighed as he glanced at the pictures. "This is not what it looks like."

"Oh, really, Leon?" Holsten did his best to sound angry. "That's reassuring. Because it looks like you're involved with an underage intern."

"She——"

"Don't." Holsten held up his hand. "Don't even try."

Bain looked like a man caught in the act. "Has someone filed a complaint?"

"Not yet. Which is why I'm here."

"What does that mean?"

"It means you're out."

"Out? What are you talking about?"

"The campaign. You're out."

The color drained from Bain's face. "You can't do that."

"Yes," Holsten insisted, "I can. And I am."

"The president will never go for it."

"Oh, he'll go for it. He wants a second term more than he wants you around. McWhinney has already named your replacement." Bain's cell phone rang. Holsten gestured with a nod. "I'd get that if I were you."

Bain took the phone from his pocket. The call was short. Bain said only yes and okay. When it was over, he returned the phone to his pocket and stared out the window. "The press will eat him alive," he said quietly.

"No." Holsten shook his head slowly. "They won't."

"Why not?"

"Because they're never going to get the story."

Bain turned to look at him. "What does that mean?"

"You're not telling them, we're not telling them. No one is telling them."

"Not telling them?" Bain had a troubled frown. "You can't expect me to keep quiet."

"We expect it," Holsten insisted, "and you'll go along with it. As far as the press will know, you're still calling the shots. Only you and I and everyone else who matters will know the truth."

"Just how do you plan to accomplish this?"

"You'll be waiting out the campaign in a cabin in Montana."

A smirk spread across Bain's face. "Do you really expect to get away with a stunt like this?"

"Yes. We do."

"I'm not keeping quiet."

"Listen, Leon." Holsten took him by the arm, pulled him close, and lowered his voice. "I had to argue like crazy to get you this." He looked Bain in the eye. "You understand what I'm saying?"

"Yes," Bain sighed.

"Tell me you understand because I don't want you to tell me later you didn't realize what was at stake. So, tell me."

"I understand," Bain sighed.

"Just be glad you aren't married."

"You should be glad I'm not married."

"Don't get cocky. Just take the deal and sit the rest of it out. You'll still get paid."

Getting paid caught Bain's attention and he seemed to relax. "So, who's in my place?"

"Aubrey Preston." The SUV came to a stop back at the hotel. Holsten reached for the door handle, then looked over at Bain. "The driver knows where to take you. Enjoy the ride. And Leon, don't ever come near the president again." Then he pushed open the door, slid from the seat, and stepped outside.

CHAPTER 50
THE NEW JERSEY SHORE

CRUSE AND LYMAN DROVE SOUTH from New York on the Garden State Parkway. A few hours later, they turned east and drove to Point Pleasant, a resort town along the Atlantic shore. At Ocean Road they made a right, then almost immediately turned left onto an unpaved alley that was squeezed between a row of traditional beach houses—two-story with white clapboard siding and screened-in sleeping porches. Cruse brought the car to a stop at the last house on the left.

Lyman glanced around warily. "You own a beach house?"

"No."

"So, what are we doing here?"

"I know the guy who owns it." Cruse opened the car door and stepped out. "Mark Ale. Lives in Bound Brook."

"And he won't mind, right?"

"He'll probably mind a lot. But he'll get over it when I send him some money and a case of beer."

They unloaded the file boxes first, then returned to the car for their luggage inside. "I hope the bed is comfortable," Lyman groaned as she took a bag from the car.

"No time to sleep," Cruse replied.

"Why not?"

"Goodall will be here before long."

Lyman stopped and stared. "You think he followed us?"

"No." Cruse answered as he continued toward the house. "But I think he's curious about what we're doing and he'll keep on until he finds us."

Lyman followed after him. "He knows about this place?"

"The car is a rental."

"So?"

"I'm sure it has a GPS locator somewhere on it. It'll take them a little while, but Foster or one of his guys will think of it and then they'll contact the rental company and then they'll show up here looking for us." Cruse held the door open while Lyman trudged inside. "So," he continued as she moved past, "while we have the time, we need to get as far into these files as we can."

With the boxes in place by the dining table, and their luggage stowed in the bedrooms, Cruse rummaged through the kitchen for a can of coffee. Before long, the aroma of coffee filled the air. When it was ready, he poured two cups and brought them to the dining room table. Then he set the boxes on the floor beside his chair and began methodically working through the files.

Lyman, seated at the opposite end of the table, attached the flash drive to her laptop and combed through the digital files. Half an hour later, she glanced down the table in Cruse's direction. "Find anything?"

"Mostly records for real estate transactions."

"No mention of Attwood?"

"No, but that doesn't mean there isn't something to this."

Lyman pushed back from the table. "I agree that Sladen was on to something, but the real question is whether it was enough to get him killed. I mean, he could have died of natural causes, in spite of what that detective says. Or it could have been a case of mistaken identity."

Cruse frowned at her. "Mistaken identity?"

"Yes," Lyman insisted. "A killer who struck the wrong person."

"That's a little too random for me. And people who die of natural causes don't usually die with traces of cyanide in their system."

"But think about it," she continued. "If someone killed Sladen, and it was because of what he knew, then the killer would also know that he was really a CIA analyst—in spite of the agency's halfhearted attempts at plausible deniability. And the killer would know that someone was going to investigate."

"Like us."

"Exactly. And then the whole thing would come down. If Sladen was killed because of what he knew, it would have been better to just ignore him."

"Or reassign him," Cruse suggested. "Stick him in a cubbyhole somewhere."

"But to do that," Lyman countered, "they would have to be on the inside."

Cruse took another file from the box. "There are a lot of things about this that don't make sense. But life doesn't always follow the neatest, cleanest, most logical path. In fact, it rarely does. And criminals are sociopaths. They don't think about things the way other people do."

"So we keep going?"

"We keep going."

"Not much further to go. We're already at the top."

"The top?"

"Attwood is a presidential appointee. That takes us all the way to the president," Lyman explained. "It doesn't get much higher than that."

"Still a lot of blank spaces between here and there."

"So, what next?"

"Keep building on the information. Fill in the blank spaces on each of those trust investors and hope we catch a break."

As Cruse turned through the pages in the file, Lyman returned to the laptop, but she kept talking while she worked. "The whole thing is just right out there in the open. They weren't even trying to hide it. If they were doing something illegal, they were pretty arrogant about it."

"Maybe they don't have to cover it up or get rid of it."

"Right," she said sarcastically. "They have a free pass?"

"If Sladen was right, then something big is about to happen. Big enough to threaten embassy employees in the entire region. Whatever that is, the people behind it know how big it is, too."

"And?"

"What if they know that what's coming will so overshadow everything else, they'll never get caught?"

"That would have to be pretty big."

They looked at each other with eyes wide open. "Iran," she whispered.

"Iran," he agreed. "An attack on Iran would eclipse everything else."

"But how do we prove it?"

Cruse tossed aside the file he'd been working on. "I don't know."

Then just as quickly, Lyman's countenance changed. "It still doesn't make sense to me. Suppose Sladen was right. Suppose something really is planned. If you don't mind orchestrating or manipulating the president, or the Pentagon, into a war with Iran, why would you care if embassy personnel are at risk? It makes no sense."

"No. It doesn't." Cruse looked through their notes. "Let me see your laptop."

"Why? I'm right in the middle of these files."

Cruse turned the laptop to face him. "I think Sladen had the same thought." He opened a file that contained information from Sladen's computer. "Look," he pointed as the file appeared on the screen. "This is information about the Office of Management Policy, Rightsizing, and Innovation." He clicked on a link, opened a page on the State Department website, and scrolled down the page. "See. This is the office that controls movement of embassy personnel. The link for it and information about it was on Sladen's computer. He knew about this guy."

"But could they move State Department personnel from one location to another without the Secretary's approval?"

"I don't know, but I know someone who can tell us."

"Who?"

Cruse pointed to the caption for a picture on the web page. "Raymond Ware."

"You think he'll talk?"

"I think I'm going to give him the chance."

A quick Google search indicated Ware lived in Falls Church, Virginia.

Cruse jotted down the address and stuffed a few items in his leather satchel. "I'm going to Falls Church. You stay here and keep working. If Mark comes by, tell him you're with me."

"You think he'll show up?"

"I don't know. But if he does, just tell him you're with me."

"Can we trust him?"

"I would trust him with my life."

CHAPTER 51
HERZLIYA, ISRAEL

HOFI SAT IN HIS OFFICE long after the staff upstairs had left for the evening. A call from the lab earlier that day indicated they were close to a result on attempts to identify the remains found in the cardboard box. Hofi chose to stay late at the office on the chance they would get the result before morning. He wanted to know first, so he could inform the family before word leaked out. He was certain the flesh in the box was that of Ohad Revach.

On his desk were reports from agents in Qom telling of what they found in the warehouse—blood, hair, fingernails, portions of three toes. From what they described, Revach must have endured hours of excruciating torture. The thought of it took Hofi back to a day years before when he had been captured by the Egyptians in the Yom Kippur War of 1973. While scouting Egyptian positions along the Suez Canal, he had been surprised by a patrol. They took him prisoner, blindfolded him, and led him into camp. Later, they transported him to a secret base near Hasna in the Egyptian desert. For the next three days he was subjected to forms of torture he'd never imagined possible. Nails driven into the ends of his fingers. Then his fingernails pulled out. When that wasn't enough, they used a hammer and broke his fingers, one at a time. Once his hands were ruined, they moved on to other body parts, each one attacked in a way that produced its own unique form of pain. Then, just when he thought they'd done all they could do, they brought out the—

A tap at the door interrupted his thought. "Yes," he called.

The door creaked open and Lior Riskin, a lab supervisor, appeared holding a single-page document. "Sorry to bother you so late," he said apologetically.

"That's all right. Are you any closer to an answer?"

"I have the results."

"Okay." Hofi sat up straight. "What was it?"

"The material in the box was human remains." Riskin's voice was almost a whisper and his eyes glanced down at the floor. "This is the report." He laid the document on the desk.

Hofi scanned the page. "You identified it as human. Were you able to determine an identity?"

"Yes, sir." Riskin pointed to the report. "It's on there. Near the bottom. The remains were that of Ohad Revach. We had his DNA already."

In spite of his years of experience, Hofi felt sick to his stomach. "All of it was of a single person?"

"Yes, sir. Not the entire body, but all of it came from a single person."

"Could you tell what part of the body was in the box?"

"Yes, sir."

"What was it?"

"Head. Heart. And …" Riskin's eyes darted away.

Hofi looked up at him. "What?" he asked insistently. "What was the rest?"

Riskin cleared his throat. "Genitals. The other element was from his genitals."

The nausea Hofi had been battling suddenly disappeared, replaced with burning anger. "We should wipe them from the face of the earth," he growled.

Tears trickled down Riskin's face. "Then their mothers would feel what our mothers feel."

"Yes!" Hofi shouted. He slapped the desk with his hand. "And their sons as our sons."

"When will it end?"

"When they are all dead."

CHAPTER 52
FALLS CHURCH, VIRGINIA

A LITTLE AFTER FOUR IN THE MORNING, Cruse arrived outside Ray Ware's house. He parked the car at the curb directly opposite the end of the driveway and reclined the seat. Certain that anyone coming from the driveway would rouse him from a nap, he folded his hands across his lap and closed his eyes. Moments later he was asleep.

An hour later Cruse was awakened by a noise from across the street. He looked up in time to see Ware as he climbed into a car and backed it down the driveway. Cruse popped the seat into an upright position and started the car. As Ware drove away, Cruse followed.

A mile or two up the road, Ware turned into the parking lot outside Caribou Coffee on Leesburg Pike. Ware parked near the door and went inside. Cruse parked a few spaces away and followed after him.

Several customers were already there and a line formed at the cashier. Ware took his place in line. While he waited, Cruse came alongside him and held his badge so Ware could see it. "We need to talk," he said quietly.

"I'm on my way to work."

"I know. That's what we need to talk about."

Ware was next in line. Cruse smiled at the cashier and gestured in Ware's direction. "Give this man whatever he wants, and I'll have a Hazelnut latte."

When their coffee was ready, Cruse guided Ware to a table that sat away from the windows. Ware glanced at his watch. "I really don't have time for this."

"You really don't have time to avoid this."

Ware appeared skeptical. "How do I even know who you are?"

"I can make that easy for you," Cruse smiled. "For the past several months, you've been moving personnel out of our embassies in the Middle East. Not just Iraq and Syria, but all of them. Jordan, Qatar, Saudi Arabia, Egypt. Some of them you've moved rather abruptly. Off on vacation, told not to return." Ware looked unsettled. "That's what you've been doing and I want to know why."

"Wow," Ware sighed. "I thought someone at State would notice. But I didn't expect the FBI would catch it."

"We didn't, actually. An analyst working in Turkey for the CIA noticed it."

"The CIA?" Ware's face lost all color. "And he called you."

"No," Cruse shook his head. "He was killed. I got curious."

Ware slumped in his chair. "He was killed? Over something I did?"

"Actually, he wrote a report about what you did. Suggested there was something big planned for the Middle East. I think that report got him killed and I think you can tell me why."

Ware shook his head. "I don't know anything about a report. Or why someone would be killed over it."

"But you do know about the relocation. You're the guy who made it happen. Right?"

"Yeah."

"How did you do that without the Secretary's approval?"

"I didn't do that on my own." Ware looked defensive. "She approved it. The Secretary approved everything I did."

His answer startled Cruse. "I haven't seen an order."

"There was no order." Ware took a sip of coffee. "When Iran started threatening to close the Strait of Hormuz, people at the Pentagon, mostly Upchurch and Elser, started pushing for a military solution." He glanced around nervously and lowered his voice. "They said we should solve that problem and the nuclear issue, too. So far, the president has resisted. But things have continued to happen over there, and Upchurch and his group have been really pushing the military solution. Trying to get the president to order an attack on Iran or let Israel do it. The secretary of state is opposed to a military solution, but she's been frozen out of the discussion. A couple of months ago, she came to me and asked me to start relocating people, quickly. She's worried there might be a war and doesn't want our people caught in the middle of it."

"Hence the reason she didn't want a formal order."

"Right," Ware nodded. "She didn't want to issue a formal order because she thought someone might try to stop her."

"So she turned to you."

"Yes. I began moving people out several months ago."

"What about the group in New York?"

Ware had a blank expression. "What group?"

"Ever hear of the Shale Oil Real Estate Investment Trust?"

"No," Ware shook his head. "Can't say that I have."

"What about Curtis McCullough, Dan Luckett, Sidney Adkins?"

"No."

"Michael Geller?"

Ware's eyes opened wider at the sound of that name. "I don't know anything about any of that, but if Geller is involved, you should talk to him."

"Why?"

"He and the president were college roommates."

"How do I find him?"

"He has an office in New York."

CHAPTER 53
BEERSHEBA, ISRAEL

YOSSI KOLLEK STEPPED FROM the shower and toweled off. Through the bathroom window he could see the sun just peeking over the hills to the east and his mind turned to the training mission they would fly that day. As a pilot in the Israeli Air Force, he'd long since come to love morning flights. Never one for sleeping late or lounging around, he enjoyed the cool freshness of the new day and the sense of awakening that came with each sunrise. Plus, morning flights left his afternoons free to do as he pleased. Now with a family, and with children approaching their teenage years, he valued the extra time at home.

Kollek glanced at the wristwatch that lay on the shelf above the sink. It was a little before six. If they followed the training schedule, they would be airborne by seven. Just then, the bathroom door opened and Avital, his wife, appeared. She looked half awake. "You remember Milli has a recital tonight?"

"Yes," he nodded. "What time?"

"Seven."

"I should be home by two."

Avital leaned around the door and kissed him, then retreated to the hallway. He heard her footsteps against the hardwood floor as she returned to bed.

When he was dressed and ready, Kollek checked on his children—Milli, their twelve-year-old daughter, and Amos, their ten-year-old son. Both of them were sound asleep. He watched them a moment through the bedroom doors, then made his way to the kitchen and out to the driveway.

Twenty minutes later, he arrived at the main gate to Ramon Airbase. A guard checked his identification card, while someone searched beneath the vehicle and dogs sniffed for explosives. Then they waved him past the gate and he drove from the checkpoint. Minutes later, he turned into the parking lot outside a nondescript hangar that sat alongside one of the runways. He grabbed his flight bag from the front seat of the car and made his way inside the building to the ready room.

As he entered the room, he expected to see the usual dry eraser boards with information and directions about the morning's training exercise. Instead, he found the base commander standing at the head of the room. Rows of seats that lined the room were filled to capacity. Men unable to sit stood along the wall taking every space all the way around. Kollek squeezed into a spot near the door. "What's going on?" he asked the man next to him.

"I don't know," he shrugged. "Looks like they called everyone in who wasn't already on the schedule."

When everyone was assembled, the commander addressed the group. "Gentlemen, we have a slight change in plans today." He nodded to a man who stood to the left. "Sergeant Zurer will be coming around with bags for your cell phones. We need you to place them in one of the bags. Seal it. Print your name on the outside and then place the sealed bag in the basket that Major Geffen will be passing around."

"Major Geffen," someone called in jest. "Totin' the basket for Zurer." Geffen responded with a good-natured smile and a mock bow. Laughter rippled through the room.

"All right," the commander said in a flat monotone. "Let's knock it off." He waited for the room to grow quiet, then continued. "From this point on, there will be no cell phones, no text messages, no email. Anyone caught with a cell phone, anyone caught making a call on a cell phone, anyone sending text messages or emails will be arrested, and I promise you it will be the end of your career."

The commander stepped aside, and Colonel Tayeb spoke up. "Okay.

There will be a change in the training schedule and we will meet back here at 0300 for the briefing. Until then, you will assemble with your flight group leaders. They will give you further instructions."

Murmuring began almost immediately as everyone realized they would have to remain on base. Kollek glanced across the room and saw Yoel Mintz leaning against the wall. He made his way to him. "What's this about?"

"Something really big."

"Another exercise?"

"I do not think so."

"Do you know?"

"No." Mintz shook his head.

"But you know something."

"No one knows anything yet."

"I'm supposed to attend my daughter's recital tonight. They'll be disappointed if I'm not there."

"No one gets off the base."

"I need to let them know I won't be home."

"The Comm Center is conveying that information right now."

Kollek was puzzled. "What are we doing?"

Mintz pushed away from the wall. "We're meeting down the hall in one of the classrooms. Get the others. I'll be down there waiting for you." He turned toward the door. "We have some details we must go over."

*   *   *

Driving from northern Virginia, Cruse reached New York City before noon. He parked the car in a deck near Times Square and walked out the exit to Seventh Avenue. With his iPhone, he obtained an address for Geller's office. It was located on the sixth floor of the IDB Bank building on Forty-Third Street. He thought about taking a taxi, then opted to walk when he realized it was only a few blocks away. Half an hour later, he arrived at Geller's office. The secretary looked up as he entered. "May I help you?"

Cruse took out his badge. "I'm with the FBI. I'd like to talk to Mr. Geller."

"I'm afraid he isn't in right now."

"When will he return?"

"Difficult to say. Shall I take a message?"

"No. I'll check back with him later."

Cruse came from the office and walked back toward the elevator. As he pressed the call button, a security guard approached from his right. "Mr. Cruse, we received a call."

"Let me guess. They want me to wait while someone arrives for me."

"Yes, sir," the guard nodded. "Someone from your office is coming to meet you."

Just then Mark White appeared from the left. He glanced in the guard's direction. "I'll take it from here." The guard backed away. White stepped closer. "You're causing quite a stir, Cruse."

"This place needs to be stirred once in a while."

"Goodall asked me to find you."

"And now you found me."

"He wants to talk to you."

"He knows how to reach me."

"He wants you to come down to the office. Now. With me."

The elevator doors opened. Cruse stepped inside. "Tell him I'll give him a report in a few days." Before White could get on, the doors closed. Cruse pressed the button for the lobby and held it to keep the elevator car from stopping.

*   *   *

Fifty miles off the coast of Oman, the *INS Kidron Valley*, an Israeli submarine, loitered at a depth of fifty meters. Powered by a diesel-electric system, the vessel was nearing the end of its battery life and its ability to remain submerged. Sometime within the next three days, it would have to surface and recharge.

The ship was under the command of Captain Harnoy, a twenty-year veteran of the Israeli Navy. He had grown up in Jerusalem and as a boy spent many hours wandering through the valley for which his ship was named. That connection was a source of great pride not only aboard the ship but in the service he and his men rendered to their country. They were as trained and professional as any sailors in any navy of any country in the world. Watching them as they performed their duties gave him a sense of confidence that together they could handle anything that came their way.

As Harnoy stood in the conning tower, basking in the moment, a voice blared over the intercom. "Con, this is radio."

Harnoy grabbed the microphone. "Radio, this is Con. Go ahead."

"Sir, we have flash traffic on the ELF."

"Roger, radio." Harnoy glanced over at Lieutenant Zukerman, a young officer on his first sea duty. "Bring the message, Lieutenant."

"Aye, sir." Zukerman started toward the radio room. Moments later he returned with a printed message. Across the top were the words *Emergency Action Memo.*

"Sir, we have a properly formatted EAM."

Commander Dorman stepped forward, took the message from Zukerman, and quickly scanned it. "Sir, I concur. The message is properly formatted."

"Very well," Harnoy nodded. "Authenticate."

Zukerman and Dorman retrieved two key cards from a locked box near the helm. Sealed in plastic, the cards contained a code known only to the Naval Command Center in Haifa, where the message originated. Zukerman and Dorman broke open the plastic cases and took out the cards. Then Dorman read the code he found listed there. "7878993LEA5428."

"I agree," Zukerman responded. "The message is authentic." He handed it to Harnoy along with one of the cards.

Harnoy compared the code on the card to the line of code at the top of the message and confirmed. "The message is authentic." Then he slumped onto a seat nearby.

The message in his hand read simply, "National Threat Assessment Command has determined that a strike against Iran is necessary. You are hereby directed to launch missiles bearing strategic ordinance targeted according to the Zebulon target package. The use of nuclear weapons is authorized."

Designed as a multipurpose vehicle, the *Kidron Valley* carried an array of sophisticated torpedoes and Harpoon anti-ship missiles. It also had a complement of Submarine Launched Cruise Missiles. Both the Harpoons and the cruise missiles could be armed with nuclear warheads, which was precisely what the EAM ordered. Harnoy read the message once more, then keyed the microphone for the PA system. "Weapons, this is the Con."

"Roger, Con, this is Weapons."

"Set condition one for strategic missile launch. Target package Zebulon."

"Aye, Con. Set condition one for strategic missile launch. Target package Zebulon."

"How long to arm the missiles?"

"Thirty minutes, sir."

"Very well. Proceed."

Zukerman turned to Harnoy. "Is this for real?"

"We have a message. It's authentic. Our job is to follow through on the orders we've been given."

"But Zebulon … Those sites are in Iran."

"I am aware of that."

"Then we're actually doing it."

"We're hitting Iran before they hit us."

"Have you ever been to Iran?"

Harnoy had a piercing gaze. "You have?"

"Once."

"And they assigned you to the submarine corps?"

Zukerman looked away. Harnoy glanced over at Dorman. "Check with Weapons. See if they can push up the launch time. We're gonna be close on the batteries."

Dorman hurried aft toward the weapons officer. Zukerman stepped closer and lowered his voice. "You're going to launch early?"

"We don't have much time. The batteries don't have enough power to take this at a leisurely pace and get us far enough away to avoid detection."

"Then perhaps we should surface and confirm our orders."

Harnoy stood. "Perhaps you should follow the orders we've received. Or I'll have you confined to the brig."

*   *   *

Geller sat behind the steering wheel of his BMW and watched as the Learjet settled onto the runway at MacArthur Airport, a commuter airport just a few miles outside Islip, halfway to the far end of Long Island. As the plane rolled to a stop on the tarmac, Geller drove between the hangars and let the BMW idle toward the plane. The engines were still turning as he steered the car alongside it and came to a stop with the hood beneath the wing.

The fuselage door opened and an attendant appeared. Moments later, Holsten stepped out and came down the steps. He walked to the car, opened the door, and climbed in on the passenger side.

"I assume everything went as planned," Geller said as he steered the car toward the gate.

"As long as we have the photographs, Leon Bain will do whatever he's told." Holsten reclined the seat back and closed his eyes. "You're sure the president will stick to the script on this?"

"He's the one who thought of it."

From the airport, they followed the Sunrise Highway along the southern edge of the island and slowly made their way toward the city. Near JFK Airport, they drove even farther south and wound their way past Rockaway Beach, then onto Flatbush Avenue. The route was a little out of the way but Holsten enjoyed seeing parts of Brooklyn he hadn't visited in a while. When they reached the Brooklyn-Queens Expressway, he expected Geller to steer the car onto the on-ramp. Instead, they turned left into the Red Hook Container Terminal.

Holsten glanced around. "What's in here?"

Geller reached behind the seat once more and this time came out with an automatic pistol. A silencer was attached to the muzzle. Before Holsten could react, Geller put the muzzle against his head and squeezed the trigger. Holsten's body slumped against the window, then Geller shot him once more.

"Sorry about that." He tucked the pistol into the pocket behind the seat. "Can't have any loose ends on this one."

Geller continued past the rows of containers until he came to a green one that was open. Two men stood by it, waiting. Geller brought the car to a stop. One of them opened the car door, slipped his hands beneath Holsten's arms, and lifted his body from the seat. The other grabbed the legs and kicked the car door closed with his foot. Together the two men lugged Holsten's body into the container as Geller drove away.

CHAPTER 54
NEW JERSEY SHORE

CRUSE ARRIVED BACK AT POINT PLEASANT a little after two in the morning. He parked the car out front and trudged up the steps to the first floor. The house was dark and quiet as he entered. Too dark, and too quiet. He walked down the hall to the bedroom where Lyman had put her luggage. The room was empty. From the looks of the bed, it had not been slept in.

In the dining room, he found the table clean and bare. The file boxes were gone, along with the laptop and flash drive. Even the bags with the unused external hard drives were gone. He stood there a moment listening to the waves as they crashed on shore behind the house and wondered what to do next. It was two in the morning. He hadn't slept in days. And everything he needed to prove his case was on that laptop or in those boxes. Without them, he was sunk.

"I might as well catch the next plane to Istanbul," he sighed.

"That's not a bad idea," a voice said. "But I have a different idea."

Cruse wheeled around to see Foster Goodall standing in the kitchen doorway. "What are you doing here?"

"I could ask you the same thing."

"Where's Lyman?"

"Not sure," Goodall shrugged. "She was already gone when we arrived."

"And the records?"

"We recovered most of them. Where have you been, Richard?"

"I had some people to talk to."

"I know you tried to find Geller. Who else did you go see?"

"Someone at State." Cruse blinked several times and rubbed his eyes. "Foster," he said, suddenly feeling weary and tired, "there's something going on. Something really big is about to happen."

"What is it?"

"I don't know. Something in the Middle East."

"An attack?"

"Yes. But that's not all of it. There's more to it than that. I just don't know what."

"Well," Goodall said, folding his arms across his chest, "from my view, you're on thin ice. You've been in tough spots before, but this one may be the last. Your career is hanging by a thread."

"I'm not worried about my career." Cruse ran his hands through his hair. "Where's Lyman? What did you do with her?"

"Like I said, I don't know where she is, and frankly, I don't care. She doesn't work for me. She's not my problem."

"She's a good agent." Cruse looked Goodall in the eye. "I got her into this. If she's in trouble, blame it on me."

"I honestly don't know where she is. But we do know how you got the warrant."

"Is Charlotte in trouble?"

"That depends."

"On what?"

"On what you decide about the offer I'm going to make."

"Which is?"

"You take a transfer to the office in El Paso, forget about Geller, Wilson, and your friend John Sladen. And we'll forget any of this ever happened."

"What about Lyman?"

"If we find her, we'll make sure she gets treated fairly."

"Nothing on her record."

"I don't know about *nothing*, but she'll still have a career."

"How do I know you're telling me the truth?"

"You don't. But, Richard, you know me. I brought you into the agency.

And I've been your boss for the past ten years. I'm also your friend and I'm telling you, as a friend, this is your only option."

Cruse looked away. "They're pretty mad?"

"Forget them. I'd shoot you myself if I thought I could get away with it." Goodall dropped his hands by his side. "Report for duty in El Paso in two days."

"Otherwise?"

"Otherwise, you'll be on the Most Wanted list. You got a problem with that?"

Cruse winced. "El Paso?"

"It's as far away as I could send you and still have you in North America. There's not an opening in Anchorage."

"But El Paso?"

"I had to go out on a limb to get you that. There are a lot of people who want you out of the bureau, and one or two who want you dead." Goodall glanced at his watch. "I have to get back to New York. They could use your expertise in El Paso."

CHAPTER 55
AL UDEID AIR BASE, QATAR

IN THE US AIR AND SPACE Operations Center, Randy Shawell stared at the screen on his desk and did his best to stay awake. Part of the North American Aerospace Defense Command, the center in Qatar was tasked with monitoring the skies above the Middle East in support of operations in the region. For the past seven hours Shawell had checked and rechecked the latest radar and satellite images, searching for the slightest indication of a threat to US and NATO forces. Thankfully he had found none. He was about to go for another cup of coffee when a red blip appeared on the screen indicating a single aircraft taking off from a base in Israel. He moved the cursor over the blip and saw it was an Israeli Eitan unmanned drone. According to information on the screen, it had just taken off from Ramon Airbase.

Roughly the size of an airliner, the Eitan was a jumbo among drones. In the world of military arms, its development was a huge coup for Israel's indigenous aircraft industry and marked the entry of Israel's military industry into the upper echelon of weapons technology. The Israeli Air Force operated several versions of the drone, most of them equipped with cameras and sensitive listening devices. They routinely flew from a base near the Lebanese border. But from the signature on the screen, created by telltale leaks of electrical impulses, this one was equipped with offensive electronic technology designed to render electrical and communications facilities inoperable.

Shawell turned to a second screen on his desk and brought up real-time images of Ramon Airbase. His heart skipped a beat at what he saw. Twenty-five aircraft, a mixture of older-model F-16s and F-15s, sat on the taxiway alongside the base's main runway. "Where are they going?" he whispered to himself as he turned back to the first screen. By then the drone was over Lebanon and had turned to the east on a path that, if continued, would take it into Syrian airspace.

"Why would they send a drone like that over Syria?" In the same instant, his heart rate quickened as he thought of an answer. "An airstrike in Syria. The Israelis are planning an airstrike against Syria."

A red phone sat to the right of the desk. It provided a direct line to NORAD headquarters in Colorado Springs. Shawell snatched the receiver from the cradle. Rusty Jackson, the watch commander in the Operations Center in Colorado answered immediately.

"NORAD watch commander."

Shawell spoke before Jackson had finished. "I'm tracking an unmanned drone out of Ramon Airbase in Israel. Heading north into Syrian airspace."

"Probably just eavesdropping."

"This one is equipped for electronic warfare. And I have twenty-five attack aircraft on the tarmac at Ramon. F-16s and 15s. Engines running. All of them armed."

"Copy that," Jackson snapped, suddenly alert and engaged. "We have the situation on the screen now."

*   *   *

At the NORAD Operations Center in Colorado, Jackson stared at the screen on the wall and watched as the Eitan drone continued eastward over Syria.

An analyst seated across the room spoke up. "Something going on?"

"Not sure. Israeli drone over Lebanon, headed into Syrian airspace."

The analyst glanced at a screen on his desk. "Equipped for electronic warfare."

"Yeah. And look at this." Jackson put up images from Ramon Airbase on a screen to the right.

"That doesn't look like a training mission," the analyst suggested.

"But where are they going?" Then their eyes met in a look of realization. "Oh no," Jackson whispered. "They're going to Iran."

"They'll never make it."

"Find me images of every Israeli air base!" Jackson shouted. "Get them on the screen now."

Two phones sat to the left of his desk. One gave him immediate access to Air Force General Spencer Murchison, the commander of NORAD. The other was a direct line to the White House situation room. He picked up the phone for Murchison. The call was answered on the second ring.

"Sir, we have a situation," Jackson began.

"What is it?" Murchison sounded sleepy and irritable.

"An Israeli drone equipped for electronic warfare headed east through Syrian airspace. Twenty-five aircraft, 15s and 16s, ready for takeoff from Ramon, armed and—"

"Alert the White House," Murchison ordered, suddenly wide awake. "I'm on my way."

Jackson hung up the phone and picked up the second receiver from the desk. Within seconds, a young Navy commander answered.

"This is Neuhaus."

"Neuhaus, this is Cheyenne Mountain. We have a situation."

*   *   *

Andrew Stanton was sound asleep when he felt a hand against his shoulder. "Mr. President," a voice called. "Mr. President."

Stanton opened his eyes to see a man dressed in a US Navy uniform standing beside the bed. "Who are you?"

"Neuhaus, sir."

"There better be a good reason for this."

"They need you downstairs, sir. In the situation room."

Stanton raised himself up on his elbows. Beyond the end of the bed he could see the door was open. A Secret Service agent stood in the sitting area outside the bedroom. Stanton looked over at Neuhaus. "What is it?"

"They need you in the situation room, sir."

Stanton pushed aside the cover, swung his legs over the side of the bed, and stood. "Where's Pete?"

"Mr. McWhinney is on his way, sir."

Ten minutes later, Stanton was dressed and headed down the hall. Flanked by his Secret Service detail and led by Neuhaus, he moved quickly to the stairs. "You don't know what this is about?"

"Sir," Neuhaus explained, "I'm the watch commander for the night. My job is to man the room and awaken you if there's a problem."

"Which you did."

"Yes, sir."

"And you don't know anything else."

"I'm not allowed to discuss it with you, sir."

*   *   *

Haden Upchurch came from his house to the driveway and crawled in the back of the limousine. He checked his watch. It was almost one in the morning. The driver steered the car to the street and turned right.

As they drove through the night toward the White House, Upchurch took out his cell phone and called Paul Catlett.

"We need to play this just right."

"Yeah," Catlett responded.

"I figure we let Beamon carry the load."

"He has a way of moving the discussion toward the correct military solution without being too overbearing."

"Right. Which is exactly what we need here."

"But we have to keep Baker out of the discussion. Once she gets going, there's no telling what she'll say."

"Beamon can handle her."

"Do we need to tell him?"

"No, he's smart enough to know that without anyone having to explain it."

"Think they're really doing it?"

Upchurch knew the question was rhetorical. They both saw the same satellite photographs. Read the same message traffic. But they were experienced players in the high-stakes intelligence game and this was how they maintained a governing consensus without explicitly saying so—establish a version of the facts and commit to it through conversation. "Yeah, they're doing it." Upchurch ended the call and leaned back, resting his head against the seat as the car moved quickly past the Capitol Building. This would be a long day and he would do it on just one hour's sleep.

*   *   *

Stanton reached the situation room to find Upchurch, Brown, Catlett, and Baker already there. Admiral Beamon, chairman of the Joint Chiefs of Staff, stood at the far end of the room, near a television screen that lined the wall. A young naval lieutenant sat at a desk in the corner, ready to assist Beamon with a smooth presentation of the latest information.

Beamon snapped to attention and those around the table stood as Stanton entered the room. "At ease," Stanton sighed. He pulled a chair from beneath the head of the table and sat down. "What's this all about?"

"Mr. President," Beamon began, "an hour ago NORAD picked up an unmanned Israeli drone as it took off from Ramon Airbase in southern Israel. The drone was equipped for electronic warfare. It flew north across Israel, through Lebanese and Syrian airspace, and is now exiting Iraq."

"You mean, moving into Iranian territory."

"Yes, sir."

"On another of their spy missions?"

"No, sir, this one is equipped for electronic warfare. Not electronic eavesdropping. We believe it's there to jam radar and communications systems ahead of these." He pointed to the screen as the image changed to show a taxiway at Ramon Airbase lined with airplanes. "Twenty-five F15s and F16s prepared to take off from Ramon Airbase. Similar numbers have already left from a dozen other sites around Israel."

"At dozens of bases?" Stanton looked surprised. "That could be over three hundred planes."

"Yes, sir."

"How many do they have left?"

"About half that many more, sir."

"Those planes were armed, I assume?"

"Yes, sir. All of them were armed. Most carried a dozen five-hundred-pound bombs."

"Where are they now?"

"Not far behind the drone, sir. They're about to enter Iranian airspace."

"We have AWACS in the area?"

"Sir, we have control of the skies throughout the entire region."

"Can they pull this off?"

"It's a smart plan," Beamon smiled. "I think they'll do some damage, sir."

In spite of the political posturing and infighting over the past several months, Stanton was relieved that Israel had finally acted. At least now they had a way forward and he didn't have to shoulder the blame for it. Israel could take the lead and bear the international criticism that would surely follow. Still, it was not in the United States' best interest for them to fail, either.

"All right," Stanton acknowledged. "What do you recommend?"

"There isn't much for us to do, sir. The drone will render Iran's air defenses incapable of effectively defending the attack. Israeli jets will drop their bombs and then head for home. The only problem they will encounter is refueling."

"How many planes will they lose?"

"Difficult to give a hard number. They have 707s that have been converted to tankers. But, as we discussed earlier, those don't give them enough capacity to refuel this many aircraft for that long a flight."

"Anything we can do to assist?"

"We have carriers in the area that could supply fuel. And some of the Israeli pilots are trained to land on our ships. But doing that would be problematic."

"What do you mean?"

"He means," Upchurch interjected, "we'd have to tell the Israelis it's okay to land. And then they would have to get there."

Stanton glanced at his watch. "Isn't there someone awake at the Israeli Embassy?"

"Of course," Baker replied.

"Mr. President," Upchurch continued, "our AWACS planes can contact those fighters directly."

"No," Stanton snapped, cutting him off. "We aren't getting in that deep. They started it; they can finish it. I'll give them the fuel they need to get home. And if their pilots get in an emergency situation, they can land on our carriers. But I'm not putting our people in a position that makes it look like we told them which targets to hit, and we're not making it look like we knew about this before it happened."

"Yes, sir."

Stanton looked down the table to Beamon. "Which carriers are in the area?"

"The *Abraham Lincoln* and the *Carl Vinson*."

"Put them on alert. Have them ready to go if this thing falls apart."

"Yes, sir."

Stanton turned to Baker. "Kathleen, you can get a message about this to the Israelis?"

She gestured with the phone already in her hand. "I have them on the line now, Mr. President."

CHAPTER 56
RAMON AIRBASE, BEERSHEBA, ISRAEL

YOSSI KOLLEK SAT IN THE COCKPIT of his F-16 and stared up at the sky. In the briefing room they said this wasn't a drill, but they didn't have to tell anyone. They all knew it as soon as they collected the cell phones and confined them to base. Now they were on the taxiway and ready to go. The Eitan drone was more than an hour ahead of them. By now it was well inside Iraqi airspace, maybe even all the way to Iran. With it, they could render radar and communications systems useless. Only the Iranian Air Force could stop the attack now, and even they were no match for what was headed their way.

On the tarmac, telltale red lights blinked on the wingtips of the planes that would accompany Yossi. Each aircraft in his group was armed with two of the most recent bunker-busting bombs. Designed to penetrate hardened underground facilities of any strength, they hung beneath the belly of the planes. On each of the wings, special racks held three five-hundred-pound bombs. More than enough firepower to destroy their assigned targets.

For an instant, Yossi's mind raced back to his family asleep in bed at home. He had missed his daughter's recital the evening before. He hoped they got the message that he was okay. In a few hours they would rise to meet the day. Breakfast, school, and his son's soccer game later in the afternoon. If he returned by … Yossi pushed the thought from his mind. *I must focus on the matter at hand,* he told himself.

From the maps Mintz used in the flight group briefing, Yossi knew this was an all-out attack, a preemptive strike to destroy Iran's nuclear capability.

Unlike the surgical bombing of the past, this time there would be no doubt about the origin of the attack. He wasn't told the extent of the mission but he was sure that dozens of other aircraft were leaving from bases all across the country. All those planes, hitting all those targets, would leave little room for ambiguity about who actually sent them or the locations they struck.

Then the radio in Yossi's flight helmet crackled. "Strike leader. You are cleared for takeoff."

"Roger," Yossi replied. "Clear for takeoff." With his right hand he nudged the throttle forward and steered the plane onto the runway. Two F-16s took up positions with him, one at either end of his wingtips.

In the headset he heard the voice of a pilot, "This is it?"

"This is it," Yossi replied. Then he shoved the throttle forward and the plane burst to life. In a matter of seconds, the three planes shot down the runway and rose into the sky. Once aloft, they circled the air base twice as the sortie assembled. When all twenty-five planes were in place, they banked to the north and headed up the Mediterranean coast.

Moments later, a voice spoke in Yossi's headset. "What about the Syrians?"

"The Americans have them covered," someone replied.

"Cut the chatter, guys," Yossi cautioned.

At the border, they entered Syrian airspace and adjusted their course to the east, on a path that took them directly over Aleppo. A few minutes later, the planes crossed into Iraqi airspace west of Tel Afar. So far, their flight had taken less than half an hour.

When they reached the border with Iran, Yossi keyed the microphone. "Departure point approaching."

One by one the group broke into teams. Yossi checked his course and confirmed the onboard computer's target information. His team was headed to a uranium processing plant at Isfahan. The others would hit the uranium enrichment plants at Natanz and Tabas, the heavy water facility at Arak, and the Russian-built reactor at Bushehr. He was glad he hadn't drawn that assignment. The team that hit Bushehr might not make it back.

By now, Yossi thought, *the prime minister has phoned the White House. No doubt the Americans will feign shock and displeasure at the plans now set in motion.*

Yossi smiled. They knew what was coming. And if they did not know in advance, they at least hoped for it. The whole world hoped for Israel to solve their Iranian problem. And now here they were, about to—

A light flashed on the control panel and a tone squawked in the headset. Yossi pressed the microphone. "Target locked."

Pilots from the planes flying with him responded, "Target acquired and locked."

Already in attack formation, the planes rolled to the left and plunged toward the drop zone. Then through the cockpit canopy, the cluster of gray steel buildings came into sight thousands of feet below.

CHAPTER 57
WASHINGTON, D.C.

WHEN PETE MCWHINNEY, the president's chief of staff, arrived in the situation room he found the table littered with coffee cups, candy wrappers, half-eaten sandwiches, and crumpled napkins. "Sorry it took so long," he said apologetically. "I was in Philadelphia for the dinner."

Stanton nodded. "How did it go?"

"Not bad." McWhinney took a seat at the corner of the table near Stanton. "They briefed me on the ride in. Is it still happening?"

"Looks like they just bombed the last sites about a half hour ago. Last of the planes are heading out of Iranian airspace right now."

"How bad is it?"

"Looks like it was an all-out preemptive strike."

"Any casualties?"

"I'm sure there were plenty on the ground."

"The Israelis," McWhinney insisted. "Did the Israelis incur casualties?"

"I don't know. We don't have an official report. I don't think anyone was shot down."

"Mr. President," McWhinney leaned closer and lowered his voice, "your Secret Service detail is outside in the hall. They want you to move over to the East Wing."

Stanton had of look of incredulity. "They want me in the Tank?"

"Yes sir, Mr. President. It's much safer."

"No way." Stanton shook his head vehemently. "I'm not going to that bunker. Brings back too many negative images of George Bush going underground on September 11. I'm not giving the Republicans that same imagery. Especially not in an election year." He tapped the tabletop with his finger for emphasis. "I'm staying right here where I am."

Admiral Beamon spoke up. "Mr. President, we're getting our first reports of damage from the attacks."

"How does it look?"

"Israeli Air Force jets armed with bunker-buster bombs hit a uranium mine at Saghand. Looks like they cratered it pretty well, sir. Heavy damage."

"What about the reactors?"

"They struck the Bushehr and Natanz reactors, the uranium processing plant at Isfahan, and the enrichment facility at Qom. In addition, three submarines, using Harpoon and cruise missiles, launched follow-on attacks against the two reactors."

"Did they take them out?" Stanton asked. "That's what we need to know."

"It's too early to tell exactly how much damage was done, but based on our initial data we think the reactors have been totally destroyed."

"What about the facility at Qom?"

"It's been damaged," Beamon grimaced, "but we're not certain it's beyond repair."

"What kind of repair?"

"They have ten centrifuge buildings at that site. The Israelis hit two of them. One was destroyed. Another sustained heavy damage but part of it is still standing. The other eight processing buildings escaped unharmed."

"What does that mean?"

Baker spoke up. "It means, Mr. President, they can continue to process uranium at that site."

"But that's just one site. Right? They're down to a single site? That ought to slow them down."

"Mr. President," Catlett interjected, "the Iranians have a stockpile of uranium that has already been enriched to twenty percent. That's the most difficult and time-consuming step in the process. Getting it from there to the necessary purity for a bomb is a simple and much quicker matter. These attacks have seriously crippled Iran's long-term program, but not the short-term. Based on our analysis of the situation, this facility could be producing weapons-grade uranium by tomorrow night."

"This was what I was talking about!" Stanton shouted. "I tried to tell Yedaya this very thing!" He struck the table with his fist. "They got us into this, then they failed to finish the job. This was always the risk they never understood."

"Sir," Beamon responded, "the Israelis hit them pretty hard."

"But they will be up and running again next week?"

"Not all of it, sir."

Stanton pointed to Catlett, "He just said they could be operational by tomorrow."

"They have a limited supply of twenty-percent uranium," Beamon explained. "It's a very limited commodity for them."

Stanton glanced at Catlett. "How much do they have, Paul?"

"Probably enough for three or four bombs, sir."

"Well, there you go." Stanton threw up his hands in frustration. "Just three or four bombs." His voice dripped with sarcasm. "What about their other facilities? The military bases and missiles."

"They were not the targets of this operation, sir," Beamon explained. "Those locations went untouched. Except for two sites that dealt with the space program, Israel confined the strikes to Iran's nuclear facilities."

"Space program?" Stanton looked puzzled. "Iran has a space program?"

"They've launched a few objects into space," Catlett offered. "Nothing that really works."

"Yet," Baker added.

"Right," Stanton agreed. "My point exactly." He looked back to Beamon. "What did they hit?"

"A launch site," Beamon continued. "And a tracking station."

"Interesting," Stanton mused. Then in the next instant he moved on. "What about the refueling option we gave them?"

"Three planes that struck a site near Shiraz in southern Iran landed on the *Abraham Lincoln*."

"Did anyone notice?"

"So far, just the crew onboard the carrier, sir."

A phone rang. The naval aide assisting Beamon took the call, then handed Beamon a note. He turned to the president. "Sir, Prime Minister Yedaya is speaking now." An image of Yedaya appeared on the screen. He stood at a podium outside a building at an undisclosed location in Tel Aviv.

"Earlier today," Yedaya began, "elements of the Israeli Air Force and Navy launched a coordinated strike against Iran's nuclear production facilities. While I regret that the failure of international attempts to curb Iran's quest for nuclear weapons has resulted in this action, I am pleased to announce that the mission was a success and that no Israeli lives have been lost in the process. Israel respects the right of every sovereign nation to protect itself. However, that same right extends also to Israel. Iranian leaders have repeatedly stated their desire to drive us into the sea and to otherwise eliminate all Jews from the planet. Having endured one Holocaust, we do not intend to sit by and watch while another is fomented against us. Our actions today, though serious and regrettable, were nevertheless necessary to ensure the security of our people. We respect the Iranian people and extend our heartfelt sympathy to the families of those who were lost or injured as a consequence of today's missions."

When he concluded his statement, Yedaya turned away from the podium and disappeared inside the building. Before his remarks could be analyzed, Rasoul Moussaoui, president of Iran, appeared on the screen, speaking from a room in the presidential palace.

"Today, the world witnessed the most heinous act of aggression in the history of mankind. An attack justified by lies and political rhetoric falsely accusing us of threatening the peace and stability of the region. I remind you that in the past fifty years, Iran has attacked no one. Yet we have been attacked now three times by our neighbors—once by the armies of Iraq and twice by Israel. Yet they say we are the threat to the region. We have repeatedly assured international authorities that our pursuit of nuclear technology is solely for peaceful purposes and we reiterate that assurance again today, even in the face of these most egregious acts of war against us. Israel had no right to attack us. And the United States had no right to assist in that attack. We are a sovereign nation with every right and privilege of self-defense and we call on the nations of the world to join us in opposing this senseless and cruel attack. Both of our aggressors will pay a price for what they have done to us today. The United States cannot aid our enemies with impunity. They cannot assist the Jews and act as if they are a friend to Islam. The principles of law and justice will not allow it."

Upchurch glanced down to avoid making eye contact with Catlett. Stanton seemed not to notice and instead looked across the room at Admiral Beamon. "I assume that was a threat."

"Yes, sir, Mr. President. That's what it was."

"Think they'll follow through on that threat?"

"Yes, sir," Beamon nodded slowly. "I think they will try. As we discussed earlier, Iran still has the same military capability it had before the attacks." His assistant handed him another note. He glanced at it and looked back at Stanton. "Reports are arriving now that indicate their missile batteries are preparing to launch."

"Do we have a plan?" Baker asked.

The image on the screen switched to a map. Beamon pointed to it. "This map shows some five hundred targets inside Iran." On the map, red dots covered every region of Iran. "All of them are essential components of Iran's military capability."

Stanton stared at the map. "Which ones are most important?"

Beamon nodded to his assistant. Most of the red dots disappeared from the screen. "About a hundred sites control ninety percent of their military capability."

Stanton pointed. "We can hit those hundred sites?"

"We can hit all five hundred," Beamon answered.

"All five hundred?"

"Yes, sir, Mr. President. You give the 'go' order and we can hit them all."

"Okay," Stanton nodded. "Let's wait and see if they actually launch a counterstrike."

CHAPTER 58
WASHINGTON, D.C.

ANN JOHNSON, THE WHITE HOUSE press secretary, stood at the podium in the briefing room and stared out at the press corps. Still well before sunrise, she'd been there for over an hour, fielding endless questions about the attack on Iran. Did Israel really act alone? What did the president know? Was the meeting last week with Yedaya a planning session for the attack? Were reports of their sharp disagreement really just a cover?

When they weren't needling her with questions about that, they were raising the incessant rumors—that Iran's refinery capacity had been eliminated, that the oil fields were on fire, that ships traversing the Strait of Hormuz were being sunk. She answered each of them with a swift, concise answer designed to convey the idea of information without actually giving any information at all. Carefully couching the slightest hint of substance in just the right language, with an ever so delicate nuance. Mentally checking every syllable before she said anything, to make certain that no unguarded word slipped past her lips.

Then Tyler Houston, a reporter from the *Ledger Daily*, raised his hand. Brainy and genuinely smarter than anyone in the room, Houston left the routine questions for other reporters, taking note of what they asked and how the questions were answered, but reserving his time for something else, something so entirely "other" that almost no one beat him to his topic. Johnson had been waiting for this moment since the briefing began. Houston would ask his questions, they would move the discussion off topic, and she could use it to wrap things up. Houston's hand went in the air and Johnson called on him.

"When commodities markets opened this morning the price of oil spiked. It's now over two hundred dollars per barrel and still climbing. Does the administration think these prices will be sustained for the foreseeable future?"

"I have no way of knowing that and neither does the president. Not right now."

"Is there any concern that oil prices this high will plunge the economy into a recession?"

"Yes, Tyler, I think it's safe to say we're all concerned about that."

"We're in an election year," he continued. "Has there been any discussion about how a downward turn in the economy might impact the president's reelection campaign?"

"As you know," Johnson began, "the president doesn't discuss campaign strategy in the Oval Office and we don't brief about it from this podium. You'd have to check with the campaign staff for a specific answer to your question. But I'm sure most political pundits would expect that a drop in the economy would have a negative effect on voter opinion of an incumbent president." Across the room, heads turned in her direction, eyes opened wide. She ignored them and continued talking. "All of which is proof positive we had nothing to do with planning the attacks on Iran or coordinating anything with Israel prior to these attacks."

From the moment she heard the words leave her mouth, she knew she had as much as admitted that the president set administration policy based on how it might affect his chances at winning reelection. She knew it and, judging by the stunned silence and startled looks, everyone in the room knew it too.

"I don't th-think that ..." Johnson stammered. "Look, it's been a long morning. I mean ..." Finally she threw up her hands in a gesture of frustration. "Never mind what I mean." She stepped from the rostrum and charged toward the door.

As she came into the hall, McWhinney was already there to meet her, his face red with anger. "What were you thinking?"

She raised her hands in the air to cut him off. "I know!" she shouted. "I know. I know. It was a stupid thing to say."

She turned toward her office. McWhinney followed. "We've been working day and night to avoid the appearance that campaign politics has any effect on White House policy decisions. And now you just handed them the biggest quote of the last four years."

"I was trying to—"

"I don't care what you were trying to do," McWhinney blurted. "What you did was give them the gaffe they need to make us all look like idiots. You told them we made decisions about Middle East policy based on political considerations."

"I just need a minute." She turned toward her office door.

McWhinney was still behind her. "You need a—"

They both came to an abrupt halt when they found Johnson's office filled with staff, their eyes glued to the television on the credenza.

"What is the meaning of this?" Johnson bellowed. "This isn't the White House TV room. You don't have anything better to do than watch television?!"

"Shhhh," someone said, gesturing for quiet.

Someone else pointed to the screen. "Talbot is at it again."

On the screen, Alex Talbot appeared on the lawn in front of a plain white church. No flags, no campaign signs, no handlers. Just Talbot and a bank of microphones.

"These are fragile times." He spoke in his most sincere voice. "In less than twelve hours our economy has gone from robust to the brink of disaster. Today, as commuters pull up to the gas pump, they're finding gas at triple and quadruple the price they would have paid just yesterday. We have folks in some states paying twenty dollars a gallon. While I support the president in his efforts to deal with this crisis, I must say, and I mean this with all sincerity, this is a situation he brought on himself and now the consequences of his actions have been visited upon us all."

A groan went up from the crowd gathered in Johnson's office. Then just as quickly, the room fell silent as Talbot continued.

"His failure to confront the growing threat of a nuclear Iran put us in this position. Because of his weak stance in the region, Iranian leaders concluded they could do anything without challenge from us. And that's just what they did, pushing their nuclear program to the brink of success in the few short years this administration has been in office. Those same failed policies led Israel to conclude that they could rely on no one but themselves to ensure the safety and security of their country. Unfortunately, presidential decisions don't exist in a vacuum. What is decided in the Oval Office has consequences far beyond that room. And now here we are, each of us once again bearing the weight of a consequence we never sought.

"But Americans are tough and we can weather this. We can get through it if we just keep working. Keep doing the things we do to earn a living and to make ends meet. This is not the time to shrink back. We have to be tough. We have to show ourselves and the world who we really are. And then we have to fix this.

"A stronger America could have prevented this situation from ever getting to the point that Israel felt so threatened, so forsaken they had to take their defense in their own hands. I urge the president to do all in his power to see this action through to its conclusion, to stand with Israel, and to support her in what will surely be an aggressive response from Iran and its allies."

Johnson looked at McWhinney. "I have to get back in there."

"No!" He took hold of her arm as she turned toward the hallway. "Let someone else do it. If you go in there, you'll have to answer follow-up questions on your earlier remark. We don't need that right now."

"I'll have to answer them tomorrow, too," Johnson countered. "You want someone else to brief tomorrow? And the day after that? And the day after that?"

McWhinney let go of her arm. "Okay," he sighed. "It's your neck."

"Yeah," she snarled, "it is my neck. And I'm just like the Israelis. No one is going to save my neck except me."

CHAPTER 59
COLORADO SPRINGS, COLORADO

AT THE NORAD OPERATIONS CENTER, deep inside Cheyenne Mountain, General Murchison finally took time to sit and gather his thoughts. He'd been there since the call roused him from sleep in the middle of the night. Now, after moving from crisis to crisis, he collapsed in his chair and picked up a Styrofoam cup filled with coffee. He sipped from it as his mind worked over the situation they now faced.

Israel obviously had inflicted significant damage on Iran, setting back their nuclear program indefinitely, but Iran emerged from those attacks with its military largely intact and unscathed. Classic strategy called for a counterstrike. Murchison had no doubt that counterattack would come. When that happened, and it most surely would come, he would face yet one more crisis—whether President Stanton would order the kind of response the situation demanded. "It won't be easy," he whispered to himself. But the consequences of not responding could be lethal. He didn't have to wait long for an answer.

A screen on the wall at the far end of the room displayed a map of the Middle East. As Murchison sat contemplating the day's events and what might happen next, a blip appeared on the portion of the map that covered Iran. In rapid succession a second blip appeared, followed by one more, then another until the map was lit up by hundreds of small white dots.

"Sir," an analyst called out, "you'll want to take a look at this."

Murchison glanced up to see the map covered with white dots. His eyes opened wide. "Missiles?"

"Yes, sir."

Murchison picked up the phone for the White House. "We have a situation," he barked. "Are they still in the room?"

"No, sir."

"Then get them back!" he shouted. "And let me speak to Admiral Beamon."

*   *   *

By the time the president and his national security team returned to the White House situation room, Iran's counterattack against Israel was well under way. Hundreds of long-range missiles, launched from deep inside Iran, rained down on key Israeli targets. American-made Patriot missiles previously deployed during the first Gulf War, along with Iron Dome, Magic Wand, and Arrow defense systems intercepted some of the incoming warheads, but many more reached their targets. Port facilities at Tel Aviv, Haifa, and Ashdod suffered heavy damage. Major highway interchanges and critical rail yards were obliterated. Key office buildings crumbled to the ground amid multiple strikes. Oil refineries were in ruins and gasoline tank farms erupted in blasts that shattered windows for miles.

As President Stanton took a seat at the head of the briefing table, Admiral Beamon once again stood before the video screen at the far end of the room.

Stanton pointed to the screen. "What do we know?"

"Within the last hour, more than two hundred Iranian missiles were launched against targets inside Israel." Beamon gestured over his shoulder to the screen. "Each of those dots you see on the map behind me represents a missile launch."

"How many actually made it to the target?"

"Too many, sir. We're still gathering information to arrive at an exact number, but the damage has been devastating."

Upchurch leaned forward from his chair. "Our reports indicate refineries, highways, rail yards, port facilities, several government buildings—all destroyed."

Stanton glanced back at Beamon. "They were actually able to hit their targets? Not just throw up some near misses?"

"Yes, sir. Unlike past attacks, this time they reached their intended targets."

Catlett spoke up. "Our analysis indicates these missile attacks showed remarkable accuracy, planning, and effectiveness."

Stanton once again turned his attention to Beamon. "Have we seen the end of it? Is that all they have?"

"No, sir. This represents their single-launch capacity, but it doesn't totally deplete their stockpile."

Catlett spoke up. "They launched them this way because they knew we would see it and they knew they might not get a chance for a second strike."

Stanton glanced back to Beamon. "We can strike back?"

"Absolutely," Beamon replied. He stepped to a phone near his end of the room. "You give the order and we can hit every location from which their missiles were launched."

"Every location?"

"Every known location. The ones they used in this attack and the ones we know about that they haven't used. We can get them all."

"Will that end it?"

"They might have a few left after that, but not many. And we can clean those up as they come online to launch."

"You're certain of this?"

"As certain as a military officer can be, sir."

"Wait," Baker blurted out. "Don't we want to talk about this? I mean, this situation is bigger than merely responding to an attack. We're about to wipe out a significant country's military. There will be casualties. Civilians will die. We can't expect to merely launch a surgical strike and get away clean. Not now. Not after all that's been said and done. We're about to get into the kind of war we've been trying to avoid."

"We've talked," Stanton snapped. "And we can't wait. If we're going to stop these attacks, we have to do it now while there's still something in Israel left to defend." No one joined the argument to support Baker and she sank back in her chair. Stanton caught Beamon's eye. "Okay," he nodded grimly. "You have the order. Do it."

*   *   *

Aboard the submarine *USS Ohio* Admiral Blundell sat in the launch chair and waited for word from his weapons officer. They'd been given the order to attack a target package inside Iran, using conventional warheads. For a moment, he'd contemplated disobeying the order and equipping the ship's missiles with nuclear warheads. But he knew his crew would never follow such an order and if he tried to force them, his chief petty officer would shoot him on sight. He glanced in the chief's direction. "What's our depth?"

"One hundred feet, sir."

"Make sure they can't see us."

"Nothing within two hundred miles of us, sir."

A voice squawked over the intercom, "Admiral, this is Weapons."

Blundell keyed his microphone. "This is the Admiral. Whadd'ya got?"

"Missiles in the tubes are armed, programmed, and ready, sir."

"Very well," Blundell replied. He turned to the firing officer seated at a panel a few feet to the right. "Mr. McClinton, you may fire at will."

"Aye aye, Admiral," McClinton responded. "Fire at will."

A row of indicator lights on the panel showed green. Then, in rapid sequence from left to right, the lights turned red as a full complement of Trident missiles launched from the ship's twenty-two tubes. Seconds later a voice came over the intercom once again. "Admiral, this is Weapons."

"Go ahead, Weapons."

"All missiles away, sir."

"Very well," Blundell responded. "Reload and prepare for a second round."

*   *   *

In New York, long before news of the Iranian counterstrike and the U.S. response reached reporters, Mattie Lewis, host of the popular cable news talk show *Political Perspective*, took a seat behind the desk on the studio set. Seated across from her was that day's guest, former Army Colonel Edwin Miller.

The floor producer counted down the seconds, then a red light appeared atop one of the cameras. Lewis looked into the lens with a serious expression. "We're continuing now with our guest, former United States Army Colonel Edwin Miller." She looked at him. "Colonel Miller, earlier today Alex Talbot took President Stanton to task for his weak foreign policy, suggesting that Israel's attack on Iran was a direct result of this administration's policy position in the Middle East. Have we forsaken Israel in her hour of need?"

"Mattie, Israel is doing our dirty work for us. Doing what we should have done all along."

"You think this was part of a planned strategy by the White House?"

"No," Miller said, shaking his head. "Not at all. In fact, it was quite the opposite. Iran has thumbed its nose at UN sanctions. Sanctions we proposed and cosponsored with a number of our allies. Yet we have done nothing to enforce those sanctions or call Iranian leadership to task for their blatant disregard for international consensus."

"So," Lewis began her next question, "when you say Israel is doing our dirty work for us, you don't think this was all a grand strategy hatched during Prime Minister Yedaya's recent White House visit?"

Miller grinned. "No, from what I've heard, the president and the prime minister nearly came to blows over that meeting. I don't think they agree on anything. At least not as it relates to policy in the Middle East."

"In his remarks earlier today about the attack, Iranian President Moussaoui made the argument that his country has never been the aggressor in the region." Lewis looked serious and earnest. "Suggesting that others have attacked them but they have attacked no one. Yet Israel still paints Iran as the regional bully. Was Iran really a threat that warranted an attack such as the one we've seen today?"

"Look," Miller responded. "There's a reason Iran has been the focus of attention. They haven't used their own army in the region, but they have sent money, weapons, and advisors to train and equip Hezbollah terrorists who do their work for them. Suicide bombers were encouraged to give their lives in senseless attacks against Israelis because Iran guaranteed substantial cash payments to the families of those who perpetrated those attacks. Material for the bombs came from Iran. Rockets regularly launched into Israel from Lebanon, Gaza, and the West Bank all came from Iran. So to say they haven't been active in the region is simply not true. But beyond that, Iran has chosen to engage in the seriously destabilizing pursuit of nuclear arms. Given their history of activism in the region, no one, Israel in particular, could afford to ignore the obvious threat."

"Will there be reprisals from Iran for this attack?" Lewis asked it as a question but the look on her face telegraphed the anticipated response.

"Most certainly." Miller paused to clear his throat. "And let me just add this to what I've already said. Arab countries in the region urged President Stanton to move against Iran. Saudi Arabia offered to underwrite the costs of a mission to bomb critical nuclear sites in Iran. Qatar offered bases for use in the effort. They all know and understand Iran's real intent is to become the dominant regional player."

"They conveyed those offers to the administration?"

"Yes," Miller nodded. "And President Stanton turned them down."

"Incredible," Lewis sighed. "So Israel has hit many locations inside Iran."

"They've inflicted severe damage on Iran's nuclear program. There may have been minimal damage at one or two locations, but the long-term effects will be important."

"What about Iran's ability to retaliate? We mentioned that earlier. You said you thought there would be a counterattack."

"Yes, and this is another point that needs to be made. This administration has steadfastly refused to provide Israel with long-range refueling tankers. As a result, the Israeli Air Force had to limit this attack to only those sites critical to the nuclear program. Iran still has the capability of launching a counterstrike—one I fear will hit Israelis very hard. Civilians, not just the military."

"And you're certain Iran will respond?"

"Yes."

"If they strike—when they strike—will President Stanton finish the job Israel began?"

"I certainly hope so." Miller had a skeptical look on his face. "But I have my doubts."

"So, we have about a minute left in this segment, where will all this end?"

"I would like to think this will end in the total annihilation of Iran's military, but I'm more prone to think Stanton will hit hard at first but fail to follow through."

"A negotiated ending?"

"Yes. And one that leaves Iran in a position to mount another nuclear challenge in the coming years."

* * *

A few hours later, Stanton was in the Oval Office preparing for a call to Prime Minister Yedaya. Stanton stood at a window and stared out at the lawn. Behind him, a door opened and Pete McWhinney entered.

"We're getting the call set up now, Mr. President."

Stanton spoke without turning around. "Has anything hit the news yet?"

"No, sir, not yet. They're still talking about whether you'll do it or not."

"Do it?"

"Whether you'll launch an attack to stop Iran from making further attacks on Israel."

"That's a sad state of affairs."

"It's cable news," McWhinney demurred.

"I'm not talking about that." Stanton turned away from the window to face McWhinney. "I'm talking about the fact that we must attack Iran to keep Iran from attacking Israel in response to Israel's attack on Iran." He shook his head in disgust. "You didn't tell me all this when you talked me into running for office."

"I thought I would break it to you gently."

The door opened, interrupting their not-so-friendly banter. Gladys

Moynihan, the president's secretary, appeared. "Mr. President, the prime minister is on the line."

Stanton moved behind the desk. McWhinney turned to leave. Stanton waved him off. "Stay," he said as he picked up the receiver.

"Mr. Prime Minister," Stanton began. "I understand you've been hit with a counterstrike."

"Yes, Mr. President," Yedaya replied. The strain in his voice was evident. "Many of our critical facilities have been destroyed. Others sustained heavy damage and we've incurred a significant number of civilian casualties."

"I'm sorry to hear that. I've ordered our forces in the region to respond. They're hitting every launch site Iran has used and all the sites we know about. And I've told them to take out any more locations that come online for a launch regardless of whether we knew about them before or not."

"Thank you, Mr. President."

"But Elazar, you have to halt any attempts at further attacks against them."

"They are attacking us," Yedaya argued.

"You attacked them. They attacked you. We hit all their launch sites. It has to end. We can't have a full-scale war. Syria won't sit quietly by. Jordan won't stay out of it. Egypt will be forced to act. It has to stop now."

"Syria has no capacity to wage war," Yedaya countered. "They are too busy fighting against their own people. As to the others, I don't think—"

"If you keep this up," Stanton interrupted, "you'll give them all plenty of reasons to forget their internal troubles and focus on you."

"Mr. President, we aren't fighting. We are defending."

"No, Elazar." Stanton was becoming angrier and more frustrated by the moment. "You're dragging us all into a war we can't win."

"Perhaps you can't win it, but we can."

Stanton was beside himself. He scowled at McWhinney, his fist tightly balled in a gesture of frustration. "We aren't in this for the same reasons. You have to know that. Our objectives are not the same."

"I understand that, Mr. President. But you must understand that Israel will do whatever she must in order to survive."

"This isn't surviving!" Stanton shouted. "This is suicide."

They continued to argue for another five minutes, then finally the call ended. Stanton hung up the phone and looked over at McWhinney. "This is insane!"

"That call could have gone better," McWhinney opined.

Stanton ignored his sarcasm. "They are playing us. Using us to do to Iran what they can't."

"Yeah," McWhinney nodded. "Just like we used them."

"We didn't use them." Stanton's eyes flashed with anger. "We didn't use them," he repeated.

"Mr. President, we knew they weren't going to sit around and wait while Iran developed a nuclear missile. And we did very little to stop Iran except to beg them to quit."

Stanton's forehead wrinkled in a scowl. "We didn't beg them."

"Well, we certainly didn't put any real pressure on them to change their actions."

"So, what are you saying?"

"We play the hand history deals us and let someone else sort it out later."

THE
SECOND
SEVEN

CHAPTER 60

EL PASO, TEXAS

AS HE HAD BEEN INSTRUCTED, Richard Cruse arrived on time at the El Paso FBI field office, dressed in the standard bureau uniform—gray suit with white shirt, muted tie, and wing-tip shoes. He was cleared by building security personnel and ushered upstairs to the office of Jimmy Thompson, the special agent in charge.

"Not sure why they sent someone with your expertise to us," Thompson began. "With all that's going on in the Middle East, I would have thought they'd keep you in New York."

"You know how it is," Cruse shrugged. "You can never tell what the FBI will do."

"That's true," Thompson laughed. "Well, anyway, we're glad to have you here. We do a lot of immigration work. Have a joint task force with Border Patrol, another with DEA. And we also do a lot of organized-crime work. Lots of guys from New York find their way down here. I'm sure you'll feel right at home once you get to know your way around." Just then a man appeared in the office doorway. He was dressed in blue jeans, a black T-shirt, and white sneakers. Thompson gestured for him to enter. "Casey Griffin. This is someone you need to meet."

Griffin entered the room. Thompson introduced him to Cruse. "You two will be working together. Casey works with the DEA Task Force."

"Certainly looks the part," Cruse observed.

"Yeah, well," Griffin nodded, "you'll get the hang of it before long." He looked over at Thompson. "Got an address I need to check out. Can I take him with me?"

"Yes," Thompson agreed. "Good idea. The two of you can get acquainted while you work." He smiled at Cruse. "Ride with Casey. See what you can learn about the work we do here in Texas."

Cruse followed Griffin down the hall to the corridor. They took the elevator to the first floor and walked to the parking deck out back. A late-model Mustang was parked on the second row. Griffin pressed a button on the key fob to unlock the doors. "Standard government car?"

"Seized it in a raid a few months ago," Griffin smiled. "Hasn't found its way to the auction yet."

From the office downtown they rode out to Turf Road, an unpaved street on the north side of town. Griffin turned the car onto a drive that led to the right and came to a stop in front of a double-wide mobile home. Cruse looked around warily. "This it?"

"Yeah." Griffin cut his eyes in Cruse's direction. "Tomorrow when you come to work, leave the suit at home."

Cruse stepped out on the passenger side and glanced over the top of the car in Griffin's direction. "You got something against suits?"

"No. But these people do," Griffin said, gesturing toward the rows of mobile homes that lined both sides of the street. "They see that jacket, they run for cover before we even get a chance." Griffin pushed the car door closed. "Take the back. I'll get the front."

Cruse moved to the left and made his way to the end of the trailer. He ducked low and stepped past a window, then checked around the back corner. Satisfied it was safe, he moved to a spot near the back door. From around front, he heard Griffin knock on the door, then heard his voice as he called out, "FBI. Open up!"

Seconds later the back door flew open and a kid darted outside. Cruse caught him with a forearm across the chest that sent the kid crashing to the ground on his back. When the boy started to move, Cruse put his foot on his chest. "Stay right there," he whispered. He drew his pistol and craned his neck to see inside. Seconds later, Griffin appeared in the doorway.

"What you got?"

"I'm not sure." Cruse reached down with his left hand, grabbed the boy by the shirt, and lifted.

The boy scrambled to his feet. "I wasn't doing nothin'," he protested.

Cruse turned him toward the wall of the trailer. Instinctively, the boy leaned forward in an arrest position. Cruse patted him down. "Who are you?"

"I ain't got to tell you nothin'."

"Then you must know, I'm about to advise you of your rights."

"Diego Sanchez," the boy sighed.

"How old are you?"

"Seventeen."

"What were you doing inside that house?"

"Nothin'. I already told you that."

Griffin came down the back steps and took Diego by the arm. "What kind of nothing were you doing in there? A little grass?"

"Are you crazy?"

"Cooking some meth?"

"You was just in there," Diego retorted. "Did you smell anything like that?"

"Then tell me what were you doing in there."

"All right," Diego groused. "A group of guys lived there. I seen them around here. Coming and going. Then I didn't see them no more. So I figured they moved on. Few days ago, I came over to see if they left anything."

"I hear this is the place to score whatever you want."

"Where'd you hear that?"

"Around."

"Well, you need a new snitch. Ain't nobody ever scored nothin' in that place."

"What makes you so sure?"

"Because the place to score is across the street."

Griffin looked deflated at the very real possibility he'd been given the wrong address. He let go of Diego's arm and stepped back. "You sure about that?"

"Of course I'm sure," Diego replied. "Everybody around here knows you go over there. Drugs. Women. I heard you could even get men if you wanted them."

"How about you become my new snitch."

"Uh-uh," Diego said, shaking his head slowly from side to side. "You start talking about those dudes and you'll wind up with a bullet in your head. They don't play."

"Well, I don't play, either. And if I find something in your file, I'm gonna be back to find you." Griffin started toward the end of the trailer. "Come on," he growled to Cruse. "Let's go."

But Cruse was curious now about who actually lived in the trailer and why they'd been given a wrong address. He looked over at Diego. "Who lived here?"

"I don't know. Just some dudes."

"How many?"

"Five or six," Diego shrugged. "Maybe a couple more."

"White guys?"

"No."

"Latinos?"

"Nah. I don't think so. Looked like they was from somewhere else. Spoke some kind of strange language. Somebody said it was Arabic or something. I don't know. They mostly kept to themselves."

"When did they leave?"

"About a week ago. I come by and saw the back door was open. Wasn't nobody here no more, so I went inside. Looked around."

"What did you find?"

"Nothin' much. Just some loose change. Few cans of food in the cabinet. I didn't really get to see it all 'cause a lady pulled up in a car and came to the door, so I ran. I came back today to see if I missed something. See what I could find. Just scrappin', you know."

Griffin was standing at the corner of the trailer. Cruse caught his eyes. "We need to take him in and see what else he knows."

"Why?"

"Trailer full of guys. Speaking a language that sounds like Arabic. In El Paso, Texas. That doesn't strike you as odd?"

"Hey," Diego argued, "I ain't goin' downtown with no feds." He shook his head. "No way."

"Why not?"

"Folks around here see me ride off with you, won't nobody talk to me again."

Cruse reached beneath his jacket and brought out a pair of handcuffs. "What if we take you in these?" Before Diego could respond, Cruse slipped the cuffs over his wrists and locked them in place. "Come on." He took Diego by the arm. "That ought to protect your reputation."

When they reached the office, Cruse put Griffin in an interrogation room. After a few more questions, he brought in a sketch artist. An hour later, they had two sketches. Cruse gave them to a technician to run through the facial-recognition software program.

In the meantime, using Diego's earlier statements about activity in the neighborhood, Griffin obtained a search warrant for the house across the street. He returned to the location with a team of agents and rounded up three suspects with connections to a Mexican drug cartel. Cruse and Diego were seated in Griffin's office, eating a hamburger, when Griffin returned.

"Make yourself at home," Griffin said sarcastically.

"No one seems to know where my office is," Cruse replied. "So we took yours."

Griffin dropped onto a chair. "The least you could have done was bring me a burger."

Cruse reached into a paper sack beside his chair, took out a hamburger still in the wrapper, and handed it to him. "Would've gotten you a shake but I didn't know when you'd get back."

"That's all right." Griffin took a bite of the burger. "I'll make do."

A bite or two later, Griffin rose from his seat on the chair and nodded for Cruse to follow. They walked out in the hallway.

"I went back inside that trailer," Griffin said, his voice little more than a whisper.

"What did you find?"

"I found this." Griffin took a slip of paper from his pocket and handed it to Cruse. On the paper was a phone number. "I ran a check on that number. It's a cell phone in Juarez. Registered to Miguel Murillo."

"You know him?"

"Yeah. Murillo works for Jose Lazcarno. Head of the biggest drug cartel in Juarez."

An office assistant appeared from around the corner. She looked over at Cruse. "We have a hit on the face-recognition software from one of those sketches."

Cruse and Griffin followed her to her desk. They watched over her shoulder as she brought the results of the scan onto the screen of her monitor. "Your sketch got a hit on someone named Ahmed Haza." She changed to another page. "We found a file on him in our database. Born in Yemen. Ties to Hezbollah. Disappeared in Lebanon during the last Israeli invasion. Thought by some to be dead."

Cruse looked at Griffin. "This isn't good. Islamic terrorists with ties to Mexican drug lords."

"You thinking they are coming into the country illegally?"

"I'm thinking that part is obvious. The real question is why?"

"The 9/11 attackers came with visas," Griffin replied. "Why wouldn't these guys?"

"That's what worries me most."

"I think I know how to help."

CHAPTER 61
TEHRAN, IRAN

DURING ISRAEL'S RAID ON IRAN, Rasoul Moussaoui remained at the presidential palace, coordinating the attack from his office on the main floor. After Iran launched its initial counterstrike, however, he and his primary advisors retreated to a steel-reinforced concrete bunker. Buried beneath a guesthouse on the palace grounds, the bunker had been constructed in the 1950s. It was equipped with running water, an electrical generator, and an air-filtration system. It offered adequate protection from conventional and chemical attacks, but it was nothing like the operations centers of most oil-rich nations.

For telephone communications, the bunker relied on a single coaxial cable connected to the city's central phone system. A second cable connected to a radio station not far away that relayed messages from government and military transmitters in the field. Crude and unstable, the systems were only nominally functional under everyday conditions. Unshielded, both had been rendered inoperable by Israeli electronic countermeasures shortly before Israel's air force attacked. In the bunker, Moussaoui and his advisors were isolated, miserably hot, and forced to rely on candles for light. News from the outside was brought to them by messengers carrying handwritten notes.

Gathered at the table with Moussaoui were the heads of the major branches of the Iranian military—Jalil Amini, the director of Intelligence and National Security, Army General Parsa Karimi, and Navy Admiral Iraj Shirdel—the same people who had advised him on military matters since he took office. Only Air Force General Akbar Imjanian was missing, the apparent victim of an unfortunate explosion that occurred while traveling on the road to Kerman shortly before Israel attacked. His replacement, a young general from Isfahan, was in the field and unable to return to Tehran. In his absence, Amini provided updates from the air force for the group in the bunker.

Moussaoui looked around and smiled. "A bit of good news. I have been informed that our Supreme Leader, Ali Tafresh, is safe and sound."

"All praise to Allah," Shirdel added.

"That is good," Amini nodded. "But our people are in grave danger."

Moussaoui leaned back in his chair. "Where do we stand now?"

"The latest reports indicate the air force has lost seventy-five percent of our missile launchers."

"As Imjanian predicted," Moussaoui sighed.

"Yes, Mr. President."

"And ancillary damage?"

"Not as bad as we are reporting to the press."

"Good." Moussaoui rested his hands on the tabletop. "I would like to now turn to our strategy going forward."

Karimi looked downcast. "What is there left to do?" He shook his head. "Conditions might not be as bad as we are reporting, but they are bad just the same. And far worse than I anticipated. In less than an hour, the Israelis all but destroyed our nuclear program. And the Americans, in even less time, eliminated our first-strike capability."

"We still have the twenty-percent uranium," Shirdel countered. "And most of the centrifuges are either operable or easily repaired." He gave Karimi a pat on the back. "We are right where we want to be, my friend."

"We have only launched the first salvo of our response." Moussaoui spoke with a cheerfulness not altogether forced as he turned again to Amini. "Perhaps you would care to explain our position."

Amini looked across the table at Karimi. "Several weeks ago, at the request of President Moussaoui, we undertook a couple of strategic initiatives. Some of which you know about. Others you do not."

"Secret measures?"

"It was necessary to keep you out of the loop," Moussaoui explained. "Because of your relationship with Imjanian."

Karimi had a look of disgust. "I can't believe I ever trusted him."

"I understand. But the two of you—one in the air force, the other in the army—were forced to work together. We did not want to risk an inadvertent disclosure to him."

Karimi looked up at Amini. "What have we done?"

"First," Amini continued, "we repositioned our submarines to the Mediterranean. They now lie off the coast of Israel."

"Israel?" Karimi looked puzzled. "Why use them against Israel now?"

"Israel was always our primary objective."

"But why not use the submarines against America? They could move undetected across the Atlantic to within easy striking distance. We could level New York City. And even if we didn't completely destroy it, their economy would collapse. They destroyed our missile sites only to protect the Jews. They must be made to pay for that."

"And they will," Moussaoui insisted. "But if we move against the U.S. directly, with our military, the U.S. will turn all of its military muscle on us. You have already witnessed how devastating that can be with just conventional arms. If we strike at them directly, with our military force, they will strike against us with all their nuclear capability, and we will cease to exist."

"We do not want an official connection to attacks on the U.S." Amini added. "Against Israel, perhaps, but not the United States. Missiles launched from a submarine would be readily detectable and they would know they came from us."

Karimi placed the fingertips of one hand against his brow and shook his head slowly from side to side. "This is an unusual strategy."

"But one that is necessary, given our circumstances." Moussaoui glanced over at Admiral Shirdel. "Are the submarines prepared to attack?"

"Yes, Mr. President," Shirdel nodded. "And they are prepared to stay as long as necessary. We have obtained permission from Tunisian authorities to resupply from Tunis."

"Very well," Moussaoui said triumphantly. "Give them the order. They may fire at will."

"Yes, Mr. President." Shirdel rose from his seat at the table and started toward the door. "I will send the message at once."

When he was gone, Moussaoui leaned close to Amini. "Contact our friends in the region. It is time for them to act."

"Yes, Mr. President." Amini nodded. "Right away."

"What about the elements of Hezbollah in Mexico? Are they in position and prepared?"

"They have already been alerted."

"We are witnessing an historic event," Moussaoui announced with pride. "The oppressed and disregarded joining together to bring Israel, the Little Satan, and America, the Great Satan, to their knees. Our fathers longed for this day, and now it is ours."

CHAPTER 62
BROOKLYN, NEW YORK

AT NOON, DANA ARKIN LOOKED OUT the window in the cab of his crane. For as far as he could see, there was nothing but rows and rows of freight containers. Red Hook Container Terminal processed as many as eight ships per day. Though not nearly the volume as Long Beach, California, it was still a large operation.

Arkin took his lunch box from beneath the seat, opened the cab door, and stepped out to a steel ladder that led down one leg of the crane to the dock below. Moving slowly, with one foot gingerly below the next, he reached the bottom in less than five minutes.

A line of containers sat fifty yards away. He made his way toward it and took a seat in the shade on the opposite side. Before long, men from the crew joined him and they sat together, eating their lunches.

Thirty minutes later, a breeze came up from the east. As it did, an odor wafted across the dock. Arkin scrunched up his nose. "What is that smell?"

"I don't know," someone replied, "but it's rotten."

"What they got in these containers, anyway?"

"Wood," someone answered. "Some kind of special wood. Going to China to make furniture out of it."

"Who told you that?"

"I seen it on one of the documents."

"They don't put wood in a container."

"They do for this wood. It's a special kind."

The breeze came up again and the odor returned. "I don't know about wood," Arkin said. "But that's a bad smell." He stood and scanned the rows of containers.

"Think you can tell by looking where it's coming from?"

Arkin shook his head. "No, but my nose can tell me." He started slowly down the container row. "My nose can tell me," he repeated. "Come on." He gestured to the others with a wave of his arm. "Let's find out where it's coming from."

They spread out along the row, smelling and checking. An hour later, someone called out, "Hey! I think it's over here."

Arkin turned in the direction of the shout and saw one of the crew members standing next to a green container. He started in that direction and soon they were all gathered by the box.

"Man," someone grimaced. "That stuff stinks."

"What would they put in a box that stinks like that?"

"What would they put in a box that stinks like that on *purpose*?"

Arkin checked the metal seal attached to the door handle. "We need to open it."

"We can't do that," someone protested. "We'll get fired."

"Anybody got a radio?" Arkin asked. "Mine's in the crane."

Someone stepped forward and handed him a radio. Arkin pressed the button to talk. "Hey, dispatch."

"Yeah."

"This is Arkin. I think we have a problem with one of the boxes."

"What kind of problem?"

"It stinks."

"What?"

"It stinks. There's a very strong odor coming from one of the boxes. I think someone should take a look inside."

"Wait a minute," the dispatcher replied. "What's the number?"

"GRXW 27372185." When the dispatcher didn't respond, Arkin keyed the radio once more. "You get that number?"

"Yeah, I got the number. But it's not on my list."

"It really stinks."

"Stand by. I'm sending someone."

Ten minutes later, a blue Chevrolet pickup truck rounded the end of the container row and drove in their direction. Through the windshield Arkin could see Bert Cooper was behind the steering wheel. "All right," Arkin said to the men around him. "This is Cooper, so be nice."

"Coop," someone said in a voice that sounded more like a yelp. "My man."

"Go easy," Arkin repeated. "He's just trying to do his job."

"But he does it so … proficiently."

"He's young," someone else added. "He'll learn."

The truck came to a stop near the box and Cooper climbed out. "Okay, Arkin, what's this—" He stopped in mid-sentence and covered his nose and mouth with his hand. "Man," he gasped, "that's bad."

"We need to open it," Arkin said in a matter-of-fact tone.

Cooper reached through the open window of the truck and retrieved a pair of wire cutters. He handed them to Arkin. "Be my guest."

While everyone else backed away, Arkin stepped to the door of the box. He clipped the metal seal on the latch and lifted the handle. The door swung open and a horde of flies rushed out. Arkin swatted at them with both hands to keep them away from his nose and mouth, but through the confusion he saw a human body on the floor of the container.

"There it is!" he shouted.

Cooper stepped forward as the last of the flies moved out of the way. "Unbelievable," he groaned.

Inside the container, the body of a man lay just a few feet from the door. He was dressed in a suit and still had on his shoes, but his eyes were sunken and maggots crawled over his face. Cooper turned away and placed a call on the radio.

"Dispatch."

"Yeah, Cooper. Go ahead."

"Call the police. We have a dead body in this container."

CHAPTER 63
NETIVOT, ISRAEL

WHEN IRANIAN MISSILES STOPPED FALLING from the sky, Michael Epstein assumed the worst was over. Still, he hesitated to leave the safety of his home. The all-clear horn had sounded late that evening but he and Daliah, his wife, had chosen to remain inside with their two small children, just in case. The windows and doors were covered in plastic carefully taped to the frame and tightly sealed in place. "Better to wait," Michael had warned, and Daliah agreed.

Through the night they listened to reports on a battery-powered radio as Tel Aviv's only working radio station kept the nation apprised of the damage. If those reports were accurate, most of the country's infrastructure had been damaged or destroyed. Netivot, it seemed, had avoided the worst of it, with only a few missiles landing in the area. Michael had heard them explode but they were on the opposite side of town.

Now, a day later, things seemed to have calmed down for good. It had been hours since the last fire truck went past, and there had been no further incidents. "We can't just sit here and do nothing," he groused.

"So go outside," Daliah replied. "What is the worst that could happen?"

"Gas," he replied dourly. "There could be gas."

"If there was gas, we would have heard by now."

"Perhaps we have not heard because everyone is dead."

"Hush," she said sharply. "The children will hear you."

"And what is wrong with that?"

"You will scare them."

"They should be scared of gas. And missiles. And the idiots who live in Gaza just a few miles down the road."

"They aren't idiots," Daliah countered.

"On a normal day, they sit in their yard and shoot rockets at us. That is not an idiot?"

"I thought you said the missiles came from Iran."

"They did. But that was last night. I am talking about the last twenty years."

"You are talking nonsense. Open the door and go outside. Before you drive us both crazy."

"I'll do it," Michael said as he turned toward the front door. "And perhaps there will be gas outside and you won't have to fuss at me anymore."

"Stop." She swatted him playfully with a towel. "All this time in the house has gassed your brain."

Michael peeled back the plastic that covered the front door of their home and stepped outside. Above, the sky was blue and sunny and seeing it lifted his spirits. Perhaps the attacks were over for good. Perhaps life would return ... well ... not exactly to normal, but as normal as one might expect when there was no electrical service and the water system was down more than it was up. But at least none of the houses on their street had been damaged.

A few minutes later, Daliah came from the house and joined him in the front yard. She scanned the neighborhood around them. "See, it's fine. We are just fine. I think we can even—" The howling sound of a rocket ripped through the sky, drowning out her voice.

Michael ducked instinctively and covered his ears with his hands. Daliah screamed and ran inside as the rocket flew past their house and landed behind them with a loud explosion. Michael ran behind the house to see where it hit. As he came around the corner, he saw across his neighbor Avishai's yard to the next street over. Smoke rose from a gaping hole in the pavement.

From behind, he heard Daliah's voice. "What did it hit?"

"The street," he pointed.

"The Iranians again?"

He shook his head. "This one was not from Iran." Michael had an angry look. "This one came from Gaza."

Just then a second rocket zipped past. Traveling on a slightly shorter arc, it landed a few feet from his neighbor Avishai's backdoor. Shards of glass flew through the air as the rear windows of the house blew out. Then, before Michael could move, a third rocket appeared. This one landed squarely in the center of Avishai's house. Seconds later the house erupted in flames.

"Call someone!" Michael exclaimed as he ran toward the burning house, shouting at the top of his voice. "Avishai! Avishai! Are you in there, Avishai?"

When he reached the house he found the back door hanging preciously by its hinges from a splintered doorframe. Michael pushed his way past and stepped inside. Heat from the flames rushed toward him. A few feet beyond the door he saw Avishai lying on the floor. Ignoring the flames that now surrounded him, Michael picked up Avishai, held him in his arms, and ran outside.

As he laid Avishai on the ground, the fire trucks arrived. Paramedics crowded around Avishai, doing their best to revive him. Michael watched a moment as they feverishly worked on his neighbor, but he could see that Avishai was in bad shape and he didn't want to watch while he died. Instead, he turned away and drifted among the firemen and the hoses that now snaked across the grass. "Why would someone do such a thing?" he mumbled to himself.

"It's happening everywhere," a fireman replied. Michael looked up to see a man standing just a few feet away, dressed in a fireman's suit. "Believe it or not," the man continued, "some places are getting it a lot worse than us."

Michael looked up to the sky and saw rockets streaking through the air. He turned slowly in a circle and saw they were coming from the west and striking in every direction. All around him houses were exploding. Flames rose in the air beneath clouds of thick black smoke. The entire village seemed to be on fire. He was about to say it was strange how all the houses were hit but not his. Then there was a loud noise and he turned in time to see the trail from a rocket headed in his direction, arcing downward on a path that took it lower and lower until it slammed into the center of his house.

At first the house didn't immediately burst into flames and Michael had hope that his wife and children were safe. He ran toward the house to see about them and in just a few seconds reached the patio. As he jerked open the back door, superheated air rushed over him. His skin felt as though it had been instantaneously blistered. He ignored the pain and plunged ahead, intent on finding his family and dragging them to safety. But two steps beyond the door, he was enveloped in a wall of orange flames. He saw his shirt turn to ashes right before his eyes and felt the melted soles of his shoes stick to the floor. And then he was no more.

*   *   *

President Stanton was just finishing a meeting on Capitol Hill with the Democrat caucus when the call came. Secret Service agents whisked him out to the car and then hurried down Pennsylvania Avenue to the White House.

McWhinney was waiting outside the West Wing entrance when the car arrived. Stanton climbed from the backseat and started toward the door. McWhinney walked at his side.

"They're launching more missiles?" Stanton frowned. "I thought I ordered our guys to take out Iran's missiles."

"Yes, Mr. President, but—"

"And to keep doing it every time they launch. How many launchers do they have?"

They were inside the building by then and headed down the hallway toward the stairs that led to the basement.

"The missiles aren't coming from Iran," McWhinney explained finally.

"Then where are they coming from?"

"From inside the disputed territories. The Gaza Strip. The West Bank. Some from Lebanon."

Stanton looked perplexed. "Civilians with rocket launchers?"

"Yes, sir."

"And Hezbollah?"

"Apparently."

"How do we respond to that? We can't start blowing up civilian houses."

"That's why we're going downstairs, Mr. President. So our people can get you up to speed on what's happening now and so we can figure this thing out."

"I'm not sending American troops into a ground war in Palestine."

"Sir," McWhinney cautioned, "you shouldn't say that yet."

"I'm not doing it, Pete." They came to a stop as they reached the bottom of the stairs. "I'll help them contain the conflict. I'll help mute Iran's military capability. But I'm not putting one US soldier on the ground."

The door to the situation room was straight ahead. A Marine guard posted in the hall outside snapped to attention, then reached to open the door. Stanton moved past him and into the room.

"Gentlemen," he smiled, and then caught Baker's eye. "Kathleen." He pulled out a chair at the end of the table and took a seat. "We're becoming regulars here."

"At least for now," Baker agreed.

"Good point." Stanton understood she meant the comment in the context of reelection.

Admiral Beamon stood at the end of the room, near the video screen. Stanton glanced down the table at him. "Admiral, what do you have for us today?"

"Sir, our AWACS planes have detected the launch of rockets from multiple locations."

"Where exactly?"

Beamon nodded to his assistant. A detailed map of Israel appeared on the video screen. He pointed to an area in the south, along the coast near the Egyptian border. "This is Gaza."

"I know a little about geography, Admiral."

Beamon continued unfazed. "We have detected as many as fifty launches from inside the Gaza Strip aimed toward towns and villages in southern Israel."

"Who's doing it?"

"It appears to be private citizens."

"Where did they get the rockets?"

"They were manufactured in Iran and distributed by Hamas."

"How?"

"Sir?" Beamon looked puzzled.

"How do they do that? How do they distribute rockets to private citizens? Does a truck ride around playing a jingle like an ice cream truck and people run out to the street to get the latest handheld rocket?"

"They find their way in. Most of the neighborhoods in Gaza are organized. They have leaders. They know who's in and who's out. And the rockets find their way into the hands of those most likely to use them."

"And then what?"

"They practice. Those stories about rockets you see on the news or in briefings—most of them are training incidents. One neighbor training another."

"We are certain of this?"

"Yes," Catlett interrupted. "Sir, in addition to data from the AWACS planes, we have satellite images of the region. Those images show rocket launches from Lebanon and from the West Bank."

"What about the Syrians? Any involvement from them?"

"No, Mr. President," Upchurch replied. "The Syrian military remains within its borders. No new movements. No troops massing for an attack."

"That seems strange."

"Yes," Catlett said, once again injecting himself into the conversation. "Our analysts found it curious, too, Mr. President."

"Will the Syrians stay put?"

"That's the big question," Baker broke into the discussion. "If they're staying out for a reason, we need to know what that reason is before we craft a response. Otherwise, our entry into the conflict will upset the status quo."

"The status quo?" Catlett's question had a scoffing tone. "I think the Syrian regime has all it can handle right now just hanging on to power in their own country. They aren't in a position to worry about Israel."

Baker focused on the president. "But our entry into this conflict might very well change all that, forcing them to forget their internal troubles and line up against us."

"You'd have to be—"

"Paul," Stanton interrupted, "I'm not putting boots on the ground in Israel. We'll give them intelligence. We'll find a way to get them arms if they need them. But absent a catastrophe larger than what you've shown me today, we're not getting into this fight."

CHAPTER 64
WASHINGTON, D.C.

AUBREY PRESTON, THE PRESIDENT'S new campaign chairman, sat at his desk in the Stanton campaign headquarters, not far from the White House, reviewing polling results with campaign staff. "I've looked at this data and it doesn't add up," he began. "With the initial incident—Israel's attack against Iran—we should have received a spike in our favorable ratings. Our numbers should have been up. Instead, our approval rating is dropping."

Laura Hanks, one of the regional coordinators, spoke up. "Our negatives have gone straight up, too." She shook her head. "Unbelievable. Three weeks ago we were fine."

"So much for rallying around the flag."

"That's because things are different," Alan Pate suggested. "This isn't like the traditional war."

"No kidding," they all chortled. "We can see that in the numbers."

"I'm serious," Alan continued. "If this was a conflict anywhere else in the world, we'd be unassailable. The election would be over and we would win. But this isn't anywhere else. This conflict is in the Middle East between two polarizing countries. We're not talking about a remote band of radicals making trouble. This is Iran and Israel. Both willing to do whatever it takes to win. And that brings up images of the apocalypse, the Second Coming, the end of time. People aren't thinking about the American flag flying high and our soldiers winning big. They're thinking about Armageddon. The imagery is totally different."

"You may be right," Laura nodded. "Our position in this thing is backwards."

Preston had a puzzled frown. "Backwards?"

"We aren't in it to protect ourselves," she explained. "We're in it to help someone else. I mean, Iran isn't preparing to attack us. At least not right now."

"Right," Alan nodded. "In the voter's mind, we're risking Armageddon for something that doesn't really involve us."

"Doesn't involve us?" someone said in a sarcastic tone. "Doesn't your car still run on gasoline?"

"Seen the price of oil today?"

"That's not what voters are thinking about." Alan leaned forward, gesturing with his hands to emphasize each point. "They may say they're thinking about the price of gas if you ask them, but their real problem is fear. And not just any fear, but fear that takes them way beyond worries about gasoline. I'm telling you, they see this as a huge risk with only a downside. They can't see the upside to this conflict. For them, it's a no-win situation. And they see us as the ones who put them in that position."

Ann Taylor, a consultant, spoke up. "Whatever the reason, the Republicans are doing a great job hammering us with this stuff." She shook her head. "Every news cycle, they hit us with something. And then kick it for two or three days."

"We have to get this story back in the right position."

"We have to get our country back in the right position."

"Someone else will have to do that," Laura countered. "We can't set policy. All we can do is set the tone and the message of the campaign."

The discussion continued around the table as each one suggested ways to divert attention from the current crisis, budget, and several proposed new television ads. In the midst of it all, Alan blurted out, "What if we found a way out of the conflict that helped both?"

The question caught everyone unaware. Laura looked across the table at him. "Helped both what?"

"Policy and politics," Alan suggested. "What if we found a way out of the conflict that solved the policy issues and the campaign issues at the same time? No one would complain about that, would they?"

"We've moved on from that," Ann said curtly. "We can't solve that problem."

Alan bristled at the comment. "I don't think—"

"No," Preston interrupted, a look of realization on his face. "Alan's on to something." He sat up straight in his chair. "If we could find a creative way to leverage this into real change, we could do something big."

"We don't even need real change," Laura added. "Just the appearance of change."

"Exactly." A smile turned up the corners of Preston's mouth. "It could change the whole election. And maybe we could find an actual solution."

"It's not our fight," someone objected. "We need to get out."

"The voters are right." Ann took up the argument. "We're risking the Great Apocalypse for something that doesn't even affect us. The president should pull the plug on our involvement. He should do that and go on television to announce it."

"No way," Preston snapped. "If he does that we're done."

"But what about the rule we set, keeping politics and policy separate?"

"What we were trying to say," Preston answered, "was that we shouldn't trade policy for politics. That's not what we're doing here." He picked up a pen from the table and pointed with it for emphasis. "Here's what we're doing. We're going to find a way to turn this situation around so that it looks like Israel and Iran created a mess, and Andrew Stanton cleaned it up."

"Won't be hard to lay blame on Israel and Iran. That's exactly what happened."

"The trick is to find a way to spin it so Stanton looks like he solved it."

"Or, better yet, to find a solution so Stanton actually does solve it."

"And that's the problem with this strategy," Taylor offered. "We can spin it on the media side, but we can't do anything about it on the policy side. We can change the way we spin it, but we can't make substantive changes in how the situation is handled on the ground. For that you'd have to get the president to act. Or at least the secretary of state."

"The president would go for it, but it would require some diplomatic legwork to get a proposal in shape for him."

"Proposal?" someone asked. "What proposal? We haven't talked about anything specific."

"Exactly," Preston noted. "And that's what I'm trying to get at. How could we bring this together so we can find out what the solution options might be?"

"Like someone said," Laura reiterated, "you need to get the secretary of state involved. She's the one person in the administration who might listen to you without turning you down out of hand."

"Fat chance of that happening," someone added.

"Why not?" Preston glared down the table toward the people seated at the far end. "Why not?" The room got quiet. "Why wouldn't the secretary of state want to solve this problem?"

"Come on, Aubrey. You know as well as we do that she's way too political to get involved in something this risky."

"She'd never go that far out on a limb."

"Well, I, for one, don't believe it," Preston retorted.   .

Laura agreed. "I think she's been trying to keep our Middle East policy out of the ditch, but Defense and the CIA keep steering everything back toward a military solution."

Preston looked over at her. "Any idea how to reach the Secretary?"

Laura reached to a stand that sat in the corner. A telephone rested there. She picked up the phone and set it on the conference table in front of Preston. He looked confused. "You mean I should just call her?"

"You're director of the president's reelection campaign. I think she'll at least take the call."

*   *   *

That afternoon, Preston reached Kathleen Baker at her office. She was reluctant to talk and more than a little wary of being drawn into domestic politics, but she agreed to see him, if for no other reason than as a professional courtesy. They met in a small study off her office in the State Department building.

"What's this all about?" she asked as they took a seat.

"The Middle East."

She looked perturbed. "If you came here thinking you could get me to go along with Catlett and Upchurch, you can leave now."

"No, no, I'm not here for anything like that. I came because we need to find a way out of this situation."

"Did you discuss this with Leon Bain?"

"No. Why?"

"We floated this idea before."

"What happened?"

"Nothing. He wouldn't take it to the president. It's an election year, you know."

"I know," Preston continued. "That's why I'm here." It was at least partly true. "To see if there isn't a way out that helps us all."

"And by all you mean ..."

"The country. Israel. Iran. The Palestinians. All of us."

"Are you serious, or is this just another ploy to draw me into supporting their current position?"

"It's not a ploy."

"And you'll take it to the president?"

"That's why I'm here," Preston responded. "To see if you'll back me up."

Baker hesitated a moment. Then her shoulders relaxed and she began again. "I'm not sure any solution will work if we add the Palestinians. Previous administrations have offered them everything they wanted and every time the offer was made, the Palestinians came back with still more demands." Baker looked skeptical. "And I'm assuming, if we could find a solution, you would want Andrew Stanton to come out on top when it's all over?"

"Well," he shrugged, "it *is* an election year."

"A negotiated settlement that gives everyone what they want, solves the situation, and lets Stanton say he did it. That's a lot to ask."

"A solution that looks presidential. One that doesn't sound like we're caving in to their demands. Those are the two big things. It has to look presidential. And can't sound like we're weak on their demands."

"They haven't made any demands," Baker stated in a matter-of-fact tone. "That's something everyone seems to have overlooked in this whole thing. Iran has made no demands. They responded only after they were attacked, and so far all they seem to want is to be left alone."

"They don't need to make demands," Preston countered. "They have Hezbollah to do their fighting for them."

"Perhaps. But as a sovereign nation, Iran has only responded, and then after provocation. Twice with Israel and once with Iraq. In each case, they were attacked and only responded to defend themselves. Since the Islamic Revolution, they've never been the aggressor."

"You think Israel was wrong?"

"Not wrong, but misguided. Israel's real problem isn't Iran. Their real problem is the Palestinians and the Palestinian quest for a state of their own. Chasing after Iran because Iran supports the Palestinians is just a waste of time and won't lead them anywhere."

"This whole thing is like a feud. It's been going on since Jews first started returning to the region."

"It's been going on a lot longer than that. Goes all the way back to Isaac and Ishmael."

"Isaac and who?"

"Never mind," Baker said. "What did you have in mind?"

"I don't know the details of the situation well enough to make a specific proposal. I was just thinking we should get President Stanton in a room with the president of Iran, at a neutral site. Let them hash this out like heads of state. Resolve their differences face-to-face. Like we did in the 1970s with the Soviet Union."

"With a press conference afterward, so you get your campaign photos."

"Why are you so stuck on the campaign? Every time we've made a point, you've given it a campaign twist."

"Because that's the way Andrew Stanton has run this administration.

Always with an eye on reelection. All that talk about no mixing policy and politics is just a lot of talk. He started running for president the day Illinois elected him to the senate and he's been running for a second term since he was inaugurated. That's one reason we got in this mess."

"Well, if we can get them in the room together, we have to get them out. And we have to do it in a way that makes it appear that Stanton solved the situation. He can't look like a leader if no one sees him leading. So, yes, we need a press conference afterward."

"You won't get Moussaoui to agree to a script and even if he does, as soon as the cameras turn on, he's going to say whatever he wants."

"I don't care, as long as we get the situation in the Middle East resolved and look presidential doing it."

Baker leaned back and crossed her legs. "I'm not sure our people are ready to see the situation with Iran as anything like the situation Nixon faced with Russia." She cut her eyes at Preston. "You realize how risky this is for an election year?"

"Yes."

"If they refuse, it helps you. But if they agree to meet, and he actually goes into the room with Stanton, you're betting a second term on one roll of the dice."

"Everything's risky in an election year."

"Yeah, but this one is a little bigger than most risks you've faced," Baker cautioned. "If Andrew can't get a deal with Moussaoui, he's going to be looking to your ability to spin it just right. And if you can't spin it, you'll get blamed for the loss."

"That's my job."

"Will the president go for something like this?"

"I think it's the only way to change the situation."

"I think you're right about that. Israel has played us right into a box."

Preston nodded. "They started it but didn't hit them with enough to actually eliminate Iran's ability to strike back. Then we had to intervene to keep Iran from blowing Israel away. And right now we look like the bad guys, but we can turn this around. Will you help?"

"We should see if they'll meet."

"How do we do that?"

"We'll have to use emissaries."

"Sweden?"

"They're the logical choice."

"They'll have to move fast."

"The Swiss can do that. I'm not sure the Iranians can. But the Swiss can move as fast as we want."

"Can we contact the Iranians without the president's approval?"

"Yes. But we'd be risking our jobs."

"I'll risk it," Preston shrugged. "What about you?"

CHAPTER 65
NEW YORK CITY

LATE THAT AFTERNOON, Mark White, one of the assistant FBI agents in Goodall's office, sat at his desk reviewing security video from the Red Hook Container Terminal. With nothing else for a lead, he did his best to track the movement of the green cargo container as it made its way to the location on the dock where it was discovered. As he scanned through yet one more video file, an aide appeared at his desk.

"The medical examiner sent over an ID on the guy in that cargo container." She dropped a single-page report on White's desk, followed by a large manila folder. The folder landed with a thud.

"What's that?" White asked, pointing to the folder.

"The dead guy's FBI file," she replied. "Apparently, we know a lot about him."

According to the medical examiner's report, the body Arkin and his crew discovered in the cargo container was that of David Holsten. Fingerprints and DNA confirmed his identity. As White read through the bureau's file, he was surprised to learn that this was *the* David Holsten, chief strategist of Andrew Stanton's successful campaign for president. He'd been cleared twice by the Secret Service—once during the campaign and a second time after the election—and he'd been thoroughly vetted by the FBI. "This is big," he whispered to himself.

"How big is it?" a voice asked.

White looked up to see Billy Dobbs standing beside him. "Got the file on the dead guy," White said dryly.

Dobbs thumped it with his finger. "Looks like we know him well."

"Yeah." White turned a page in the file to reveal a photograph of Holsten. "Look familiar?"

"That's the dead guy?"

"Yeah."

"Man," Dobbs sighed. "That's David Holsten. I didn't recognize him from the photos in the morgue."

"The maggots had done a number on him by the time they found him."

"I guess so," Dobbs retorted. "We have to tell somebody. The press will be all over this."

"Think they already know?"

"Probably. Is Goodall in his office?"

"Yeah."

"Well, come on." Dobbs gestured. "Let's tell him now. We can go together."

*   *   *

Daryrush Kashfi sat on the bed and waited. He'd been there in the house for the past two weeks, never going outside. Confined to the bedroom, the curtains drawn tight against the windows. Leaving the room only for trips to the toilet across the hall and meals in the kitchen. Now the time had arrived. He had his bag packed, a well-worn leather case with his papers inside and one change of clothes. The case had been his father's and Daryrush had taken it when he left home in Yemen for the trip to Mexico. That seemed like a long time ago. Yet here he was, in Juarez, waiting to cross to the United States and fulfill the mission he'd prayed for since childhood, to bring the Jihad to American homes and visit upon them the wrath of Allah. A wrath made all the more vengeful by their profligate lifestyle and merciless oppression of the poor.

Suddenly there was a knock at the door and then it opened slowly. Juan Rivera appeared. "It is time. Bring your things. You are next."

With little hesitation, Daryrush picked up his leather case from the bed and started toward the door. He left the room and followed Rivera down the hall to the kitchen, then around the corner to a doorway that led to an attached garage. On the far side of the garage a closet was built into the corner from rough, unfinished plywood. Inside, a hole had been cut through the concrete floor. Deep and wide, a ladder led down into it. Daryrush made his way toward it and leaned over for a look inside.

The hole was illuminated by a bare light bulb that dangled from the ceiling. Through the glare, he saw that the ladder led down perhaps ten meters. At the bottom of the hole an opening led off to the right through a tunnel that appeared to be even darker and danker.

"It's okay," Rivera assured him. "Once you get into the tunnel, your eyes will adjust." He stepped to one side of the hole and reached out with his hand. "Give me your case. I'll hold it while you climb down and toss it to you when you get to the bottom." Daryrush hesitated. Rivera smiled. "Look, I've been with you for two weeks. You think I'm going to rip you off now?"

Daryrush handed the case to Rivera, turned around to face the ladder, and stepped onto the top rung. He reached with his foot and felt for the next rung below, placed his foot there, and shifted his weight to it. Then he moved his right foot into place on the rung below that. Slowly and methodically, he made his way down the ladder, one rung at a time, until he reached the bottom. He looked up, smiling triumphantly, and held out his hands to receive the leather case.

As promised, Rivera dropped it over the edge into the hole. The case landed squarely in Daryrush's outstretched arms. He gripped the handle with his right hand and swung the case to his side. Then he glanced up one last time and tossed a timid wave. Rivera acknowledged him with a nod, then moved away from the hole. Left to face the darkness of the tunnel alone, Daryrush crouched low and started inside.

Forty-five minutes later, he emerged in the basement of a house. He exited from the tunnel and raised himself up to his full height, relieved to finally be able to stand up all the way. Seated in the room were his friends, Mana Pejman and Bahram Kooshan. They had traveled with him on the freighter from Somalia. Daryrush took a seat next to them. "Where are we?"

"Texas," Pejman replied with a laugh. "Was the tunnel that long to you?"

"We are not far from Houston," Kooshan offered.

"This is a different way than we planned." Daryrush looked worried. "I do not like changes."

"Relax," Pejman soothed. "Shahin made the arrangements. Everyone has been paid. We are in a good place."

"That bothers me, too."

"What? That we are in a good place? That bothers you?"

"No," Daryrush said, shaking his head. "It bothers me that they have already been paid."

"Why would that bother you?"

"If they have been paid, what incentive do they have to get us there safely?"

"Shahin brought the money." Pejman had a defiant look. "They would not dare oppose him."

"How do you know this? How do you know Shahin paid?"

"I saw him." There was a hint of indignation in his voice. "Do you doubt he would do as he said?"

"I did not expect him to come in person. You saw Shahin?"

"Yes."

"I knew he would come," Kooshan smiled. "He would not send us on such an important mission without coming to participate himself."

"And you must remember," Pejman continued. "We have taken an oath to Allah, in the presence of Shahin. If we do not arrive at our destination by tomorrow, Shahin will want to know why. And if he does not like the answer, he will bring more destruction to Lazcarno than we could possibly imagine."

A creaking sound caught Daryrush's attention and he jerked his head to the left. For the first time he noticed a staircase that descended behind a water heater in the center of the room. Moments later, a man appeared on the bottom step. "The car will take you now."

Daryrush stood with Pejman and Kooshan and together they started toward him.

*   *   *

In New York, Dobbs and White found Goodall standing at the window in his office. Dobbs rapped his knuckle on the doorframe as they entered. Goodall turned to face them.

"I received a call just now," Goodall informed, not waiting for them to speak. "Any guess who it was from?"

"Not a clue," Dobbs replied. "We wanted to update you on the body they found at Red Hook."

"I heard," Goodall answered dourly. "The call was from the *Times*. One of their people is doing a report for the morning paper. They wanted a comment."

"What did you tell them?"

"What do you think I told them?" Goodall shoved the chair back from his desk and dropped onto it. "How does the *Times* find out before I even know?"

"They just brought us the report," White explained. "As soon as we saw it was Holsten, Dobbs and I came right up here."

"The *Times* knows about an FBI investigation before the FBI."

"That was the Manhattan medical examiner trying to beat us to the punch," Dobbs suggested. "This isn't the first time they've done it."

"Are they going with the story?" White asked.

"They're going with it, but they'll hold off two days."

"Two days?"

"That's all we can get without going to court and asking for an order."

"We don't even know what this is about."

"Then get busy. And bring me the file."

"You want the file?"

"I'd like to know a little something about this guy before I call the director."

CHAPTER 66
MEDITERRANEAN SEA

FIVE MILES OFF THE COAST OF HAIFA, Israel, Captain Fallahi looked through the periscope of the *Tareq*, the newest of the Iranian Navy's Kilo Class submarines. A smile spread across his face. "I see it. One hundred meters off our bow."

Commander Kazemi, the ship's executive officer, had a skeptical look. "You are certain it is an Israeli ship?"

"It's flying an Israeli flag. See for yourself," Fallahi said, motioning to the periscope.

Kazemi leaned forward and peered through the eyepiece. After a moment, he stepped back. "Okay," he acquiesced finally. "It is an Israeli ship."

Fallahi turned to the ship's weapons officer seated on the right. "Prepare to fire tubes one and two."

"Aye, Captain. Preparing to fire tubes one and two."

"Load missiles in tubes three and four."

"Aye, Captain. Loading missiles in tubes three and four."

Kazemi looked puzzled. "Missiles?"

"When we fire on the freighter," Fallahi explained, "we will give away our position."

"But by the time anyone responds, we will be long gone."

"Yes," Fallahi nodded. "But we must be prepared to act quickly. When their ships leave port to check on the freighter, we will reposition ourselves behind them and attack again. They will never know what hit them." He turned back to the periscope. "Weapons officer. How are those tubes coming?"

"Torpedoes in tubes one and two. Armed and ready, sir."

"Stand by to fire."

"Aye. Standing by to fire."

Kazemi grabbed Fallahi's arm. "You will launch the missiles against the rescue ships?"

"No," Fallahi said, shaking his head. "Only an Israeli Jew would be so barbaric." He pressed his eyes against the eyepiece, adjusted the periscope, then leaned back, smiling. "I shall launch the missiles against this." He gestured again toward the periscope.

Once more, Kazemi peered through the scope. In the viewing glass he saw the large, rounded dome of an LNG tanker. He stared at it a moment, then turned to Fallahi, a startled look on his face. "You will destroy the city."

"I know," Fallahi smiled with pride. "That is why this ship was built."

"But lives will be lost. Civilian lives."

"And how many Iranian civilians lost their lives to the Israeli attacks?"

"That ships holds liquefied natural gas. It's lying in port. When you strike it with a missile, it will explode with the force of a small nuclear bomb."

"Exactly my strategy." Fallahi eased Kazemi aside and rested his forehead against the pad above the eyepiece. He slid his thumb over the firing button on the periscope handle. Through the eyepiece, he focused on the crosshairs of the ship's sighting device and trained them over the freighter amidships. Then he slowly depressed the firing button. There was a swishing sound of air as the torpedo left the tube. "One away."

"Tube one away."

Fallahi pressed the firing button once more and again there was the swishing sound of air. "Tube two away."

"All tubes away," the weapons officer reported.

Fallahi continued to watch through the periscope as the seconds ticked by. Then an explosion ripped through the tanker's bow. A second explosion erupted near the center of the ship. Thick black smoke rose in the air.

Fallahi stepped back. "Down periscope."

"Down periscope," someone repeated, and the periscope lowered from the conning tower.

"Make your depth fifty meters," Fallahi ordered. "Steer east on a heading of eighty-six degrees. Flank speed."

"Aye, Captain. Steering east. Heading eighty-six degrees. Flank speed."

"Weapons. Are the missiles armed?"

"Armed and ready with the targeting package."

"Very well," Fallahi replied. "Launch all tubes."

"Launching tubes three and four." There was the sound of rushing air, and the ship rocked from side to side. "All tubes away."

*   *   *

On a hill above the city of Haifa, Ayelet Brosh sat at a table sipping a cup of hot tea. From the second-floor balcony of her home she had a clear view of downtown from the seashore in the south to the port to the north. What she saw that morning did not look good, but she refused to let it dissuade her from following her normal routine.

To the south, smoke rose from the ruins of an office building. It had taken a direct hit from a missile the day before and smoldered most of the afternoon. Sometime in the night, it finally collapsed. In the north, flames still burned out of control from a fuel tank that had been struck about the same time as the office building. The water system was offline and the electricity was out, but the gas line to her home still worked and she'd managed to light a burner on the stove. Tea in the morning was important to her. "They might destroy this city and bring its ashes down on my head," she said to herself, "but they will not destroy me. I will not allow it. God," she said, pointing heavenward, "will not permit it."

Then from somewhere down the hill there came a deep, rumbling noise. Low and powerful, she felt it vibrating through the balcony floor, growing more powerful by the moment. The cup on the table rattled in its saucer. As the sound grew stronger, the cup bounced in the air, struck the table hard, and rolled to the floor, where it shattered into pieces. Ayelet glanced around, her eyes darting to the left and right in desperate attempt to figure out what was happening.

Dazed and confused, she glanced over the balcony ledge and looked down below. At the port, several miles to the north, she saw a huge white column rising into the air. Thick and roiling, it rose straight up from the ground, higher and higher. Then it began to slow and the top rounded off like the cap of a giant mushroom.

Seconds later, a pulsing shock wave rocked her backward. She banged into the chair where she'd been sitting and tumbled over, landing with a thud on the balcony floor. In the same instant, glass in the windows shattered into a million pieces. The shards, propelled at a speed too fast to calculate, penetrated the walls of her living room and bedroom, shredding the wallboard into strips of backing paper that dangled from the studs that once held it in place.

Dazed but still conscious, Ayelet struggled to her feet and glanced around to find the balcony was bare. The table was gone, along with the chairs and the shattered pieces of the cup and saucer. All of it gone and the balcony floor swept cleaner than any broom could sweep.

Agitated, confused, and disoriented, she staggered over to the balcony ledge to look out at the city. What she saw drained all resolve from her soul.

Down the hill below her, the city lay in ruins. Every building from Kiryat Yam in the north to Kfar Galim in the south was gone, reduced to rubble by the biggest, most powerful explosion she'd ever witnessed. All that was left were piles of concrete and twisted steel. Even the trees were gone and, worse still, there was not a single person in sight. No sound of traffic on the highway. No wailing sirens from the fire trucks coming to rescue them. Only the silent whisper of the morning breeze as it drifted past.

In anguish, she turned away and looked up at the sky. And that's when she saw the roof of her house was gone, leaving only the bare wooden frame in place. She stared at it a moment, mouth agape, hands lightly against her cheeks. Then with all her might she screamed as loudly as she could, "WHY?!" She took a deep, gasping breath and doubled over, screaming again. "Why do they do this to us?!" Then she raised up for yet one more breath and looked up to heaven, screaming all the louder, "Why do you let them do this?!"

CHAPTER 67
WASHINGTON, D.C.

A LITTLE BEFORE LUNCH, President Stanton met in the Cabinet Room with a group of high school students from Indiana. The visit had been scheduled months in advance and when the school decided to make the trip in spite of the trouble raging in the Middle East, Stanton saw it as a chance to demonstrate to the public that they had nothing to fear. Aubrey Preston had tried to talk him out of it, arguing that the Republicans would use it to show how out of touch he was with the nation's sense of urgency regarding Israel and a conflict that induced images of Armageddon, but Stanton would not be deterred.

With the group seated around the conference table, he launched into a long-winded recitation of the history of the White House. Somewhere between a story about the burning of the building by the British in the War of 1812 and the real story of Andrew Jackson's giant block of cheese, Pete McWhinney appeared at the door. From the look on his face, Stanton knew there was more trouble.

McWhinney came to his side. "We have a situation," he whispered.

"Now?" Stanton frowned.

"Yes, sir. We need to get downstairs."

Stanton shook his head. "Have them brief me in the Oval Office."

"We really need to do this downstairs."

"Pete, I've been down to that room at least once in each of the last three days. I'm not going down there today. Have Admiral Beamon brief me in the office. I'll be in there shortly." He turned back to the group. "Now," he smiled, "where was I?"

"Cheese," someone said.

Half an hour later, Mrs. Moynihan appeared at the Cabinet Room door. She caught Stanton's eye and arched an eyebrow. He turned to the group. "Well, gang, as much as I would like to stay and visit, I have to go now and attend to the nation's business. But I've arranged for you all to have lunch in the White House cafeteria, and if I can squeeze in a few minutes, I'll stop by and see how you're doing." The group burst into applause and Stanton left the room.

Mrs. Moynihan ushered him down the hall. "Admiral Beamon has been waiting fifteen minutes, Mr. President."

"Admiral Beamon works for me, Mrs. Moynihan."

"I'm just helping you stay on schedule, Mr. President."

"Yes, Mrs. Moynihan. I appreciate that."

When Stanton reached the office, he found Admiral Beamon seated on the sofa, one arm draped over a leather briefcase that sat beside him. Pete McWhinney joined them and stood near the door.

"Sorry about the delay," Stanton apologized. "I got a little carried away with a group of high school students."

"I'm sure it was more entertaining than what we've been discussing."

"A welcome relief, actually." Stanton took a seat in a chair near one end of the sofa. "What's happened?"

"Sir, a few hours ago, an explosion at the port of Haifa leveled the city."

Stanton looked puzzled. "Haifa?"

"Yes, sir."

"How bad was it?"

"Most of the city's central district has been obliterated." Beamon opened his briefcase and took out a photograph. "This is an image from our satellite."

Stanton picked up the photo and stared at it. "It looks like a nuclear bomb."

"Yes, sir," Beamon nodded. "It does."

Stanton glanced at him over the top of the picture. "Was it?"

"We can't rule that out definitively, but our analysts think it was actually a missile strike against an LNG tanker. The *Imperial St. Marie*, a tanker owned by Imperial Oil Company, was tied up at the port."

"Where did the missile come from?"

"That's the bigger issue." Beamon leaned forward, resting his elbows on his knees. "The Israelis insist the missile was launched from a submarine in the Mediterranean."

"What do we say?"

"We don't know yet. Our satellites didn't pick up anything at the time. We're still researching the matter."

"Anything we can do?" Stanton leaned back in his chair. "I mean, obviously we'll give them whatever humanitarian aid they need. But militarily, is there anything we can do now?"

"The Israeli Navy has deployed missile cruisers to the region. They're out there looking for Iranian submarines. They would like our help."

"They've formally requested it?"

"Yes, sir," McWhinney answered. "Secretary Baker received a written request less than an hour ago."

Stanton looked over at Beamon. "Convene a meeting of the Joint Chiefs. I want to discuss this with them before I do anything."

"Yes, sir."

CHAPTER 68

EL PASO, TEXAS

THAT AFTERNOON, TONY PETERSON took Cruse and Griffin aside. "Listen, I have a guy who told me about seeing some people in Juarez he thinks are from the Middle East. I think I can get him to meet with you and look at those photos. You want to talk to him?"

"Sure," Cruse answered.

"I'm interested," Griffin added. "But there's only one thing." He looked over at Cruse. "You gotta lose the suit."

A few hours later, Cruse and Griffin rode across town to Casa Itzel Café on Radford Street in north El Paso. They parked the car in an alley around the corner and went inside. Peterson was seated alone at a table in back. "Where's your guy?" Griffin asked as he slid onto a chair.

"He's in back. This is where he works."

Cruse took a seat on the opposite side of the table, his back to the wall, with a clear view of the front door. He glanced around, checking the room. "The food any good here?"

"I don't know," Peterson shrugged. "I never eat here." He pointed to Cruse's jeans. "I see you decided to get comfortable."

"Two days in El Paso," Cruse chuckled. "And already I'm forgetting New York."

"I read your file," Griffin quipped. "You weren't in New York that much."

"Keep it quiet," Peterson cautioned. "This is a safe place but you never know who's listening."

"So," Cruse continued, "let's talk to your guy."

"Okay, sit tight and let me check with him."

Cruse and Griffin did their best to look inconspicuous as Peterson disappeared in back. A few minutes later, he returned to his seat at the table. "He's a little nervous about talking."

"Come on," Griffin growled. "We're here. He's gonna give us nothing?"

"He's really worried about cooperating."

"What you got on him?"

"Not much. He's just someone I know," Peterson explained. "Doesn't like what happened to the neighborhoods after the cartels moved in. Tries to help."

"Let me talk to him," Cruse suggested.

"If you're going, I'm going, too," Griffin insisted.

"I don't know." Peterson looked wary. "I think if we gang up on him, we won't get anywhere."

"We won't do that," Griffin insisted. "Cruse will do the talking. I'll do the listening."

"Okay," Peterson said reluctantly. "He's in back at the sink. His name's Remedios Tamayo."

Cruse and Griffin rose from the seats at the table and crossed the room to the kitchen. A man stood at a sink in the corner, washing pots and pans. He wore white pants and a white t-shirt with an apron over the top. He glanced over his shoulder as they approached. "I told you this might not be a good time for this."

"Remedios Tamayo," Cruse said quietly. "We just want to ask you some questions."

Tamayo turned far enough to see them. His eyes were wide with a look of concern. "Where's Peterson?"

"Out front," Cruse motioned.

"We'll be busy soon." Tamayo turned back to the sink. "I ain't got time now."

Cruse moved beside him and took a picture from his pocket. "You know him?"

"No. Never seen him before."

Cruse took out another photo. This one was a picture of Ahmed Haza. "How about him?" Tamayo glanced at it but said nothing. "How do you know him?" Cruse persisted.

"I didn't say I knew him."

"But you recognize him."

"Yeah, I've seen him."

"Where?"

"Around."

"Around where?"

"I saw him in Juarez," Tamayo sighed. He picked up a pot from the floor and shoved it into the sink. "A couple of days ago. But that's all I got to say."

Cruse didn't stop. "Donde en Juárez?"

"Una tienda."

"Which store? What was he doing?"

"I don't know. Buying something, I guess. They looked like—" Tamayo stopped in midsentence. "That's it." He waved his hands in protest. "I've said too much already."

"They?" Cruse pressed the issue. "They who? Who was he with?"

"I can't tell you that." Tamayo shook his head. "I can't tell you."

"You mean you won't."

"I mean," Tamayo hissed, "if they find out I said this much, I'm a dead man. If I tell you more, they'll kill everybody I know."

"If I tell them you talked," Cruse replied, "you'll be a dead man anyway."

Tamayo looked him in the eye. "You wouldn't do that to me."

"Who was he with?"

"You don't understand."

"Lo entiendo perfectamente," Cruse said quickly. "Who was he with?"

"Okay." Tamayo heaved a dejected sigh. He pointed to the second picture still in Cruse's hand. "That guy was with Juan Rivera."

"And who is that?"

"I know him," Griffin said, leaning closer. He caught Cruse's eye. "We got enough. Let's go."

When they came from the kitchen, the table where they'd been sitting was empty. Peterson was nowhere in sight. Cruse and Griffin walked outside and made their way to the car. When they were seated inside, Cruse looked over at him. "So, who is Juan Rivera?"

"He works for Miguel Murillo."

"That's the second time we've heard that name."

"Yeah," Griffin nodded. "We should get over to Juarez and see what else we can find out."

"Isn't that dangerous?"

Griffin backed the car into the street. "Every day is dangerous down here."

CHAPTER 69
WASHINGTON, D.C.

ANDREW STANTON was on the golf course at Andrews Air Force Base, squeezing in a quick nine holes of golf, when he received a call from McWhinney telling him of yet one more incident that required his attention. Stanton played out the hole, took a seat on a nearby golf cart, and rode back to the clubhouse. His limousine was waiting when he arrived. Twenty minutes later, the motorcade came to a stop on the driveway outside the entrance to the West Wing. Stanton bounded from the car, moved quickly inside the building, and took the steps to the basement. McWhinney and the national security team were waiting as he took a seat at the head of the conference table.

Stanton glanced down the table to Admiral Beamon. "What do we have this time?"

"Mr. President, less than an hour ago, an Iranian submarine lobbed antiship missiles into Tel Aviv." Images appeared on the screen behind him. He pointed to them as he spoke. "Those missiles struck a water-treatment facility, essential components of the telephone system, and a power-generation plant."

"Casualties?"

"Still counting, sir."

"This is an outrage!" Upchurch fumed.

"I share your indignation, Haden," Stanton replied coolly. "But Israel can hardly complain if Iran strikes back. After all, Israel struck first."

"Mr. President, Israel did strike first. But only because we didn't."

"You think we should have."

"I've made that very clear."

"You've also made it clear that you think we didn't strike Iran's nuclear facilities because I'm weak."

"Yes," Upchurch nodded bravely. "But not weak because you're afraid of war. Weak because you're afraid of the voters."

"I remind you that you work for me."

Upchurch took a deep breath and spoke in a calm and even tone. "They've wiped out Haifa. Now they're moving against Tel Aviv. Mr. President, we have to hit back and hit back hard enough to make them stop."

"We've already bombed every missile site in Iran," Baker jumped into the conversation. "What more do you suggest we do?"

"There has to be a way to make them stop."

"Bombing something isn't going to do that," Baker argued. "What more can we hit?"

"Mosques," Upchurch listed calmly. "Hospitals. Playgrounds. Make them pay."

"Are you crazy?"

"And while we're at it," Stanton countered sarcastically, "why not the orphanages, too." His voice grew louder and harder with each word. "Get them while they're young. Before they hear the name of Allah. Before they find out about car bombs and suicide bombs." He was shouting now. "Before they have time to learn to hate us for our stupidity!"

"What they need most is intelligence," Catlett offered. "Information. Useable information."

"That's right, Mr. President," Beamon said. "We need to—"

"We need to use some intelligence instead of just talking about it!" Stanton yelled, his face red, the veins in his neck bulging. "I'm tired of coming down here every day, multiple times every day, and hearing the same proposals from the same talking heads who have nothing at risk in this game!"

"Gentlemen," McWhinney intervened. "Could you excuse us a moment?" He turned to Stanton. "Come with me, please." He rose from his seat at the table and gestured for Stanton to do likewise. Reluctantly he followed McWhinney out to the hallway.

"You know," Stanton complained, "every time you do that, it looks like I'm the schoolboy getting taken to the hall by his teacher."

"You would rather we shouted at each other in there?"

"I'm tired, Pete."

"We're all tired, Mr. President. But we have to just—"

"No!" Stanton shouted, cutting him off. "I'm tired of this. Of coming down here and talking about solving someone else's problem. I didn't tell Yedaya to bomb Iran. I didn't lead him on to think we would cover for his mistakes if he did. I did the exact opposite. I told him not to do it. I denied him the refueling tankers he needed to do it right. And I warned him there would be consequences if he went ahead and did it anyway. Now there are consequences and the American people are paying the price for it. American people, Pete. Paying the price for something Israel did."

"Listen to me, Upchurch is right." McWhinney did his best to remain calm. "We need to find a way to stop the conflict. But we have to think about this in practical terms, too."

"Practical terms? You mean the election?"

"Yes," McWhinney nodded. "I mean the election."

"This is the situation room," Stanton snapped. "I may be a jerk about some things, but this is the White House situation room."

"No, sir," McWhinney disagreed. "It's the hallway in the White House basement, which is why I brought you out here." He gestured toward the door to the situation room. "In there we talk about military strategy and options. Out here we talk about our political lives."

Stanton turned toward the door. "I don't want to do this now."

McWhinney took him gently by the elbow. "If we don't get reelected, we don't get to do the things we talked about. Education, safety net for the poor, realigning the economy, new forms of energy—all of that is lost. Winning the election is as important as winning this military situation we face."

"So what are you saying?"

"I'm saying, oil costs are rising and that's bad enough, but people will understand. We can get past that. But if you turn your back on Israel, we lose the vote in New York, probably Pennsylvania, most of the South, including Florida. We can't win the election with that scenario."

"So Israel has us in a corner."

"They do for now. If we can get past this, we can deal with Israel later."

"How do we get past it?"

"We take it one step at a time."

"That's how we got into most of the wars of the past two centuries."

"And it's how we're going to find our way forward in this one."

"Okay." Stanton took a deep breath. "Let's go back in there."

A guard opened the door. Stanton and McWhinney entered the situation room. Stanton looked over at Admiral Beamon as he took a seat. "So where are we with this? Have the Israelis asked for our help?"

"There's been no formal request," Beamon replied. "And there's not likely to be."

"Why is that?"

"These are proud people, Mr. President. They've already asked us to help them once."

"What do we know about this latest strike? Anything more than the other one?"

"Unlike with the explosion at Haifa, this time our systems detected the missiles as soon as they broke the water. Every indication tells us they were launched by a Kilo Class submarine of the Iranian Navy loitering off the Israeli coast right there. Most likely, it was the *Tareq*." Beamon pointed to a place on the map. "Our analysts say it's sitting right there. The Israelis are searching for it but they don't have the capacity to locate it. Unless they stumble across it, the submarine will be free to escape."

Catlett spoke up. "Or continue the attack."

Stanton nodded. "We have the information they need?"

"Yes, sir," Beamon assured him. "We know precisely where it's located."

"Okay," Stanton affirmed. "Give it to them. Give them the information, but don't join in the attack."

"Yes, sir, Mr. President." Beamon stepped to a phone at the end of the table.

CHAPTER 70
JUAREZ, MEXICO

LATE THAT AFTERNOON, Cruse and Griffin took a pickup truck from the FBI motor pool and drove across the border to a cafe on Pablo Lopez Street at the southern edge of the city. They parked in back and went inside. Griffin chose a table near the front, where they could see the street without being conspicuous.

Cruse glanced around. "You sure this is the place?"

"This is the neighborhood," Griffin replied. "That store across the street is where Tamayo said he saw Ahmed Haza."

Cruse looked in that direction. "The butcher shop?"

"The sign says carniceria, but it has more than just meat."

"You come down here a lot?"

"Not too much. Don't want my face to get too familiar."

They ordered food and ate while keeping an eye on the street. In a little while, a car stopped on the corner. The passenger door opened and a man got out.

"Look familiar?" Cruse asked, watching through the window.

"No." Griffin leaned to one side. "I can't see the driver."

"Neither can I."

While the vehicle sat idling, the man closed the car door and went inside the store. In a few minutes he returned. As he walked toward the car, the car backed toward him, changing the angle of view from the café window. When he opened the door to get inside, Griffin and Cruse had a clear view of the driver seated behind the steering wheel.

"That's him."

"Who?"

"Rivera." Griffin stood. "Pay for the food. I'll get the truck."

While Cruse tossed some money on the table, Griffin disappeared out the back door of the café. Cruse took one last sip from his drink and followed after him. When he came out to the street, the car was still sitting at the corner but while he watched, the car turned right and drove away, moving at a slow idle.

By the time Griffin came with the truck, the car was out of sight. Cruse climbed inside. "They went that way." He pointed to the right. "But they turned down a side street."

"Which one?"

"I'll show you."

Several blocks later, Cruse pointed again to the right. "This is the street." Griffin made the turn and pressed the gas pedal. The truck surged ahead. "Don't get too close," Cruse cautioned.

"I've done this before."

A few minutes later, the car turned left down a dusty unpaved street. Griffin continued to the next corner and turned there. They both watched out the window at the next cross street. "There he is," Cruse indicated.

Griffin seemed unfazed. "Like I told you, I've done this before."

At the next corner, they paused and waited to see the car as it passed through the intersection on the street one block to the left. When the car didn't appear, they turned left, rode quickly to the next corner, and turned left again. "It should be in here," Griffin decided.

"Yep," Cruse said, signaling. "Parked by that house."

The car sat in front of a house on the left side of the street, near the middle of the block. Griffin and Cruse drove past it and continued on for two more blocks. Then they doubled back on a parallel street until they reached a spot directly behind the house. Griffin parked the truck in an empty lot and switched off the engine.

"What do we do now?" Cruse asked.

"Sneak up behind the house and see what we can find out. Maybe get a peek inside."

"We don't need a warrant?"

"This is Mexico," Griffin chuckled. "I don't think a warrant would do us much good now."

Cruse and Griffin stepped from the truck, eased the doors closed, and started across the lot toward an alley. Moving quietly, they worked their way up the alley to a shed. A bare, grassless yard lay between it and the house with a hedgerow to the left and two cars parked to the right.

From the corner of the shack they could see the windows along the back wall of the house were open and screenless. People moved back and forth inside. "You take the window on that end," Griffin said, motioning to the left. "I'll go this way." And he started around the shack toward the end of the house to the right.

Cruse crouched, ducked behind the hedgerow, and hurried to the house. He waited there a moment, listening to make sure he hadn't been seen, then raised himself up to see over the sill.

Inside was the kitchen. A table with chairs sat near the center of the room with a counter and sink on the opposite side. Two men stood at the sink. They were talking, but Cruse couldn't understand what they said.

At the table were four men, all of them with dark hair, olive complexion, and sharp features. Cruse was certain they were from the Middle East. Then a cell phone rang. He glanced to the right to see it was Griffin's, and he was desperately trying to turn it off.

Suddenly a head popped out through the open window above Cruse, followed by a torso, as a man reached out with his hand and grabbed hold of Cruse's hair. Instinctively, Cruse reached for the man's arm, pulled him through the window opening, and struck him across the throat. The man rolled to one side, gasping for breath. Cruse turned away and ran for the shed where they'd been hiding before.

A gunshot rang out, followed by two more. Bullets struck the dirt to Cruse's left and right. As he reached the shack, a round struck the wooden frame of the structure, showering him with splinters. Still, he did not stop but continued down the alley, doing his best to keep the shack positioned on a line of sight between him and the house, and working equally hard to keep his legs pumping as fast as they would go.

Cruse reached the truck first. He opened the driver's door and climbed inside. Griffin, running from the opposite side of the house, made it as a hail of bullets struck the side of the truck. He wasted no time trying to get inside the cab but instead dove over the side and landed in the bed of the truck. "Go!" he shouted. "Go! Go! Go!" He drew his pistol from the holster on his ankle, held it above the edge of the truck, and squeezed off five rounds. By then Cruse had the truck in gear. He backed it from the lot and continued down the street, driving in reverse. At the first intersection, he whipped the rear of the truck into the cross street, slammed the gearshift into drive, and stomped on the gas pedal. The truck shot forward down the street as the men from the house appeared on foot behind them.

CHAPTER 71
TEHRAN, IRAN

JALIL AMINI, DIRECTOR OF INTELLIGENCE and National Security, found Rasoul Moussaoui sitting alone on a bench beneath a large oak tree on the palace grounds. Amini walked quickly toward him and took a seat beside him. "It is not good for you to be out here all alone. Where are your bodyguards?"

"I sent them back to the palace. I needed the peace and quiet." Moussaoui gazed up through the tree's bare branches at the sky above. "And I needed the air. It is stuffy inside."

"We have new developments." Amini's voice sounded even more serious than usual.

Moussaoui seemed not to hear him. "How long before electricity is restored?"

"I do not know."

"Have you asked?"

"Yes," Amini nodded. "I have asked. But no one seems to know. We have generators for the lights. Haven't they turned them on?"

"We have electricity here, but the system is down across the city, and having electric lights only makes the lack of them everywhere else all the more obvious." Moussaoui looked over at Amini. "What is it this time? What did you come to tell me?"

"The Israelis found our submarines."

Moussaoui's eyes widened. "And?"

Amini looked away. "They sank them all."

"The Israelis did this?" Moussaoui was puzzled. "They located all of our submarines?"

"Yes."

Moussaoui's eyes narrowed. "The Americans," he seethed. "They must have helped."

"Yes," Amini nodded. "Admiral Shirdel is all but certain they provided assistance."

"Do we have proof?"

"We have radio traffic recorded by operatives in Lebanon. But it is encrypted and scrambled and we can't decipher it. Their missiles took out our central computing facility that normally handles such things. Sources tell us the transmissions are from an American AWACS plane operating in the area."

"It is voice?"

"Yes, but digitized and all we hear are sounds."

Moussaoui looked him in the eye. "Did the Americans sink our ships?"

"Admiral Shirdel does not think so."

"But they gave Israel the necessary information."

"Yes," Amini nodded. "Israeli ships sank them, but it was made possible only with information supplied by the U.S. Without the Americans, the Israelis never would have found them."

"It makes no difference." Moussaoui rested his back against the trunk of the tree and crossed his legs. "Whether they attacked our ships directly, or provided Israel with the necessary means. It is the same conduct they use to justify their own actions against us." He placed his hands at his side and closed his eyes. "They say we use Hezbollah to do our toughest work. And we say America uses Israel to execute its policy of oppression against the people of Palestine. They justify their attacks against us on that basis. And we shall use the same to justify our own." He opened his eyes and once again looked over at Amini. "Our people are already crossing the border from Mexico?"

"Yes."

"Tell them they are free to act." Moussaoui folded his arms across his chest and closed his eyes.

CHAPTER 72
WASHINGTON, D.C.

THAT EVENING, AUBREY PRESTON met with President Stanton in the residence upstairs at the White House. Stanton appeared distracted, on edge, and he stood while they talked. "We're in the middle of a situation. I don't have long. What's this all about?"

"It's about that. About the situation."

Stanton looked puzzled. "What about it?"

"We were looking at the numbers and they're not good."

"Numbers?"

"Polling numbers."

Stanton's forehead wrinkled in an angry frown. "We've been over this a thousand times, Aubrey. Before you moved to the campaign. After you moved to the campaign. Way back when we were just thinking about the campaign. I can't set policy based on polling numbers. How many times do I have to tell you guys that?"

"You won't be president if you don't pay attention to the polling results."

"What are you telling me? I'm going to lose?"

"With most armed conflicts, presidents experience a rise in popularity. Voters generally support the military. When the troops are deployed, there's a corresponding rise in popular patriotism. That generally carries over to the president who commands those troops. That's not happening this time."

"I'm aware of that," Stanton nodded. "Voters perceive the Middle East as a trap. The stakes are too high. There's too much risk. All downside. No upside."

"Yes, sir, but it's more than that. They see this in biblical terms. The end. Or at least flirting with the end."

"So, what does all that mean for the campaign?"

"We need to explore options that solve both problems at the same time. A strategy that gets us out of this conflict, rather than deeper into it. An approach that makes you look like the leader we all know you to be. A problem solver. Israel and Iran got themselves into this, we show them how to resolve it without engaging in a ground war."

"I'm listening." Stanton took a seat in a chair near the door. He gestured for Preston to sit, as well. "But I think you're talking about negotiating our way out of this, and that would be tricky."

"Not a settlement," Preston said, taking a seat in a nearby chair. "A solution. Something that actually resolves the underlying issues."

"Won't work," Stanton said, shaking his head. "The Republicans will label it as surrender. Talbot would see right through it."

"Compromise. Not surrender."

"That's the same thing," Stanton said with an arrogant smirk. "Worse, in fact."

"There's always compromise in every solution."

"Listen, I know to all you wise guys it looks like I've just been feeling my way through this the past few days, groping like a blind man who's lost his way," Stanton said sarcastically, the tension rising in his voice. "But I do know one thing for certain. In an election year, compromise will be viewed as surrender. And whether voters understand the nature of this conflict or not, surrender will cost us the election."

"A solution, Mr. President. We're finding a solution."

"Oh, come on!" Stanton shouted, unable to contain his frustration any longer. "This is just more of the same political-speak I got from Leon Bain. Redefining words to mean something they don't. Every phrase nuanced until it breaks. I need more than that!"

"No, sir," Preston insisted. "I'm not talking about spin. I'm suggesting an actual solution that resolves all the underlying issues. One that appears sane, just, and reasonable. A solution that walks us back from the brink of the apocalypse and leaves the Middle East safe, secure, and at peace."

Stanton arched an eyebrow. "If you can do that, you can be president tomorrow."

"No, sir." Preston shook his head. "I can't do that, but you can. And when you do, you will be seen as one of the most heroic figures in the history of the republic. A genuine leader. A statesman the likes of which we haven't seen in decades."

Stanton rubbed his chin. "What do you propose?"

"A meeting."

Stanton's frustration level rose immediately. "I've been in meetings with generals and admirals every day for the past week. Who do you want me to meet with?"

"The president of Iran."

Stanton was startled. "What?"

"In secret," Preston added quickly. "At an undisclosed, neutral site. Just the two of you at the table."

"You're out of your mind," Stanton said quietly. "I should fire you on the spot."

"Sir, to get out of this situation, both politically and strategically, we have to change the nature of the conflict. Meeting with Moussaoui will do just that."

"Talbot will eat me alive."

"Talbot won't find out about it until it's over and done and by then the press will be talking about you with terms like *statesmanship, honor,* and *duty.* Talbot will be irrelevant."

"Nah." Stanton shook his head. "Things like this have a way of getting out. Someone always knows."

"Secretary Baker is onboard with the idea."

Stanton looked curious. "Kathleen agreed to this?"

"She's willing to explore it."

"What about Upchurch?"

"I haven't talked to him, and I don't think we can."

"We can't make a move like this without talking to him. He's the secretary of defense. One of the most powerful positions in the cabinet. Besides, a move like this would directly affect his department."

"If we tell him we're even considering this, he'll leak it and the whole thing will blow up in our faces."

"Upchurch is a jerk sometimes but he's a good man." Stanton spoke with a reassuring tone. "He can keep a secret."

"Upchurch is just what you said. He's the secretary of defense," Preston countered. "This war is exactly what he needs. He'll do anything to keep control of it and prevent it from sliding over to State."

"It's a conflict." Stanton took a professorial tone. "You said it right the first time."

"Sir?"

"You said 'war' just now. Technically, it's not a war until we make a formal declaration and Congress approves. Until then, it's a conflict."

"Yes, sir."

"Are you going to be in town for a day or two?"

"Yes, sir."

"I'll tell McWhinney to set up a meeting with Kathleen Baker." Stanton rose from his chair. "You'll be there with us."

"Yes, sir," Preston replied, standing as well.

"I have to go." Stanton opened the door and gestured for Preston to follow. "They'll be looking for me downstairs."

CHAPTER 73
EL PASO, TEXAS

LATE THAT NIGHT THERE WAS a knock on the door of Cruse's apartment. He took an automatic pistol from the dresser drawer, walked quietly to the living room, and peered out the peephole to see Foster Goodall standing outside.

"I did what you said," Cruse began as he opened the door. "I reported and I've been minding my own business."

"I know." Goodall stepped around Cruse and entered the apartment. "I'm not here because you messed up."

Cruse shut the door. "Then why are you here?"

"We need you back in New York."

"No. You need me right here." Cruse moved to the sofa and picked up a photograph that was lying there. "I've been to Juarez. Hezbollah has people on the border. Take a look at this." He handed Goodall the photo. "Remember this guy?"

"Ahmed Haza," Goodall mused as he studied the picture. "I thought he was dead."

"So did every other Western intelligence agency." Cruse dropped onto the sofa. "But he's here."

Goodall took a seat in a chair to the left. "Where did you get this picture?"

"Routine drug case. Someone saw someone. We put him with a sketch artist. Ran the sketch through our face-recognition program." He pointed to the photo. "That came out of the database."

"And he's in Juarez?"

"Just a few miles across the border." Cruse leaned forward. "This is bad, Foster. Mexican drug cartel. Known operatives from the Middle East. That could work in both directions and none of it good. I mean, Hezbollah, teaming up with the drug cartels, brings lots of muscle into the drug trade. And it gives Hezbollah access to ways to easily cross our border from Mexico."

"That's all interesting." Foster tossed the photograph on the sofa next to Cruse. "And on a normal day I would join you. But I need your help."

"With what?"

"We found a body in a cargo container at Red Hook."

"Who is it?"

"David Holsten."

"Worked for Stanton's campaign?"

"Yeah. Chose to avoid a White House position. Continued to consult instead. Word on the street is, he was working with Michael Geller. Know anything about that?"

"Not much," Cruse grinned. "You guys didn't let me get that far."

"If you were back in New York, where would you go with this?"

"I'd go right back where I left off and start asking questions."

"The shale oil thing? The trust?"

"Yeah. And I'd start with Geller."

"Okay." Goodall stood. "Do it."

"I'm here, Foster. You told me to come down here, mind my own business, and maybe I wouldn't end up in prison." Cruse also stood. "This place is crawling with bad guys. I can spend the rest of my career right here."

"Whatever's happening here is not your problem. Not now. You're going back with me."

"Just like that?"

"Holsten was the president's friend. Four years ago, he had access to everything. He developed a network of friends. Powerful friends that gave him contact with almost anyone in the world. We're trying to figure out what the killer was after and whether the president is in danger. We need your help."

"That sounds like a job for the Secret Service."

"Right now it's everybody's job. Pack a bag."

"You've cleared it?"

"Would I be here if I hadn't?"

"Okay. What time's the flight in the morning?"

"We're leaving now. I have a plane waiting. Get your bag. We gotta go."

CHAPTER 74
NEW YORK CITY

EARLY IN THE MORNING, Cruse and Goodall arrived at JFK Airport. They were met on the tarmac by a car and driver. On the ride downtown, they reviewed the Holsten file one last time.

"How long was he in that container?" Cruse asked as he stared at the crime scene photographs.

"Not quite a week, as best they can determine so far."

"I wouldn't have recognized him."

"Those steel boxes are like ovens. Holsten's body deteriorated quickly." Goodall reached into the pocket of his jacket. "Here." He handed Cruse a photograph. "Take this with you." The picture showed Holsten from a year earlier, dressed in a business suit, standing on the sidewalk outside the Harvard Club. "Maybe that will jog someone's memory."

Cruse took it from him. "I think it will take more than this to get them to remember." He tucked the photo into his pocket. "Knowing the guy ended up dead in a container box could give lots of people a reason to forget."

"That reminds me," Goodall continued. "A reporter from the *Times* got wind of Holsten's death. The paper was set to run a story on it, but we managed to hold them off. No one outside our office and the medical examiner's office knows he's dead."

"How'd you pull that off?"

"Initially they said they'd give us two days. I told them that we'd give them exclusive access to the entire story if they would simply put their coverage on hold until we were ready."

"And they agreed to that?"

"Well," Goodall shrugged, "it didn't hurt that the Secret Service was telling them the same thing."

"Holsten's family doesn't know he's dead?"

"No one knows. So when you talk to people, don't mention that he's dead. Just tell them we're looking for him. Want to talk to him. Not in any trouble. Just looking into something that happened before he started working for the president. Keep it ambiguous."

Half an hour later, they arrived on the street outside the FBI office in lower Manhattan. As the car came to a stop at the curb, Goodall turned to Cruse. "You know where to begin?"

"Yes. Are you going to cover me on this?"

"Cover what?"

"Last time I tried to talk to these people, they called the White House."

"That won't be a problem this time. But if you do have trouble, give me a call."

"What do I do about a place to stay?"

"We have an apartment in midtown. You can stay there. I'll tell the office to set it up for you and get someone to drop your bag there." Goodall opened the door. "Hank will take you to your first stop. Just tell him where to go." Then he pushed the car door shut, stepped out to the sidewalk, and was gone.

Hank, the driver, glanced up in the rearview mirror and caught Cruse's eye. "Where to?"

"The IDB Bank building on Forty-Third Street."

Hank steered the car away from the curb into traffic. A few minutes later, they arrived at the address. Cruse climbed from the car, crossed the sidewalk to the lobby entrance, and made his way to the elevator. On the sixth floor, he once again entered Geller's office. Geller's secretary smiled up at him. "You're back again, I see," recalling his earlier visit to the office.

"Is Mr. Geller in today?"

"No, I'm afraid he's not. I did tell him you were looking for him earlier, though."

"That's okay." Cruse took a chair from the far side of the room and moved it near her desk. He sat down and looked over at her. "I can talk to you just as well."

"I'm busy. Really busy."

Cruse took out the photograph of Holsten and showed it to her. "Ever seen him before?"

Her eyes opened wide and the corners of her mouth turned up in a brief microexpression of recognition, then quickly returned to normal. "No, I don't think I have."

"You realize that lying to an FBI agent, even about an unrelated matter, is a federal offense."

"And you realize," she said without emotion, "that what I don't know, I can't tell you."

"Ever seen him with Mr. Geller?"

"No."

"Ever seen him on your own, without Mr. Geller?"

"No."

"Does Mr. Geller know him?"

"You'd have to ask him."

"Fair enough." Cruse stood and turned toward the door. "Tell Mr. Geller I'll be back. This isn't going away."

In the lobby downstairs, Cruse called Mark White at the FBI office and asked him to track down an address for Curtis McCullough, one of the investors in the Shale Oil Trust.

"He and his wife have a residence on Long Island. But they keep an apartment at the Carlyle Hotel."

"Upper East Side?"

"Yeah. Madison and Seventy-Sixth Street."

"If you see my luggage sitting around the office, it's supposed to go to an apartment."

"Goodall got it all set up already. Come by when you get a chance and I'll give you the key."

On the street, Cruse hailed a taxi and rode uptown to the Carlyle. He took the elevator up to McCullough's apartment and knocked on the door. A middle-aged woman greeted him.

"Yes?" she said with a smile.

"Mrs. McCullough?"

"Who wants to know?"

"Richard Cruse." He flashed his badge. "I'm with the FBI."

"Oh." She had a worried look. "What's this about?"

"I'm looking for your husband, Curtis. Is he around?"

"No. He's not. Why are you looking for him?"

Cruse took the photograph from his pocket. "Actually, I'm interested in this man." He handed her the photo. "Have you ever seen him?"

"David Holsten?" Her eyes opened wide. "Sure. We know him. I mean, I haven't seen him in a while, but I know him." She gave the photo back to Cruse. "Is he in some kind of trouble?"

"We're just investigating an incident that happened during a campaign a few years ago. Trying to track down information." Cruse tucked the picture into his pocket. "Your husband knows him?"

"Yes. Of course." A frown creased her forehead. "What's this about?"

"What about Michael Geller? Did he know Mr. Holsten?"

Her face was clouded with contempt. "Don't get me started on Geller."

"What about him?"

"That guy's a creep."

"How so?"

"I don't know. He's just a creep. I don't like him."

"Did he know Holsten?"

"Yes. Of course."

"How well?"

"They were together all the time. They're all in some kind of business deal together. Geller. David. Curtis. Several other men. Why are you asking all these questions?"

"We think Mr. Geller and your husband might be able to help us."

She gestured over her shoulder. "You want me to see if I can find Curtis?"

"Yeah." Cruse was surprised by her response. "Sure."

She backed away from the door. "Come on inside. No point in standing out there." When Cruse was in the apartment, she shut the door behind him and gestured to the left toward the living room. "Just wait in there. I'll be right back." Then she disappeared down the hall.

While she was gone, Cruse looked around the room. Bookcases lined the wall opposite the doorway. Three framed photographs rested on one of the shelves. He made his way in that direction and studied the pictures.

In a few minutes, Mrs. McCullough returned. "Curtis said he doesn't have time to talk to you today." She had a sheepish look. "He's not very happy with me for letting you into the apartment, either."

"I'm sorry about that."

"Oh, I don't care." She waved her hand. "Actually, I'm glad for the company. Gets kind of lonely up here sometimes."

"Yes, ma'am. I was just—"

"Wait." Her face brightened with a look of realization. "This is a picture of David right here." She reached past Cruse and took one of the framed photographs from the shelf. The picture showed three men standing together, each of them holding a golf club. "That's David standing next to Curtis," she said, tapping the photo with her finger. "They were in a golf tournament together." She pointed to the third man. "That's Michael Geller. They all played together that day. Some kind of fund-raiser, I think. Out in the Hamptons."

Cruse looked at it a moment. "Any way I could get a copy of this?"

"Oh," she exclaimed, "you can have this one." She turned the frame over and pulled the back loose. The photograph came free with it and she handed it to him.

"You're sure about this?"

"Please," she insisted. "Curtis loves that picture, but I hate it. If you take it, I'll have a place for a picture of Gabby."

"Who's Gabby?"

"Our beautiful British Shorthair cat."

*   *   *

From McCullough's apartment at the Carlyle, Cruse went back to the corner on Forty-Third Street near the IDB Bank building. He found a bench across the street near a hot dog stand and took a seat.

Thirty minutes later, Geller's assistant emerged from the building and walked up the sidewalk to the right. He followed after her, keeping a safe distance until she turned and entered Annie Moore's, a restaurant just down from Grand Central Terminal. She took a seat near the window. He slipped onto a chair across from her.

"Mr. Cruse!" His sudden appearance startled her. "I told you before. I have nothing to say to you."

"I think you do." He took the photograph of Geller, Holsten, and McCullough from his pocket. "You told me you didn't know David Holsten."

"That's right."

"And when I asked if Mr. Geller knew him, you said I'd have to ask Geller."

"That's what I said."

He held the photograph so she could see it. "I believe this is a picture of Geller, Holsten, and McCullough, is it not?"

Her eyes darkened. "What do you want with me?"

"Geller knows David Holsten."

"Obviously."

"And you know David Holsten."

"And what does that prove?"

"Why would you resist even admitting that you know the guy?"

"Okay," she sighed. "I know him. Are you satisfied?"

"When's the last time you saw David Holsten?"

"About a week ago."

"Where did you see him?"

"In the office."

"With Geller?"

"I can't remember, exactly. They're both in and out all the time."

"What was he doing in the office that last day you saw him?"

"He and Mr. Geller were talking about a meeting they both planned to attend."

335

"What kind of meeting?"

"I don't know. Probably about their oil investment."

"The Shale Oil Trust?"

"Yes. How do you know about that?"

"Where was the meeting?"

"The Harvard Club."

"Did they leave together for that meeting?"

"I don't think so. I think the meeting was later that day."

"Does Mr. Weiss know David Holsten?"

"Mr. Weiss?"

"Yes. Does he know David Holsten?"

"Yes."

"How do you know that?"

"They work together on political campaigns. David and Mr. Weiss take care of the mechanics of it. The politics."

"And Mr. Geller?"

"Mr. Geller and his group provide the money. What are you getting at, Mr. Cruse?"

"What does Weiss add?"

"He provides manpower and the Jewish vote."

"They're heavily involved in politics?"

"I'd say so."

"How much so?"

"Mr. Holsten isn't officially connected to the president anymore, but he's out there working for him just the same. They've built an extensive organization in the city. Almost enough to control the vote in all five boroughs."

"Which gives Weiss a lot of pull at the White House."

"Which gives Weiss a lot of pull in many places, Mr. Cruse."

CHAPTER 75

BOSTON

NORMAN BLUNDELL CHECKED the morning traffic in his rearview mirror and steered his pickup truck into the lane to his left. He reached for the radio on the dash panel and pressed a button, changing to an all-news station. As he did, he noticed the time. "Almost nine," he grumbled. "I should have been there an hour ago." The freeway was more congested than usual and already he'd spent half an hour stuck in the bumper-to-bumper delay of a fender-bender.

A carpenter by trade, Blundell was on his way to meet a potential client who wanted a price on renovating office space near Logan Airport. He'd gotten a late start because his wife's car broke down and he had to drive her to work. The morning had been a whirlwind of activity even before then, getting their two children ready for school and preparing for the day. Even if everything had gone according to schedule he would have been a few minutes late for the meeting. Now he was very late.

At the entrance to the Ted Williams Tunnel he changed lanes again, moving to the far-right lane. The meeting was at a building on Harborside Drive. To get there, he had to take the first exit past the tunnel. If he missed it, he would have to go all the way to Franklin Street before he could turn around.

Just inside the tunnel, the truck's headlights came on. Tires on the right side of the truck made a roaring noise as they crossed over a drain cover buried in the pavement near the tunnel wall. The noise repeated as they crossed another, then another in quick, rhythmic succession. A slower car appeared up ahead. Blundell lifted his foot from the gas pedal and checked his side mirror in anticipation of moving around the car. As he reached up to flip on the turn signal, something in the mirror caught his eye. He looked again and saw a column of water spewing from the drain behind him. It shot straight up to the roof with a force so strong that it blasted ceiling tiles free, scattering them in every direction and sending broken pieces showering down on all four lanes of traffic.

The sound of screeching tires brought his attention back to the front and he looked out the windshield in time to see cars in front of him sliding sideways as water spewed from the drains in the roadway up ahead. He swerved to the left to avoid the next one, scraped against the car beside him, then cut back to the right to avoid a taxi that was stopped in the middle of the road. As he came around the taxi, he saw why everyone was trying to stop. A wall of water was rushing straight toward them with tremendous force, sweeping trailer trucks, delivery trucks, cars, and buses ahead of it.

Blundell brought the truck to a stop and put it in reverse but before he could get it moving, the water reached him. A city bus, carried along by the crest of the onrushing tide, came crashing down on the hood of his truck. As it came toward him, he saw the driver staring down at him through the bus window, eyes wide with fear, mouth open in a terrified scream. Then the bus rolled over and the roof of the pickup slammed down against Blundell's head. Pain shot down his neck into his spine and out to his fingertips, then everything went strangely dark.

*   *   *

Within minutes of the first signs of trouble in the tunnel, the alarm rang at the firehouse on D Street. Engine Company 39 sprang into action. Two ladder trucks and a paramedic unit rolled from the building and sped toward the freeway. Close behind them was a mobile command center.

Seated on the passenger side of the command center cab was Bob Montgomery. At twenty-three, he was the youngest man in company. On a routine day he would have ridden with the crew in one of the ladder trucks, but that month he was working a training rotation. He was assigned as an assistant to Neil Harris, the command center driver.

As they turned onto the freeway entrance ramp, the radio squawked with message traffic from other companies responding to the alarm. Montgomery looked over at Harris. "That's Company 7. How many does that make?"

"Three."

"This must be a big accident."

"I think it's more than an accident."

"They had a chain reaction down in Milton last—"

Montgomery stopped in midsentence as they reached the highway descent toward the tunnel entrance. In front of them, the pavement ended at the edge of a dark pool of roiling seawater, flowing from the mouth of what had been the tunnel as if bubbling up from a deep mysterious spring. Water from the opening washed over the top of the retaining wall that lined both sides of the highway, flowed over the grassy slope behind it, and cascaded down to the service road below. Floating on the surface of the water were body parts—arms, legs, and limbless torsos—ripped apart by the force of the water as it rushed into the tunnel from the bay, then surged violently down the long tube toward the openings at either end, grinding and shredding everything in its path.

Montgomery stared at the scene a moment, then jerked open the cab door, hung his head through the opening, and vomited.

"Get a hold of yourself, rookie," Harris cracked. "This is gonna be a long day. You can't start hurling every time you see an arm or a leg lying around."

"What happened?" Montgomery gasped.

"I don't know," Harris replied in a matter-of-fact tone. "Looks like the tunnel filled up with water. From the way it's flowing I'd say there's a hole in it the size of this truck." He shoved open the door and started out. "Come on. We got injured people to take care of. Let's go."

"Injured?" Montgomery exclaimed. "They're not injured. They're dead."

"Not all of them," Harris called as he slammed the door shut. "Come on."

Montgomery raised his head from between his knees and glanced out the windshield of the truck. Between their position and the water, a dozen cars and trucks were piled in a knot against the guardrail on the right. Four more vehicles were perched atop the retaining wall to the left. Through the shattered glass of one he saw people moving around inside. He sat there staring, for a moment not sure if he was awake or dreaming.

Then Harris shouted at him, "Hey! Get out of that truck and get moving!"

Reluctantly, Montgomery pushed the door open wider and climbed to the ground, being careful to step over his own vomit.

Behind them, trucks from Company 7 arrived. They took up a position a quarter mile away, parking a tanker and a ladder truck sideways across the highway, blocking access and creating a perimeter for the scene. The highway beyond them was clogged with traffic and jammed with emergency vehicles trying to reach the tunnel. Before long, television crews arrived and then a crowd of curious onlookers.

Montgomery did his best to focus on the work at hand, getting the command center up and running and assisting with removing the injured. An hour into the effort, the injured were gone but the area was crawling with people as teams worked to locate the human remains coughed by the water. In the midst of that effort, two ambulances inched their way past the fire trucks from Company 7 and rolled slowly toward Montgomery's position. He watched as they came closer, making their way carefully through the sea of rescue workers. While still twenty yards away, the ambulances came to a halt, lights flashing, engines running.

Suddenly, both ambulances erupted in simultaneous explosions that ripped them apart and sent shrapnel flying in every direction. Montgomery watched in horror as firemen, paramedics, and volunteers were mowed down as if strafed by fire from an automatic weapon. Mouth agape at the scene before him, a piece of hot metal ripped through Montgomery's cheek. Another sliced through his thigh. Then a third struck him squarely between the eyes, tore through the skin of his forehead, and shattered his skull. He collapsed backward, fell to the pavement, and was gone.

*　　*　　*

In Washington, President Stanton sat in an upholstered chair near the sofa in the Oval Office. With him that morning were Ralph Ligon, the director of National Intelligence, and Jean Brown, the national security advisor, delivering the morning intelligence briefing.

In the midst of their discussion there was a light tap at the door, then it opened and McWhinney appeared. He moved quickly across the room to Stanton's side and leaned near his ear. "They need you downstairs."

"We're in the middle of something."

"I know, but they need you now, sir."

Just then, Jean Brown's cell phone rang, followed in the next instant by the phone in Ligon's pocket. While they were distracted, McWhinney nudged Stanton and gestured for him to follow. Stanton rose from the chair and started toward the door. As they passed by Gladys Moynihan's desk, Stanton caught sight of an image on the television screen in her office.

"What's that?" he asked, pointing.

"There's been an explosion in Boston."

"Explosion? What kind of explosion?"

"The FBI thinks it might be a terrorist attack."

"What did they hit?"

"The tunnel."

"The tunnel?"

"Yes, sir. It's not good."

CHAPTER 76
BOSTON

AT THE FBI OFFICE on Cambridge Street, Beverly Ogilvie, the special agent in charge, activated the office's operations command center. With video, voice, and data links, she was in constant contact with every federal law enforcement agency in the nation. To staff the center, she drew on the best analysts from the region and put them to work combing through the evidence being collected at the scene.

"Okay," she said, glancing around the room. "What do we have?"

Gina Bradford spoke up. "We have video from cameras inside the tunnel."

"What do they show?"

"Three blasts breeching the tunnel wall."

Ogilvie moved to Gina's desk and stood there watching as images on the monitor showed eruptions from three locations along the tunnel wall.

"That's an explosion?"

"No doubt about it," Gina nodded. She replayed the video frame by frame. "See the debris pattern?" She tapped the screen with her finger. "Pieces of the wall flew all the way across four lanes to the opposite side of the tunnel, before the water started pouring in."

"And that tells you?"

"The water wasn't the cause of the breech in the wall." Gina looked at Ogilvie. "There were three explosions along the tunnel wall." She pointed back at the screen. "All of them timed to detonate simultaneously. Followed by the two vehicles that detonated after emergency crews responded to the scene."

"This was a well-planned attack."

"Yes."

"What's behind the wall at those locations in the tunnel? Do we have a diagram of the place?"

"I have it," Gina offered.

"Show me what's in those places." Ogilvie pointed. "Right where the blasts occurred. What's behind the wall?"

Gina brought up a diagram of the tunnel and scrolled down the page. "Looks like those locations are maintenance areas. Pumps. Exhaust fans."

Ogilvie walked back to the center of the room. "I think we can say with a fair degree of certainty that this was a deliberate attack."

"A terrorist attack?"

"Not terror. Not yet."

Kent McCloud spoke up. "I've got video from inside those rooms."

Ogilvie moved toward him. "What does it show?"

McCloud pointed to the screen. "This is the footage from this morning." He pointed to the screen. "Two men come from behind that pump. They go out that door."

Ogilvie turned back to the room. "Anyone got video from outside the tunnel service buildings?"

Ed Thomas, seated two desks away, called out, "I have it. Looks like they left in a pickup truck." Images on his monitor showed two men as they left the building and climbed into the cab of a truck.

Ogilvie studied it a moment. "Enhance the picture. Can you get a license number?"

"Got it." Thomas pointed to the screen. "XTM 8448."

"Run it."

He typed in the number and searched the Massachusetts license plate database. Seconds later the results appeared on the screen. "Registered to Arthur Hayes at 228 Howland Street in Roxbury. But the truck was reported stolen from that address two days ago."

"Doesn't matter," Ogilvie replied. "Send someone to that address." She looked across the room to a desk near the corner. Brian Sanders was seated there. Bruce McIntyre leaned over his shoulder pointing to something on the screen. "You two," she called. "Sanders and McIntyre. Go talk to the owner. Find out what he has to say."

"Yes, ma'am," Sanders answered.

They were almost to the door when Thomas called out, "Ma'am, you might want to wait on that. Boston police located the truck."

"Where'd they find it?"

"Corner of Beale Street and South Central Avenue. In Wollaston. Located it about half an hour ago."

"How'd they get it ahead of us?"

"I don't know," Thomas shook his head. "But they're there now, processing the scene. Looks like they have a fatality."

"A body?"

"Yes, ma'am."

Ogilvie glanced in McIntyre's direction. "Go!" she ordered. "What are you waiting for? Check out the truck, then talk to the owner."

*   *   *

When Sanders and McIntyre arrived at the store on Beale Street, they found the pickup truck parked in an alley near the store's rear entrance. A slender man with dark hair and olive complexion was slumped over the steering wheel. Blood still oozed from a gunshot wound to his forehead. The area around the truck was cordoned off with yellow crime scene tape, and a detective stood near the driver's door. He glanced up as Sanders and McIntyre approached. "Don't even think about it," he growled.

"What?"

"This is my crime scene and you're not getting it."

"One call downtown and I can have whatever I want," Sanders argued.

"Not this time," the detective grinned. "This time you go through me."

"Yeah?"

"Yeah. Make your call and get in line." The detective gestured with a nod to the left. McIntyre looked in that direction and saw Will Hedges, a Secret Service agent, leaning against the hood of a car parked nearby on the sidewalk. Hedges gave a meek wave of his hand. McIntyre walked over to him.

"Freezing you out, too?"

"Yeah. And good luck getting anything out of that detective. I've worked with him before."

"Who's the dead guy?"

"I don't know," Hedges shrugged. "They won't say."

"We'll see about that." McIntyre took his cell phone from his pocket and placed a call. Two minutes later, the detective's phone rang. After a short conversation he glanced in McIntyre's direction and waved him over.

"Okay," he scowled. "So you know how to make a call."

McIntyre and Sanders stepped toward the truck. Hedges followed. The detective talked while he continued to work. "I got prints from the truck and the dead guy. We already ran them and came up empty. If you guys can help us, I'll cut you in on the case."

"Not a problem," McIntyre replied. "Email the file to me and I'll have someone get right on it."

*   *   *

In the White House situation room, the screen on the wall opposite the door showed live images from the tunnel in Boston. Ralph Ligon stood to one side, prepared to answer questions. Admiral Beamon sat at the table across from Paul Catlett. President Stanton stood near the opposite end of the table.

"They blew up the tunnel and then they detonated two ambulances in the midst of the responders." Stanton fumed. "If this was Iran, I'm going to blow something up."

"And just exactly what does that mean?" Kathleen Baker turned to face him. "What are you going to blow up? We've already hit their military targets. You want to start killing innocent civilians, too?"

"I don't know but I'm—"

"This has gone far enough, Mr. President. We have to find a way to dial this down. Not up."

"They attacked us on our own soil," Jean Brown joined the argument. "On our own soil. We can't let that go unpunished."

"But who do we punish?"

"Iran," Upchurch said flatly. "They did it. They get to pay the tab."

"Mr. President," Ligon interjected, "we have images from inside the tunnel. Before the blast."

The screen divided in half with one side still providing live footage from the scene while the other half showed video recorded at the moment the water rushed into the tunnel. Everyone in the room watched as explosions ripped through the tunnel walls.

"Charges were placed in an area near the two sump pumps and an exhaust fan," Ligon explained, pointing to the screen. "We've identified two suspects. One of them has been found."

Stanton rubbed his forehead. "What does he have to say?"

"He's dead, sir."

"Dead?" Stanton's eyes were wide. "Who is he?"

"Javad Bizhani. He's from Pakistan."

"Do we have anything on him?"

"Arrived on a student visa. Attended class, then disappeared. Apparently used several aliases. The FBI is in the process of tracking those down now."

One of Ligon's assistants was seated near the screen. He caught Ligon's attention and handed him a message. Ligon glanced at it, then spoke up. "Mr. President, we have something else you ought to see." Ligon nodded to the staff member. "Put it on the screen."

The screen on the wall divided once again with the live feed from Boston on the left and video from inside the tunnel on the right. In the center between those images was a television news broadcast. "This is from Aljazeera," Ligon explained. "They ran it ten minutes ago."

They all watched as the broadcast played video of a young man dressed in Islamic revolutionary garb reading a statement about his determination to inflict pain on the Great Satan in an effort to bring all who lived there to a true faith in Allah.

"Great Satan," Stanton gestured toward the screen. "That would be us he's talking about?"

"Yes, sir," Catlett replied.

"Who is this young man? Why are we watching this?"

"This is Javad Bizhani."

"And we think he is responsible for the attack in Boston."

"One of the suspects," Ligon replied.

"You said he's from Pakistan. Who is he working with? Al'Qaida? The Taliban?"

"No, sir," Catlett spoke up. "They don't have the resources to pull off something like this."

"Who, then?"

"Hezbollah."

"With Iran's help."

"Most likely."

"In response to our missile strikes against them."

"Yes, Mr. President."

"We attacked them to defend Israel. Now they've attacked us."

"Yes, sir."

"But we can't prove for a fact that Iran had anything to do with it."

"Not to a mathematical certainty," Upchurch offered. "Not now, at least."

"Mr. President," Brown added, "we don't need mathematical certainty. No one will blame us for responding. We must defend ourselves."

"And by that you mean …?"

"Military action."

"Troops?"

"Definitely," Upchurch offered. "Troops on the ground."

Stanton had a pained expression. "On the ground in Iran."

"Yes, sir."

Stanton looked over at McWhinney and nodded toward the door. "Let's step outside."

In the hallway, Stanton shouted angrily, "What are they doing? We are getting sucked deeper and deeper into one more Middle Eastern war. We just finished two. Now they want to send us back over there to fight in Iran, of all places. We can't win a war like that."

"Mr. President, they attacked us."

"No, Pete. They didn't attack us. The Iranian Army did not attack us. The Iranian Air Force did not attack us. The Iranian Navy in their rowboats did not invade us." Stanton wagged his finger for emphasis. "Islamic fundamentalists, perhaps. But we can't make a case that this was the action of the nation of Iran. I know it. You know it." He pointed toward the door. "And everyone in that room knows it. They are playing with us."

"I don't think Iran is playing with us. I think they're deadly serious."

"Not Iran, Pete. Them!" he shouted. "The people in that room! They're the ones doing a number on us."

"So, what do you want to do?"

Stanton took a deep breath and tried to calm his emotions. "I want you to set up a meeting with Kathleen Baker. Make sure Aubrey Preston is there."

"He's political. He's with the campaign."

"I know who he is," Stanton snapped. "This isn't about politics."

"Then what is it?"

"Set up the meeting."

"Mr. President. We can't—"

"Set up the meeting, Pete."

"We can't do it. Someone will see it. The press will see her there. With Aubrey. It'll look like whatever you're doing is being done because of politics."

"Fine," Stanton snarled. "Get us a room at Blair House." He turned away to enter the situation room. "It can look like we're sleeping together."

"Mr. President?"

Stanton stepped back from the door and stood just inches from McWhinney. His voice was low but tense. "Set up the meeting, Pete. And keep it quiet. And if Upchurch finds out about it, you'll both be looking for a new job."

CHAPTER 77

NEW YORK CITY

FROM HIS MEETING at the restaurant with Geller's assistant, Cruse rode to the Harvard Club. An attendant at the door pointed him toward the director's office. "Mr. Swanson," he said. "Third door on the right."

A receptionist met him as he came into the office. "I'm sorry, but Mr. Swanson doesn't see anyone without an appointment."

"I think he'll see me." Cruse flashed his badge. "FBI. Tell Mr. Swanson I'm waiting."

Just then a door opened and a man appeared. Tall and broad-shouldered, he wore a dark suit that was impeccably tailored with a white shirt and silk tie. "I'm Mr. Swanson. How may I assist the FBI?"

"I would like to review your security tapes."

"For what purpose?"

"So I don't have to get a warrant and seize them all."

"Oh. Very well. Right this way."

Swanson escorted him down the hall to the security officer's station and introduced them. "Mr. Easterling will get you whatever you need."

When he was gone, Cruse and Easterling got down to business. "Call me Brownie," Easterling smiled. "What do you want to see?"

Without much effort at all, they located images of Geller as he arrived at the building with Holsten. "I saw some interior cameras when I came in." Cruse pointed to the date stamp at the bottom of the screen for the exterior images. "Can you show me the files from those cameras for the same date?"

"Sure," Easterling retorted.

Moments later, images from the file appeared on the screen. Easterling scanned through them to a section that showed Geller and Holsten as they emerged from the elevator, then walked together down the hall. Near the far end, they turned left into a room.

"What's in that room?" Cruse asked.

"It's the Crimson Room."

"Crimson Room?"

"Yeah, you know. Harvard Crimson. Crimson and White."

"Oh. Is there a white room?"

"Nah," Easterling said, shaking his head. "Just Crimson. It's a meeting room. Popular place. Has a wet bar and its own restrooms. We use it a lot."

"You rent it out?"

"Yes. Need to see the records?"

"That would be helpful."

A review of the room reservation file showed it had been reserved frequently by Henry Wilson. "I'll need copies of these records," Cruse instructed.

"No problem."

From the Harvard Club, Cruse took a taxi to Henry Wilson's office. They met in a conference room that offered a panoramic view of the Hudson River. "Back again?" Wilson asked sarcastically.

"Yes."

"Does your boss know you're here?"

"He sent me."

"I doubt that," Wilson chuckled.

"His name is Foster Goodall. He's the—"

"I know who he is."

"Then give him a call."

Wilson stepped to a table in the corner and picked up the phone. Cruse followed and took a seat near the desk. After a moment with Goodall on the phone, Wilson hung up.

"So, what do you want this time?"

Cruse took out the photo of Holsten and held it for Wilson to see. "You know him?"

"Yeah," Wilson shrugged. "I know him. Everyone knows him. He's David Holsten." He leaned back in his chair. "Haven't seen him in a while, though. Something happen to him?"

"I have video of Holsten entering a room at the Harvard Club with Michael Geller."

"Yeah," Wilson shrugged once more. "So what? No big secret about it."

"Club records say you reserved the room on numerous occasions."

"Look, they're part of an investment group, okay? The Shale Oil Trust you were here about before. That's all. Just an investment group. Geller and Holsten arrived together. They came together, they left together. That's all I know."

"When's the last time you saw Holsten?"

"A week ago. Ten days. He was going to see someone."

"Who?"

"I don't know."

"Yes, you do."

Wilson looked away. "He was going to see Leon Bain."

"The president's campaign advisor?"

"Yes."

"Why would Holsten go to see Bain?"

"Holsten used to work for the president. Now he works for Geller. They pull the strings."

"The strings?"

"On Andrew Stanton's campaign. They're the ones calling the shots. Not Bain or that guy they have in there now."

"Why would Stanton have them running the campaign?"

"What's the one thing that always determines how campaigns are run, Mr. Cruse?"

"Money."

"You answered your own question."

Cruse left Wilson's office and descended into the nearest subway tunnel. He paid the fare and took a seat on the first train that arrived at the platform. With the rhythmic clack of the wheels against the rail in the background, he

SEVEN DAYS

let his mind focus on what Wilson had told him. Bain, the president's reelection campaign, Holsten, all working for Michael Geller. A man with ties running deep in directions no president of the United States should ever want to go. Yet there it was and now he had to decide what to do next.

"There's no option about that," he whispered finally. The next thing was the next thing to do. Go see Geller. Confront him. See what happened. That's how they always worked it. You followed the evidence wherever it took you. Track down all leads. Talk to every witness. Michael Geller was next.

At the next subway station, Cruse stepped from the train and made his way up to the street. A few minutes later, he reached Times Square. A news crawler on a building at the corner showed a steady stream of headlines. As he watched, information about the explosions in the tunnel in Boston moved past. He took out his cell phone and called Goodall.

"Anything I need to know?" Cruse asked.

"Looks like a terrorist attack," Goodall responded. "Aljazeera has a video of a bomber who apparently took credit for it. They aren't certain he's actually the guy who did it but the group he's with has ties to Hezbollah. Look, I gotta run. This place is crazy. You need some help?"

"Not right now. Do you need me to come in?"

"No. Keep doing what you're doing. I'll catch up with you in a little while and you can fill me in."

"Okay. But this thing goes pretty far."

"How far?"

"High."

"How high?"

"I'm thinking it reaches the top." Cruse waited but there was no response. "You there?"

"Yeah. I'm here."

"What do you want me to do?"

"Work it. Do what's next."

352

CHAPTER 78
SAN DIEGO, CALIFORNIA

LUIS CASTILLO, A STRUCTURAL TECHNICIAN, walked along the base of the dam at Alvarado Water Treatment Plant, making his twice-monthly inspection. A concrete barrage dam, the structure consisted of a series of gates and buttresses that stretched across a gulch once known as Alvarado Creek. Behind the dam was Lake Murray, a popular recreational area for hikers and boaters.

Castillo checked the surface of the dam carefully, but he'd worked as a technician long enough to know that the real danger wasn't the dam itself but the ground on which the dam rested. Water had a way of finding the lowest point possible. If there was a crack, a gap, a sliver of an opening in the footing beneath the dam, water from the lake would find it. Once that happened, the dam could very quickly lose its structural integrity.

The first buttress seemed in good shape, as did the gate beside it. As he came to the second buttress, he opened a service door on the side to check the floor around the motor that lifted one of the gates. He took a flashlight from his hip, stepped into the motor room, and moved along the wall to the right. At the back corner, he turned left and walked behind the gate motor. As he did, the beam of his flashlight fell across a black duffel bag. One end of it appeared damp and he knelt beside it, curious to see what was inside. He unzipped the top and pushed it open to find the bag was packed full with blocks of plastic explosives, each of them wired to a detonator. Castillo stared at it a moment, his palms suddenly sweaty, his heart beating wildly. Then he stood, backed slowly toward the door, and stepped outside.

From the base of the dam, he ran across the road to the primary pump building. He jerked open the door and shouted as loud as possible, "There's a bomb in the dam!"

Dwight Carmichael, a pump room manager, was seated in his office to the left of the door. He glanced up from his desk. "Luis, have you been drinking on the job?"

"No, sir," Luis insisted. "There's a bomb. In the dam. By the gate motor in the second buttress. Call somebody."

"What kind of bomb?"

"A duffel bag filled with explosives."

Carmichael came from behind his desk, a look of alarm spreading across his face. "Are you sure?"

"Yes, sir. Come on. You can see for yourself."

The two men ran across the road to the room at the base of the second buttress. As they came around the end of the gate motor, the beam of Carmichael's flashlight fell on the black duffel bag. Wires protruded from the opening at the top, and through the gap in the zipper he saw the detonator.

"Okay," Carmichael said, trying his best to sound calm. "Okay. Let's get out of here and call someone. We need to notify the police."

When they were out of the room, Carmichael took his cell phone from the clip on his belt and called the system operator.

"This is Carmichael at Alvarado. We have an emergency. There is an explosive device in one of the gate motor rooms."

"Dwight, are you being funny." Her voice had a flirting lilt. "'Cause if you are, I gotta tell you, that is a subject way too serious to be funny."

"Listen to me," he snapped. "There's a duffel bag with a bomb inside and it's sitting beside one of the gate motors. Right in the center of the dam."

"Oh no!" she gasped.

"Oh yes. Get the police. The fire department. Call everyone you can think of. And tell them to bring the bomb team."

Carmichael ended the call and returned the phone to his hip. "Okay, Luis. We need to stay calm."

"We need to get out of here. That thing could blow any minute and when it does, all that water's gonna come rushing right out here on top of us."

"We can't run," Carmichael cautioned. "We can't run. If we run, the thing blows and lots of people lose their lives."

"If we don't run and it blows, *we're* gonna lose *our* lives."

"That's the way it goes," Carmichael grimaced. "That's the job we signed up for." He bumped Luis on the shoulder with his fist. "Come on. We need to check the other rooms."

"What for?"

"To see if there's a bomb in them."

At the second buttress they found the same thing, a duffel bag filled with plastic explosives wired to a detonator. A check of the third room revealed another. Carmichael and Castillo retreated again to the road. "This is bad." Castillo shook his head slowly. "If they explode, that dam will go. There'll be no stopping the water."

"Yeah," Carmichael sighed. "I know."

From down by the freeway, the wail of sirens rose up the hill as emergency vehicles wound their way up the slope toward the dam. Within the hour, police units and fire trucks lined the road. ATF and FBI agents combed every inch of ground around the dam searching for evidence. SWAT units blanketed the area. And inside the three gate motor rooms, teams from the bomb squad worked to defuse the bombs.

Television reporters began to arrive shortly after the first police cars. At first they wandered among the emergency crews, asking questions, taking pictures, and recording the investigation as it unfolded. When the FBI arrived, easy access came to a halt. They established a perimeter well down from the dam and limited access to only essential personnel. Most of the news teams were staged on a hilltop behind a residence at the end of Del Cerro Boulevard that overlooked the gulch. From there they had a commanding view straight down the slope to the dam. A few ventured into the community, interviewing worried residents as they loaded their possessions into cars and trucks for the ride to safety. But most just stood on the hilltop, talking incessantly about the potential for destruction and the area below the dam that would be most affected.

Late that afternoon, Carmichael found Castillo. "They want us to give an interview."

"An interview? To the media?"

"Yeah."

"With television?"

"Yes."

"I don't know anything," Castillo said, shaking his head. "I wouldn't know what to say."

"Chief thinks it would be good for viewers to see the face of the person who found the bombs."

Castillo was wary. "He wants me to talk to reporters? Before we talk to the lawyers?"

"I'm just doing what they tell me, Luis. Department policy says they can't make you give an interview. So if you don't want to do it, that's your choice. But the chief asked me to find you and take you to do an interview. So here I am, delivering the message."

Castillo frowned. "He must have a friend at the television station."

Carmichael seemed to ignore the comment. "There's really not much to it. They'll just ask you a few questions. You tell them what you know. What you don't know, you just say, 'I don't know.'"

"All right," Castillo sighed. "I guess if the chief wants me to."

"Good," Carmichael smiled. "Come on."

Carmichael led the way around the pump building to a pickup truck that was parked in back. He got in behind the steering wheel. Castillo climbed in on the passenger side. They drove down the hill to Airoso Avenue, then continued alongside the freeway. At Del Cerro Avenue, they turned back up the hill and rode to the top at the opposite side of the dam. Carmichael parked the truck near the edge of the pavement at the end of the street.

A group of reporters was gathered at the brow of the hill fifty yards to the right. As Carmichael and Castillo came from the truck, a woman started toward them. She wore a navy skirt, off-white top, and high-heeled shoes that made her calf muscles stand out with every step.

"I knew it," Castillo groused.

"What?"

"Chief's friends with a woman at the television station."

"Why do you say that?"

"Look at her. If she asked, wouldn't *you* send me for an interview?"

By then she was just a few feet away. "You must be Luis." She smiled at Castillo.

"Yes, ma'am," he replied. "I am."

"I appreciate you doing this." She nodded in Carmichael's direction. "Thank you for bringing him up, Dwight." She glanced back at Castillo. "We'll be just a minute while we get the camera set up." Then she stepped away to help get things arranged.

When she was out of earshot, Castillo looked over at Carmichael. "I see now what really happened."

"What?" Carmichael's eyes darted away. "What are you talking about?"

"It wasn't the chief with the friend. It was you."

"What do you mean?"

"You're the one with the friend at the TV station."

Carmichael leaned close. "She's a new reporter. Just getting started. Don't make a scene."

"You dating her?"

"Not exactly."

"You mean not yet."

The reporter returned. "Luis, if you could stand over here with your back toward the dam."

"Yes, ma'am." Castillo cut his eyes at Carmichael. "Whatever you need."

Carmichael gestured with a jerk of his head and mouthed the words, "Be nice."

"Just stand right here." Jenny took Castillo by the shoulders and gently maneuvered him into position, then glanced back at the cameraman. "Is that good?"

"Yeah."

Castillo looked her in the eye. "I don't know your name."

"Jenny, Jenny Monroe. I'll ask you some questions. Keep your eyes on me and talk to me when you answer. Don't worry about the camera."

"Okay."

Then she cleared her throat, put the microphone near her lips, and began. "In an exclusive Channel Two interview, we're talking this afternoon with Luis Castillo, the Water Department employee who discovered the bombs planted inside the dam. Luis, could you describe for us—"

Suddenly, an explosion shook the ground beneath their feet. Castillo turned toward the gulch in time to see the center section of the dam crack open. Seconds later two more explosions erupted. The face of the dam ripped open and water poured through. As the water cascaded over the broken dam, sections of concrete on either side of the breach collapsed, releasing a wall of water that tumbled down the hillside.

A hundred yards below the dam, the onrushing water collided with the first row of houses. Without a pause, it swept the houses off their foundations and splintered them to pieces. Broken boards and mangled plywood now collected at the head of the wave. Pushed by the momentum of the lake as it emptied down the slope, cars, trucks, and boats were gobbled up. Then trees and still more houses added to the sludge as the wall of water grew to tidal proportions.

When it reached the freeway, the water seemed to pause a moment as it lapped at the elevated roadbed. The area alongside the pavement quickly filled and the water surged over the highway with undiminished force. Guardrails were ripped from their posts. Cars and trucks were swept away.

In the commercial section across the road, the accumulating debris formed a battering ram that tore through a row of retail shops and slammed into the side of Alvarado Hospital. Water piled against the side of the emergency room wing, then splashed onto the roof two stories above the ground. For a moment it seemed even the hospital would not stand. Then up the gulch, the water receded and the lakebed appeared. Moments later, the wave that struck the hospital retreated, too, bringing with it windows, doors, tables, and chairs that were sucked from the rooms inside.

Castillo stood with his mouth wide open, staring down at the barren path from the dam to the hospital. Less than a minute before, it had been green and lush. Houses beneath the trees had stood there for years. Now there was nothing.

Finally Carmichael shook him. "Come on. We gotta get down there." And they started toward the truck.

CHAPTER 79

NEW YORK CITY

AS EVENING APPROACHED, Cruse made his way to the FBI apartment on Thirty-First Street. That night, as he lounged on the sofa watching the news, his cell phone rang. He glanced at the screen to see the call was from Lyman.

"Where are you?" he asked, surprised that she would contact him. "Goodall will can us both if he finds out we talked."

"Forget Goodall. Is that why you haven't tried to find me?"

"Just doing my job. Where are you?"

"I'm watching Geller."

"Geller? Where are you?"

"Brooklyn."

"Does Goodall know where you are?"

"I don't work for Goodall. My supervisor is at the embassy in Ankara."

"You need to leave. If he finds you out there working this case, it won't matter where your supervisor's located. He'll make it rough on you."

"Don't you want to know who Geller is meeting with?"

"Who is it?"

"Meet me and I'll show you."

"Where?"

"Junior's in Brooklyn."

Half an hour later, Cruse arrived at Junior's Restaurant, a Brooklyn landmark on the corner of Flatbush and DeKalb Avenues. Lyman was seated at a table with a view of the street. He took a seat across from her.

"What happened at the beach house?"

"I saw Goodall and his guys coming. So I took the records that seemed the most important and got away."

"You've been working on the case since then?"

"Yes. I saw you at Henry Wilson's office today. Get anything out of him?"

"Not really." Cruse glanced around the restaurant, checking, then looked back at her. "So, who was Geller meeting with?"

She took a photograph from her pocket and held it for Cruse to see. "Do you know this man?"

"No. Who is he?"

"His name is Naseem Musa."

"That's who Geller was meeting with?"

"Yes."

"Who is Naseem Musa?"

"Ever hear of Amin el-Husseini?"

"The Grand Mufti of Jerusalem?"

"Yes," she smiled, "during the days of the British Mandate. You do know a little something about the region."

"I've spent most of my career with the bureau there."

"During World War II, Hitler promised el-Husseini control of the Middle East if he would recruit the Arabs to fight the Allies. El-Husseini did a pretty good job of gathering volunteers, but we all know how that story ultimately turned out. When Hitler died, el-Husseini's dream died, too."

"What does that have to do with Geller?"

"I kept digging on Geller."

"You said there wasn't anything."

"Right," she nodded. "The trail went cold on his mother's side of the family. It took a little work but I found out why. His mother's family came to America under the name Kaltenburg, a name they assumed after the war. Their real name was Kaltenbrunner. Geller's grandfather was Hans Kaltenbrunner, one of Hitler's closest advisors. He died shortly after the war, before he could be tried at Nuremburg."

"So, what did you find from following him?"

She gestured with the photograph. "Musa is a Muslim cleric. He claims to be the legitimate heir of el-Husseini and the rightful Grand Mufti of Jerusalem. He hasn't been able to convince anyone to agree with him, but he keeps trying, hoping someone will give him the official title."

"What's so important about that?"

"One of the region's biggest problems is a lack of unified leadership. Each neighborhood follows someone else. There is no central, unifying figure. If Musa was the Grand Mufti, he would be the supreme Muslim leader of Palestine. Arguably the leader of the entire region that once comprised the British Mandate. Everyone would follow him."

"Why was Geller meeting with him?"

"I don't know, but maybe you should ask Geller."

CHAPTER 80
WASHINGTON, D.C.

EARLY IN THE MORNING, Andrew Stanton left the White House and crossed the street to Blair House. Adrian Lane, a nominee for the Fifth Circuit Court of Appeals, was waiting for him there. They paused for photographs with reporter pool photographers, then retired to a room upstairs. When they were alone and the door was closed, Stanton turned to him.

"Adrian, thanks for coming on such short notice."

"I'm always glad to help out, Mr. President."

"You understand I won't be meeting with you today."

"Yes, sir. I understand."

The door opened and two assistants from the White House entered. "You'll be appearing next week before the Senate. These gentlemen will help you go over your testimony."

"Yes, Mr. President."

Stanton left the room and walked across the hall and down to the next floor. Aubrey Preston and Kathleen Baker were waiting for him in a corner room.

"This better be good," he warned as they all took a seat.

"It's very simple," Baker began. "You meet Iranian President Moussaoui at a neutral site. Somewhere safe. So neither of you feels threatened."

"You have a place in mind?"

"The island of Majorca."

"Okay. Will Spain agree?"

"We floated the idea of a meeting in Madrid, just to get the discussion started. They are agreeable to host it. I don't think they'll object if we change the location to Majorca."

"One can hope. But I still have a problem with the meeting. Won't this look like we're negotiating with terrorists?"

"Iran is a sovereign nation. You and the president of Iran are heads of state. We're not negotiating. We're meeting to discuss our differences and see if there is any common ground."

"That sounds good to us, but I'm not sure it'll fly with voters. Assuming that isn't a problem, how do we reach the Iranians with an idea like this?"

"The Swiss will act as our go-between."

"They know about this?"

"Yes. They're ready."

"And we can trust them to keep it out of the press?"

"Yes, sir. They won't talk."

"What about the Iranians? What's to keep them from leaking it, or just flat out disclosing it? They've hit us pretty hard. We're handing them a big fat pitch to hit out of the park. Who's to say they won't torch us with this?"

"They won't know who they're meeting."

Stanton looked perplexed. "Excuse me?"

"We'll set it up as a meeting between me and Moussaoui. Once they're in the room, we'll bring you in."

"Think that'll work?"

"I think it's the only way to keep them from talking ahead of time."

"And what keeps them from talking after we meet?"

"We'll work on that after they agree to talk."

"Okay. Set it up."

CHAPTER 81

LOS ANGELES

THROUGHOUT THE PREVIOUS DAY and into the night, people stopped by Life Church to pray and meditate. Located on Portola Parkway, in the Lake Forest section of the city, the church had become the focal point of the community's response to the tragedies in Boston and San Diego, now overwhelmingly viewed as terrorist attacks. In response to the spontaneous acts of faith offered by those who came to the church, the ministry staff decided something more deliberate should be done. They prevailed upon Ronnie Baze, pastor of the church, to join them for a community prayer service and publicized it through messages posted on Internet social sites. Within hours those messages went viral, generating millions of hits to the sites.

For his part, Baze was reluctant at first. His speaking schedule kept him more than busy and he wasn't convinced the matter warranted his attention, but when reporters started calling with questions about the service, he became interested. Now he sat in his study, putting the final touches on remarks he planned to make later that morning at what had blossomed into a regional prayer service.

In the midst of his preparation, someone knocked on the office door. "Yeah," he called without glancing up from the notepad on his desk.

The door opened and Sally, his secretary, appeared. "You gotta see this." Her eyes were alive with excitement. "You have to take a look."

"A look at what?"

"The people." She moved toward a window on the wall to the right. "They're showing up from everywhere."

"Where are they now?"

"In the parking lot."

"The parking lot?" Baze had a puzzled frown. "What are they doing out there?"

"Standing in line to get into the building." She reached the window and raised the blinds. "Look."

Baze squinted against the morning sunlight, but through the glare he saw a crowd of hundreds gathering in the parking lot. He rose from his chair and came to the window. "Have they opened the doors yet?"

"Yes. All the pews on the sanctuary floor are full. These people out here are waiting in line for a seat in the balcony."

Baze came away from the window, crossed the office, and walked out to the hallway. Three doors down from his office he came to the sound room and went inside. A window looked out on the sanctuary and through it he saw the pews on the ground level were filled to capacity and up above people were slowly filing into the balcony. Down front, near the altar, television cameras were posted on either side of the building. Baze stared in awe.

*   *   *

Three blocks from the church, Daryrush Kashfi sat behind the steering wheel of a van painted with the red-and-white logo of Rancho Mirage Heating and Air. He adjusted the visor of his cap to shade against the glare of the morning sun and turned the van from El Toro Road onto Portola Parkway. Dressed in gray uniform coveralls, he looked like any other air-conditioning repairman, but in back of the van he carried a much different cargo.

A little way down the street, he came to the parking lot entrance at Life Church. He paused for oncoming traffic, then turned left and idled toward the building. Across the way he saw a crowd of several hundred people shuffling toward the building entrance. He smiled at the sight of it and knew there must be many more inside. "Allah has made a way," he whispered to himself.

At the far side of the parking lot, he turned left and followed the driveway around to the back of the building. A dozen parking spaces lined the area between the driveway and the building. Three cars were parked there. Daryrush frowned as he noticed a shiny new Lexus in the space marked *Pastor*.

"They could sell that car and feed a thousand families with the price," he grumbled. "Instead, they drive past the poor and never notice them."

Beyond the row of parking spaces he came to a fenced area that held one of the building's eight air-conditioning units. He turned the van to the left, brought it to a stop, then shifted into reverse and carefully backed it alongside the fence. When it was in place, he switched off the engine, climbed over the console, and let himself out through the passenger door on the opposite side.

Standing there, with the door open, he stripped off his shirt and pants and tossed them onto the seat. He threw in the cap as well and gently closed the door. Then he turned away and started across the campus lawn toward El Toro Road.

A few minutes later he reached the street. Fifty yards to the right, a car was parked on the shoulder of the pavement. He walked toward it, doing his best to remain calm. When he reached it, he opened the door and got in on the passenger side. The driver smiled over at him. "All is well?"

"Yes," Daryrush nodded. "All is well."

"The others are waiting. Everyone is in place."

"Good."

"But we must hurry. We must be far away when you make the call."

"No," Daryrush cautioned. "We cannot risk being stopped by the police. Drive with the traffic, the same as we practiced it. We must not call attention to ourselves."

"When you place that call we will be the focus of everyone's attention."

"Look around," Daryrush said with a broad sweep of his hand. "We are but one more car in the morning traffic. No one suspects a thing."

As he spoke, Daryrush took a cell phone from his pocket, dialed a number, and pressed the button to place the call. A moment later he heard a ringtone, and then from behind them came the rumbling sound of an explosion.

* * *

In Washington, D.C., Kathleen Baker watched from the backseat as the car in which she was riding turned onto Cathedral Avenue. A few blocks later, they rolled quietly through the gate at the Swiss Embassy. When the car came to a stop, she took a briefcase from the seat beside her, stepped out beneath the portico, and walked quickly through the building's side entrance.

From the reception lobby she was ushered upstairs to the office of Jonas Druey, Switzerland's ambassador to the United States.

"Jonas," she said without emotion, "we are grateful for your assistance."

"I am always happy to assist your country."

"This may still blow up in our faces. You might find yourself mentioned in a news report."

"I am not afraid to fail in an attempt to do the extraordinary. You have the letter?"

Baker opened the briefcase and took out a linen envelope. Sealed with red wax, it bore an imprint of the Great Seal of the United States. "You will deliver this to President Moussaoui?"

"Certainly."

"It has to go directly to Moussaoui. Not Amini or anyone else. Just Moussaoui."

"I understand." Jonas held out his hand. Baker laid the letter on his open palm. "It is our pleasure to make the delivery."

"How quickly can you do it?"

"As expeditiously as possible."

"Very well," Baker nodded. "Time is of the essence."

"I have made it our top priority."

As Baker turned to leave she caught sight of a television mounted on the wall to the right. On the screen were images of a large building. Smoke rose from behind it and people were seen rushing from the doorway into the parking lot. A caption at the bottom of the screen identified it as Life Church in Los Angeles.

While Baker watched, a news reporter appeared on screen. Behind her, an ambulance worked its way across the parking lot and into the center of the crowd. To the right, a police car inched slowly along the edge of the lot between the crowd and the building.

"We're here outside Life Church," the reporter began, "where moments ago an explosion ripped through the back of the building. Worshippers gathered for a community prayer service now stand in the parking lot wondering if they, too, have become the next victims of an apparent—"

Suddenly a loud roaring sound overwhelmed the reporter's voice and images on the screen shook as the ambulance exploded. In an instant, nails packed around the explosives sliced through the crowd in a deadly barrage. Hundreds collapsed on the pavement in a bloody, flesh-strewn mass.

Panicked, those who still could move turned to run but before they could get out of the way, the police car behind them exploded. Shrapnel from the trunk and rear seat struck hundreds more, sending them to the pavement in anguish.

The remainder of the crowd, now frantic, started in the opposite direction only to find their way blocked by a fire truck. As they moved around it, the truck exploded, littering the parking lot with body parts and mangled corpses.

Baker stood in the ambassador's office, staring at the screen in disbelief. A tear appeared at the corner of her eye and rolled down her check. Druey came to her side and touched her gently on the elbow. "Madam Secretary, I am so sorry. Is there anything I can do?"

She wiped her eye with the back of her hand. "Get that message to the Iranians as fast as humanly possible," she ordered grimly.

"Certainly," he nodded.

CHAPTER 82

NEW YORK CITY

UNABLE TO REACH GOODALL by phone, Cruse went to the FBI office in lower Manhattan. He arrived to find the place alive with activity. Phones rang constantly and the air was thick with the incessant sound of agents talking, pleading, arguing, and shouting as they worked their contacts trying to figure out whether events in Boston, San Diego, and Los Angeles were related and what might be coming next.

Cruse made his way down the hall and found Goodall in his office, standing at the window, reading a memo. "You got a minute?"

"Only a minute," Goodall answered, glancing over his shoulder in Cruse's direction. "That's about all I have. You in trouble?"

"Not really," Cruse replied in a tentative voice.

"Then what is it? I can tell you want something."

"I need a search warrant."

"A search warrant?" Goodall turned away from the window and leaned against the corner of the desk. "For what?"

"Michael Geller's apartment and car."

"That's a serious matter." Goodall laid aside the memo and folded his arms across his chest. "What basis do you have for it?"

"Geller was the last person to see Holsten alive. I can't find him and I have reason to believe they were together when Holsten was killed."

"Is that information reliable?"

"Yes," Cruse nodded. "It's as close as we're gonna get."

"Okay." Goodall reached across the desk and picked up the phone. "But there'll be trouble. And when this blows up, we'll both take the hit."

"Maybe not."

"What do you mean?"

"There's a lot going on now." Cruse gestured to no place in particular. "Maybe no one will notice."

"Oh, they'll notice." Goodall arched an eyebrow as he dialed a number. "Anytime a close personal friend of the president gets served with a search warrant, people notice."

"Can you spare a couple of guys to go with me?"

"Yeah. Get White and Dobbs with you." Someone on the other end of the line answered the call. Goodall moved around his desk toward his chair. "This is Goodall. I need a search warrant." He took a seat. "I'll send the details in a minute." He hung up the phone and looked back at Cruse. "You'll get your warrant, but don't toss the place. Just look around."

"Right."

*   *   *

With White and Dobbs accompanying him, Cruse arrived at Geller's Park Avenue apartment. Geller wasn't home so they executed the warrant on the housekeeper and began moving from room to room.

In the study, Cruse found maps of Israel showing several versions of a divided country. One of the maps was rather old and showed the British Mandate covering all of the area that included present-day Israel, Jordan, and Lebanon. Another appeared to be an official United Nations publication showing the boundary lines drawn in 1948, which carved out half the former Mandate as the countries of Jordan and Lebanon. The other half formed the state of Israel. A third map showed the present division of the region.

A fourth map, however, gave Cruse pause for concern. It showed the area divided with the eastern half of present-day Israel under Palestinian control, having East Jerusalem as its capital. The western half was under Israeli control, with Tel Aviv as the capital.

While White and Dobbs continued to search the apartment, Cruse unrolled the maps on Geller's desk and studied them closely. "This first one divided the region in half," he whispered to himself. "Jordan and Lebanon were the original Palestinian refuge. Yet for the last fifty years they've been acting as if they are a people without a country. Their argument isn't against Israel. It's really against Jordan and Lebanon for stealing their heritage." He traced the lines on the third and fourth maps. "Yet either of these two maps would reduce Israel—once again—to roughly half its present size." His forehead wrinkled in a frown. "But who created these maps?"

When White and Dobbs finished searching the remainder of the apartment, they joined Cruse in the study, carrying a laptop and cell phone. Cruse glanced at them. "That's all you found?"

"It's more than you have," White said, looking toward the maps.

Cruse rolled them up and tucked them under his arm. "I'll take the maps," he smiled. "Even if they aren't much."

"Do they relate to the case?"

"I don't know," Cruse shrugged. "But I'm going to take them for now and see where it leads." He started toward the door. "Let's see if his car is in the garage."

In the parking garage beneath the building, they located Geller's car—a BMW parked in a numbered space reserved for him. Cruse glanced inside through the windows but saw nothing suspicious.

"Think we should pry open the truck?" White asked.

"No." Cruse shook his head. "Let's take it back to the office and get the lab to go through it."

An hour later a rollback truck arrived. While the driver loaded the car, Geller arrived. "What is the meaning of this?" he protested.

"Mr. Geller, we have a search warrant for your apartment and your car." Cruse took the warrant from his pocket and handed it to him. "This *is* your car, right?"

"Yes, it's my car," Geller replied with an indignant tone. "And I'll have your job for this."

"Probably not," Cruse smiled. "We'll need you to come with us. We have some questions we'd like to ask you."

"You're arresting me?"

"We need to talk to you."

"I'm not going anywhere with you."

"Very well." Cruse reached behind his back and took a pair of handcuffs from his belt. Then he grasped Geller by the arm and turned him around. "Mr. Geller, I'm taking you into custody for questioning in the death of David Holsten."

"I want my lawyer."

"That's not happening. Mr. Holsten's death is part of a terrorism investigation." White shot Cruse a worried look. Cruse ignored him and guided Geller toward a car parked a few spaces away. "You can talk, or not, Mr. Geller, but you're not getting access to a lawyer."

"I'm an American citizen."

"No lawyer." Cruse opened the door and nudged Geller toward the backseat. "Watch your head." Cruse slammed the door shut and looked over at White. "I don't care if the Patriot Act applies or not. He doesn't get a lawyer."

"But he's right."

"About what?"

"This *is* still America."

"No lawyer," Cruse snapped.

CHAPTER 83

ST. LOUIS

MANA PEJMAN TURNED the delivery truck onto Brentwood Boulevard and drove south. Just past Clayton Road he turned into the parking lot at the mall and let the truck idle around the northern end of the complex. When he reached the back, he turned left and continued down the backside of the shops, past service areas reserved for deliveries. Finally he came to a sign that marked the rear entrance to Tiny Tots, a children's clothing store. He slowed the truck to a crawl and turned right, brought it to a stop, then backed it toward the loading dock behind the store. When the truck was in place, he set the parking brake, switched off the engine, and climbed from the cab.

Without looking back, he walked from the service area to a car parked in a space thirty yards away. He opened the door, got in behind the steering wheel, and felt under the floor mat for the key. He found it, started the car's engine, and drove away from the building.

When he reached the opposite end of the mall, he took a cell phone from his pocket, scrolled down the contacts list, and pressed a button. He waited to hear the phone on the other end ring, then a smile broke across his face. "Allah has blessed us with victory," he whispered.

On the second ring he heard a loud boom behind him as the delivery truck exploded. The force of the blast tore a gaping hole in the back wall of the store. A shockwave generated by the bomb blew debris through the interior of the store, pushing clothes, racks, and fixtures crashing through the front windows into the mall corridor.

*　　*　　*

At the opposite end of the mall, Mindy Lewis was in the Home and Hearth store with her five-year-old daughter, Angela, when the blast rocked the building. She felt the concussion against her chest and glanced up as a window in front shattered. In the next instant, tiny slivers of glass peppered her arms and cheeks. Instinctively, she ducked low and reached out for her daughter. From the corner of her mouth she tasted blood and looked down to see tiny crimson droplets form on her arms.

Naturally curious, she turned away from her daughter and looked toward the mall corridor. For a moment she thought about walking in that direction to see what had happened. But just then smoke rolled toward them, followed by screams and shouts and the sound of footsteps as people ran to get out of the way. From the back of her mind she remembered reading an article in a magazine about catastrophic events. Those who survived were almost always the ones who moved quickly away from the scene. So instead of walking to the corridor to see what happened, she grabbed her daughter by the arm and turned toward the nearest exit.

"Come on," she pleaded with Angela. "We have to get out of here."

"But, Mommy," Angela protested, "your arm is bleeding."

"I'm okay. Come on. We have to hurry."

"Where are we going?"

"Home."

At the opposite end of the store, they came to the counter with the cash register. A clerk called out to them as they hurried past, "You can't go out that way." Mindy ignored him and rushed past the counter into the stock room. A red Exit sign hung from the wall and she turned in that direction. Moments later, she pushed open the door and led Angela out to a delivery bay on the front side of the mall.

"Come on," Mindy urged once more. "We have to hurry."

"But you said we would get some ice cream," Angela protested. "And we haven't had lunch."

"I think that will have to wait."

"But you promised."

"I know." Mindy led her across the mall drive to the parking lot. "I know."

In the parking lot, they joined other shoppers gathered in clusters not far from the building. Most of them chattered nervously, rehashing details about where they were when the explosion occurred. Others watched in silence as fire trucks and emergency crews arrived on the scene. Mindy and Angela stood with them for a moment, watching as a team of paramedics unloaded their gear and rushed inside.

As the team moved toward the mall entrance, Mindy noticed three city buses parked there. They looked like any other city bus, but the sign above the windshield on each of them read, Out of Service. The sight of them left her uneasy and she had an overwhelming urge to run. She pushed the feeling aside but couldn't keep her eyes off the buses. Then she saw a man moving inside. He wore a white T-shirt and stared out the window toward the parking lot as people continued to hurry from the mall.

Mindy glanced down at Angela. "Let's go," she tugged on her daughter's arm.

"What happened? What are those firemen doing?"

"They're going inside to help people who were hurt."

"Was there a fire?"

"Sort of."

"What was it?"

"I'll explain it in the car." Mindy tightened her grip on Angela's arm and walked in hurried, quick steps. "We have to go."

"Mommy, you're walking too fast."

Mindy reached down and scooped up Angela in her arms, then she quickened her pace as they made their way toward a gray minivan parked twenty yards away. When they reached the van she snatched open the side door and dropped Angela onto the seat. Then she slammed the door shut and got in on the driver's side.

"Mommy," Angela cried. "You didn't buckle my seat belt."

"We'll get it later."

"But you said the policeman would get us if you didn't."

"It'll be all right this time."

Mindy put the key in the ignition and started the engine. Then she put the car in gear and started across the parking lot toward the street. As she drove, she glanced in the rearview mirror at the buses parked near the mall. Suddenly all three erupted in a violent explosion. Fire shot in every direction and smoke billowed into the air. Pieces of the buses were flung into the air and windows shattered in nearby cars. There were loud screams from people in the crowd and many collapsed to the pavement. Mindy gasped at the sight of it, then turned her attention out the front windshield and pressed her foot against the gas pedal.

The van shot forward as a cloud of thick black smoke swirled around them. Shrapnel from the blast pinged against the van and she heard a thumping sound on the roof. Still, Mindy kept her foot pressed hard against the gas pedal, and the van picked up speed.

At the far side of the parking lot she jammed her foot on the brake pedal and brought the van to a stop for the turn onto Brentwood Boulevard. As she waited impatiently for a gap in traffic, a blob of dark red blood appeared at the top of the windshield and trickled down to the wipers, followed by a severed human leg as it slid down the bloody trail and tumbled onto the hood.

CHAPTER 84
THE WHITE HOUSE

ANDREW STANTON SAT BEHIND HIS DESK in the Oval Office and listened while Stewart Whilden from the FBI briefed him with the latest information from Los Angeles.

"The initial bomb was contained in a van that exploded in back of the church," Whilden explained. "Several witnesses report seeing a van at the church that morning and two men were seen driving away from the church just before the blast. The church has security cameras and we're going through recordings from them now. There are also several traffic cameras on the road in front of the church. Our analysts are going through that, too."

Stanton nodded in response. "Any names come up?"

"We have three key suspects. All from the Middle East."

"You don't want to give me names?"

"No, sir," Whilden answered. "Not now."

"What about San Diego and Boston?"

"I'm not up to speed on the latest from those locations, sir. They told me to brief you on Los Angeles."

There was a knock at the door, then it opened and Pete McWhinney entered the room. He came around the end of the desk and leaned close to Stanton.

"Michael Geller has been arrested, Mr. President."

Stanton looked surprised. "Michael Geller? What for?"

"He hasn't been charged yet, sir. The FBI is holding him in New York."

Stanton looked over at Whilden. "Excuse me just a minute." Then he rose from his seat at the desk and walked out to the colonnade that led past the Rose Garden. McWhinney followed and when they were outside Stanton turned to him. "What's this all about?"

"They say they're holding him on terror-related charges, but they're really investigating the death of David Holsten."

Stanton's eyes opened wide in a startled look. "David Holsten is dead?"

"Yes, Mr. President. His body was discovered three days ago. The FBI has kept it a secret while they investigate."

"What happened to him?"

"He was shot and his body was hidden in a cargo container. Port workers in New York discovered it."

Stanton sagged onto a bench near the garden. "We wouldn't be here without David," he sighed.

"No, Mr. President, we wouldn't."

"Does his wife know?"

"I'm not sure. I can find out, but I don't think so. We wouldn't have found out if they hadn't arrested Michael."

"Who's his lawyer?"

"They won't let him have access to counsel."

"Why not?"

"They're holding him under provisions of the Patriot Act. He can't talk to anyone right now."

Stanton looked perplexed. "And they think Michael murdered David Holsten?"

"Apparently."

"That's impossible. They were best friends."

"No," McWhinney demurred. "Not best friends."

"Well, they certainly weren't best enemies." Stanton rested his hands at his side and stared down at the walkway. "This isn't good, Pete."

"No, sir," McWhinney agreed. "It's not good."

"They have Geller? A lot could come undone if he speaks."

"Right."

"Can you check on that?"

"Mr. President, I don't think—"

"I'm not asking you to fix it, Pete. I'm asking you to check into the problem. We need to know what we're dealing with here. Especially with Michael and his ... contacts."

"Yes, sir."

Stanton shook his head. "We need to end this thing with Israel." He looked up at McWhinney. "Geller, Holsten ... it has to end. We can't afford to keep going. Not now."

"Geller is going to call you and ask for help, sir."

"No." Stanton shook his head. "Michael wouldn't do that."

"Yes, he would. And he will. And when he does, you have to turn him down."

"I'll put him off."

"No." McWhinney was adamant. "You can't take the call."

"You mean cut him off?"

"Yes, sir."

"Won't that just make things worse?"

"I'll take care of—"

A door to the Oval Office opened and Mrs. Moynihan appeared. "Mr. President, there's something in here you need to see."

"In a minute."

"I think you should come now."

Reluctantly, Stanton rose from the bench and walked with McWhinney into Mrs. Moynihan's office. On the television near her desk they saw images from the mall in St. Louis.

"When did this happen?"

"Within the hour," Moynihan answered.

"This is a coordinated attack," McWhinney added. "First Boston, then San Diego, Los Angeles. And now St. Louis. They're making us pay for supporting Israel."

Stanton glanced at Mrs. Moynihan. "Tell the secretary of state I need to see her."

"Certainly, Mr. President. When shall I tell her to come?"

"Now," Stanton replied as he turned toward the door to the Oval Office. "We're going to end this now."

CHAPTER 85
NEW YORK CITY

AN EXAMINATION OF GELLER'S CELL PHONE revealed a long list of phone numbers. Among them was a number for Franz Baer. When Cruse checked on the name, he learned Baer was a resident alien from Germany who had lived in the U.S. for the past thirty years.

Using Goodall's name, he obtained a car from the bureau motor pool and rode out to Baer's home in The Hamptons. When Cruse arrived, he was led by the housekeeper to Baer's study. "Mr. Baer will be in to see you shortly," she assured.

While he waited, Cruse studied the photographs that hung on the wall. He was standing near the windows, staring at a photograph of a man talking to Adolph Hitler, when Baer entered the room.

"That one is interesting." Baer pointed to the picture. "That's my uncle standing next to Adolph Hitler."

"You are proud of him?"

"Yes. Of course. Shouldn't everyone be proud of their uncle? He was a Nazi. Not a crime to be a Nazi, at least not in the United States."

Cruse turned away to face him. "Is that why you came here? So no one would harass you for being a Nazi?"

"I could be a Nazi anywhere."

"You could be a Nazi anywhere so long as you kept quiet about it and didn't associate with other known Nazis. In Germany, the Nazi Party has been outlawed."

"Well, then," Baer said with a thin, tight smile. "It is a good thing we are not in Germany."

"I suppose."

"You may not like the Nazi Party, Mr. Cruse. You may not care for me in particular. But in America, it is not against the law to be either one."

"How do you know my name? I don't believe I introduced myself."

"I know many things. You're one of them."

"Do you know Michael Geller?"

"Yes. I know him well." Baer pointed to another picture on the wall, this one of two men standing by a car with Hitler. "That's his grandfather in that one."

Cruse glanced in the direction he pointed but took a picture of Musa from his pocket and held it for Baer to see. "What about this man? Do you know him?"

"No." Baer's eyes darted away. "Can't say that I do."

"His name is Naseem Musa."

"Never heard of him."

"Claims to be the rightful successor to the Grand Mufti of Jerusalem."

"Many have made that claim."

"Any reason why Geller would be associating with him?"

"You'd have to ask Geller."

A desk sat at the opposite end of the room. Baer moved behind it and took a seat. Several large pieces of paper were rolled up and lying there. He unrolled one and found it was a map. "This is the same map I saw in Geller's apartment."

"I don't doubt it."

Cruse unrolled another. "This one, too."

Baer smiled. "Geller drew that one."

"For what?"

"For the agreement."

"What agreement?"

"The agreement to end this current conflict between Iran and Israel."

"What does Geller have to do with that?"

"Oh, it's his dream. To finally end the Arab-Israeli conflict." Baer nodded toward the maps. "He sent those to me just the other day."

"There's an agreement?"

Baer nodded. "It is being worked out even as we speak."

"Israel will never agree to a deal."

"It is not their deal to make. Your president will make it for us."

"Us?"

"The Führer promised to give the Arabs a homeland in Palestine." Baer had an arrogant smile. "America will make good on that promise."

Cruse had a puzzled frown. "Why are you telling me this?"

Baer leaned closer and lowered his voice. "Because," he said, wagging his finger at Cruse, "there is nothing you can do to stop it." He leaned away and chuckled. "No need to keep it secret now."

*   *   *

From Baer's house, Cruse drove back to Manhattan and parked his car in the garage beneath the building. As he stepped from the car, an attendant approached. "Mr. Goodall wants to see you."

Cruse took the elevator up to the office. Goodall was waiting when he arrived. "Let's go for a walk. I need to get out of here for a few minutes."

They rode the elevator back to the lobby and walked out to the street. As they stepped away from the building, Goodall turned to Cruse. "I understand you went to see Franz Baer today."

"Yes."

"Learn anything interesting?"

"Michael Geller is the grandson of a Nazi officer."

"I'm sure there are many grandsons of Nazi officers."

"Yeah, but this guy wasn't just any Nazi officer. Geller's grandfather was one of Hitler's closest confidants."

"Interesting."

"No kidding! It's really interesting when you realize Geller and Andrew Stanton were college roommates. Geller is one of this president's closest friends."

"There's nothing illegal about having friends with a past."

"Well, this friend has a map of a partitioning of Israel that doesn't yet exist."

"I'm not sure I follow you."

"This is how they end the conflict with Israel and Iran."

"How *who* ends it?"

"The president. Look, if I'm right, then this whole thing—Israel's attack on Iran, Iran's response, the attacks we've had the last few days—is all part of the same thing. It's all related and this is how it ends. This is how Iran makes Israel pay."

"What's how it ends?"

"The division of Israel I saw on that map. They're going to carve it up."

"You seem convinced."

"I am. And I never thought of it this way until just now."

"What way?"

"This whole nuclear program thing is a ruse."

"A ruse? For what?"

"To get Israel to bomb them. I bet Iran never even had a nuclear program at all."

"Why?"

"If Israel bombs Iran, then Iran can portray Israel as the bad guy. The whole world sees it that way."

"Which is exactly what happened."

"Right. So then Iran can counterattack against Israel and no one will object because everyone understands—Israel went first."

"Iran was just defending itself."

"But then the U.S. intervened and launched strikes against Iran in an attempt to force them to stop. Now the U.S. is in the middle of the conflict, only we're in it as a negative player."

"We're one of the bad guys."

"Exactly. And Iran can respond to us, too."

"The explosions in Boston, San Diego, and the others."

"Which is what we saw in Juarez. Men from the Middle East crossing the border into the U.S."

"But how does that figure into Geller and Baer and the maps?"

"We can either find a way to end the conflict that Iran will accept, or endure continual bombings, as many Middle Eastern countries do today."

"But this is America. We aren't going to have people terrorizing our cities."

"So, we posture ourselves as the tough guy standing up to the bully, then we make a deal. That's how we've always done it. We bombed Iran; now we're going to make a deal."

"Which is?"

"Which is what I saw on those maps drawn by the president's best friend. Land for peace. Half of Israel for a Palestinian state and they get the United States to make it happen."

"Nice theory," Goodall replied. "But it's impossible. We'd have to force Israel to do it."

"We already have a huge flotilla in the region."

CHAPTER 86
WASHINGTON, D.C.

LATE THAT EVENING, KATHLEEN BAKER arrived at the White House. Mrs. Moynihan ushered her into the Oval Office, then closed the door behind her. Stanton sat in an upholstered chair near a sofa across from the desk. On his lap was a file and he was hunched over it, reading. He glanced up as she entered the room.

"Any word from the Swiss on a response?"

"Not yet."

"Have a seat." He motioned to the sofa. "Why the delay?"

She took a seat across from him. "I'm sure this caught the Iranians off guard. It's a brilliant move, but I'm sure it was as unexpected for them as it was for me."

"We're all set on our plan?"

"Yes, sir."

"Think they'll go for it?"

"I hope so."

"We have to find a way to end this thing, Kathleen." Stanton looked determined. "We can't have people blowing up buildings in our cities. There's no way to end it with a military strike. We have to get to the source, to the cause behind the cause. Did you see those pictures from St. Louis today?"

"Yes, Mr. President."

"It was horrible." He had a pained expression. "And at a shopping mall, of all places. That gets to the heart of who we are, and if we have to make a deal, then that's the price we must pay."

"Yes, Mr. President. Are you sure you're prepared to make a deal?"

"I am," Stanton nodded. "But are you?"

"It's not my call," Baker frowned. "That's up to you."

"Yes, but you'll be there, too." Stanton crossed his legs. "This could get rather uncomfortable."

"What do you mean?"

"They're going to want concessions on Palestine."

"So," she shrugged, "we can concede without giving up the entire store."

"They're going to ask for land."

"They always do."

"And they'll want official recognition."

Baker leaned back. "Are we prepared to officially recognize the Palestinian Authority?"

Stanton arched an eyebrow. "Isn't that what it will take?"

"Israel will object."

"Israel started this," Stanton scowled. "We're just cleaning up their mess. They can get over it. I'll send them parts and munitions, but I'm not giving them innocent civilian lives."

"Do you know how you're going to sell it to them?"

"Sell it to them?" Stanton's face turned red. "We've got terrorists attacking our cities," he fumed, his voice growing louder with every word. "Terrorists right here in America, killing our people. I don't have to sell anything to Israel. I can point an ICBM in their direction and tell them they can agree or die!"

"Mr. President," Baker replied with a calm, even tone, "I don't think that's how we want to treat them."

"It's how they treat us," Stanton retorted. "They do whatever they want and expect us to support them. And they never once consider what's best for the United States—or anyone else, for that matter. They only think about what's best for Israel. But if we think only about what's best for America, then we are somehow acting unjustly. And then they play the Holocaust card."

"I don't think that's what they did here."

"Sure it is," Stanton insisted. "They bombed Iran without so much as a wink or a nod in our direction, but they left themselves wide open to a counterstrike. If they want to chart their own course, they can pay the price for it themselves. I'm not bailing them out of jail with a deal that isn't in our favor."

Baker looked him in the eye. "Did you really want to know about the attack on Iran in advance?"

"I wanted to know with enough time to stop them."

"And that's why they didn't tell you."

"And I'm saying we can both play that game." Stanton gestured with his index finger. "They don't tell me in advance, they feel no obligation to respect me as a participant, and I don't respect them. Not anymore."

CHAPTER 87
NEW YORK CITY

KEMAL BEYAR STOOD AT A WINDOW of his sixth-floor apartment and looked across the street toward the Dreyson Science Building. Located on the campus of Columbia University, the building sat at the far end of a paved courtyard. As he looked out the window that morning, students moved across the courtyard on their way to class. Others sat on benches that lined the walkways, chatting with friends, reading, listening to music. Across the courtyard to the right, Arash Abadi appeared, walking alone as he made his way toward the building entrance. Abadi, a student from Afghanistan, was in his first year at the university.

Beyar took a cell phone from a table by the window and placed a call. Moments later, Arash answered. "You are okay?" Beyar asked.

"I am sweating."

"That is just the excitement."

"I don't feel well."

"Relax," Beyar said, doing his best to sound cheerful. "Soon Allah will greet you with open arms."

"And Allah shall be praised."

"You are a courageous servant of God."

"And Allah shall be praised."

With his free hand, Beyar picked up a pair of binoculars and watched as Abadi reached the steps and entered the building. When he was out of sight, Beyar laid the phone on a table near the window and turned to the bed. An automatic rifle lay there with three extra magazines and a box of cartridges. He tossed the binoculars onto a pillow, picked up the rifle, and flipped the selector switch to automatic.

As he returned to the window, he heard Arash's voice from the cell phone. "I don't know about this."

Beyar propped the rifle on his shoulder, holding it in place with one hand, and snatched up the phone. "You can do this. You must do it."

"But I am afraid."

"Everyone is afraid. But fear is a lie. The brave ones are the ones who do not give in to the fear. They push through to the truly heroic. Allah is counting on you. We're all counting on you."

From the phone, Beyar heard only silence, then in a loud voice Arash shouted, "Allah is God and him only will I serve!" There was a scream, followed by the sound of scuffling, then the phone went dead. Beyar stepped quickly to the window and opened it.

Moments later, the doors of the science building flew open and students rushed outside. As they came into the courtyard, Beyar knelt and propped his elbow on the windowsill. With the rifle gripped tightly in his left hand, he sighted down the barrel, trained it on the chest of a girl in jeans, and squeezed the trigger with his right index finger. First one, then two and three shots fired. With each report, he felt more and more adrenaline rushing through his body. A smile swept across his face. His body trembled with excitement and he held the trigger tightly, squeezing it all the way back as far as it would go. Bullets poured from the barrel in a long, lethal burst.

Down on the courtyard, little tufts of dust rose from the pavement as some of the bullets missed their targets and struck the bricks that formed the courtyard walkways. But most of the shots struck human flesh, and soon the area below him was dotted with bleeding bodies as shot after shot rang out from the rifle.

When the magazine emptied, he jerked it from the bottom of the rifle, tossed it on the bed, and picked up a fresh one. Reloaded and ready, he continued firing on anyone who moved, then he turned his aim on the cars that passed by. A city bus approached and he swung the rifle in that direction, took careful aim at the driver, and let loose another burst. The windshield exploded and through the opening he saw the driver slump to the left, dangling by the strap of her seat belt. The bus veered sharply right, jumped the curb, and plowed through the courtyard, crushing the bodies of fallen students beneath its wheels. Beyar laughed as he watched it career forward and slam to a stop against the brick wall of the science building.

A taxi came next, followed by a beer truck, then three more taxis. Beyar took them all out with shots through the drivers' windows. When traffic stopped coming, he turned his rifle on the windows of the surrounding buildings, working from floor to floor, window to window, putting rounds through each one of them.

Half an hour after he started, the sound of footsteps rumbled up the stairwell through the apartment building. Beyar knew what was about to happen and he smiled to himself at the thought of it. "Come on," he whispered. "I have something special just for you."

He turned back to the window and squeezed the trigger hard, once more sending a hail of gunfire, this time into an ice cream store on the ground floor of a building on the corner. As the glass in the store windows shattered, Beyar heard the ripping sound of the door to his apartment splintering apart.

Footsteps rushed down the hallway toward him. As they drew near, Beyar dropped the rifle out the window and turned with his hands in the air. A man appeared in the bedroom doorway. He held a pistol in his hand and pointed it at Beyar's chest. "On the floor," he yelled. "On the floor now!"

Beyar grinned as he dropped to his knees and spread out flat on the carpet. The room quickly filled with men dressed in combat gear. One of them stepped on Beyar's arm while a second put a knee in the center of his back. "You piece of scum," someone growled. "We ought to carve you up right here." Beyar did not reply. Instead, he listened intently past the voices and from the corner of the room he heard a faint clicking noise. The others seemed not to notice, but Beyar heard it and the sound of it sent an irrepressible grin from ear to ear across his face. One of the men saw it.

"What are you grinning about?" *WHAP!* A fist struck Beyar on the side of his skull. "You want to laugh? I'll give you something to laugh about."

Beyar turned to answer him and saw the man's fist cocked in the air, ready for one more punch. Then there was an explosion and from every direction flames filled the room. Seconds later, three more explosions ripped through the apartment and it was engulfed in white-hot flames. Clothes on the backs of the men in the room burst into flames. The plastic stocks on their rifles and the grips of their pistols melted. And as the heat sapped his strength, Beyar heard their anguished cries as the flames consumed their flesh.

CHAPTER 88

WASHINGTON, D.C.

JONAS DRUEY, THE SWISS AMBASSADOR, arrived without fanfare at the State Department building. He was met at the underground entrance by an aide and escorted upstairs to a private study off the Secretary's official office. Kathleen Baker was waiting for him when he arrived.

"Is there a problem?"

"That all depends."

"On what."

"On the nature of their reply."

"When can we expect it?"

Druey took an envelope from his pocket and handed it to her. "You said you wanted it done quickly."

"Yes, we did." She opened the envelope and read the note she found inside. "They want to negotiate about the site."

"At least they didn't say no."

"We can't negotiate. We don't have time. If this is going to work, I need to meet them now."

"You have a location?"

"Majorca."

"Excellent choice," Druey nodded. "I have a positive relationship with the Spanish legation. Shall I make inquiries on your behalf?"

"If it will get the president of Iran to the meeting."

"It has to be Moussaoui?"

"Yes."

"Very well. I shall let you know what I find."

*　　*　　*

At the White House, McWhinney came to the Oval Office and informed Stanton of the shooting in New York. While they talked, Mrs. Moynihan entered the room. "Mr. President, there's a call from Michael Geller."

McWhinney looked alarmed. "Mr. President, you—"

"I know." Stanton looked in McWhinney's direction. He then turned back to Mrs. Moynihan. "I'm busy."

"Very well," she said, and left the room.

When she was gone, Stanton looked over at McWhinney. "I thought he would have known better than to call me. He knows I can't get involved."

McWhinney backed away and gestured toward the door. "Let's step outside for a moment."

Stanton rose from his chair and followed McWhinney out to the colonnade. When they were safely beyond the office, McWhinney turned to him. "I asked around about Geller."

"And?"

"He's not handling detention very well."

Stanton looked concerned. "They think he'll talk?"

"From what I'm hearing, he's making plans to divulge everything he knows about us."

"They'll never let that happen."

"That's what I'm counting on."

"You talked to someone?"

"Mr. President," McWhinney sighed, "you really don't want to know about this."

CHAPTER 89
NEW YORK CITY

IN THE BUREAU'S MANHATTAN OFFICE the pace was even more hectic than before as agents worked with local police to find out who was behind the attack at Columbia University and whether any more attempts were planned. Cruse avoided being drawn into the details of that effort and instead focused on Geller, the murder of Holsten, and the things he learned from talking to Baer. He was convinced they were all related and that somehow the maps he'd found in Geller's apartment pointed toward an answer to the questions that troubled him.

With workspace at a premium, he set up shop in the break room and did his best to fend off the curiosity of his fellow agents. He unrolled the maps on a table near the window and studied the details yet one more time. Shortly before ten that morning, Mark White entered the room. "I have the report from Geller's car."

Cruse glanced in his direction. "What's it say?"

"The lab found traces of blood on the upholstery and the carpet." White dropped the printed report on the table. "DNA matches Holsten. Goodall thinks we should turn everything over to the DA's office so they get a warrant and formally charge Geller with murder."

"Let me read this first," Cruse suggested. He picked up the report and stared at the pages, pretending to read them carefully. But he had no intention of delving into its details. He was certain Geller had killed Holsten and just as certain they could get a conviction on a murder charge. But if Goodall turned the case over to the DA's office on a murder charge, they would be forced to allow Geller access to a lawyer and that would be the end of any discussion they might have about Franz Baer and the maps.

Cruse hurriedly rolled up the maps and stashed them in Goodall's office. Then he took the elevator down to the lobby and walked out to Worth Street. Geller was being held in the Metropolitan Correctional Center, a federal detention facility on Park Row, five blocks away. The walk took less than fifteen minutes. He was cleared through the security checkpoint at the entrance and made his way to the central desk.

"I'm here to see Michael Geller." Cruse flashed his badge. "I need him in an interview room so I can talk to him face-to-face."

The clerk picked up a clipboard and ran her finger down a list of names. "He's not on the list."

"What do you mean he's not here? I brought him in myself."

"He's not on the census list." She turned to a computer monitor. "Spell the last name."

"G-E-L-L-E-R."

"Maybe he made bail."

"There was no bail!" Cruse shouted. "Find out what happened to him."

The clerk stared at the monitor a moment, then stepped away from the desk and disappeared through a door on the far side of the room. A few minutes later a man appeared.

"You were asking about Michael Geller?"

"Yes." Cruse showed his badge once more. "I brought him in yesterday."

"Mr. Geller is dead."

"Dead?" Cruse was dismayed. "Are you sure?"

"Found him in his cell last night."

"How did he die?"

"You'd have to ask the ME about that."

Cruse charged from the jail and walked two blocks up Worth Street to the medical examiner's office. Ben Cameron, the examiner's assistant, was on duty. When Cruse asked to see Geller's body, Cameron escorted him to the morgue's cooler in the basement. Individual compartment doors lined the wall, each of them numbered. Cameron had Geller's file in his hand and he opened it to check the location of the body. Then he grasped the handle of a cooler door and pulled it open. "This should be your man."

Inside the compartment, a body lay on a metal tray. Mounted on rollers, the tray slid in and out to provide access. Cameron grasped the end of the tray and pulled it out. The corpse that lay atop the tray was covered with a white sheet. He turned back the sheet and looked over at Cruse. "There you go."

Suddenly Cruse had doubts. "You sure this is Geller?"

"Fingerprints matched."

Cruse was surprised. "You checked the prints?"

"No. Not me. I cut 'em open and look inside. One of your guys did the prints."

"One of my guys? Who?"

Cameron glanced at the file again. "Actually, it was a woman. Sandra Lyman."

"Lyman?" Cruse's eyes opened wide. "When was she in here?"

"Last night. Right after they brought the body down."

"You're sure it was Lyman?"

"Yes. I'm sure. It's right here in the file."

"Did you see her down here?"

"I saw her but I didn't talk to her."

Cruse looked down at the body again. "Did you do a toxicology screen?"

"Yes. Came back negative for the usual substances."

"So, how did he die?"

"Heart attack."

"You're sure?"

"You keep asking me that." Cameron's voice betrayed his growing sense of frustration. "Yes," he insisted. "I'm sure. Would you like to come down here next time and do your own autopsies?"

"I would if I could. Did you check for cyanide?"

"Nothing indicated he was poisoned."

"Still have your samples?"

"Yes. But I don't think it'll do much good now," Cameron shrugged.

"Why not?"

"Cyanide dissipates rapidly."

"You can't find traces of it?"

"Maybe."

"Good. Check for it and call me with the results. And Ben," Cruse said, looking him in the eye, "don't tell anyone else."

*   *   *

Cruse left the medical examiner's office and started up the street. As he walked, he scrolled through the call list on his cell phone, looking for the number from which Lyman had called two nights before. When he located it, he placed a call to her but it went unanswered. He tried again and spent the remainder of the afternoon searching the city for her, including the neighborhood in Brooklyn around Flatbush Avenue where they'd met the last time, but she was nowhere to be found. Finally, as the afternoon turned to evening, he returned to the midtown apartment where he'd been staying. As he stepped out of the taxi and started across the sidewalk, a voice called to him.

"Cruse." He looked up to see Lyman standing in an alley next to the building. She waved him over. Cruse took a few steps in her direction, then stopped while he was still a safe distance away. "What?" she asked. "Aren't you glad to see me?"

"I would have been until a few hours ago."

She looked puzzled. "What happened?"

"I went to the lockup to see Geller."

"Oh." Her countenance dropped.

"You killed him," Cruse said flatly.

"Well," she smiled, "I think that would be difficult to prove."

"Probably not."

A car came to a stop at the curb behind Cruse. Lyman gestured toward it. "Let's go for a ride."

"I don't think so."

Lyman pulled back her jacket to reveal an automatic pistol in the waistband of her jeans. "Maybe you should get in the car." She started slowly toward him. "Don't make this difficult."

Cruse took a few halting steps backward, then turned away and ran up the street. At the corner he glanced back over his shoulder and saw the car just a few yards behind. It accelerated, swerved around traffic, and came alongside him. Cruse turned the corner and ran as fast as his legs would carry him, but the car kept pace. Then, in the middle of the block, Lyman stepped out of an alley. Cruse darted to the left in front of traffic and cut to the opposite side of the street. From behind him a shot rang out. A bullet zipped past his head and struck a street sign that was mounted to a pole near the curb. Startled by the near-miss, he cut to the left and stepped inside a grocery market. As he walked quickly down the aisle, he reached into his pocket for a cell phone and called Goodall.

"I've been looking for you," Goodall declared. "Where are you?"

"I'm running," Cruse panted.

"What's wrong?"

"Lyman's after me."

"That's why I'm calling. We finally got a report on her from Ankara. She's not an FBI agent."

Cruse stood behind a potato chip rack and watched the front of the store. "Who is she?"

"We don't know yet."

From his hiding place in the store Cruse caught sight of Lyman on the sidewalk out front. "I gotta go."

"Where are you?"

"Around the corner from the apartment."

Cruse ended the call, shoved the phone in his pocket, and worked his way to the front of the store. From a spot behind a shelf, he looked out through the window again, checking. When he didn't see Lyman, he stepped to the door and started outside, intending to run back toward the apartment building, but as he came from the store he found himself face-to-face with Lyman.

"You should have known better than to run." She held the pistol in her right hand, just inside her jacket, and gestured with a nod toward the car. "Now let's go."

The car was parked at the curb and the driver stepped out. "Let's go," he said, taking Cruse by the arm.

Suddenly, Mark White appeared from the right. He placed the muzzle of his pistol against the driver's head. "Against the car," White ordered. The driver let go of Cruse's arm and White shoved him toward the rear fender of the car.

At the same time, Billy Dobbs appeared at Lyman's side. He took hold of her hand that held the pistol. "I'll take that from you now."

But with a quick move, she shrugged free and pointed the pistol at him. "Back off," she hissed, and Dobbs took a step back. Then she pointed the pistol toward Cruse. "You finally figured it out?"

"You were just playing me the whole time," Cruse cursed.

"When they decided to get Sladen out of the way, they knew you'd be curious about what happened. I was there to keep tabs on you."

"By letting me investigate?"

"I read up on you. Best way to keep you from seeing too much is to keep you busy."

"You're not that clever, or that crazy. If you were really working for someone else, you would have just shot me on the spot."

"That would have been too obvious and too messy. And it would have attracted way too much attention. Besides," she grinned, "if you talked, what would you tell them? Nazis from World War II control the US president? How many would believe you? They won't even believe you now." She glanced at White and Dobbs. "Go ahead. Tell them your theory. See how far it gets you."

"Who do you work for?"

"There are some things I'm not going to tell you."

Goodall stepped from the alley behind her. "It will go easier on you if you put the gun down."

Lyman glanced over her shoulder in his direction, then turned with her back to the wall, pointing the gun alternately toward Goodall, then Dobbs, then Cruse. "Is that the same deal you offered Geller?" she said nervously. "Talk and it'll go easier for you?"

Cruse spoke up. "You killed him."

"Yes. I killed him. Michael couldn't handle being locked up. He was about to talk."

"And what was he going to say?"

"What you already know."

"Which is?"

"Like I said," she grinned. "The Nazis own your president."

"What did you have on him?"

"On who? Andrew Stanton? We didn't have anything on him," she scoffed. "He had it on himself."

"What are you talking about?"

"He wanted to be president. We made it possible."

"That's all?"

"That was more than enough. We supplied the money; we owned his soul. We still own it." Goodall stepped closer. She pointed the pistol in his direction. "We own him and he's going to put an end to the Jews."

"That'll never happen."

"Oh yes it will. And there is nothing you can do to stop it."

She inched to the left, waving Goodall away with the gun. When she reached the corner of the building, she slipped away and ran up the alley. White and Dobbs ran after her. Patrol cars arrived and soon policemen were everywhere. Goodall gave the driver to one of them while the others ran up the alley after Dobbs and White. A few minutes later, there was an exchange of gunfire from the next street over.

By the time Goodall and Cruse arrived on the scene, Lyman was seated beside a paramedic van, bleeding from a wound to her shoulder. A policeman stood nearby and others milled about, talking and laughing.

Lyman looked up at Cruse. "So, tell me, how does it feel to lose?"

"Ask yourself that question."

Her eyes darted to Goodall, then back to Cruse. "Think again."

"I don't need to think. I know."

"Without me, you have nothing. No case, no theory, and no way to stop us."

"But I have you."

"Not yet." Suddenly she leaped to her feet, grabbed a pistol from the holster of a policeman, and pointed it toward Cruse. Before she could shoot, Dobbs stepped from behind a patrol car. Pistol in hand, he squeezed off two quick shots. The first struck Lyman squarely in the chest. The second hit her between the eyes. Her body crumpled to the sidewalk.

An hour later, while evidence technicians finished examining the scene, Goodall took Cruse by the arm and led him away. "Are you okay?"

"Yeah," Cruse nodded. "I'm fine. But I gotta tell you, I never suspected she wasn't an agent." He ran his hands through his hair. "And I have no clue what's going on here."

"I think you understand more than that," Goodall offered reassuringly. "She got in your head, didn't she?"

"I guess," Cruse sighed.

"Well," Goodall continued, "she was right about one thing, though."

"What's that?"

"Without her, we don't have much of a case."

"What do you mean?" Cruse frowned.

"She was the link to every other piece of information you have."

"Now whose head is she in? She's just like every other sociopath. She couldn't stand it that she might die without everyone knowing what she'd done. But she's not nearly as important as all that."

"I'm not so sure. Think about the case. Geller's dead. Holsten's dead. She's dead. Sladen's dead. All the good guys are dead. All the bad guys are dead. There's nothing left."

"What about Baer?"

"He's an old man from another generation."

"And he's in the United States."

"Right," Goodall nodded. "He's in the United States, where he can be a Nazi or a Muslim, or anything else he wants to be."

"Did they really buy the president?"

"I don't know, but that's not the important thing," Goodall suggested.

"What is?"

"Whether you can prove it."

"I don't know."

"And that's my point." Goodall pointed with his index finger for emphasis. "You have nothing. There's nothing you can do."

"Maybe."

Goodall looked worried. "What does that mean?"

"Maybe there's nothing I can do through the judicial system, but there is one thing I can do."

"What?"

"I can stop the president from making that deal with Iran."

"How? You don't even know for sure that there *is* a deal."

Cruse stepped away. "Watch the news."

Goodall stopped and stared after him. "Watch the news? What are you going to do?"

"You'll see." Cruse started across the street.

"I bailed you out once," Goodall shouted. "I can't do it again."

Cruse ignored him, turned the corner, and was gone.

CHAPTER 90
WASHINGTON, D.C.

LATER THAT EVENING, Kathleen Baker attended a reception for foreign journalists held at the Capital Hilton. She worked the room, making sure to greet everyone while chatting about nothing at all of substance. In the midst of a conversation with a reporter from London, her cell phone rang. The call was from Jonas Druey, the Swiss ambassador. She stepped into the hall to take it.

"We have a response," Druey reported. "Shall I tell you over the phone? It's not complicated."

"Where are you?"

"At my office."

"Can we meet?"

"Yes," Druey replied. "I'll be here awhile longer."

"I'll be right over."

Baker left the hotel and walked out to her car. Less than half an hour later, she arrived at the Swiss embassy. Druey met her in a room on the first floor. She was anxious to hear the response.

"What did they say?"

"It's really very simple," Druey exclaimed. "I could have told you over the phone."

"No," she said, shaking her head. "This is better. I couldn't risk someone overhearing us. What did they say?"

"The meeting is set for the island of Majorca. You and Moussaoui. You may each bring staff to assist with the meeting, but there is to be no press of any kind. Absolute secrecy is a must."

"This is great!" she beamed, grabbing him by the shoulders. "Just great."

"But there is one catch," Druey cautioned.

"What's that?"

"The meeting takes place tomorrow."

"Tomorrow?" Baker frowned. "Why tomorrow?"

"I don't know. They just said if you can be there tomorrow, they will meet with you."

"And you told them yes?"

"Of course. I assured them you would be there by noon." Druey had a thoughtful look. "I hope that leaves enough time."

"I do, too. I better get moving." Baker stepped away, then returned just as quickly and kissed him on the cheek. "Thank you."

"My pleasure," he smiled.

CHAPTER 91

CALVIA, MAJORCA

AFTER TRAVELING ALL NIGHT, Kathleen Baker arrived just before noon at the Hospes Maricel hotel on the southwestern shore of the island. Accompanied by three staff members, she entered a third-floor meeting room, where she found Rasoul Moussaoui, the president of Iran, seated at a long conference table. He was flanked by six aides, three on either side, and body guards stood near the windows.

Moussaoui stood as she entered and reached across the table to shake her hand. "I am glad we have this opportunity to meet."

"Yes, I hope we can make some real progress."

Moussaoui let go of her hand and eased back into his chair. As he did so, the door opened again and Andrew Stanton entered, followed by an entourage of aides and assistants.

"I hope you don't mind," Stanton said, smiling over at Moussaoui. "I thought maybe we should cut through the confusion and get right down to the issues at hand." He extended his hand to Moussaoui, who stood and shook it.

"I am sorry." Moussaoui was clearly caught off guard. "I was not expecting you."

"I knew for this to work it would be best for both of us if no one knew I was coming."

"Yes," Moussaoui declared. "Perhaps that is true." An aide leaned near him to whisper something, but Moussaoui cut him off with a wave of his hand. "I am happy to discuss matters with you, but I think we should do that alone."

"I agree." Stanton took a seat at the table. "We can wait while our people leave the room." Moussaoui joined him and the two sat across from each other in stony silence.

Baker stepped toward the door, accompanied by her staff and those who came with Stanton. As they filed from the room, Moussaoui's aides rose from the table and followed them out. Only the bodyguards were left and Moussaoui gestured for them to leave as well.

When the room was finally empty, Stanton leaned forward with both hands resting on the table. "You went too far," he said, his voice low and serious.

Moussaoui seemed confused. "Too far?"

"The church in Los Angeles. The dam in San Diego. Those weren't part of the plan."

"I knew of no plan," Moussaoui shrugged. "Certainly none with you."

"You had a plan with Geller and Naseem Musa." Stanton tapped the tabletop with his finger. "And it didn't include bombing civilians."

"That is true. None of our Iranian civilians were supposed to die, either." Moussaoui leaned forward, his face close to Stanton's. "Yet, thanks to your bombs and missiles, thousands of innocent men, women, and children in my country will no longer see the sunrise." The two men stared at each other a moment, then Moussaoui leaned back in his chair. "I understand Geller is dead."

The comment caught Stanton by surprise. Moussaoui was better connected than he thought. He looked away and did his best not to show it. "You'll have to take that up with Naseem Musa. I came here to reach an agreement. I'm willing to talk about all options."

"I'm not sure I am so well prepared."

"That's okay," Stanton said with a stern look. "I'll make it easy for you. If you back out now, and leave without a serious attempt at peace, you won't have a country to return to."

Moussaoui's eyebrows narrowed. "Are you threatening me?"

"I am offering you an opportunity to resolve issues that have plagued your region for centuries," Stanton explained. "And I am giving you a chance to look like a statesman rather than a thug. To come in from the cold, dark past and join us in the Community of Nations. Now, let's finish this and actually do something for our people."

"Very well," Moussaoui uttered thoughtfully. "What are you offering?"

"We will agree to full sovereignty for the West Bank and the removal of all Jewish settlements from the area. But you have to call off the attacks on the United States and take measures to ensure they never happen again."

"Unlike the accusations in your so-called free press, we do not control everyone who wishes to destroy you."

"But you control the ones attacking us now. This went way beyond the plan and you know it. This was a deliberate attempt to take advantage of the situation at my expense."

"Well," Moussaoui began in a contemplative voice, "I'm afraid the plan has changed."

"Changed?" Stanton frowned. "What do you mean?"

"As you suggested earlier, things have gotten out of hand."

"And what does that mean?"

"Your bombs and missiles destroyed mosques, water systems, electrical generating facilities. Our country is in ruin."

"You were taking advantage of the situation by attacking Israel in an all-out blitz. They hit military targets. You went straight for the civilians. We couldn't just sit back and watch. You knew the stakes when you chose that option."

"We were counterattacking in response to their unprovoked treachery."

"Okay." Stanton took a deep breath and swallowed. "What more do you want?"

Moussaoui took a piece of paper from his pocket. "We made a list."

*   *   *

In the afternoon, Stanton and Moussaoui emerged from their meeting.

They shook hands in the hall, then walked away in opposite directions. As Stanton moved down the hall toward the elevator, Kathleen Baker caught up with him. "What happened?"

"Ride with me to the airplane. I'll tell you about it in the car."

An aide met them in the lobby and escorted them to the front door, where they were joined by Secret Service agents. Stanton's limousine was parked nearby and they were whisked safely to the backseat. Moments later, the motorcade drove from the hotel to the highway and headed toward the airport.

"We made a deal," Stanton pronounced finally.

"What kind of deal?"

"We agreed to normalize relations with each other. Exchange ambassadors. The whole thing."

"Okay," Baker said slowly. "Do they understand we may have to get congressional approval for some of that?"

"We didn't get into the details of how to do it, but there's more."

"More? How much more?"

"We are agreeing to recognize Palestinian sovereignty over the full area of the West Bank." Baker groaned and shook her head. Stanton ignored her and kept talking. "Gaza becomes an autonomous region of Israel, with Gaza residents having full Israeli citizenship or the option of moving to the West Bank. Palestinians who wish to return to the West Bank from other regions of the world may do so without interference from Israel."

"Yedaya will never agree to that."

"We've agreed to sponsor a UN resolution establishing the Palestinian state with East Jerusalem as the capital."

"He won't agree to that, either."

"Kathleen," Stanton said, turning to face her. "None of the permanent members will object to the resolution and it will easily pass the full assembly. They've all wanted to do something just like this since the beginning. The only reason it hasn't happened before is because we've always used our veto to stop it. Yedaya can agree to the terms of this deal, or they can find a new prime minister."

"Okay." Baker had a troubled look on her face. "When does all of this go into effect?"

"We'll introduce the resolution at the next UN session."

"Good," she sighed. "That gives us a little time to get things together."

"Not really," Stanton stated dryly. "We're announcing the agreement at the White House tomorrow."

Baker's mouth fell open. "Tomorrow?"

"Yes. Tomorrow. At a joint press conference. Pete's already setting it up."

"But that gives Israel no time to prepare."

Stanton's eyes flashed. "They gave us no time to prepare when they started all this," he snarled. "I don't feel obliged to give them time now that we're ending it."

CHAPTER 92
MARYLAND

A CHECK OF TALBOT'S SCHEDULE indicated he was campaigning that week in western Pennsylvania. Cruse drove in that direction, hoping to catch up with him at a rally scheduled for later that day in Pittsburgh. At a truck stop on Interstate 70, west of Hagerstown, he stopped to eat. He parked the car near the restaurant entrance and went inside. When he came out, Goodall was waiting for him.

"Get in back." Goodall motioned toward the backseat of Cruse's car.

"Why?"

An agent appeared beside the car. Goodall pointed in his direction. "Give him the keys. He'll drive. We need to talk." Cruse tossed the agent his keys and got in back with Goodall.

From the truck stop parking lot, they drove north, away from the highway. "You're going the wrong way," Cruse complained.

"Relax," Goodall soothed. "This will only take a minute. Are you driving out to find Talbot?"

"I can't let them get away with it. Not now. Not after all that's happened and what I've found out."

"What you *think* you've found out," Goodall corrected.

"It doesn't matter," Cruse continued. "I have to tell someone what I think is going on. Someone who's in a position to do something about it."

"And I can't let you get away with it," Goodall responded.

Cruse jerked his head in Goodall's direction, his eyes open wide, a look of concern on his face. "What do you mean? What are you talking about—can't let me get away with it?"

"I mean, this operation is too critical to our national interests to allow you to disclose it to Talbot."

"You?" Cruse had a look of disbelief. "You're with them?"

Goodall drew a pistol from the holster beneath his jacket, pointed it toward Cruse, and pulled the trigger. The bullet ripped through Cruse's chest and he slumped against the door on the far side of the car. He gasped for breath, and Goodall squeezed off a second round that struck the center of Cruse's forehead. His body went limp, slid from the seat, and crumpled on the floor. Goodall caught the driver's eye in the mirror. "Make a right on that dirt road." He gestured out the front windshield. "Not too fast. We don't want to kick up a lot of dust."

The driver nodded in response as he closed the car to make the turn.

CHAPTER 93
WASHINGTON, D.C.

IN THE AFTERNOON, Andrew Stanton and Rasoul Moussaoui appeared at a joint press conference in the East Room of the White House. The key players were there, including Haden Upchurch, Kathleen Baker, Jean Brown, and Aubrey Preston. Seated one row behind them was Moussaoui's advisors—Jalil Amini, the Iranian director of Intelligence and National Security, Army General Parsa Karimi, and Admiral Iraj Shirdel of the Iranian Navy. Seated next to Shirdel was Naseem Musa, the presumptive Grand Mufti of Jerusalem.

Stanton took the microphone first. "Today we have reached a strategic juncture, not just in the resolution of the current Middle Eastern conflict, but a crucial juncture in the road toward true world peace. Today, through the joint efforts of President Moussaoui—who has worked diligently and faithfully to protect the interests of his people—and our own national security team, we are announcing a comprehensive agreement that resolves the crucial problem that has plagued the Middle East since the day Abraham mounted a camel and set out from Ur on a trip, the result of which has affected every generation since. This agreement, when fully implemented, will assure a permanent homeland for the Palestinian people, while simultaneously guaranteeing the safety and security of Israel, Iran, and their respective neighbors.

"With this agreement, we put in motion the apparatus that will establish a sovereign Palestinian state, in the area now known as the West Bank, with its capital in East Jerusalem. I am delighted to have worked with President Moussaoui on this effort. His insight, foresight, and wisdom made this agreement possible, and I want to personally thank him for joining me in the mutual sacrifices necessary to reach this historic agreement."

Those gathered in the room applauded Stanton's remarks, then Moussaoui took the podium. "It is a sad day when nations find themselves compelled to wage war as the last means of protecting their sovereignty and ensuring peace and safety for their people. Perhaps no other phenomena of human nature speaks to our need of God so much as that we who desire peace must rely on the means of war to obtain it. Perhaps today we have at last turned a corner on that effort. Perhaps today we have liberated generations to come from the need to constantly make war against the forces of tyranny in our effort to release the forces of liberty. Thanks to the foresight of President Stanton, we have resolved the differences that face us in our own era, and we have pushed back that day of war beyond the horizon of the generations we represent here today. But time and history alone will decide how permanent and lasting those changes may be."

The applause for Moussaoui was polite but muted, and after an awkward moment before the crowd, Stanton guided him toward a large table that had been positioned to the left of the podium. Two chairs were placed there, and on the table were duplicate copies of a joint communique that summarized the agreement along the lines Stanton outlined to Baker the day before. As the press and invited guests looked on, Moussaoui and Stanton took a seat at the table and, with great flair, signed the copy of the communique before them, then exchanged them and signed again. When they were finished, they stood, shook hands, and received once more the polite applause of those gathered before them.

While Stanton and Moussaoui shook hands with dignitaries and posed for photographs, Kathleen Baker glanced over her shoulder to see Naseem Musa as he leaned close to Jalil Amini. Straining her ears, she heard the exchange between them.

"Allah has blessed us this day," Musa said with pride.

"Yes," Amini nodded. "He has turned our enemies in our favor. With the help of the Americans, we will drive our enemies into the sea, just as you said."

"Soon there will be one less flag flying over Jerusalem. And then we will turn our attention fully to the Americans and finish the job we have only now begun."

"One flag down," Amini beamed. "One more to go."

ACKNOWLEDGEMENTS

My deepest gratitude and sincere thanks to Joe Hilley, Lanelle Shaw-Young, Arlen Young, Peter Gloege, Janna Nysewander, and a host of people who had input in making this book happen. Thank you for the hours and hours of time devoted to making Seven Days possible.